INVITATION TO
DEVON

INVITATION TO
DEVON

Joy David

Quiller Press
LONDON

Illustrations by Emma Macleod-Johnstone
and Louise Robson

Copyright © 1991 Joy David

First published by
Quiller Press Limited
46 Lillie Road
London SW6 1TN

ISBN 1 970948 52 1

Produced by Hugh Tempest-Radford *Book Producers*

Typeset by BP Integraphics and printed in
Great Britain by The Bath Press, Avon

Contents

Acknowledgements

The author would like to thank Sheila Burns and Janie Macleod-Johnstone for their devoted and determined research, the dedication of the illustrators, Emma Macleod-Johnstone and Louise Robson, and Jamie Macleod-Johnstone for the idea that sparked off this and the other series of books that I have written and will write. I would thank also the hundreds of people who generously gave me their time when I went to see them. So much information did I gather, that I overan the number of words I was permitted to put in the book; what has been omitted will find its way in another time.

Introduction

When I was invited to write **'An Invitation to Devon'** I had the mixed feelings that I always experience when being asked to a party. Would I enjoy it, would I feel out of place, would I find the people dull or would they think I was a bore. Maybe I would meet someone new.

I accepted. Devon was the host and I found myself a welcome guest amongst some of the most interesting and exciting people I have ever met in any of my travels around the globe, let alone in the United Kingdom—but they were by no means all Devonians.

People make a party and for me people have made this book an enjoyable experience. I hope you will agree.

Devon and Cornwall

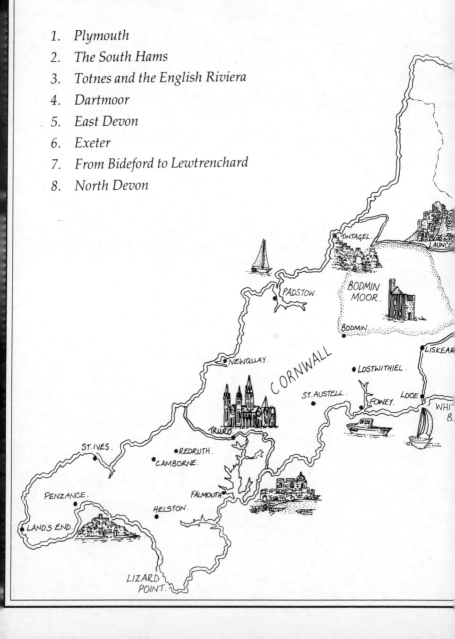

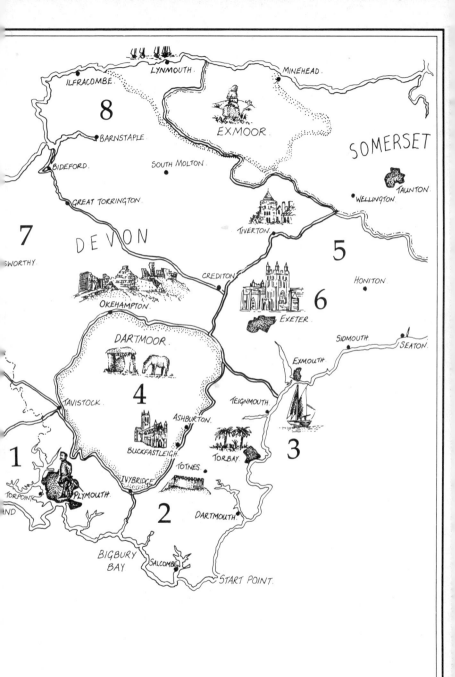

CHAPTER 1

Plymouth

32 Langage Farm Dairy Products, Plympton. Tel. No. (0752) 337723.
17 Langdon Court Country Hotel, Down Thomas, Plymouth. Tel. No. (0752) 862358.
22 Lanterns, Cornwall Street, Plymouth. Tel. No. (0752) 665516.
3 Mayflower International Marina, Plymouth. (0752) 556633.
18 Millstone Country Hotel, Roborough, Plymouth. (0752) 773734.
18 Moorland Links Hotel, Yelverton. Tel. No. (0822) 852245.
9 The New Continental Hotel, Plymouth. Tel. No. (0752) 220782.
22 Piermasters Restaurant, Barbican. Tel. No. (0752) 229345.
26 The Polytechnic Bookshop, Plymouth. Tel. No. (0752) 669199
21 The Tamar Hotel, Crownhill, Plymouth. Tel. No. (0750) 771445.
5 Trattoria Pescatore Restaurant, Stonehouse, Plymouth. Tel. No. (0752) 600201.

35 Saltram House, Plymouth. Tel. No. (0752) 336546.

I could have invited you to join me anywhere in Devon, the journey's intent being to take a look at, and be inquisitive and about, its places and people. My decision to begin in Plymouth was a lazy one admittedly; it is my home town and there seemed no better place to start.

When I was asked to write this book neither I nor my publishers were sure what would would result from my travels. What emerged, once I started visiting people, were fascinating tales of their lives and businesses. The outcome is that I have ended up with a book that certainly tells you about good places to stay, eat, drink and see but also gives you an insight into the fabric of their existence.

The Hoe and Plymouth Sound

There is no finer vantage point than Plymouth Hoe to take in the brilliance of Plymouth Sound on a sunlit day, its waters dotted with the white and often brightly coloured sails of the innumerable boating enthusiasts who flock to the Marinas and Yacht Clubs here.

It is an incomparable sight, with the Cornish coastline clearly visible on the right, and the purple flecked cliffs and fields of Bovisand and Mountbatten rising sharply to the left. Even on the wettest, windiest day in winter it is awe inspiring to stand watching the seas thrash the rocks beneath, scattering the spray from the foam-tipped waves over the sea wall.

Plymouth has been host to many people over the centuries. Catherine of Aragon first stepped ashore in Plymouth when she came to this country to marry the unfortunate Prince Arthur, brother of Henry VIII.

She would have seen a very different Plymouth to the one we know today. The narrow winding streets of the Barbican, where Catherine landed, would have been unpaved. I doubt if any of the buildings now exist. Southside Street, now the main thoroughfare of the busy Barbican, is first recorded in 1591.

What an exciting place this city must have been in the time of Drake and Hawkins. It was from Plymouth that Drake sailed on the 19th July 1588 to defeat the Armada, and it was on Plymouth Hoe that he played his famous game of bowls. I do not have much difficulty in conjuring up the scene when I stand there today.

Plymouth has always been at its zenith when there is trouble on the horizon. In between times, such as the lessening of the Spanish threat in the 17th century, and the prospect of French invasion during the Napoleonic Wars, the glory of this naval town diminished, but always it had its wonderful harbour and coastline. The construction of the Breakwater by Rennie (1812–1840) gave Plymouth one of the largest and safest harbours in Britain.

Two other towns had grown up alongside Plymouth over the years, Devonport and Stonehouse, and by the beginning of the 20th century they were one continuous mass of buildings married together in 1914 under the name of Plymouth. Nonetheless, each has managed to keep its own personality. In keeping with its seagoing tradition, the Dockyard grew and flourished and until the last decade was the largest employer in the city. Now, under private management, it has shed a vast number of its work force and the city has had to look elsewhere for its prosperity. In some ways this has been no bad thing. The wave of new industry brought into Plymouth to redress the balance has breathed fresh life and blood into the city. The property developers, reshaping the environment, work with almost as much intensity as after the terrible bombing of 1941, when the centre was gutted. The bombing, horrific as it was, made way for a new city centre to grow, dispensing with the colourful, old narrow streets that would have crucified commerce.

There will never be a time when the sea does not influence life in Plymouth. Instead of harbouring men-of-war it is a haven for yachtsmen and where they are marinas flourish.

I have a great affection for **Mayflower Marina** on the Devonport side of the city. Tucked away from the hustle and bustle of commercial life in Richmond Walk, it offers a wonderful anchorage for yachtsmen, and more importantly, offers them total security. It has marvellous facilities, including shower rooms which are designed as individual bathrooms rather than communal bathing houses. Quite an innovation and one that I would like to see emulated by many more marinas.

I am probably sticking my neck out when I say that if there were more people like Don Bird, the Managing Director of the Mayflower Marina, and his Board of Directors, who understand and are dedicated to the welfare of yachtsmen, there would be far less criticism from our fellow Europeans. So many marina developers do not appear to have the slightest interest in sailing, but concentrate on the marina's land asset and its profits. Breweries are being restrained when they try to monopolise the market, I hope the same thing will happen to the dominant marina developers.

Don Bird recognises the need to have close association with European marinas. It is his drive that has led to the formation of The Yacht Harbours Association which aims to ensure high standards in every marina. For example, apart from its facilities for showering that are the envy of many, it also has the safest berths and the most efficient security of any Marina in the country. These are the sort of standards that T.Y.H.A. sets out to achieve. Mayflower marina is also a member of the Trans-Manche Association which brings our European yachting friends into a closer relationship.

Much of Don's spare time is spent meeting with his colleagues both sides of the Channel. He works extremely hard at building these links, but he does admit that it is no hardship to go to France, Spain or Holland where he is always welcome and right royally entertained! The interesting point is that most of the European Marinas are owned by their respective local councils, and private developers are not encouraged. Whatever changes for the better come from these Associations will have been instigated by Don's indefatigable enthusiasm and work.

Belief that Plymouth must tackle new markets or stifle is high on the list of Don's priorities. He is not always a fan of the City Fathers; recently they turned down an application for the extension of the Mayflower marina on what, in his opinion, was a whim. What is even more aggravating, apart from putting his plans back for six months, the rejection of this extension has deprived Plymouth City Lifeboat of its much needed home.

Down in this neck of the woods is **The Artillery Tower**. It is not the easiest place to find but if you go down to the Stonehouse end of Union Street you will come to a roundabout. Turn left into Durnford Street and just keep going until you can go no further.

The Tower is one of three, erected just before the turn of the 15th century by Sir Piers Edgcumbe. This was the central tower and the largest. The purpose was to provide the main defence of Plymouth Sound; seven sided and built of limestone its walls are up to 5ft thick! The upper chamber gave it secondary fire power and living quarters, and the lower chamber housed the three main artillery pieces mounted on large blocks.

With this history , just imagine what it feels like to dine at a table in what was the Gunners quarters. It has slightly altered, of course, the doors to the restaurant and the sea wall were constructed during the 19th century. Built up from the beach the wall provided a sea defence, leaving the Artillery Tower the seaward side. Storms have battered against it for over 500 years and none have been able to erode the building, although the storm on the 16th December 1989 managed to flood the restaurant and break its storm shutters. The old building stood firm, and somehow 22 people still enjoyed a first class dinner!

There is a murder hole over one of the doors which was used to deter invaders by the persuasive means of pouring boiling oil on their heads. This is only used today for repelling unwelcome visitors or for those who do not pay their bill!!

The young owners of this exceptional restaurant are Andrew and Sue Camper, who are the chefs, and David Perry, who looks after the front of the house. They are an excellent team, working tremendously well in a building which has every conceivable inch of space utilised. You will never find a vast menu at The Artillery Tower but the food is of a very high quality, beautifully presented and delicious.

The named choices on the menu amused me. It talks of 'Murder-hole' Mushrooms, Smugglers' Shrimps, Soup of the Sound, followed perhaps by a Leap of Salmon or a Swim of Trout, even a Majesty of Fillet, a Frolic of Lamb or a Flight of Duck.

Durnford Street is an area of Plymouth which has more listed buildings than anywhere else. After you have lunched at The Artillery Tower, which is between 12 noon and 2pm, a stroll along here will not go amiss. The sea is never far away on one side and on the other is the fairly impressive Stonehouse Barracks home of the Royal Marines.

During the war years, Sunday morning Church Parades were *de riguer* in the Barracks. It cocked a snoot at Jerry, who had probably bombed the hell out of the city the night before. One Sunday morning I was invited, as the guest of a rather dashing young Marine Captain, to watch the parade and have drinks in the mess afterwards. It was a fairly normal happening but this morning the young man, who shall be nameless, was in charge of the parade.

Immaculately turned out he stepped forward, sword raised to report the parade correct to the Commanding Officer, only to catch his highly polished toe cap in a small shrapnel hole, the aftermath of the previous night's bombing. He fell, sword still at the salute, slid several feet forward and without batting an eyelid stood up and carried on as if nothing had happened. Totally unnecessary story really but it epitomises the unshakeability of this tough force.

Round the corner from the barracks, in Admiralty Street, is another eating house. It is not a street in which one would expect to find the stylish **Trattoria Pescatore**, owned by Piero and Rita Caligari. The building is old and the Caligaris have enhanced its antiquity by the rich, yet subtle, decor.

Stonehouse Barracks

They are committed to their profession and it shows, not only in the food which is a delight, but in their insistence of high standards from their suppliers. Piero openly admits to impatience if he does not get what he wants, when he wants it.

Their *clientele* comes from discerning local people who have discovered them and told their friends. There is plenty of parking space and it is quite safe to leave your car overnight if you are tempted to have a little more wine than you ought. In the summer months you can sit outside in what is no more than a flower filled passageway. I loved it and was not alone in my admiration. It won a Plymouth in Bloom award.

The Royal William Victualling Yard closeby stands as a monument to its architect John Rennie and one of England's finest 19th-century buildings. It is vast and spartan but with such majesty that it will be tragic if it does not find a purpose. The question is what should be done with it? At the moment it is totally wasted. The Royal Marines use it to house their landing craft but otherwise it is neglected and falling into disrepair. I have heard it suggested that it could be used for a University or for a Conference Centre but my vote would certainly go to a Maritime Museum. It is strange that Plymouth with all its seafaring history does not have one.

Staying in the vicinity, at the bottom of Cremyll Street is Admiral's Hard; from here a little passenger ferry crosses the river to Cremyll. It takes ten minutes but once landed on the other side you are in Cornwall and a stone's throw from Mount Edgcumbe Park, the 16th-century seat of the Earls of that name. I lived a few miles away from here in my childhood and memories of the hours of pleasure spent in Mount Edgcumbe Park still live on. The house suffered badly during the war

The Folly at Mount Edgcumbe overlooking the sea with the distant backdrop of Plymouth

years and was almost completely destroyed by fire but it has been rebuilt. The Orangery is quite beautiful and a delightful place to take tea on a summer's afternoon.

It has the distinction of being the first landscaped park in Cornwall and covers over 800 acres, some formal but mostly open parkland or rugged cliffs, the latter are reached through the enchanted woods of Penlee out to a point from which you can survey the whole of Plymouth Sound.

I stood there, many years ago, watching Mountbatten bring a war battered destroyer limping into Devonport Dockyard for repairs. Before that, I used to watch the great liners anchor in the bay, the *Ile de France*, the *Normandie*, the *Queen Mary*, the Dutch liners *Vollendam* and *Rotterdam*. Tenders came out to the ships to take the passengers ashore in Millbay Docks and to the awaiting boat train. The might of the Royal Navy steamed past this point, led by the dignified battleships: H.M.S. *Rodney, Nelson, Royal Oak* and *Hood* accompanied by their flotillas of escorting destroyers. Jane's Fighting Ships was a regular Christmas present for me and I knew every ship by name, gunpower and tonnage. Those were the days when seaplanes anchored beneath Mount Batten and every now and again you would see one of them scurry across the water until it had enough speed to lift its great bulk into the air.

Between Penlee Point and Mount Edgcumbe lie the twin villages of Kingsand and Cawsand which have changed very little in hundreds of years and once infamous for smuggling .For about 150 years, between 1700 and 1850, no less than 50 vessels operated out of Cawsand alone. Smuggling was as much an industry as fishing or farming.

The Chief Customs officer in Plymouth estimated in 1804 that an average of 17,000 casks of spirits were smuggled into Kingsand and Cawsand every year, and such was the skill of the villagers that the task of the Exciseman was virtually impossible. There are innumerable secluded coves and narrow inlets which made landing easy and, once in the villages, the warren of houses provided immediate concealment.

If you want somewhere to eat that is picturesque and has stunning views it would be hard to beat the Criterion Restaurant in Garrett Street, Cawsand. The Ship Inn across the narrow street used to be a favourite holiday haunt of Gracie Fields. You have to leave your car in the car park at the top of the village and walk down but it is worth the effort.

I am now talking about motorised transport rather than shank's pony, by which mode of travel we arrived here in the first place. You will have to come across the Torpoint Ferry from Plymouth to reach these two villages by car. It is not all that far and very rewarding, especially if you take the opportunity to come along the stunning coast road via Tregantle, Polhawn and Rame Head. The latter has a little church on the headland that goes back to the 12th century and is still candle lit on the rare occasions it is used. Its gravestones look out over the sea and the beautiful church is filled with the spirit of the past.

If I were visiting Plymouth, where would I choose to stay? It is not easy to be objective about this, and would depend on what I wanted to do and obviously how much I was prepared to pay. My choice is personal preference but I hope it is catholic enough to produce something for everyone.

From a purely business point of view, I would choose **The Copthorne**

The Copthorne Hotel

in Western Approach, right in the heart of the city centre. It looks nothing from the outside but when you walk through the doors it has a pleasing mixture of cool efficiency and comfort. There is nothing ostentatious about it but the soft colours of the furnishings, predominantly strawberry, lend warmth. Part of a group, it has only been open for three years but in that time has made quite an impact.

Its steadily increasing business is down to the enthusiasm and dedication of the General Manager, Patrick Maw. He is one of those nice men who openly admits he always does things he likes best first of all in any day and leaves the unpleasant tasks for later. Fortunately, his assistant works the opposite way and between them they have a successful relationship which communicates itself to the staff.

The two restaurants are meeting places for business people, as indeed are the excellently-equipped seminar rooms, used by many companies. In keeping with the Copthorne's four star status it has a Leisure Club, 'Plymsoles', and its facilities are free of charge to guests. The hotel has different special weekend packages which are well worth investigating.

Patrick Maw had several very interesting observations as a newcomer to Plymouth, having only been here 12 months. From a family point of view he thought the area was a wonderful place in which to live, although not the city itself. He has found a charming home just across the border in Cornwall, and the sheer pleasure of his drive into work in the early mornings has become a bonus rather than a bore.

His comments on the influx into Plymouth businesses of some very bright people who having moved here, delight in the environment and then refuse promotion because of it, struck another chord. It is sad that promotion opportunities do not exist so far down in the South-West and perhaps it is something that should be addressed.

I was interested in Patrick Maw's approach to the acquisition of new business. It always intrigues me that we build more and more hotels in one place but do not increase, to any great extent, the population. So how does one fill the bed space? He admitted that he did get slightly anxious about the possibility of further new hotels in Plymouth and he does recognise that there are only so many slices you can get out of any cake. To ensure that the Copthorne gets its fair share he is using his knowledge and especial interest in Germany to attract Germans, and this is proving successful.

The other city centre hotel I like is **The New Continental**, at the opposite end of Western Approach going towards the Hoe.

When I was a child there were few foreigners living in the city and certainly none who were prominent businessmen. How that has changed in the the last 30 years. It all started with the arrival of Steve Hajiyiani, the patriarch of the Greek Cypriot family who dominate the club, hotel and catering world and have done for many years. He arrived in Plymouth in 1953 and started off in a small cafe in King Street, not the most salubrious of the city's streets, but from that little acorn a mighty dynasty has grown and Plymouth currently benefits from extremely good Greek restaurants.

The Hajiyiani flagship, The New Continental Hotel, which five years ago was one of the most run down hotels in Plymouth, has been reborn.

New bedrooms, as I write, are being built to add onto the already excellent rooms; the total will shortly be 99 rooms. The Executive Restaurant caters for the business fraternity, especially at lunchtime. You can enjoy a first class meal without the anxiety of wondering how outrageous the bill will be.

Dinner Dances are a very popular feature. Perhaps not the elegant and rather formal affairs of the past but a delightful evening out. Conversely, there is the relaxed and extremely popular bar beneath, The Grapevine, which is packed out night after night attracting people of the 25–40 age group, well dressed and prepared to have a thoroughly good time.

One of the first improvements the Hajiyianis made when they acquired the New Continental was to build on a Leisure Club where full membership is offered to families.

Every weekday functions take place and it is a recognised venue for companies wanting one day seminars. All the facilities are available, including a special day delegate rate.

In Plymouth there are two hotels which have outstanding views.The **Mayflower Post House**, standing to the right of Plymouth Hoe, looks out over the entire Sound. Unfortunately, it is quite the ugliest building. Such a wonderful site surely merited something better. However, I have spent many happy hours sitting in its lounge and drinking coffee whilst revelling in the sheer sparkling beauty of the sea ahead of me.

Its close neighbour is **The Grand Hotel**, a mere bowl's throw from where Sir Francis Drake played his famous game. A fine hotel built in the mid-1800's. It is of majestic proportions delighting the eye from the outside, and decorated with charm and style inside, providing 46 distinctive bedrooms, 24 of which face the sea.

The Grand Hotel

The land next to it used to be the headquarters of the Royal Western Yacht Club before it was bombed during the war. Since then there have been many ideas for building on the site but at last, after a great fight, The Grand has been granted planning permission to build an extension which will be completed in 1993. The facade will match the existing building, behind which will be another 77 bedrooms, a further restaurant, cocktail bar and the added bonus of a Banqueting Hall and Conference facilities which will accommodate 600 people. The plans allow for the building of a Leisure Complex including a swimming pool with a convertible roof, two squash courts, a sauna, and gymnasium, all available to residents as well as non residents on a membership basis.

The Grand has some excellent weekend breaks on offer with special rates featuring all kinds of interesting activities, such as clay shooting, hot air ballooning, and dry slope skiing.

One former and prominent guest of the Grand managed to draw a crowd of a 100,000 people to Plymouth Hoe in 1889. He was William Ewart Gladstone, who had already served three terms as Prime Minister. In answer to the massive crowd he came out onto the balcony and addressed a few words to them. They probably could not even hear this frail, silver haired old man but he was a charismatic figure they would never forget. One wonders if John Major would command such an audience on a cold winter's night?

Gladstone might have been very surprised to know that less than 200 yards along the Hoe from the Grand Hotel, and just over a quarter of a century later, Parliament's first woman member, Nancy Astor, would take up residence with her husband in Elliott Terrace. An elegant house with wonderful views, which the Astor's gave to the City of Plymouth and is now used for official entertaining and visiting VIPs.

For anyone who cannot afford the luxury of staying somewhere like the Grand, there is a friendly family hotel almost around the corner in Citadel Road. It has a Cornish name **'The Kynance'**, which it acquired from an inscription the owners found on the wall. When first opened, the name attracted Cornish guests because they believed they were staying in a hotel run by Cornish compatriots. The strong bond between the Cornish and their fierce pride in the County is easy to underestimate, and to understand if bred elsewhere. As an example: a true Cornish couple living in Plymouth will actually go over the Tamar Bridge into the county for the birth of their children rather than risk them being born Devonians.

The Kynance started out as a small bed and breakfast establishment, run by Dorothy and Eric Brown . In 1954, they were both young and neither had the slightest idea of how to manage a hotel, but they loved the area and felt they could make a success of it. It was not long before it began to thrive. People stayed longer in those days, cars were fewer in number and more people made use of trains and coaches. A hotel, therefore, sited almost on Plymouth Hoe and without costing an arm and a leg was ideal.

It was quite amusing talking to Dorothy's daughter, Margaret, who helped from an early age. I think the sixties are only moments ago but for her it seems another age altogether. She recalls seeing women in long nightdresses and men in nightshirts wearing night caps. Chamber pots were still in use and early morning tea was brought round to each room.

Trade boomed for the Kynance until the late sixties when, without warning, it started to slack off. The regular clientele of representatives from carpet companies, cigarette firms and even rubber glove manufacturers from the Bristol area were a huge part of the Brown's trade and every month more and more began to disappear. Access to Plymouth had become fast and easy. It was no longer necessary to stay overnight.

It took two years before business picked up again and in a totally different way with the arrival of coach parties of young people from France. The children and their escorts enjoyed the friendliness of the Kynance and gradually, what had been a small commercial hotel found itself with a large contract with Brittany Ferries and a booming European trade. Its good reputation has also attracted a number of famous bands including The Bay City Rollers, Thin Lizzy and Brian Ferry, so you can see it can be all things to all people.

Dorothy Brown was one of the instigators of the Plymouth Hotel and Restaurant Association which has done much to improve the standard and service of Plymouth's hotels. It probably seems strange to most people these days that many hotels did not even have running water in the bedrooms in the sixties, let alone the en-suite facilities which are the norm today.

A really old fashioned place in which to stay is **The Hoe Guest House** in Grand Parade. It has only four quaint bedrooms, although they do have such modern facilities as televisions and wash basins. The guests share the two bathrooms. I was enchanted with the place. Mrs Grindon, the owner, is a happy-go-lucky woman who enjoys having guests in her home but has no intention whatsoever of allowing anyone to persuade her to modernise the house. She says that, if she did, all the personal touches of the past would go. Take a look at the original bells by the beds that were used once to call the servants. These, I hasten to add, are no longer connected.

Breakfast is served in a delightful room with a view across Plymouth Sound that is breathtaking.

On the outskirts of Plymouth we are spoilt for choice because of some particularly fine hotels and country houses. The ones I have chosen are those for which I have a soft spot and where you will find something distinctively different in each case. In order not to show any prejudicial preference, I am writing about them in alphabetical order.

Suddenly, **Alston Hall**, near Holbeton, has awoken from its slumbers like a sleeping beauty after being given the kiss of life from two enterprising, articulate and exciting hoteliers, Peter Higgins and William Woyka. For years I have watched this lovely house, built in 1906, deteriorate. I was thrilled, therefore, to step through the front door into the Grand

Alston Hall

Hall with its superb panelling, to be greeted by Peter Higgins, who, with his partner, has begun to redress the ill treatment the house endured for the last 20 years.

Alston Hall is little more than 20 minutes from Plymouth on a turning off the Kingsbridge Road. To get to it you go just beyond Yealmpton, over a little humped back bridge and then take a turn to the right, signposted Dunstone and The Shire Horse Centre. The lanes are narrow and the hedges leafy allowing occasional glimpses of the rolling country-side beyond. Continuing along this road for a few miles, you come to a small hamlet where the signpost will say Newton Ferrers, Noss Mayo and Stoke Beach straight ahead. Along this road you will see a turning to the right, clearly marked Alston Hall.

The plans for its revitalisation were well underway the soft autumn morning when I called. The emphasis is centred on ensuring that it becomes a gracious country house that has visitors, avoiding the preten-sions of the profuse new breed of self dubbed country houses. Special weekends are a part of the plan. An Opera weekend is one occasion which should be superb. Imagine dining in this truly lovely house and then relaxing to the strains of *La Bohème* perhaps, coming from the Minstrels Gallery. A black-tie occasion, of course, done with style and without ostentation.

Slowly but surely the gardens are being given new life and order. New peony trees have been planted; the rose garden, once a delightful place to sit and enjoy the soft petalled beauty of the flowers and absorb their scent, has been replanted and hopefully by the time you read this book will be well on its way to emulate past glory.

I can see Alston Hall blossoming. Corporate entertaining will become quite a major feature I am sure. What company could resist such an attractive situation with every conceivable facility as well?

Twenty years ago we used to take our children to Alston Hall on Sundays for lunch and to swim or perhaps sit around the pool basking in the sun and enjoying a super cream tea. I thought those days had gone forever but with the arrival of Peter and William, they have not. Plymouth is lucky to have acquired another perfectly tuned string to its bow.

When you come face to face with a hotelier with as much experience as Robert Maund, you are meeting a total professional. With his wife Maureen, he owns the Grade I listed **Boringdon Hall**, at Plympton.

Boringdon Hall

You come up the small approach road lined with trees and see before you this magical place which has passed through many renowned owners. King Edgar granted the manor to St Peter of Plympton in 956 AD, Henry VIII granted it to his friend, the Earl of Southampton, who sold it to the Duke of Suffolk, father of the fated Lady Jane Grey.

The house later passed to John Parker, who undertook the remodelling into an elegant Elizabethan manor and built the pretty village of Colebrook. Upon completing Boringdon's restyling, Parker held a great banquet at which the guest of honour was Sir Francis Drake, who brought with him Sir John Hawkins, Richard Grenville and Sir Walter Raleigh. It must have been a splendid occasion. A later Parker commissioned the magnificent Coat of Arms of King Charles I, which dominates the Great Hall to this day; the loyalty of the family to the crown, however, lost them ownership of the house during the Civil Wars.

Because of the intricate nature of the building you can dine in a number of different settings, each beautiful and gracious, sometimes intimate, sometimes in a grand manner. It seems almost impertinent to comment on the food and wine but not to do so would be to insult the skill of the first class chefs and the excellence of the wines.

The bedrooms exemplify the Elizabethan era, with four-poster beds and furniture reminiscent of the period. You may sleep in a room where once Queen Elizabeth I stayed during her progress through the West Country in 1588. Today she might stand back and marvel at the modern comforts of en-suite bathrooms, central heating and satellite television, but she would recognise the rooms which have changed very little.

The little plaque just to the right of the front door as you enter the Hall says, 'Please take care and note the unevenness of the floors.' Floors that have been there since the day Boringdon was first built and would give a spirit-level apoplexy. Robert Maund told me that it states on the deeds that Boringdon Hall is open to anyone who just wants to wander round; they have a legal right to do so.

I remember **Elfordleigh** as a rather tatty hotel, set in magnificent grounds with wonderful views and a golf course, approached from the winding hill that leads up out of Colebrook village past Boringdon Hall.

Elfordleigh Hotel

The approach and the views have not changed. It is still a wonderful setting, but what a transformation in the building. From the shell of the original hotel, Robert and Tina Palace have created a hotel, country club and leisure centre that many would love to copy but few would succeed. They have had courage, dedication and immense flair to achieve the result. Elfordleigh has three purposes. If you were to ask Penny Ratcliffe, their very able Marketing Manager, which takes priority, I am not sure what she would say. She can afford to be equally enthusiastic about all of them.

To understand Elfordleigh one has to look at its history. For many years it was just a mediocre hotel and a golf club. The latter was, and still is, supported by keen golfers and, therefore, it was not the easiest task in the world to get them to accept the intrusion of other sports into their insular midst. Today, no new members are taken just for golf. If you join Elfordleigh—and you would be foolish not to—then all the sporting facilities are available to you and your family all the year round. This does not mean that the golfers have become second class citizens - quite the opposite, they have their own locker room, bar and restaurant.

I could see what a marvellous place it would be for business people in the local community. Here they may unwind after a hectic day, or bring their family for Sunday lunch and to enjoy the tennis on one of the three all weather courts, play squash maybe, or escape to the golf course while the children swim, either indoors, or in the heated outdoor pool.

I was taken on a conducted tour through the various activity areas: the twelve piece gym where even the cushions on the machines are more than comfortably padded to take some of the pain out of exercising reluctant muscles, the solarium, the sauna, the showers and changing rooms are all furnished and equipped with the same consideration for comfort and restful to the eyes.

A full time, fully qualified beautician works in a room which just begs the client to relax and enjoy a massage, a facial or a complete top to toe treatment. The games rooms have a full-size snooker table, billiard tables, and table tennis. They lead into a small bar which is for the exclusive use of the golf club members and beyond to a bright, rustic dining room where good inexpensive food is served daily in delightful surroundings.

In the hotel is the Churchill Restaurant which has rich mahogany panelling on its walls and bears some super prints, not only of Churchill but of elder statesmen of days gone by. Tina Palace's ability to colour co-ordinate with great sensitivity has led her to furnish it with deep maroon tablecloths and carpets and dark wood chairs and tables. A further dining room is set in a semi-circular conservatory which catches all the sun and would be delightful for meals in the spring, summer and autumn.

Finally, the function rooms are superb. The main room opens up onto a patio with steps leading down into the grounds. What a glorious view there is from here. Wonderful for conference and seminar purposes with its own bar and ante-room and for which every modern training need is available, but on the lovely summer's morning that I was there, my thoughts went to how super it would be for a wedding reception. I have to admit falling in love with Elfordleigh.

Apart from the sheer pleasure of looking at somewhere like this, I get almost as much delight in talking to the people who work there. The staff are well trained and take it as a natural part of their day's work to be courteous and helpful to everyone, but it was my chatter with Penny Ratcliffe that I particularly enjoyed. I like to know what is going on in the marketing world and this astute lady is extremely observant. She makes it her business, in the nicest possible way, to know what is happening in other hotels, not to ape them, but to ensure that Elfordleigh is always on top.

It is her I have to thank for the tip that a glass of wine taken in the comfort of the bar in the Copthorne about 6.30pm in the evening not only enables you to watch the scene as the business fraternity gather before an evening out or before going home, but it makes doing the weekly shopping chore next door at Sainsburys a pleasure!

In our conversations about hotels we have talked of those on the edge of Plymouth but not about **Langdon Court** at Wembury which, although it is only six miles from the city centre, is so peaceful it could be in the back of beyond. What I want to tell you about is the history

Langdon Court

of this fine house. Imagine that you had walked along the beach and climbed up the valley until you came to the old carriage drive. You would probably be puffed if you were not very fit but you would be rewarded by the sight of this mellow mansion standing in some seven acres of land.

The house has been there since the 15th century. It has seen trouble and strife, times of peace and certainly times of change. Elizabeth I owned it and then, in 1564, she granted Langdon to Vincent Calmody for his 'Services to the Navy'. In many ways these services are still continued by the present owners, Sheila Barnes and Alan and Ann Cox, who play host regularly to naval officers from the Commonwealth and other navies attending courses at H.M.S. *Cambridge* just down the road.

It is probable that Vincent Calmody took advantage of the dissolved priory of Plympton to build Langdon, more or less as it is today. We do know he was granted the right to all buildings, building material, stone and timber on that site. His son, Josias, married Katherine Courtenay of Ugbrooke and through her became a very wealthy man. His fortune was inherited by his son, Shilston who, having been knighted in 1618, turned his back on the monarch and fought for the Parliamentarians in the Civil War. Plymouth of course was in the hands of the Roundheads and besieged by Charles I and his men. Justice was done though—Shilston met his fitting deserts at the battle of Forde Abbey, near Axminster, on February 13th 1645, just before the siege of Plymouth ended.

Being so close to Plymouth it is quite possible that Charles, who personally led two attacks on the city, may have slept at Langdon Court.

No one seems to know quite what happened to Langdon Court after that particular period until the Restoration, except that it was destroyed and rebuilt, which is proven by the date 1668 on either side of the front door. Each succeeding owner has altered the house, sometimes extensively. In 1856 Josias Pollefexen Calmody decided that if an Englishman's home was his castle then it should look like one, and this accounts for the castellated tower and extension on the north-west corner.

The interior has some truly lovely features. Above all I love the wide, graceful stairs with polished oak bannisters and wall panelling.

Dining in the restaurant is to dine in style. The room is particularly beautiful, with granite mullions and lovely polished mahogany doors.

The grounds are a delight too, with Elizabethan walled gardens, unchanged for centuries. A marvellous place for wedding photographs; indeed, receptions are very popular here and it takes no imagination to understand why. For me, I would take advantage of the weekend bargain breaks if I could, because to stay at Langdon amidst such grandeur, yet live simply and comfortably, would do nothing but restore one's faith in life and give one the energy to take the slings and arrows.

Once upon a time a very nice detached house stood back from the Roborough road; time and financial circumstances made it necessary to divide the house into two. Vic Wilkinson and his wife purchased one half with a costly mortgage but always felt they would like to obtain the other half of the house. Three years later it became available. They bought it and subsequently spent some months turning it back into one house in order to open **Millstone Country House Hotel**.

It is a delight. Plenty of parking space inside the walls of the garden. Indoors it is very much like an informal home and it is this that has brought it continuing success, with mainly business people from the nearby, but unseen, business parks, industrial estates and hospitals providing the clientele.

The garden is not vast but it is tranquil, abundant with blooms and with a backdrop of trees screening it from any other building. Traffic rushes by in the main road but I felt as if it did not exist.

As I turned off the main Roborough to Yelverton road where a sign said **Moorland Links Hotel**, it was if I was reliving my young days. The Hotel during the war years and immediately afterwards was the Mecca for the young set on a Saturday night. War or no war, evening dress was the order of the day and somehow all the girls managed to be attired in pretty creations, frequently made from curtains or materials that had lain unnoticed in trunks in the loft for years. Clothes were rationed so we all had to make do with whatever materials we could find. Sometimes we dined, sometimes we just came for the dancing

Moorland Links Hotel

to Frank Fuge's orchestra. Romance was always in the air, accentuated no doubt by the urgency of war. On Saturday nights we forgot that our partners could well be sailing or flying into battle the next day. They were so very precious, carefree moments; our time for fun and we made the most of it.

The gardens seemed eternally lovely, and now on this return visit many moons later, with the sun shining and the rich colours of the moors offering a backdrop, the vista was still superb. I wondered as I went through the door how much had changed in the ensuing years. There, still, was the ladies cloakroom on the right, the focal point for discussion and exchange of so many girlish secrets. The reception desk on the left seemed just the same but from there on everything was different and, I have to admit, infinitely for the better. Every possible use has been made of the rooms. The delightful restaurant looks out over a large lawn fringed with oak trees. The Gunroom bar is well appointed. Colour schemes have been carefully and beautifully co-ordinated which gives the whole hotel a sense of being cherished.

The bedrooms I found especially pleasing. I understand that Mr Jenkins, the Manager, is responsible for the furnishings. It is not only the immaculate appearance of the rooms that struck me, it was the individual touches that make them special. He has great taste and an eye for detail. Each bed is crowned with pretty drapes that match those at the windows, and nice pieces of furniture dress each chamber, including comfortable chairs.

Who uses this hotel? Mainly business people who are relocating to Plymouth or down on business at one of the industrial estates which are a short drive away. If I had worked flat out all day, I can think of no more charming place to which to return than the Moorland Links. The food is excellent, the wine list intriguing and the staff are there to cosset you.

As in many good hotels today, great emphasis is put on the facilities for conferences and seminars. The excellent geographical situation of Plymouth, with its motorway connections across the West Country, and direct roads from all neighbouring counties: Cornwall, Somerset and Avon, makes the Moorland Links Hotel a natural venue. When I was there Irene Brown, who looks after much of this side of the business, was planning a new product launch for one of the major car companies using a marquee set in the grounds to display the vehicles. Local companies regularly book rooms at the hotel for day meetings and every conceivable piece of equipment is available, including a helicopter landing facility.

With more and more people taking to the air, it was very important for Plymouth to acquire its own airport and, even more important, a company who would be prepared to operate from it. Within striking distance of both the Millstone and the Moorland Links is **Plymouth City Airport**, Boringdon and Elfordleigh are not too far distant either. In fact to get to any of the hotels I have mentioned a taxi fare will not break the bank.

A city without an airport would be worse than Easter without Eggs! Plymouth could have found itself in this situation in 1975 when property speculators did everything in their power to prevent Brymon Airways

Plymouth City Airport

from taking over Plymouth Airport. They did not succeed and the company has a long lease which should secure its future.

Way before the 1939–45 war the City Fathers had been brave enough to look at the question of air transport out of Plymouth. As far back as 1923, the Chamber of Commerce had the concept in mind to take mail which had crossed the Atlantic by ship, from Plymouth to London. From there it could be transferred to a regular air service to Europe, within seven hours of arriving by sea. It sounds very tame now but in those days it was quite a feat.

From a small grass plot at Chelson Meadow—now the refuse tip for the city—Alan Cobham, who became one of the best known airmen ever, took off on a proving flight to Croydon. This was successful and the city council started looking for a suitable site. Roborough appeared the ideal spot and from then onwards the airport has grown.

After the war it was used by small airlines and had resident planes belonging to Britannia Royal Naval College who used it for training. Dennis Teague, who is an aviation historian and has written some first class books on our local aerodromes, said to me when we met in The Dome early last year, "It might be fair to say that Roborough played a more important part in the Falklands conflict than it did in the war, because every Naval Sea Harrier and helicopter pilot received their basic training in the Chipmunks based here." Not many people know that!

It is the success that **Brymon Airways** have made of the City Airport that has brought much business to Plymouth. They persevered where many fell away. The service offered is efficient and enables business people to make a trip to London and return in the same day. They have consistently introduced new routes, although, sadly, Brymon are unable to expand much further in Plymouth, but they are going to operate out of Bristol Airport which will involve new routes and aircraft.

It was never my intention to look especially for women to write about in this book but I am delighted to find in my travels far more than I realised who have fascinating stories to tell and who not only run their families but hold down demanding roles. Diane Lovell of **The Tamar Hotel** in Crownhill, Plymouth is an example. This attractive lady helps her husband run a very busy pub, as she has done for more than 20 years, but this is only part of her life.

I would not describe her as a typical publican. She certainly does some very unusual things. For example, quite recently she saw a Wedgwood dinner service at a Trade Show, fell in love with the pattern and decided to build a separate restaurant upstairs in the pub, incorporating the colours of the dinner service, and thus 'Reflections' was born. This small intimate restaurant is only open to non-smokers; she won't even allow her husband in!

The soft peach-and-green shades in the carpet and the wallpapers tone perfectly with the Wedgwood. The rattan chairs have pretty cushions, all complementing the decor, and the overall atmosphere is one of charm and friendliness—almost as though it does not belong to the busy bars downstairs. Diane never advertises but slowly and surely she is building a very contented clientele who enjoy the good food and wine and love the caring attention that she shows them, together with her right hand Sheila and her staff.

Reflections is used frequently for special occasions, like Golden Weddings. Diane takes the trouble to go out to people's homes to talk the details over with the celebrants who, having reached 50 years of marriage or more, are no longer young. She tries to make it easy for them to plan their special day. A very caring lady.

You would think that all this activity would be enough for any one person, wouldn't you? Not so, just a little while ago Diane found herself dissatisfied with her knowledge and decided to go back to school to get some 'A' levels. Needless to say she succeeded and is about to embark. on a pyschology course. Probably very useful when you are dealing with quite a large staff and a vast number of customers!

I have no doubt that Diane would have achieved much of this without her husband, but it is his support which has allowed her to give so much of her time to charitable work. He is the epitome of a good land-lord, full of fun and charm, and with that assured air of being able to control any given situation.

It is a little difficult today to see how the Tamar could once have been a coaching inn. The Plymouth Leat used to run past its doors and in the time of the Civil Wars, a battle raged outside. Nowadays Crownhill is part of Plymouth city but its local shopping area, of which the pub is a part, still has the atmosphere of a village street.

Eating out in the centre of Plymouth offers a wide choice of establishments and cuisine. Strangely the only missing factor is a MacDonalds! Is that a good or a bad thing I do not know. I have a sneaking liking for Kentucky fried chicken and fish and chips rather than the burger type of operation.

One of my favourite places to eat is **Lanterns** in Cornwall Street, owned by Greek partners, Tony Yiannocou, Peter and Emilio Solomon. This is a fun place to be where the food is essentially Greek but the menu has a whole range of dishes for those who prefer the more staid English food. I have never tasted lamb more tender or delicious, done in the Greek manner.

Situated right in the middle of one of the busy shopping streets in the centre of the city, it is like stepping into an informal club. At lunchtime and in the evenings there are devotees who would not go anywhere else. The waiters are constant in their attention to their clientele, most of whom they know by name. One of the great characters is Andreas Charalambous, a lively man who exudes a warmth and enthusiasm for the business - and you rapidly become aware that football is his great love. Plymouth Argyle and Torquay United players and managers are constant visitors.

If there are two or more of you visiting Lanterns, try Meze, a delicious and challenging feast of most Greek dishes. You will have just about everything put in front of you, and eat as much as you wish, allowing plenty of time to be able to fully appreciate quite the nicest way of sampling the excellent food.

If you are counting the pennies then this has to be one of the best value for money places in the city, with ebullient Greek hospitality thrown in for good measure.

The Barbican, apart from its wealth of history, is somewhere that any visitor must explore and has many eating houses. It depends on my frame of mind and my companions as to which one I would go to given no restriction on money. I would probably toss a coin and choose between Piermasters down at the far end of Southside Street, almost next to the Fish Market, or Hosteria Romana at the other end. Each has its virtues. Stephen Williams owns and is the chef at **Piermasters**, and he is quite brilliant. The informal and simple interior makes for relaxed conversation. The menu of the day is always on the blackboard and majors on fish, and at some point during your meal Stephen will emerge from the kitchens, looking immaculate in his chef's clothing, with always a word for each of his customers. It's a nice place to go, good value but not cheap. It is beloved by the sailing fraternity and used by businessmen at lunchtime.

An Italian who arrived in Plymouth 30 years ago still speaks English with a charming Italian accent but this gifted man has mastered many more languages and is currently learning Japanese. Why? Because he is Enrico, a successful restaurateur who owns the delectable **Hosteria Romana**. The Japanese have quite a strong foothold in Plymouth where their Toshiba factory employs a large number of the city's work force. At management level they dine frequently in this entrancing building and it is in order to show them the courtesy, which Enrico offers to everyone, that he has added Japanese to his repertoire.

Southside Street is always busy and yet when you walk into the courtyard of Hosteria Romana, the hustle and bustle has disappeared as if by magic. There are plants everywhere and the rough hewn stone walls offer shelter to the tables, with their rich marble tops, and chairs where you can sit and enjoy a pre-dinner aperitif.

Inside, the restaurant is on two levels with the upper part forming a gallery. It is a warm hearted place. Enrico has an Italian staff who have been with him for years and know the majority of their customers. Food is all important to Italians and the nine chefs make sure that every dish comes to the table beautifully prepared with fresh produce.

Hosteria Romana also has a small Albergo along one side of the courtyard where, in the simple but comfortable rooms, one can stay and feel that you are not in Plymouth but in some romantic part of Italy.

Enrico is an entertaining conversationalist to whom one could listen for hours. His agile mind covers many topics. Ask him about clothes and he will tell you that he cannot buy what he wants in Plymouth. According to him there is not a good class men's clothing shop. Where can he buy his linen shirts, his cotton socks? Rome, of course.

The Barbican will give you endless hours of delight as you wander, but to learn more simply of the history of this City which has filled so many pages in history books, I would suggest a visit to Plymouth Dome on the Hoe which has fourteen different exhibition areas describing all the stages of Plymouth's history using the latest audio-visual technique.

The Barbican still retains its medieval street pattern and has a number of buildings dating from that time. The Elizabethan House has a wealth of original features as does the Merchants House which brings to life Plymouth's social and economic history, but the oldest is Prysten House in Finwell Street built in 1490,

Isambard Kingdon Brunel was responsible for building the **Fish Market** on the Barbican. He would be horrified to know that because of the corrosive action of the sea there is no support for the cast-iron posts which keep the building upstanding, and so, shortly, the market is to move to the opposite side of the water. It will be a godsend to the fishing community because of the improved facilities, but the loss to the Barbican of yet more character is appalling.

The Fish Market. The Barbican

The market building cannot be destroyed because it is listed. The starlings are well aware of this and continue to make their nests in the cast-iron posts, but with no more trawlers coming in to the quayside, pubs like The Dolphin, where today you can listen to the talk of these men of the sea, will find they have a change of clientele.

I talked with the uncrowned king of the Barbican, Fred Brimacombe, who politely tipped his cap to me as I introduced myself but did not stop filleting his fish! The busiest time of day is the early morning and Fred's rugged, smiling face is to be seen there from some ungodly hour every morning. He has been associated with the fish market all his life. In his young days he used to be on the quay skinning the dogfish before he went to school—which did not endear him to his teachers who objected to the lingering smell!

Barbican quayside

On the quayside is **The Barbican Gallery**, a delightful old Georgian .warehouse which has been converted by Bill and Sheila Hodges into a fine, well stocked gallery. It was established in 1970 and specialises in the sale of watercolours by living painters. The range of pictures on show includes oil paintings by Gerry Hillman and Clem Spencer, together with selected oils by other West Country artists. Bill Hodges is a mine of information and very precise thoughts about the Barbican. He mourns the loss of the village atmosphere which went with the disappearance of the post office, the chemist, the butcher, the baker and the candlestickmaker.

I do speak in jest when I say the loss of the baker, because the Barbican still has Jackas, which makes the most fabulous bread in ovens that have been baking for literally hundreds of years.

If you enjoy Beryl Cook's work, Bill and Sheila almost always show her paintings and it is not unusual to see the lady there in person.

Robert Lenkiewicz also has a studio on the Barbican and this controversial artist is frequently to be seen walking about. His flowing mane of hair and piercing eyes make him easily recognisable. The Gallery has just produced a new print of his, *A Self Portrait*, which marks a new development for them. They are now a publishing member of the Fine Art Trade Guild and they expect this to be the first of many. Bill told me that they intend to publish paintings by artists whose work has a particular interest or appeal to people living, working or visiting the West of England.

If you find Robert Lenkiewicz interesting take a look at the enormous mural at the end of the Parade. It says much about him and is evidence for all to see of his undisputed talent. I find his work disturbing and sometimes distasteful but no one can doubt his burning ideals. I suppose it is because much of it hits out at the establishment who do not do enough for the under privileged members of society. One has to admire him, not only as a talented artist but for his philanthropy and the giving of his time to those who are less fortunate.

As you come to the end of Southside Street you enter Notte Street. It may not look very impressive today but it has housed many famous people in its time. Just opposite the entrance to Hoe Gate Street, one street up from Southside Street, was the residence of William Cookworthy, one of the town's most respected citizens. He was a chemist and mineralogist of national importance. To his house came people like the great Doctor Johnson. Captain James Cook dined with him the night before he sailed on the epic voyage of the *Endeavour*. John Smeaton lived with him whilst he was building the Eddystone lighthouse.

Coming up towards the City Centre you will see St Andrews, the mother church. Virtually destroyed by the bombing, only the outer walls and pillars remained, but it never gave up the fight against evil. From the ruins came a place of worship with the word 'Resurgam' firmly in place over the fire blackened door. Today it is the liveliest Anglican church in the city, a beautiful setting for its congregation and clergy, with the constant reminder of the Blitz in the wooden Cross on the altar made from the charred remains. It is open every day for services and private prayer or just to sit and rest awhile, whilst the brilliant colours of the John Piper glass windows let in the sun's rays.

Next door is the ancient Guildhall, which also suffered during the Blitz, but is now at peace with the world.

Across the main road of Royal Parade with its Gydnia Fountain at the top, the modern shopping area of Plymouth looks wistfully at the beauty of the old buildings. No one could possibly endow the architecture of the post-war Plymouth with great praise. The lay-out is splendid and extremely practical but that is all. Much is done to make Plymouth beautiful with flowers everywhere, and it is this that catches the eye and warms the heart rather than the buildings.

Every conceivable multiple retailer is in evidence and a regiment of shoe shops, but if you skirt the edges of the streets which run parallel to each other you will come to Mayflower Street where there are one or two nice specialist shops. **Francesca's** is a small, distinguished dress shop which always has something unlike anything the big stores offer. Almost next door is **The Polytechnic Bookshop** which has a wide range, although selective because of its limited space, and across the road is a shop for men which I am quite sure would acquire Enrico's special socks or shirts if only he would ask them.

Just tucked in amongst these shops is **La Croqembouche**, certainly the best tea room in the city, serving wonderful cakes and pastries and light meals too. If you wander a little down the road towards The Armada Centre, just look to your left and you will get a tremendous view sweeping right through the streets up to Plymouth Hoe and the War Memorial.

The Armada Centre gave Plymouth its first taste of undercover 'mall' shopping. Dominated by Sainsburys, the Mecca for thousands of shopping Plymothians every week, including myself—after the glass of wine in the Copthorne, of course—the Armada Centre is a thriving world of its own with a host of different types of shop within, its elegant modern walls including Jaeger, Laura Ashley and Benetton.

Without doubt **Dingles** is the city's most prestigious store and one with a fascinating history.

I watched with a strange equanimity the bombs raining down on Plymouth in 1941. I was in the midst of it; there was nowhere to hide and so we just carried on. It is history now that much of the city was devastated and a new city centre rose slowly from the ashes over two decades. Even now there are still areas being rebuilt. Dingles, part of the House of Fraser group, was the first major store to emerge - indeed it was the first new department store to open in Great Britain since 1938. It was on a prime site and on the opening day, September 1st 1951, nearly 40,000 people visited the store. Nylons, groceries and tinned fruits were in great demand, still a major luxury after the deprivations of the war years. Some people came simply to ride on the escalators, a novelty in Plymouth and the first to be installed in a West Country shop.

Almost forty years later, on the evening of December 19th 1988, a small fire broke out on the 3rd floor and, in spite of the valiant efforts of 120 firemen, Dingles was a charred shell by morning. The awful bombing in 1941 left me dry eyed but this senseless fire started by a mindless, militant rights group got to me and I have to confess to feeling quite tearful. If I had that sort of gut feeling how devastated the staff of Dingles must have been when they arrived for work.

Peter Fairweather, the General Manager, told me that he and his senior management had spent all night watching the fire getting a firmer hold. At the beginning they thought it would be localised and they were busy planning how to open up for business in the morning—but that was not to be. In fact Peter wondered if the store would ever open again. This was not a pessimistic thought, merely practical. The site is prestigious and would command a high market value which, together with the insurance, might have been a more attractive option for the main board directors. He was agreeably surprised when the reaction was, 'How soon can we reopen?'

From that moment on, Peter Fairweather and his staff rolled up their sleeves, started clearing away the debris and, just like the war years, found a way to carry on. After the raids of 1941 Dingles managed to house various departments in large private houses around the city. This time it was slightly different. On January 19th 1989, 5,000 people queued up for the opening of Dingles' fire clearance sale, in temporary premises secured at Estover. The old Habitat premises in Campbell Court were purchased as an outlet for furnishings and electrical goods, and the ground and first floors at Royal Parade were finally re-opened at the end of March.

There is no question in Peter Fairweather's mind that without the intense loyalty of his staff this would never have come about. He is a modest man and I believe that whereas he is absolutely right about his staff, many of whom have been with Dingles for years—whole families of them—it is his ability to lead from the front that was the catalyst.

September 1990 has seen the store fully re-opened in all its glory. The original estimate was £13.2 million; I wonder what the final figure was.

Dingles has always had just that something extra. A store of which Plymouth is extremely proud. Paradoxically if you asked Plymothians how often they actually shopped in Dingles the majority would tell you never. I made it my business to do a mini market research on this and found that those who did not buy from Dingles were the most vociferous about the need for Plymouth to have such a prestigious store. Cock-eyed thinking really but perhaps it is because Plymouth historically has been a city where the average wage was low and Dingles seemed out of reach.

Debenhams is the other major store just up from Dingles in Royal Parade. They were true friends to the beleaguered Dingles after the fire.

I wonder how many people know that Dingles only came into being because in 1880 a 39 year-old-Cornishman, Edward Dingle, became dissatisfied with his job as manager of Spooners, a drapery store in Bedford Street and now part of Debenhams. He left the store and started business for himself. Within a year he was employing thirteen shop assistants, twelve dressmakers and two boys. I would take an even bet that if you were permitted to go through Dingles' staff records you would probably find relations of the original assistants still working for the store.

When I walked through the stylish black door at the entrance to **Barretts** in Princess Street, it had a sense of style and space, created by light, colour and the clever arrangement of the bar. Plymouth, as we know, is blessed with two particularly talented and internationally known artists, Beryl Cook and Robert Lenkiewicz, who are unusual in their approach to their work. They are friends of Stephen Barrett who has chosen to use their works to highlight the decor.

The cafe-restaurant is the brain child of this talented restaurateur, and whilst I sat waiting to have a chat with him I was glad of the time to observe. The whole ambience of the place is hard to define but it has an air of its own, quite unique and certainly out of the ordinary in Plymouth. I watched his young and very competent staff getting organised for the lunchtime session. These are girls who have been taught by Stephen to have a love for, and understanding of, both wines and food. He makes sure they have the opportunity to learn as much as possible, and, if their interest is there, that they attend courses and obtain diplomas. That is how seriously he views his business.

The market he aims for is 'professional' and it is here you will see the legal beagles from the Law Courts, the local solicitors and accountants, the bank executives—interlinked harmoniously with the theatre fraternity. Plymouth's Theatre Royal is just across the way.

I found talking to Stephen fascinating. He has carefully studied his market place and seen the need to serve healthy food, free from additives. What is the good of getting meat from a super butcher if you do not know what happens at the abattoir?

He is currently carrying out research on the allergy factor in wine. People quite frequently say they are allergic to red wine. It is a sweeping statement and probably untrue. What they are allergic to is the additives in the wine so, hey presto, Barretts will shortly have organic wine.

Having heard much of **Chez Nous** over the last decade or so but never having visited it myself, I was not sure exactly where along Frankfurt Gate I would find this highly acclaimed venue. Once outside the door I noted a discreet sign tucked away proclaiming the restaurant's identity.

Le Patron, Jacques Marchal, was there to greet me. The interior was a pleasant discovery, typically French: elegant, informal and friendly; a reflection of Jacques' style of cooking—*cuisine spontanée*. In Jacques words, Chez Nous is 'not necessarily the place to be seen, but it is the place to be'.

Jacques, as the chef, and Suzanne Marchal, his wife and acting front of house, have been running their place since 1980; a successful and happy partnership. He had previously been trained in his native country

Fresh Lobster. Chez Nous

with various culinary experiences under his hat, including the Cafe Royal in London. By the seventies he was ready for a change and chose Plymouth.

There is no leather bound, flamboyant menu to illustrate the selection available—rather a simple blackboard menu at the back of the restaurant. This is because *cuisine spontanée* is based on fresh, local produce according to season and availability.

The man himself is a pleasant contradiction, typically gallic with an arrogant charm and dry humour, yet without the 'snobbish' prejudices one might expect. He appreciates a personal regard for style but no one is condemned or judged by their manner or dress -only their appreciation of the meal once tried. He does not, however, take affront if someone is put off by the decor and menu. He admits that the home counties have a more sophisticated palate more naturally suited to his style of restaurant and cuisine than the local populace. In his opinion it is simply a case of those outside of the South East having been bred to different habits—we are all products of our environment. Chez Nous provides the opportunity to try something different, to gently break local habits.

What would he want to go on and do now that he has so successfully run his own establishment? Chez Nous is featured in all of the leading food guides and is the only venue in Devon to hold a Michelin star. Without hesitation, Jacques replied, to travel to Japan and study there in a monastery for a year, to learn the Japanese culinary art and the philosophy which is an integral part. Would Jacques Marchal then return to open his own Japanese restaurant? No, Plymouth is not big enough to support that or other minority cuisines. For example, really good American style fast food places can be excellent, but they would not and have not worked here.

The 28 cover restaurant relies upon the business world for a large part of its trade. Jacques looks to them for approximately 10 covers at lunchtime and of an evening the theatre crowd is a popular market.

He encourages his customers to eat as they please, possibly to enjoy a pre-theatre starter and to return at the end of the evening for their entree. His approach obviously works as the majority of his customers, approximately 70% from outside of town, are repeat business who come again and again, introducing on occasions new converts. Indeed, this has resulted in many a famous face from very far and wide, sitting in discreet corners of the room, sampling and delighting in the food. No fuss is made and no publicity is sought—word of mouth is sufficient for the Marchals.

Jacques recognises the growth of the city and the county, which can only be good news for him, but not if it is at the expense of what attracted him in the first place. So long as his enjoyment of the many splendid walks around Plymouth can continue, who knows what the future holds for him? With this, his family and his restaurant, at present he is more than content.

When people talk about **The Bank** in Plymouth, it is not what you think. Once it was the main branch of Lloyds Bank but today it is a busy pub, a meeting place for many during the day and the evening. Right next to the Theatre Royal it always attracts a wide range of people.

Derry's Clock and the Bank

I remember it as a bank when it faced the Plymouth branch of the Bank of England, where once I worked. Not many people even remember that such a building existed.

The Bank of England was the élite of the banking world before nationalisation; one did not apply to them to work, one was asked. Female employees had to conform to the strictest of codes. We wore either black, grey or navy-blue clothes; nail varnish was colourless. It was almost a sackable offence to come to work without wearing a hat and gloves. We were treated extremely well and given dowries when we left to marry. I created the cardinal sin by eloping from there one Thursday afternoon to marry my first husband at the Plymouth registry office.I even had the temerity to take one of the bank porters along as a witness. It took months for Threadneedle Street to decide whether I could stay on and if I still had the right to a dowry. They were forgiving!

Those were the days when no one gave a second thought to security when it came to transferring money from one place to another. We used to go on journeys taking money in tea chests from one Bank of England branch to another without any protection whatsoever. The journey would start at Plymouth station with the tea chests, containing thousands of pounds, being loaded into a van on the train. We would sit in a compartment next to it, and that was that. We got paid 'danger money'—a whole £5 per trip!

In Stoke village, a residential part of the city, there is a restaurant worth visiting, even if it is out of the way. Called **The Dining Room**, it is not spectacular in its decor but it serves delicious food and has an excellent staff who are caring and attentive. The chef definitely has a flair for sauces. I want to tell you a story about this place which I hope will encourage you to go there and not the reverse.

I had long wanted to visit the Dining Room and went there one Wednesday evening. It was empty. We were greeted by a charming young waitress, Polly, who showed us to a table in the window. We looked at the menu and decided to order wine whilst we made up our minds what we would eat. Polly took the order and after a while came back to say they didn't have our choice in stock. I asked what she would recommend as a substitute which threw her into confusion. Off she went to the back somewhere and eventually emerged with the chef who, in a somewhat embarrassed manner, said that neither he nor Polly had any idea what was in the bins, so would we like to follow him and take a look for ourselves. Unusual, we thought, but nonetheless we were happy to do so.

Having had a splendid time looking at their stock and taking note of the immaculate state of the kitchen, we chose a bottle. The wine needed to breathe so we decided to have a sherry. More confusion and I eventually said, "Look, lead me to the bar and I will choose." Into schooners went a good Amontillado and Tio Pepe. To cut a long story short we discovered that the previous night the manager had done a moonlight flit taking more than just himself!

The chef John and young Polly were left to cope and neither of them even knew how to operate the till, let alone the wines. Having told us, they relaxed and we had a super meal. We asked them to join us over coffee and we got round to talking about jobs. They asked me what I did, to which I replied, "Write about restaurants!"

Two well established businesses interest me greatly. Both have come into their own in new markets in recent years. The first is **Langage Farm Dairy Products** which gives the word, diversification, a new meaning.

Since 1959 Len Harvey has been running Langage Farm, originally with his father, James, and subsequently with his wife, Elizabeth, and their three children, James, Wendy and David. This is no ordinary dairy farm. The 200 acres are put to a far greater use. The Jersey and Channel Island herd are still there and probably remain the most important factor, as you will see.

To reach the farm I drove on the outskirts of Langage Industrial Estate and came to a small lane sign posted to the farm. Driving into the courtyard was amazing. Instead of the agricultural scene I expected, I found a hive of activity. People were coming and going from a farm shop, delivery vans were in and out, kitchens were at work producing superb cheese cakes amongst the various goodies on sale. Ice-creams of a remarkable range of flavours were being devoured by customers, sitting in the sun at rustic tables. Not the norm for a farm, I thought to myself.

It all started when Len and his wife decided to try selling a little cream around about 1980. This was received extremely well and so they developed other dairy products, selling them both wholesale and retail. Such was the success that first of all a creamery was built, followed by the necessary cooling rooms, and then, in 1985, Elizabeth marketed some of her wonderful ice-cream recipes and the Langage Farm Products really took off. Now they are sold all over Devon and Cornwall, each packaged in the very smart Langage Farm covers complete with their logo—a dairy cow of course.

All this has grown almost by accident. Len Harvey told me there really was no business plan when they started. Gradually the business has grown, sometimes painfully, but each year has brought them more success.

What exactly do you conjure up in your mind when you hear the phrase 'Garden Centre'. I tend to think of it being a nursery where I can buy plants. This is probably so in many cases but at **Endsleigh Garden Centre**, on the main A38 at Ivybridge, one learns that it is so much more.

I spent an enjoyable time talking to the owner and driving force behind this business, Robin Taylor, but before I introduced myself I wandered around the eight-acre site which has been skilfully utilised to cover comprehensive needs. Originally, Robin and his brother bought just four acres in 1972, in order to establish a garden centre outlet for plants raised on their father's nursery at Endsleigh, Tavistock. So enlargement to twice their acreage could have meant a hotch potch, instead of which it is laid out in a remarkably logical manner.

There is a central sales area of some 30,000 square feet, with a two-acre outdoor plant sales area on the south side. Specialist franchises are

Blooms from the Endsleigh Garden Centre

almost all on the north boundary of the site. Car parking is very easy. There are 350 spaces at the moment but it is planned for a further 150 to meet the increasing number of people who regularly come from Plymouth, Torbay and Exeter to enjoy the Centre, and get advice on the many aspects of gardens and gardening.

I was particularly impressed by the four information centres, staffed by intelligent, helpful people who do not treat one like an idiot when asking for assistance.

I learnt, later on, that one of the features of Endsleigh is the team spirit the staff have. Robin Taylor is insistent that courtesy is shown to all customers. He is the sort of chap who does not expect anyone to do anything he would not do himself.

He was quite open with me and said that it was not the love of plants that brought him into the business but strictly as a viable economic proposition. I believe it was this approach to it that has brought him such success today. He is objective and not a dreamer.

It is this objectivity that made him look seriously at the benefits of employing selected specialists on a franchise basis in order to ensure that Endsleigh could offer a comprehensive service to its customers. There are several such enterprises now covering aquatics and ponds, pools and saunas, garden buildings, conservatories and horticultural machinery, as well as an aviary and animal centre, where I spotted chipmunks!

Catering is also franchised. Mrs Rossiter operates the tea room which has just been rehoused and is now part of the main sales area. Over the years she acquired quite a following in her little 1930s tearoom which held a collection of more than 100 old teapots.

For some time I have heard people talk of **Dinnaton** and have never been sure exactly what it was or even where it was. A telephone call to Ray Taylor, the Sports Manager, soon organised a chance for me to go and see for myself.

Dinnaton is a Sporting and Country Club that has evolved around some old farm buildings set in 30 acres of Dartmoor National Park. It is only 15 minutes drive from Plymouth; quite easy to find if you take the second exit on the roundabout as you come off the A38 at Ivybridge, almost across the main road from Endsleigh. As I turned into the complex I was slightly disappointed by the exterior. It is functional but not pleasing to the eye; however, inside it is friendly and extremely well equipped.

The heated swimming pool is a popular venue for a vast cross- section of people, from mums with small children to serious swimmers practising for competitions. Added to this are squash courts, match play snooker tables, a multi purpose gym, and a health suite in which there is a sauna and steam rooms, sunbeds and massage treatments. Courses are run by Ray Taylor to ensure that people know how to use the equipment in the gym correctly. How vital this is and so often disregarded.

The club's well appointed bar and coffee lounge, both of which overlook the swimming pool, are in constant use. It is quite amusing watching the swimmers whilst one relaxes with a drink or one of the delicious home-made meals which are available throughout the day.

Golf is an important activity and the driving range attracts people who want to improve their play. Before the summer of 1991, outdoor tennis courts should be ready.

Behind the sports complex the attractive old farm buildings have been converted into Dinnaton's Haywain restaurant. It is charming and intimate for meals or for a formal banquet, wedding, anniversary or company dinner.

Alongside the Haywain, luxury accommodation has been built into the old stables. There are six double bedrooms, all en-suite; ideal to stay in if you come for a wedding or a company affair. When you stay at Dinnaton you automatically receive complimentary membership of the club's facilities.

Whilst I was out here I popped into **The Hunting Lodge**, which is literally down the road from Dinnaton. At lunchtime the big restaurant is shut but in the large, interesting bar good pub food is served from 12 noon until 2pm. It is an increasingly busy time for Richard Odgers and his staff because more and more people from the industrial estate, just behind them, have discovered what excellent value the food is. The most expensive item is a grilled sirloin steak at £8.50, but sandwiches start at £1.40. There are always vegetarian dishes and a special children's menu.

It is at night that the Hunting Lodge shines. The candlelit restaurant is open, complete with its beams and rafters. The menu is not extensive but it concentrates on first class grills to which one can add an extra sauce if required. Live music and dancing are part of the entertainment on Saturday nights.

Richard Odgers's enthusiasm for his business is the paramount influence here but he openly admits that without his staff his job would be a lot harder.

Being nosey I wanted to know why Richard had chosen the Hunting Lodge as his first venture into ownership. The response was interesting. He was a troubleshooter, going to pubs that were in need of better management and taking on the task for approximately 12 months before moving on. Finally he ended up at the Hunting Lodge where the previous owners were near to retirement. He agreed to stay slightly longer than his norm, on the understanding that he would get the chance of buying it when they retired.

It was nearly three years before the deal was done, by which time he had been able to assess the potential and also decide what needed doing to improve the place. Out went the rather dark green furniture to be replaced by the warmth of red and brown. The bars were altered and intriguing stencils appeared on the walls. Old stonework was uncovered, the small dance area changed. New loos, attractively decorated, took over from the rather tatty ones. In short, much was done to make it the nice pub and restaurant that it is today.

If you have ever organised a staff outing or an office Christmas lunch you will appreciate the efficient way in which the Hunting Lodge works. Organisers take on the task willingly and know that they will have satisfied customers on the day. How is it done? Simply ensuring that constructive discussions take place early on. Everyone orders the meal of their choice in advance and then Richard ensures that a copy of each person's choice is given to the organiser, with a copy for the guest; the final copy remaining with the Hunting Lodge. A coach is available if it is required to ferry people—indeed every little detail is covered.

To finish this chapter on Plymouth I want you to come with me to **Saltram House**, not only because of its beauty but to introduce you to some of the traumas that beset those who care for our heritage - in this case, the National Trust.

You approach it along a sweeping drive which prepares you for the beauty of this Grade I listed, Georgian house, built in the 16th century by the Bagg family.

The National Trust does not like to think of Saltram as a museum, but as a home. It is their wish that visitors should feel that they have arrived whilst the family is out. Everyday silver is left out, as if it were going to be used, and everything has been arranged in the house as it would be, if it was lived in. You can wander along the stone flagged floors, marvel at the beautiful and ornate pieces that adorn the walls, ceilings and floors. It is quite blissful but a nightmare for those who have to care for it.

Mr Ludford, the recently arrived administrator, has already acquired an astounding knowledge of the history of the house. He told me that

Saltram House

the National Trust administrators are changing their ways and running the Trust as a more commercial venture. It is quite obvious that increasing sums of money are needed if we are to conserve our national heritage. The sad thing is that the greater the public's interest in our wonderful houses, the more people visit them, and the influx of people can cause more harm than monetary gain because of the resulting damage to the buildings and their contents.

How are they handling Saltram? Well, treating it in many ways as families would have done in the great days of country houses. Often they were only lived in for a few months of the year and the remainder of the time shutters were closed and furniture covered. Practically the same thing occurs at Saltram today. The house is open from April or Easter, whichever is the sooner, and closes for the winter months from October.

Saltram over the years has suffered much wear and tear, more so now with such an increase of visitors than in the previous decade. A lot of the furnishings have been damaged by sunlight. The silk wall hangings, Chinese wallpapers and original carpets are very fragile. These carpets cannot be walked on so special carpets are laid down for the visitors.

To protect the colours of carpets, upholstery, paintings and textiles, the windows are fitted with ultraviolet filters and the light is controlled by drawing Holland blinds. Every evening the shutters are closed and all the silver is put away. Every morning, just before opening, the shutters are opened. This is just one way of conserving these wonderful historical artefacts.

The humidity of the house has to be kept constant and low all year long; it has to be monitored every day. If the level rises suddenly this can result in untold damage.

The house is spring cleaned from January until opening time by specialists taking the utmost care. One of the servants in the time of the Morley's (the last family to live at Saltram) is now one of the seven residents of the house and she can remember when the carpets used to be dragged outside in the early morning, turned over and dragged over the dew to clean them. There is no use of ordinary furniture polish, which contains acrylic and would ruin the wood. Special polish is used just once a year. Scaffolding is put up to clean the high shelves and ceilings. The vacuum cleaner has a piece of netting attached to it to catch any precious pieces that might fall off the ceiling, ornament or painting. The offending piece is then rescued and taken to the restoration room for repair.

Contingency plans against any eventuality have been taken by the National Trust. The library contains irreplaceable material, the oldest book being the *Neuronbourg Chronicle*, and there are some superb Rembrandt etchings to add to everything else of beauty and antiquity. If, God forbid, they were damaged by water following a fire, then Saltram has the co-operation of a blast freezing company who would blast freeze everything that was damaged by water and remove them to cold storage until such time as the conservationists could use their special techniques to dry them out. I had no idea what a complex task caring for this sort of property could be. It was an eye opener, and has made me even more appreciative of all that is done to allow the general public the sheer joy of sharing the wonder of our heritage.

One of Saltram's major assets is the park. As the house becomes more and more fragile, entertainment is transferred outside. Saltram has hosted Anglo-American fairs, paid for by the organisers. The Lions Club, one of Plymouth's very active fund raisers, takes advantage of the setting too on occasions—and pays for the privilege, of course. In the near future it is hoped to use the courtyard and stables as an attraction with, perhaps, a carriage to take people round the estate. On most, days the park is free for use by anyone, but is closed from dusk to dawn.

The National Trust have been imaginative and hard working in seeking monies to help maintain this beautiful house. One of their fund raising enterprises is a series of concerts, mainly of classical music, held either in the Saloon by candlelight or in the Orangery. Imagine the tones of a harpsichord playing Mozart, fragile light flickering over breathtaking scenery, with the stillness of an autumn evening catching each note. The whole house is lit by candles for these splendid occasions and visitors are allowed to look around. Wonderful! What better way to finish this part of an Invitation to Devon.

CHAPTER 2

The South Hams

The A379 out of Plymouth leads you to one of the prettiest areas in the whole of Devon. It is far quieter than its next door neighbour, Torbay, and for the most part less commercial. I found my explorations delightful, tantalising and rewarding. Strictly speaking Ermington is not in the South Hams. In fact it has great difficulty today knowing quite where it belongs because of its proximity to the ever encroaching boundaries of Plymouth. I wanted to look at the work of a remarkable lady, Violet Pinwill, whose father was the vicar of the parish church for over half a century.

The church has a crooked spire which leans precariously from its 13th century tower, almost as if it is trying to bend down to touch the wooded valley of the River Erme which lies below. Inside there is so much beauty, but the most impressive feature is the carved woodwork, old and new. Violet Pinwill is responsible for the new and you can see her intricate work in almost every corner of the church.

Trout farms have always fascinated me and it was with pleasure that I set off to meet Christopher Trant at **The Mill Leat Trout Farm**. It

Ermington church

is an established business which was started by Christopher's father in 1979. This one is situated on the outskirts of Ermington in lovely, lush countryside. It takes its name from the Leat, or watercourse, that runs down to the River Erme. The mill ceased being operative some years back and even the grinding stones have been removed but the old building flourishes. It is the home of several enterprising businesses which have grouped themselves around the trout farm.

People come from quite a wide catchment area to catch and collect their trout. Beautiful, plump fish that are delicious to eat. Youngsters come here and are taught how to catch a fish and once they get the hang of it they come back time and again, bringing their parents with them, of course.

Much of the work is done for catering establishments who ring up and order daily. It is Christopher who has to go out rain or shine and catch the fish ready for the customer to collect or have delivered.

Over the years trout has not only become more popular with the general public but the price has come down to acceptable levels. Pound for pound it is probably as cheap as any fish in the market today. Running this farm takes a lot of skill and knowledge. It looks simple enough when you stand on the little wooden bridge looking down at the fish pens, but, for Christopher Trant to feel he was sufficiently well informed to cope, it meant a post graduate course on Fresh Water Biology.

Mill Leat is open all the year round but during the winter it is open from 9–5pm for five-and-a-half days and in the summer everyday from 9–5.30pm. It is an enjoyable outing.

Fifty yards on from the junction of the A379 with the B3210 I came to **Flete House**, which, although it takes its name from the Saxon 'top of the tide', has no structure left of those times. It is a beautiful and interesting house to visit, open May to September on Wednesdays and Thursdays between 2–4pm.

The present house was founded in Tudor times and occupied by the Hele family who lived there until the 18th century when it was bequeathed to John Bulteel. The Bulteels, over the next centuries, added to the house until it was transformed into a neo-Gothic house complete with battlements. By the late 19th century the Bulteel fortune had been dissipated and in 1863 Flete was up for sale, complete with an estate of 5000 acres. This time it came into the hands of an Australian sheep-farmer who stayed only a matter of ten years or so.

Meanwhile Georgina Bulteel married Henry Bingham Mildmay, whose ancestor had been Chancellor of the Exchequer to Elizabeth 1. They lived at the nearby estate of Mothecombe and when the Australian got bored with Flete she urged her husband to buy it. It had been badly neglected so the architect Norman Shaw was commissioned to carry out renovations. By 1881 the Mildmay family moved in and Flete became the centre of glittering gatherings. Many distinguished visitors came to Flete, including Queen Victoria's daughter, the Crown Princess of Germany, our present Queen's parents, Queen Mary and Edward VIII when he was Prince of Wales.

The Mildmay's loved horses and riding. The second Lord Mildmay was a talented steeplechase jockey and almost won the Grand National in 1936 on 'Davy Jones'. In tragic and slightly mysterious circumstances he was drowned in 1950 and, as there was no male heir, his sister Helen inherited. There was no way she could maintain Flete and it was about to be demolished when a wonderful solution was found. The Country House Association rented the house for the sum of one shilling in 1961 and set about converting the interior into 38 apartments for retired people. The grand reception rooms are for the use of all the residents and it is these which are open to the public.

The gardens are lovely. Grassy slopes are joined with cedars of Lebanon and many other trees. Each path takes you to some focal point.

Tucked between wings built in the 18th century, the Tudor manor is almost intact and here, in front of what was once the main entrance, is a most unusual garden. Made by setting different coloured pebbles in geometric patterns, it is a copy, I believe, of one made for Bess of Hardwick in Elizabethan times.

It was quite difficult to make up my mind after that which way I wanted to go, but because the weather was glorious, I opted for the coast, which via Modbury was only a few miles away.

Modbury is built on the slopes of a valley and has four main streets intersecting at right angles. The main street is full of nice buildings and innumerable little shops. It is always a busy place but the free car park just off the bottom of the main street makes it easy to bide a while and take note.

Having climbed up and down the main street, which I warn you is steep, you will be in need of sustenance so a visit to **The Exeter Inn** would be a good idea. You will find evidence of the Civil War here. It was used as the headquarters of the Royalist forces under the

The Exeter Inn and Modbury

command of General John Trevanion, prior to the battle of Modbury. Replicas of the coats of arms of the General and his senior officers are on display.

Roger Stephens took over the Exeter Inn about eighteen months ago and has spent a fortune on refurbishing it. It has all been done in keeping with the 14th century building. It is full of character, low ceilings, rich dark beams, wooden settles and tables. Managing it is a charming lady called Margaret, who is a splendid hostess. She has that gift of remembering people's names and their likes and dislikes.

The menu is ever changing with daily specials going up on the large blackboards around the bar. A bowl of home-made fresh mint and vegetable soup, followed by a delicious pasta dish, sounded good to me. The portions were extremely generous, served very quickly and excellent value for money.

It would be pleasant to stay there, whilst becoming acquainted with the many super places within easy reach. There are six well appointed bedrooms, each with a different decor and very comfortable four-poster beds.

The road from Modbury, towards the sea, winds its way towards Kingsbridge but every so often there is a turning right, which will take you down a narrow lane to a beach. The first one is Kingston which boasts **The Dolphin Inn**, a popular place serving good food and hospitality. A short walk from there will take you to Wonwell beach which I think is at its best in the winter or early spring, when you can walk along its deserted sandy stretch almost to Bigbury on Sea.

I have never been enthusiastic about Bigbury as a beach but it does give immense pleasure to thousands of people every summer who come for holidays or make the seventeen mile journey from Plymouth, to enjoy a day on the sands. It is quite heavily commercialised. What is exciting though is **Burgh Island**, which lies off the coast and is accessible by foot across the sand at low tide and by sea tractor from the car park at high tide.

Small and magical, the island was first inhabited in AD 900 by a Monastic order who built a chapel on the summit, consecrated as St Michael de la Burgh. Slowly a fishing community came into being and by the 14th century it was thriving. There is only one cottage left today and that is now **The Pilchard Inn**, a delightful port of call after a walk across the sands.

The island belongs to the Porters, two charming and very courageous people who bought it in 1985, spending every penny they had. It was not just the island that they wanted, it was the hotel that had been built in 1929 by the theatrical impresario, Archibald Netherfield, who had designed it to entertain his famous friends. Agatha Christie stayed there regularly. In fact, two of her books *Evil under the Sun* and *Ten Little Nigger Boys*, were written in one of the splendidly ornate rooms. Noel Coward came for three days and stayed three weeks. On his recommendation the Mountbattens and Edward and Mrs Simpson stayed there once or twice. By the mid-1930s it had become the 'in' place to be and known as the smartest hotel west of the Ritz.

By the time the Porters arrived the hotel was in an appalling state of decay, having been closed since 1955. Their task ever since has been the restoration of the hotel in the 1920s Art Deco style. Their love affair with the island and the hotel became almost a cult story with magazines and newspapers, so when they re-opened in March 1988, the word had spread across the world. People came from London, New York, Los Angeles and Europe and loved every moment of their stay. What had seemed almost an impossible dream had become true for the Porters.

You will find that Saturday nights are particularly good fun. Everyone dresses in 1920s style and the live music rapidly gets people in the mood for dancing to tunes of the era. The food is excellent, the friendly informality superb and the Porters are wonderful hosts.

Back in the little village of Bigbury, two miles away from the sea there is a quaint and interesting church which dates from the 12th century. Take a close look at the lectern and you will see that it has an eagle's head on a gilded owl! It was given to Ashburton four hundred years ago by a bishop whose symbol it was, and so it was made in that image. However, when it arrived at Bigbury, the parishioners took exception to its owlishness. Off came the owl's head and on went the eagle's.

There are several brass portraits but I preferred the one on slate of an Elizabethan and his wife. Mrs Pearse wears a hooped dress and her husband, John, stands beside her. It is the inscription which amused me. It says:

Pearse, being pierced by death, does peace obtain

About half a mile away is the hamlet of St Ann's Chapel with a nice pub, **The Pickwick Inn**, which was built around parts of a 14th-century chapel named after the Celtic Goddess, St Anne. Not a nice lady to know. The mainstay of her diet was babies, apparently. The decapitated remains were found in a nearby well. It seems quite logical, having heard this, to be told that the pub is haunted. Not by the Celtic lady, thank heavens, but by a gentle soul who has not been seen recently yet whose harmless presence is very definitely felt.

Back on the main A379 just a few miles down the road going towards Kingsbridge there is a turn to the right which will take you to the village of Thurlestone.

If you were to ask most Plymothians where Thurlestone was they would probably ask, 'Where did you say?' Yet it is within three-quarters of an hour's drive. It stands on the craggy South Hams coastline with marvellous views of Thurlestone Rock, an extraordinary natural arch on the seashore, and Bigbury Bay, with its vast expanse of sands. On a summer's day it is a still, calm haven, but the winter winds rise and the seas thunder in, roaring through the rock and pounding the shore, creating a noise that is peculiarly its own.

Thurlestone still manages to sit in splendid isolation in spite of the advent of the not too distant motorway. I can just imagine what it must have been like when Plymouth was a day away and there was no means of transport other than the horse. What a glorious place for the smuggler!

If you talk to people in the village they will tell you stories of how the Excisemen were foiled and how the old parson would turn a blind eye to fifty or more kegs of wine finding their way to the roof of the

Cottages in Thurlestone Village

church for safekeeping. He naturally expected to receive his payment in the form of a keg or two. It was as natural as baking bread for the villagers to take part in these nefarious activities—in common with the whole of the south coast which had its favourite spots and baiting the Excisemen was the sport of the day.

Sport today is mainly golf. Although Thurlestone's course is not of championship quality, it is one of the most sought after in the county and one of the most difficult to play.

The village is a gentle place with its cluster of cottages and nice houses. The church is a fine looking building albeit a slight hotch-potch of architecture. It stems from the 13th century and has been considerably altered over the years, but it is obviously much loved and well attended. It sits on a slightly raised position looking down the slope, lined with old gravestones, towards the village inn. It is here that in some ways my visit to Thurlestone begins, because the inn was once a farmhouse, and in 1896, in that farmhouse, Margaret Amelia and William John Grose saw the possibility of running a boarding house to accommodate golfers playing on the newly opened links nearby. From that moment four generations of the Grose family have worked consistently to produce what is **The Thurlestone Hotel** today.

If you are privileged enough to take a look at an early visitors book you will read endless testimonials to the comfort and hospitality of the house. As you read, you will see that many people returned year after year, some to spend the whole summer and some just to take

Thurlestone Hotel

advantage of the two weeks annual holiday, but no entry is less than enthusiastic. Not much has changed, once people have discovered the delights of this superb hotel, they too come back again and again.

Because of this the weather is almost immaterial. Even in the worst of winter it would still be enjoyable. Witness to this is an entry dated January 12th 1901:

> Sundays wind I'll ne'er forget
> Monday's frost was hard, you bet,
> Tuesday's snow four inches thick
> Wednesday's mud how it did stick
> Thursday's rainy windy day
> Friday balmy like May
> Saturday we went away
> Oh! if we could only stay!!

There is something about privately owned hotels that cannot be beaten. David Grose and his brother Graham are the inspiration behind the business today but they are only emulating the standards that their great-grandmother Margaret Amelia started all those years ago.

Have you ever noticed the difference in the welcome you get in this sort of hotel rather than one belonging to a major group? It starts at the reception desk. At the Thurlestone you are greeted with a warm smile and you feel like an important person. In the other sort almost always the receptionist never really looks at you. It is almost name, rank and number. She takes your name, her face is averted to gaze at the computer screen. She produces a card, asks a couple of questions and hands you a key. You have become room 107 or whatever.

Staff at the Thurlestone do not change all that often and one can understand why. Like the Palace in Torquay, they belong to and are as proud of their hotel as the Grose family.

Another narrow lane off the A379, a little nearer to Salcombe this time, will take you down to Hope Cove. So many people miss Thurlestone and Hope Cove because they are tucked away but it is so rewarding to go to them. There is nothing much to do at Hope Cove except enjoy the sea and sand, water ski a little or just take off in a boat.

Fishing was once the main source of income for the village, especially for mackerel and pilchards. Huge shoals used to be caught not far off shore. In fact, the first little bay below Bolt Tail is still known as Pilchards Cove. The few remaining fishermen take their boats out to catch lobsters and crabs which are eagerly awaited by locals and visitors—they are also sent far afield.

There is a little single storey building near the old lifeboat house which was once a rest room for fishermen. It is known now as the reading room, where a daily paper is placed for anyone to read. The little square is a pleasure to be in with its thatched cottages and cobbles and the small, rather austere Wesleyan chapel.

Inner Hope is sheltered by Bolt Tail, which rises sharply at the far end of Bigbury Bay. You can still see the outlines of an ancient Iron Age fort. Outer Hope is the focal point of village life, with a thatched cottage, post office where you can buy almost anything, two inns, a restaurant and cottages.

Once having seen Hope Cove you will want to stay. **The Cottage Hotel**, set in two acres of grounds with a wonderful position overlooking the bay, is the answer. The hotel's gardens wind down to the private beach where you can bathe in safety or take romantic walks along the cliffs to other sandy beaches, rocky coves and wooded valleys, each with its own spectacular sea views.

The Cottage Hotel

The Cottage Hotel has been developed in stages since 1927 from a small late 19th century cottage to the 35 bedroomed hotel it is today. I was interested to hear the story behind it. The owners, Mr and Mrs Ireland, bought the hotel seventeen years ago and run it with their family and Mrs Bazzano, who fell under the spell of this delightful place purely by accident. After living in Italy for some time and then flying off to Australia, she finally came to rest in England, where she was introduced to hotel administration by a hotelier friend of hers. Happy to live anywhere, she found her way to the Cottage, where she has been contentedly ensconced for the last seventeen years.

It provides a relaxing atmosphere for everyone who stays here, with accommodation to suit large or small families. There are de-luxe rooms overlooking Bigbury Bay together with standard rooms, all attractively furnished and fully equipped with every modern facility.

There are three lounges, two with old brick fireplaces, wood panelling and oak beams. The third is a small television lounge. The timbers of the famous tall ship, wrecked along the coast nearly fifty years ago, were used to build the 'Herzogin Cecilie' cabin, where you can sit and enjoy a drink from a well stocked bar.

The restaurant seats over a hundred people comfortably and is renowned for the excellence of its cuisine. At lunchtime there are bar meals, leaving the restaurant for the greater formality of an evening meal. Dances are held or films shown during the season and there is a recreation room with its own bar, full-size table tennis and play facilities for children. The hotel is near two golf courses and special terms are available for golfing breaks. You can sail or fish from the breakwaters, hire a boat or take off for Salcombe, Kingsbridge or Thurlestone. Plymouth, Torquay and Dartmoor are only an hour away.

Another good hotel is **The Tanfield**, owned by the resident proprietors Mr and Mrs Ward—two friendly people who for years ran residential homes in Plymouth. Theirs is a comfortable hotel where everyone feels relaxed, almost as if you were at home. This nice atmosphere has been created by satisfied customers returning year after year and treating it as such. One of the differences here is that pets are more than welcome. Both the Wards have a love of animals and they get quite a number of bookings from people with similar outlooks. The rooms are well furnished and the food is plentiful, with great care taken over any dietary needs.

And so to Salcombe, a place that never fails to stir my soul with its beauty. Its harbour is always full of all sorts and sizes of marine craft. Yachtsmen throughout the world make for the shelter of this wonderful estuary. The little town that, not so many years ago, was a self-supporting working community who all knew each other, has become very much the centre for people with second homes. It has taken a lot away from the comfort of the locals, although the amount of visitors certainly makes the tills ring—or buzz or whatever it is they do today.

While we are talking about businesses let me tell you about **Salcombe Dairy**. Ever since my visit to Langage Farm I have been hellbent on discovering who else in Devon is dedicated to the making of true ice-cream. Salcombe produced the answer. Quite surprising really because it is not the most accessible of places but here, right in the middle of a car park, I found Salcombe Dairy and learnt more about ice-cream in an hour from talking to Peter Stannard, the Sales Manager of this

View from Salcombe

efficient and prosperous business, than I have done in a lifetime. If the proof of the pudding is in the eating then the apricot ice-cream cornet I licked with avidity substantiates Salcombe Dairy's claim to be one of the top independent makers of ice-cream in the country.

When Peter Howard, the owner, first started making this fabulous ice-cream, he had to charge almost three times as much as any other ice-cream producer. The reason was that the ingredients were top notch and he was not prepared to cut corners. Rum and Raisin for example, was not made using a rum essence but by soaking the raisins in genuine Lamb's Navy Rum overnight.

The retail price did not seem to matter once people had sampled the ice-cream. The demand became greater and the company expanded into its present premises from which it has produced more and more varieties of ice-cream. Never once has the quality suffered.

Peter Stannard has tremendous enthusiasm for his task and constantly creates new outlets for this excellent product. I went to the Theatre Royal in Bath a couple of weeks ago and there, to my delight, Salcombe Dairy ice-cream was on sale in the interval. It is not only on sale in the West either; go to Sadlers Wells or to watch the Davis Cup at Queens and a pound to a penny you will find it there.

The success of the business has meant that the management have had to find new premises and are moving to South Brent. It is a practical move because it is just off the A38 and will make life a lot easier for their deliveries. Getting from Salcombe to the A38 can take up to an hour on a busy summer's day. I sensed a certain sadness though in the thought that they were leaving Salcombe where the business had first been conceived, but I was reassured when they told me that they would always have a presence in Salcombe.

I wondered what had brought the two Peters into this fairly volatile business and the answer came back: 'What else would two ex-Union

Castle men do?' I had no answer for that. It reminded me of the true story about two Naval Captains of two destroyers coming up the Medway into Chatham. They collided. Signals flew between the two ships. The first said, 'What are you going to do now?' The second replied, 'Buy a farm'!

Salcombe is full of memories. Tennyson adored it. The harbour entrance has the ruined wall of a medieval castle which guarded shipping 450 years ago and stood for King Charles against Cromwell. The little town is delightful to walk through and almost all the time you will catch glimpses of the ever changing scenery and colours of the estuary. It is a place to stand and stare and certainly to stay if you can. There are many hotels, pubs and guest houses which offer excellent accommodation but for true peace and serenity there is only one place I would go.

You may well wonder if you are actually running out of road before you come to the **Tides Reach Hotel** but then suddenly round a corner you come upon a tree-fringed sandy cove and there it is, set in what has to be one of the most beautiful and natural surroundings in the British Isles.

It is a well appointed hotel built in the mid-thirties. Like so many good hotels it is run by the owners, Mr and Mrs Roy Edwards. The Edwards family have been hoteliers for generations. Roy escaped at one time to become a Civil Engineer but returned to the fold a few years ago. He has never regretted it and the impeccable standards of the hotel has proved that he did not make a mistake. Staff training is a major ingredient in the success of this hotel. Smiling receptionists greet you and somehow manage to remember the names of guests when they next meet.

The Tides Reach is entirely devoted to the holiday industry. They do not have business functions and whilst non-residents are welcome, it is always the residents who take pride of place. This is quite unusual today. So many hotels I find are putting much effort into attracting alternative business. The successful way in which the hotel is run seems to prove that they are absolutely right to stick to their policy.

One of the drawbacks in staying in Salcombe is the lack of parking facilities. The great advantage at Tides Reach is the big car park, and for boat owners they have a dinghy park and their own moorings just off the beach. You can forget your car in the summer and take the ferry from the beach into Salcombe. It takes about ten minutes and you can go further up the estuary if you wish to go to Kingsbridge or across the water to the beautiful beaches and walks on the other side.

With its own boathouse right on the beach the hotel provides facilities for windsurfing, water skiing, sailing and canoeing. I can imagine a good many people coming here to stay and not bothering to leave the little bay. Even if the weather is not kind there is still the pool and leisure complex with all its amenities to while away the time.

It would almost be an impertinence to suppose that the food here could be anything but excellent. It is and is complemented by a fine wine list at amazingly reasonable prices.

Tides Reach would be lovely at any time of the year but probably at its best in the early summer before the main holiday crowds descend. June is a good month. The weather is usually reasonable and all the services like the ferry into Salcombe are available.

Just across the estuary from Salcombe is East Portlemouth. The easiest way to get to it is by the little ferry from Salcombe, which runs during the summer months. To get there by road you have to go right round the top of the estuary and then face the nightmare of traffic in narrow lanes. The beaches are the real attraction but everywhere there is something to see. The National Trust own the cliffs and you can walk as far as Prawle Point, Devon's southernmost tip.

Had you come by car, more narrow lanes would take you to East Prawle and then to the ghost village of Hallsands, which hangs over the sea disappearing more every year. This once prosperous little fishing village died in a storm in 1917 when it was washed away. It is something that should not have happened. Shingle was needed for the Dockyard in Plymouth and at Hallsands it was easy to dredge. The loss of the shingle gave the village no protection from the savage sea.

If you wander the lanes going northwards for a few miles you will come to Beesands where the fishermen's cottages are right on the shore. It is a nice way to while away a lazy hour watching the fishing boats being launched from the foreshore.

Torcross is a place, tranquil in summer, which turns to the seething fury of a witches cauldron when the ferocious gale force winds and thundering seas shake the exposed coastline. It is the beginning of an

Lobster Pots at Beesands

area which was totally taken over by the Americans in World War II. At one end of the village there is a Sherman tank which was raised from the sea just off shore in 1984, forty years after it was sunk in rehearsals for the D-Day Normandy landings. 749 Americans lost their lives off this beach when preying German E Boats pounced on them unawares.

It is very hard to believe Slapton Sands and Torcross were the hub of the American activity in 1943–4. The beach was in constant use for practising the amphibious landings. Whole villages were evacuated and the villagers found homes elsewhere. In recent years an obelisk has been erected to commemorate this piece of history.

Behind is the Slapton Ley Nature Reserve which is both beautiful and full of wildlife. There is a Field Studies Centre too.

I suggest continuing along this route, through the village of Strete, perhaps stopping at the little cove below Stoke Fleming where Warwick

Slapton Lea Nature Reserve

the Kingmaker is said to have landed. It is a small world of its own and, strangely, named Blackpool.

Kingsbridge is charming. It rises steeply from the Salcombe estuary— one of my favourite boat trips is up the estuary from Salcombe to Kingsbridge. The tower of the church stands on massive 13th century arches; much of the rest of the church is anything from the 15th century to the nave and aisles of the 20th century.

There has always been a rule for the rich and one for the poor. To prove the point there is an inscription on the wall outside the priest's doorway which must have been there for hundreds of years. It says:

> Here lies I at the chancel door,
> Here lies I because I am poor,
> The farther in the more you'll pay
> Here I lie as warm as they.

One little monument by Flaxman touched my heart; it is of a baby clinging to two women, in memory of a mother who died on her way home from India.

For such a small town it has produced some remarkable people. George Montague, whose collection of animals and birds is in the British Museum; John Hicks, the Protestant minister who was persuaded to march under Monmouth to Sedgemoor and, after defeat, found a hiding place with Lady Alice Lisle at Ellingham in Hampshire. She, poor soul, had no idea that he was escaping and, when he was discovered, she was hauled off to Winchester for tried by the brutal Judge Jefferies, who sentenced her to death.

Another famous man of the town was William Cookworthy who found a way of using Cornish China clay to make English porcelain. He is remembered in the Cookworthy Museum of Rural Life, in Fore Street. Housed in a wonderful 17th century school building, it has period costumes, porcelain, old local photographs, a complete Victorian pharmacy and a magical world of dolls houses and toys which delight children of all ages.

A business very much bound up with fish is **Salcombe Smokers** who produce the delicious Salcombe Smokies—smoked mackerel to those of you who do not not know. What a fascinating business it is and, unbelievably, until two years ago the present owners, Mr and Mrs Benson and their sons Chad and Bruce, had never attempted the smoking process.

I tried to find out from them how it was done but the recipe they use is very much a secret and one that they hope will be handed down to the next generation of Bensons. What I did learn was that almost anything can be smoked, although they haven't tried flat fish yet! Whether it is mackerel, salmon, haddock, or even prawns (which are fantastic smoked), it is always done with oak chips. These the Bensons obtain from Dartington Mill from the hand carvings and sometimes, slightly ghoulishly, from the undertaker after he has finished planing a coffin. Oak is apparently the best wood to use for this because it leaves no after taste. None of the smoked fish has any artificial colour in it.

The smoking is done downstairs from the shop in four massive kilns. Mackerel need three fires to smoke them and every fish varies in the length of time it has to be smoked. Salmon is the most difficult; it takes three days using one fire, and the fish are laid in salt for some hours before smoking. The salmon is not usually local but brought from the Shetland Isles because the Bensons say it is the best.

For people who had been in the smoking business for such a short time they were extremely knowledgeable and successful. When they took it over, the business was run down, but in their first year the turnover was up by 50%. The locals started coming in for wet and smoked fish and in this, their second year, the business has been phenomenal.

Success only comes from hard work and certainly the Bensons do their share of that. They have a thriving mail order side with fish, cleverly packaged, being sent through the post.

Bruce Benson goes out to hotels, pubs, delicatessens and wholesalers, acting as the salesman and delivery man. He is a likeable young man who gets on well with his customers. Chad is very proud of his title as 'Head Smoker'. He also says he is the chief taster—essential to ensure the fish are absolutely tip-top.

Mr Benson told me that some years ago he actually came to this shop to apply for a post. He already had considerable experience in wet fish but the owner told him that he didn't have a hope in hell of getting a job in the shop!!

I would not be surprised to see this business expand very soon, especially into the export market. I hope that they will still keep the family touch which contributes to their success.

The Smokers are members of the Devon Fare Group, whose Chairman is Roger Curnock of the Bel Alp Hotel at Haytor, whom you will meet a little further on in this book.

Devon Fare is a bit like a Guild. It is a group of small businesses who got together to help each other promote the food of the county. It is subsidised at the moment by Devon County Council but is going to have to stand on its own financial feet very shortly. There is a very pleasant lady, Margaret Drake, who runs the Group and if anyone would like to know more, do give her a ring on Bovey Tracey (0626) 833583.

When you have done with wandering, a walk along the quay on the Dartmouth road will bring you to **The Crabshell Inn**. Its original purpose was to serve the men who worked on the barges moored on the quayside. It still has that air of the sea about it and is a great place to have a drink or a meal. On good days you can sit outside and watch the activity of the estuary. I was slightly put off by the new motel which has grown up alongside it, which does offer good accommodation, however. It just seemed to detract from the old pub, but once inside you are in the world of a real inn.

The A381 takes you from Kingsbridge to Dartmouth, if you want to wander then you may be tempted by a signpost that says **Buckland Tout Saints**, which is dominated by a hotel of the same name forming part of an estate whose written history goes back for nine centuries. Built by Sir John Southcote in 1690, it is an elegant Queen Anne manor house set amidst rolling hills. The atmosphere is one of gracious country-house living. I have never stayed, or eaten there, but those who have tell me it is wonderful and that the food is a gastronomic delight.

Further up the A381 it is definitely worth going into Blackawton, a large village which gets its name because the local building slate turns black when it is wet. I went there to see **The Woodland Leisure Park** which, in its first year, has won the title of not only the best Touring

Buckland Tout Saints Hotel

and Camping Site in the South West but also for the whole country. It is owned by the Bendall family who consist of mother and seven children. A remarkable dynasty whose aims seem to be excellence and fun. Three of her children work in the Woodland Leisure Park which developed because they saw the need to diversify from the farm of 168 acres that they had owned for twenty years.

The Bendall's creative ability has enabled them to design both the park and caravan park together with some beautiful landscaped gardens. It is an idyllic place to stay. I think it is an incredible achievement to have gained so much recognition in their first season. It is set in a secluded valley with sixty acres devoted to action packed adventure— or tranquillity at the other end of the scale. There are hundreds of animals and birds in Noah's Ark Paddock and Under Cover Animal Farm. There is Ern the Emu and Ho the Hog and an animal for every child to love. You can see one of the most comprehensive collections of water fowl and poultry. Go to the Honey Farm and watch half a million bees working the miracle of the honey. I discovered how bees make glue and learnt why they dance. It is quite an experience.

Children will be constantly occupied hurling themselves off the triple drop slide, or for the smaller ones investigating the Toddlers Play village. If you are a fit father then you may feel up to challenging your son on the Green Beret Commando Course. A large pond entices you to get into a Jolly Pedallo and take to the water. By the time you have tackled the Screamer Death Slide, Action Track 1 & 2 Tube Slides and the Tarzan swings you will probably be ready for a drink if not a meal in the excellent cafe. If you would rather bring your own food, the Picnic Field is designed for just that.

I have to admit that a gentle meander along the Woodland Paths and the Monk's Nature Trail was a bit more suited to my age but it did not prevent me from enjoying everyone else's frenetic activity.

Although I was not there to see it, I understand that there are spectacular Entertainment Days with live performers, Treasure Hunts, Displays and Fun Days.

It really is a tremendous day out for anyone, even if they do not want to pitch a tent or bring a caravan for a longer stay. The pitches are level and excellent. It is all terraced, so there is a sense of space. The facility building has free showers, electric points, bathroom for young and old, disabled facilities, hairdryers, water points, chemical disposal point and Calor gas. Well behaved dogs are more than welcome and the country shop is stocked with just about everything you need.

The Bendall's are a charming family and genuinely want people to enjoy themselves, not being in it only for financial gain. They are quite rightly proud and elated with the awards they have won, but having met them I am certain they will not sit complacently on their laurels.

Just before I tell you about Dartmouth, let us back track two miles to Stoke Fleming, which stands three hundred feet above Start Bay. Its streets are narrow and a walk along the cliffs will leave you spellbound. You can almost imagine that you are in Atlantis when you see traces of a submerged forest along the shore, and the great rocks called, for some unknown reason, the Dancing Beggars. It is a village of little activity; not the place to stay if you need entertaining but the sheer beauty of the surroundings is invitation enough.

Blackpool Sands

To stay in **Stoke Lodge Hotel** which overlooks the peaceful village is a rare treat. The Lodge was bought by Mrs Meyer and her son some ten years ago. It was quite a challenge, a totally new experience for both of them, although the son owned a restaurant in Dartmouth, and still does—the Scarlet Geranium, next to the Harbour Book Shop . It has the most wonderful cakes which are made on the premises.

Stoke Lodge was in a sad and sorry state when they started their programme of refurbishment but a decade of dedicated, and sometimes inspired work has produced a truly lovely hotel. It is a place that never closes and remains busy throughout the year because of its comfort and very high standards. To prove the point I can tell you that to stay at Stoke Lodge for Christmas you have to book about one year in advance. I am not in the least surprised.

A huge dining room, which is both comfortable and despite its size remains intimate, is one of the additions. There is an indoor and an outdoor swimming pool, and a jacuzzi, sauna, sunbeds, gym and spa baths you can see how well equipped it is.

There are twenty four bedrooms with different degrees of comfort. You can have either a standard room, a sea view room, four-poster or single room, or—the epitome of luxury—a Garden Suite. Apart from not having a view, there is no room in the hotel that is not extremely comfortable, well furnished and fitted with every modern facility.

The most important asset, the Mayer's feel, is the excellence of their food. They believe that it is essential for their visitors, returning in the evening after a day out, keenly anticipating a wonderful meal, not to be disappointed. It is a compliment to the Mayer's that so many people, having once visited the hotel and its restaurant, do come back again and again.

It is not only residents who value Stoke Lodge. There are frequently 150 or so who come for Sunday lunch at any time of the year. Having seen the menu and the range it covers, all for £7.25 including coffee, I am amazed that there are not more.

The grounds live up to the same immaculate order of the hotel and there is nothing nicer than a quiet stroll round the colourful flower beds and on to the village pond, which is part of the grounds of Stoke Lodge.

Turning the car around I made tracks for Dartmouth which you approach from the top of a steep hill. If the traffic permits, it is a great place to stop for a moment because of the stunning panoramic view you get of the town and the river.

Dartmouth is a 'show stopper'. Its dramatic scenery is heightened by the tiers of houses which cling for dear life to the hillside overlooking the river Dart. I have never thought of it as being a very comfortable place to live because of the endless hills, but nonetheless it is a town I love visiting.

The waterfront is always busy no matter what the time of the year. In the summer the pleasure traffic on the river is accompanied by the thousands of boats of the yachting fraternity. There are constant passenger and car ferries crossing the busy river to Kingswear on the other side, from whence it is an easy run into Torbay. A lot of people come down to Kinsgwear and leave their cars there, then take the ferry across

View of Dartmouth

to explore the delights of this very old town which has seen more history than most. There is a method in their madness. Dartmouth is one of the most difficult places to park in the season.

The town was important as early as 1147 when it was used as a point of assembly for the Second Crusade. Much of the waterfront land has since been reclaimed making the New Quay. As late as 1567 ships were still tied up to the churchyard wall of St Saviours. This is quite the most interesting church in the town. It was dedicated in 1372 but much altered in the late 15th century and again in the 1630s. If you take a look at the magnificent west gallery and take a guess at what it would cost to build today, you will be astonished to know that at that time it cost just £15.

Because of the sheltered deep-water, the harbour has always been sought after and in the 12th century Dartmouth rose to being the fourth most important town in Devon after Exeter, Plymouth and Barnstaple. All the cloth trade from Totnes came down the Dart; wine from France was the main import and wealthy merchants and shipmasters made it their home. John Hawley was the greatest of them all and his driving force took the town forward. Chaucer visited in 1373 and his meeting with Hawley probably inspired him to use the man as the Schipman in the Canterbury Tales.

After Hawley's death, Dartmouth lost its way until around about 1580, when trade again flourished and many of the wonderful buildings, which fill the eye with pleasure, were built between this time and 1643. Much of the old town has either been preserved or restored. I wandered along the Butterwalk, revelling in the black-and-white houses and shops and then along the frontage of the Quay, passing the Castle Hotel, a favourite place for meeting one's friends and having morning coffee.

On this visit there were three people I wanted to meet. The first was Joyce Molyneux at **The Carved Angel** on South Embankment. This quiet, modest and charming lady is a legend in her own lifetime. It

The Butterwalk at Dartmouth

does not matter where I go in the country, if I mention her name to anyone who enjoys good food, they know her.

Ten years ago she created this wonderful restaurant in a nice old building. The wide window, overlooking the street and the river, allows anyone to look in, whereupon they will see tables, simply laid with crisp linen and fresh flowers. It is not the most atmospheric of places but that is of no importance. The food is out of this world. It is an eating experience. Not the place to go unless you are prepared to spend money, but what a gastronomic investment!

When I sat down to talk to her at a table in the window, it was after the luncheon trade had finished. She was relaxed and I soon discovered she has a keen sense of humour. We chatted away about her love of cooking which she inherited from her father, who used to enjoy cooking for his family. I got the feeling that the creation of superb, balanced and beautifully presented food was as necessary to her as breathing in and breathing out, which is why she is so successful.

We talked of her philosophy on running a good restaurant. The emphasis came down strongly in favour of team work. Every member of her staff is capable of doing any of the jobs required to produce the end result. It is a system the Japanese have used for years and they have made it work so, in the same way, there is a rotation here.

Joyce never minds if people just pop in at lunchtime for one course or even a bowl of the super Provençal fish soup and a cup of coffee. She told me about the Americans who tend to order in quite a strange way to us. One will have a three course meal, the other just one dish, a third a bowl of soup and the fourth perhaps a cup of coffee. This causes no problem at all. Wisely, she understands that not everyone can afford to indulge themselves at the prices she has to charge but she would rather they enjoyed something than not come at all.

Just round the corner from here is **The Harbour Bookshop**, once owned by Christopher Milne, son of A. A. Milne who has enchanted children of all ages with his Christopher Robin and Pooh Bear stories. Since I became a grandmother I have become further acquainted with these books, though more often on video than read. I think I know every word and every picture in *Pooh Bear and the Blustery Day*!

All the years that Christopher Milne had this bookshop he was constantly asked about the books and his father. It must have been quite a cross to bear.

In recent years the bookshop has changed hands and is now owned by Bruce and Nicolette Coward, two dedicated booksellers. They made the decision ten years ago to up sticks from London, where they were both involved in publishing. They wanted a better environment in which to raise their children. Nicolette has family connections in this part of the country so when they knew that Christopher Milne wanted to sell, they seized the opportunity.

The shop is marvellously stocked with every imaginable kind of book. The space is limited but much skill has been used in ensuring there is a space for children to hunt out their favourite books, or discover new friends, whilst their parents browse in peace.

I asked Nicolette where most of their trade came from and she told me it was local, with a boost from tourists in the season, but they had also built up a considerable mail order business, especially in books for yachtsmen. Their mailing goes all over the world and they feel that the ex patriates become their friends. In fact they have been entertained by customers when they themselves have been abroad.

Even after ten years Bruce still finds himself being asked if he is Christopher Robin, but he takes it as a compliment. This busy shop must be very hard work but I felt it was a labour of love as well as a living.

Up the steps by the side of the Harbour Bookshop, I found my next port of call, **The Cherub Inn**, the oldest building in Dartmouth. It has not been a pub all that long—since 1972 in fact. Dartmouth is very lucky that this incredibly beautiful building has survived. It was almost destroyed when fire swept the southern end of Higher Street in 1864 and narrowly escaped bombing during the second world war when the north side of the street was hit.

To the passer-by in 1958 the Cherub looked derelict but the gaze of one, Mr Cresswell Mullett, fell upon it. He delved deeper, found the original framework and, stripping away the thick plaster, revealed the extremely rare wooden windows in the north wall of the first floor. He discovered that the house was built mainly of ship's timbers and was originally a merchant's house. His restoration has ensured that it is now a Grade 1 listed building and that people like myself are lucky enough to be able to enjoy the entrancing atmosphere of the inn.

The bar downstairs is only small but it is brimming with character and a deep sense of history. Upstairs, there is an equally charming, low beamed room where you can dine at nice solid tables. There is one table up here, number six, which is always in demand by couples. It is in a romantic corner, but it also has a ghost which hovers around it and quite frequently makes an appearance—or at least, its presence felt. In a perfectly friendly manner I hasten to add.

The food is good, not wildly expensive and there is an emphasis on fish, which is locally caught. If you like oysters, then try the Salcombe variety, which are luscious. I love salmon and would always opt for River Dart salmon if it was available. If you do not like fish then prime charcoal grilled steaks, chicken and game in season, are always available.

Every day there are specials on the blackboard which can be eaten either in the bar or in the little restaurant. I think they are tremendous value, especially when you have the privilege of eating your choice in such a fabulous place.

For malt whisky lovers, this would be paradise—there are no less than forty from which to choose.

Janet and John Hill, together with their son Steven, run the Cherub. I asked Janet about it because, when I looked at the narrow, three storey building, I realised it must be incredibly hard on the legs having to climb up and downstairs with regularity. Her answer was in the affirmative. Yes, it was excruciatingly hard on the legs but the sheer joy of working in such an incredible place made up for it.

The Hills bought the Cherub just over a year ago, having previously owned and run the Ilsham Valley Hotel in Torquay. They were very popular there and it has not taken them long to establish themselves in Dartmouth either. They are the right sort of caring people to have such a treasured piece of our heritage in their possession.

The Cherub has a little card which is given to people telling them of its history and on the back there is a quotation from Thackeray's *Memorials of Gourmandising* which I want to print here because it applies so much to the Cherub and the Carved Angel:

Sir, respect your dinner!
Idolize it; enjoy it properly
You will be many hours in the week, weeks in the year
and many years in your life, happier if you do.

I am quite sure if I asked the Economic Growth Department of Devon County Council they would tell me that Dartmouth worries them because of its lack of railway facilities and the strangulated site along the water's edge which discourages any large new industrial development. The Amenities Committee would shake their heads at the lack of golf clubs, beaches and other amenities, but I have never yet met anyone who has not found Dartmouth entrancing and been totally happy with what it offers. The town does not look depressed or dejected. Its citizens seem to prosper and it manages to maintain high-class shops, so there cannot be much wrong. I hope it will never change.

The saving economic grace is probably Britannia Royal Naval College, a splendid red brick building which dominates the town. It looks down from its majestic height onto the river and the town beneath. It is the home for all basic naval officer training, both male and female. Gone are the days when boys used to come here at the age of thirteen to finish their schooling and be trained as young naval officers at the same time. Today's young men and women are never less than eighteen and frequently graduates.

Royal Brittania Naval College

The decision to build the college was made by the Admiralty in 1896 and the foundation stone laid by Edward VII on 7th March 1902. Since then it has produced some famous naval officers, amongst them Prince Philip. It was here that he first met our Queen when, as Princess Elizabeth, she came with her parents, King George VI and Queen Elizabeth, to the college for the spectacular passing out parade. This takes place on the quarterdeck of the college every year but not always in the presence of the monarch!

Along the quayside you will see notices advertising river trips up to Totnes and elsewhere. If you have time, take to the water, for the trip covers some of the most beautiful scenery in the county. On a sunny day the brilliant blue of the water finds it hard to compete with the endless variation of greens to be seen in the trees and fields. You will see Dittisham, a village of thatched stone cottages winding through plum orchards and daffodil fields down to the river. From the quay by an old inn, a passenger ferry plies its trade, signalling its approach by ringing a large brass bell.

It is the epitome of a peaceful English scene but remember that this river, arguably the most beautiful in England, has been the means of bringing wealth to many places throughout our history.

CHAPTER 3

Totnes and the English Riviera

PLACES OF INTEREST

77   Perils of the Deep, The Quay, Brixham. Tel. No. (08045)
101 Powderham Castle, Kenton, Exeter. Tel. No. (0626) 890243
100 Teign Valley Glass Studios & House of Marbles, Teignmouth. Tel.
     No. 0626 773534
82   Torre Abbey, Torquay. (0803) 293593
66   Totnes Motor Museum, Totnes. Tel. No. (0803) 862777

When you leave Dartmouth on one of the river boats, your eventual
destination will be Totnes, historically one of the finest towns in the
country. On one night in August 1990 tragedy struck it. The centre
of the main street was gutted by fire. Fortunately, no lives were lost
and, thanks to the diligence and skill of the firemen, far less was
destroyed than otherwise would have been. Gone is the distinctive
arch that hung from one side of the street to the other and with it
some of the finest linenfold panelling anywhere. We are told that given
time much of the arch and the clock can be restored. In fact, in less
than forty-eight hours after the disaster, clockmakers from all over
the country were in touch with the Mayor offering help in the restoration.

Totnes, first mentioned in the reign of Edgar about 959, was probably
a small settlement. Since then many tales are told of this busy little
town, which is not much more than one long street climbing up a hill
by the River Dart, including the true story of a Totnes boy, William
John Wills, who grew up to be the first Englishman to cross Australia—
and perished in so doing. An obelisk to the memory of his name stands
at the foot of the main street. What a poignant story it is.

William Wills, born in 1834, was the son of a doctor and he too became
a doctor. Both men eventually emigrated and set up practice in Mel-
bourne, but William had itchy feet and longed for the open life. With
his friend Burke he planned the expedition to cross Australia from south
to north, something never done before.

It took them four months to reach Cooper's Creek and there they
left supplies, instructing those remaining to stay three months. Wills
and Burke with six camels and two men went northwards, reaching
the mouth of the Flinders River on February 12th 1861 — mission accom-
plished! On the way back they were delayed by the illness of one of
their men and stayed with him until he died.

At Cooper's Creek they found the holding party had left that very
day taking the stores with them. Wills would have followed them but
Burke was insistent on seeking help from an up-country station which
they never found. By this time, near to starvation, they staggered back
to Cooper's Creek to find that the holding party had returned in their
absence but had departed once more.

With death staring them in the face Wills insisted that Burke should
go on without him, bringing back help if possible. He was left with
a starvation diet which would last eight days. Burke struggled on but

dropped dead. A man called King who was with him managed to survive and was rescued. A party immediately set out to find Wills but it was too late. He lay, dead, with his diary open beside him in which he had faithfully recounted one of the bravest expeditions ever undertaken by man. The small obelisk in Totnes is a humbling memorial.

There is also on Harper's Hill the trace of the prehistoric Icknield Way, and a stone marked by an arrow in Fore Street claims to be the landing place of Brut. It is called Brut's stone and when he stepped ashore he is supposed to have said:

> Here I sit and here I rest
> And this town shall be called Totnes

The only time it ever gains recognition nowadays is when the mayor of Totnes stands on it at the beginning of a reign to proclaim the new sovereign.

The old Butterwalk always beckons, with its pillars supporting the projecting houses, most of which were built in the 16th century. Today it is the home of a number of busy small shops.

Totnes Butterwalk

That great architect, Sir Gilbert Scott, thought that the stone screens, in the church, built 500 years ago, were some of the finest of their date in any parish church. The church has a sense of timelessness about it and to sit in one of the old pews breathing in the beauty makes one closer to one's Creator.

The 16th-century Guildhall teaches one that life was extremely rich in Totnes back in the late 14th century. A plaque bearing the name of every mayor since 1377 underlines this. It is a sombre building of grey stone with a slate roof and a verandah on pillars full of an odd collection of pieces of Totnes history.

If you want to know about the making of cheeses of all kinds visit **The Ticklemore Cheese Shop**, No 1 Ticklemore Street, which has been on the go for four years. Sarie Cooper, the owner and her husband have been making cheese for ten years. The idea was to make the cheese actually on the premises in the belief that it would attract people. A novel idea, which can teach an ignoramus like myself much about the craft of cheese making.

It was cheese with a difference, made from sheep's milk. Milk from sheep is rather special because it can only be obtained for about four months in the year, although the yield is twice as much as from a cow. This, of course, makes the cheese seasonal. In order to get the milk, the lambs have to be weaned after six weeks. The cheese can then be stored until Christmas but once it has gone, there is no more until the following Spring.

Sarie also makes goat's cheese because the milk is very similar. Ticklemore produces a hard cheese, or a blue cheese—Beenleigh Blue—which is very strong and rich and also a smoked cheese. Having tasted them all I have decided that the goat's cheese, Ticklemore goats, Blue Harbourne and fresh goat's cheese, have a definite and distinctive tang of their own, far more so than the sheep's cheese.

Ticklemore Cheese Shop sells over sixty different varieties. They are all farmhouse cheeses, some of which they make themselves. They have been persuaded to add one or two Continental cheeses to the range to satisfy their customers. Sarie seriously wants to concentrate on selling nothing but cheese rather than enter the delicatessen market, of which there are several in the area.

They actually do have delicatessen owners as their customers but the backbone of the business is the local hotels and restaurants whose customers in turn ask where the cheeses they serve come from.

The demand for Ticklemore cheeses grows everyday and they deliver as far away as London. Indeed there are occasions when they have to turn business away.

Of the several good hostelries in the town, I have always enjoyed the **Seven Stars**, an early 19th century building of great charm which offers both accommodation and good food in the bar and the restaurant. I have had a great deal of fun there on the evenings when they have an Old Time Music Hall. It is an occasion when you get a number of regulars who know the form and encourage the rest of the audience to participate.

If you want a fascinating hour or two spent amongst the well known and much loved Austin 7, the exotic Talbot Lago, Voisin, Aston Martin or Alfa Romeo, let alone a collection of early bicycles and a motor-cycle gallery, you will find them all in **The Totnes Motor Museum** at Steamer Quay, near the old bridge.

It was first opened in 1970 in a converted cider warehouse. There are two floors of exhibits, with something to interest every age - from the child's pedal car to the unique racing Grand Prix cars. You will regret having thrown away the toy cars you once owned when you see what prized exhibits they are today. I can remember my father bringing me models back from London when I was a child. Models which, if I had kept, would be worth a small fortune today. How careless my generation were.

The main theme of the museum is Vintage, Sports and Racing Cars spanning some eighty years of motoring. The cars are kept in running order and, in the case of the racing cars, can be seen on the major race circuits of England and Europe, often at Grand Prix meetings. The history of the cars fascinates everyone who sees them. Some more interesting than others, of course, like Fangio's Le Mans car, one was raced by a Prince, some by famous racing drivers and even an Amphicar for crossing the river.

The Motor Museum opens every day from Easter to October, 10–5pm.

Just north of Totnes, on the A381 at Littlehempston, there is a nice pub, **The Pig and Whistle**. It has been a hostelry for four hundred

Pig and Whistle, Littlehempston

years serving travellers. As with all inns of that age, it belonged to a monastery and was also a blacksmiths. One of the monks got left behind at the dissolution and still haunts the pub today.

Steeped in history, full of character, warmth and charm, the Pig and Whistle is always worth visiting. The beer is well kept and the food excellent. I have spent many happy hours there enjoying not only the company of my friends but of the regulars who never make visitors feel intruders.

The Pig and Whistle is an easy run out of Totnes. Just far enough to make you feel you have been on an outing, but equally good if you just want to pop out for lunch instead of staying in the town.

Littlehempston lies in a delightful valley where Gatcombe Brook and the little River Hems join forces to flow towards the Dart. It has a 15th-century church which is almost unchanged and fills one with wonder at the skill of the craftsmen of the time. There are three 15th-century screens and the barrel roofs, with carved bosses, are something to be remembered.

Whilst I was visiting Totnes I took the opportunity to drive up the Kingsbridge road, firstly to Harberton where a stream flows by the churchyard and a 16th-century inn looks welcoming. I wanted to take a look at the fantastic 15th-century screen placed from wall to wall. It has to be one of the finest possessions of the church in the whole of the county. It is of medieval craftsmanship and has four rows of cresting running along it. The traceried bays and the long vaulting are all decorated with small carvings and painted in red, gold, green and blue. There are two great buttresses with fine canopies and below are forty-four paintings of saints which are on metal and were added in the late 19th century when the screen was restored. There must be a minimum of a thousand distinct pieces of carving in this screen.

Originally the village was part of the parish of Harberton but came into its own when the mills along the banks of the river needed power. There are only a couple of mills surviving today: Hill Mill was once an edge tool works about a mile upstream and today this is a delightful restaurant and hotel—but the other **'Crowdy Mill'** was my destination.

This family-owned, commercially-worked flour mill is situated in the valley of the River Harbourne. There has been a mill on the site for seven hundred years and the current one for two hundred. The entrance is over a wooden bridge and into a courtyard which embraces a setting seemingly hardly unchanged in all that time.

I was greeted by two eager members of the family, Dizzy and Gussie the springer spaniels, followed by their master, Keith Benton. I was shown around to see first hand the mystery and magic of traditional production of stoneground flour by natural water power. The process was briefly explained and underlined that it was neither quick nor light work. Wheat carefully selected for its flavour and quality, is taken by sack from the silo to the mill and put in the grain elevators up to the winnower to sieve the chaff from the grain. After careful cleaning it is put back into sacks and onto the hoist to travel to the top of the mill and into the hopper from which the wheat is fed onto the genuine old French Burr mill-stones, turned by the power produced from the water wheel. The result is 100% flour but not the finished product.

It is then taken to another hopper and into what is known as a dresser, which sorts the bran out. The bran gets bagged separately for animal feed. The rest is fed into a further hopper to produce either self-raising or malted grain flour. Malted grain is possibly better known as granary flour, but Crowdy Mill cannot use that description. Although widely used by us in the common vernacular, 'granary' is a copyrighted brand title by one of the bakery conglomerates.

Having had my eyes opened, Keith's mother, Anne, was kind enough to ask me to join them for a cup of tea in the pleasant, countrified kitchen of their home. It was Mrs Benton who originally bought the mill in 1988, six years after it had been carefully restored. A year later Keith joined her having left the very different world of London's Soho media industry. Devon offered him something new, a challenge in relatively clean air, rolling countryside and healthier living - and above all a slower and saner way of life. With his 'green' conscience, it was a chance to live within a working village and environment which provided wildlife, scenery and an energy-conserving business.

With careful marketing and the quality of the products, the family has built up an acclaimed business supplying schools, prestigious bakers and restaurants. Joyce Molyneux was telling me that she uses it in the Carved Angel in Dartmouth and I know that the Seafood Restaurant in Padstow is another delighted customer. There are also many retail outlets in the South West.

Despite the hard work and long hours, the Bentons have found, in Devon, a lifestyle which satisfies them, a business which is successful and fulfilling and a part of England that is known as 'God's own'.

One mile from the centre of Totnes on the A381 take the road sign-posted Ashprington and you will come to **Bowden House**. It has played a quite remarkable part in the history of Totnes. It was in Norman times that it became important when Judhael, the first Norman lord of the town, gave his daughter's hand in marriage to a member of the de Broase family and for the next hundred and thirty years Bowden was the home of the Lords of the Manor of Totnes. It had a varied career after that until in the mid 15th century it was purchased by a wealthy financier who, earning £520 a year, was reputedly the richest man in Devon. He spent a fortune converting the medieval house into a Tudor brick mansion in keeping with his wealth. He was a great philanthropist who genuinely cared for people. No one had any idea how much he did for the poor until some years ago twenty vast bread ovens were discovered in the house, from which, in times of need, bread was baked for hundreds of people and given away freely.

After his death, his son, who had been knighted at the Coronation of James I, lost much of the family money and in 1704 the house was sold to another successful businessman, Nicholas Trist, whose mother had been a member of the de Broase family (now known as Browse).

Nicholas was an arrogant man who constantly fell out with Totnes council, not least because of his insistence that the family should sit in pews on the north side of the church, which was the customary area occupied by the Mayor and dignitaries of the borough. On one

Bowden House

Sunday morning he marched into church during a service and had the parishioners forcibly ejected from the pews that he wanted. Having achieved his mission, he expected the service to carry on as normal. Later, he sent his blacksmith to place locks on his chosen pews.

From that day for ten years, there was complete estrangement between himself and the town until finding themselves in financial difficulties, the Mayor and council had to ask him for help. To his credit Trist stepped in and saved the town from ruin. I will bet that he never allowed them to forget his beneficence.

The house had varying fortunes after the Trists were forced to sell because of gambling debts. In the 1880s it was bought by the Singer family—of sewing machine fame—who lived in their magnificent mansion 'Oldway' at Paignton. It was used as a stud farm and even had its own racecourse. Today it is the Petersen family who are the owners, and it is to them that we are indebted for the privilege of seeing this fine house with its mixture of styles.

I was taken on a tour of the house by a guide dressed in Georgian costume. She had a great knowledge and love of the house. Watch out in the pretty Victorian pink bedroom where two ghosts, who are as much a part of the house as the family, tend to make their presence felt. One is said to have warm hands!

The most recent addition to the house is a purpose-built British Photographic Museum which houses well over a thousand cameras. There are miniature models less than two inches high, early movie equipment and the enormous Victorian portrait cameras.

It is open Tuesday, Wednesday and Thursday from April to October, plus Bank Holiday Sundays and Mondays, from 11–6, and from 2–4.30pm there are guided tours of the house. The grounds are lovely and you can get refreshments in the house or picnic in the grounds if you prefer.

No-one should ever come to Totnes without making a little detour to the west and visiting Dartington. It is a village but with a difference. There is no such thing as the village square but you will discover, if you are diligent, just how many virtues it has.

The old manor was once surrounded by almost five square miles of wooded and agricultural land, with its farms and hamlets gathered under its wings, linked by trade, industry and religion. As early as 1152 it is recorded that it had a priest and it is quite possible that there was a church at the site of Dartington Hall long before that was built.

One of the oldest pubs in England is here, **The Cott Inn**, which was nearly destroyed by fire a short time ago but, like Phoenix, has risen from the ashes. It used to give refreshment to passing traders of wool, tin and hides as they travelled one of the oldest trade routes in the country between Totnes and Ashburton. Cott is not the shortened version of cottage but comes from Johannes Cott, a wealthy merchant who lived here.

Dartington Hall has been the pivot since Saxon time. It flourished under the Normans, in Tudor times Raleigh advised the owner about the planning of the gardens and in the 17th century it was extensively modernised. It took World War I to bring it to its knees and until 1925 most of its fine farmland was derelict and the great hall was a sorry ruin.

Then a miracle happened: an American lady, Dorothy Elmhirst and her husband settled here with her husband Leonard to carry out a clause in the will which had made her rich. The clause stated that a very large proportion of her inheritance should be spent on education. It

Dartington Hall

was the start of an experiment with activities spread over three thousand acres, along the lovely valley of the Bidwell Brook. There were mills and workshops, her college taught the natural industries of the country-side, experts taught forestry and farming, gardening and pottery. New businesses were started—cider mill, saw mill and tweed mill. A new school was founded and an arts centre established attracting artists and performers from around the world.

The Elizabethan house was reborn, with a fireplace sixteen feet wide in the 600-year-old hall and a banqueting hall with magnificent timbers of an even earlier date. It was an estate bursting with energy and an example to everyone.

Sadly, time has not been kind to it. The Dartington Hall school was closed amidst a lot of controversy; the mills no longer exist. A business park stands where the sawmills were, but the Cider Press Centre displays and retails beautiful crafted goods and is well worth seeing. The Hall is still very much alive and is a Mecca for a variety of people who attend courses there. Anything from a day course on the use of word processors to a residential week making music.

Many of you will own or have seen the beautiful Dartington glass but do not be too disappointed when you find it is not made here but in Torrington, North Devon.

You are in the vicinity of several castles. Totnes was first built before history began and is now a crumbling mass of stones of the Norman era. It stands high up on a mound with part of a moat round it, and in the keep are two staircases and a small chamber.

Compton Castle bursts upon you as a complete and very welcome surprise as you drive along a quiet lane one mile north of Marldon. It is probably the best example of a fortified manor house left in the county. Now the property of the National Trust, it is still occupied by and administered by Mr and Mrs Gilbert, whose family home it has been since the 14th century—with the exception of a time between 1800, when it was sold, and its purchase by Commander Gilbert who lovingly and carefully restored it over a period of years. He was a direct descendant of Sir Humphrey Gilbert who gave Britain its first colony, Newfoundland. Sir Humphrey was also half brother to Sir Walter Raleigh.

I think the true story of how Compton came back into the hands of the Gilberts is incredibly romantic. About the beginning of the 20th century Walter Raleigh Gilbert, a young naval cadet on his way back to the naval college at Dartmouth, saw the ruined property and made up his mind that he would buy back the old family home one day. It took him another twenty-six years to realise that dream and then with the help and support of his wife, Elizabeth, he set about the daunting task, room by room. I wonder how many times they must have wondered if the unrelenting work would ever come to an end. We have much to thank them for. Compton Castle is a great house.

There have been several periods of rebuilding since Geoffrey Gilbert erected it in 1330–40. He was able to do so because he had married the Compton heiress. Of that period the solar, the cellar and some foundations of the great hall remain. Extensive changes were made between 1450–75 and much of the house that you will delight in visiting, dates from this time. It was almost another forty years before anything else was added and then three of the five machicolated towers were added. If you do not know what 'machicolated' means do not worry; neither did I until I first heard it when I visited the Artillery Tower restaurant in Plymouth, where unwanted visitors received machicolations—it is the pouring of any repellent like boiling oil, slops or any other horrific fluid down a chute onto the unfortunates below.

Compton Castle is open on Monday, Wednesday and Thursday from 10–12.15 and 2–5 from Easter Monday until the end of October.

Berry Pomeroy belongs to the Duke of Somerset and has been owned by only two families since the Norman Conquest—the Pomeroys and the Seymours, whose descendent the present Duke is. It is one of the most romantic ruins in the whole of Devon and haunted without doubt. You can feel it when you walk around. Television South West filmed

Berry Pomeroy Castle

there quite recently and felt a presence whilst they were doing so. You don't believe in such things? Well, I wonder why when they tried to play back the film, the screen was blank!

Time now for Torbay—a place with which I have a love-hate relationship. I suppose it is the same with anywhere which looks for a large proportion of its income from tourism. The love bit comes from the incredible beauty of the bay which sweeps grandly from Brixham to Dawlish Warren, encompassing Babbacombe Bay en route. The hate lies in some of the devastation that has been caused by thoughtlessness and the pursuit of commercialism which could have been avoided.

It is cheating slightly if we start this journey at Kingswear, but just imagine that you have come across the River Dart on the ferry to Kingswear. The little boat clunks its way across the busy river and you drive ashore only minutes later to find yourself in a little town, one mile from the mouth of the River Dart. The town itself is not of much interest but it allows you to drive up the winding road above the River Dart catching glimpses of this unfailingly beautiful estuary.

If you want to pause awhile, as I sometimes do, I try to call up a picture of what it might have been like in the 12th century when a gradual movement of people from the hills surrounding Dartmouth and Kingswear began to make new homes alongside the harbour in order to carry out business with France and eventually America. Much of it was connected with the fishing industry, but as time went by wines and silks took over. Smuggling was rife and there would always have been the danger of invaders from the Continent.

There is a curious granite tower, the Daymark, built in 1864 by the Dart Harbour Commissioners. It replaced a chapel that was not only a place of worship but helped guide sailors into the harbour entrance, which is difficult to see from a ship. If the tide is on the ebb and the winds blowing, it is also very treacherous. The tower is octagonal and stands eighty feet high and can have been of no possible use except in daytime.

The arrival of the railway in 1864 changed the life of Kingswear totally. In order to build a station the slipway had to be widened, and old buildings ruthlessly demolished. Much of Tudor Kingswear disappeared. In the 1960s the Kingswear to Paignton line was closed but that loss was soon repaired by the arrival of **The Dart Valley Railway**, a private company who have operated ever since.

We are very lucky that, in the last thirty years, enthusiastic railway buffs have helped make the steam railway one of the most celebrated tourist attractions.The Dart Valley Light Railway operates two steam lines, the Dart Valley Railway between Buckfastleigh and Totnes, and the Torbay and Dartmouth Railway between Paignton and Kingswear; both conjure up images of travel in history, each rich with nostalgia for the prosperous days of the Great Western Railway, providing a sentimental insight into the journeys of yesteryear.

The Dart Valley Railway continues to portray the line as it was in the Great Western days. Steam is the boss, the guards with their whistles and green flags still control the trains. The Great Western locomotives stand proud and majestic; however apart from the smell and smoke it is impossible to recreate every detail. Some of the GWR engines have had their day and have to be replaced by more recent engines, although the elderly and fragile are preserved.

When you take a trip on either of the two lines, not only do you feel the great sense of love that has been poured into them over the years, but you also witness some of the most breathtaking scenery in

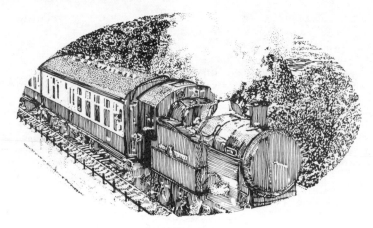

Dart Valley Railway

Britain. The Buckfastleigh line passes over the river Dart, through Staverton Station, used on several occasions for television and film serials including *The Hound of the Baskervilles*. The journey ends at Totnes BR station; at this point you can take one of the River Dart boats from the steamer quay near the town for a trip into Dartmouth and then take the train back on the Torbay and Dartmouth line.

Not only is the train ride a memorable experience but so are the ten acres of riverside grounds that form a leisure park, workshops where engines undergo repair, a museum and the Free Flight Butterfly Centre.

Paignton station is situated right in the middle of the seaside resort. It is where Agatha Christie's fictitious character, Hercule Poirot, a neat little man with military stance and stiff well-behaved moustache, travelled in 1939 with Captain Hastings in the novel *The ABC Murders* and in 1956 in *Dead Man's Folly*. Today the Model Railway can be found at the station and it is a must for all the family.

The first stop along this line is Goodrington Sands and then on to Churston, another port of call for Poirot. Agatha Christie often used Churston station, riding the train to Paignton before driving to appointments in London.

From Churston to Kingswear, the line crosses the high ground separating Torbay from the Dart Valley and starts coasting downhill into wooded rolling country, disappearing suddenly into the Greenway Tunnel, 495 yards long; once back in daylight the view stretches for miles right across to Dittisham and down towards Dartmouth. As the train approaches the town, sailing fanatics will be in awe of the masses of yachts that lie in the harbour, and you can see for yourself why this part is named Onedin Line country—for this is the location for many of the shots used in the famous television series. Kingswear is the final stop.

The trains only run during the basic holiday season at Easter and May to October on the Paignton line, and at Easter, May bank holidays and from June to mid-September on the Buckfastleigh line. Work is

Bayards Cove, Dartmouth

still carried out throughout the year in maintenance and spreading the word around so that more people become aware of the facilities on offer. Without passengers the trains will not survive.

Brixham has always been the home of fishermen, whose houses perch into the side of the hills leading to Higher Brixham. Some are close to the harbour or open onto the little streets or steps bringing their occupants to the seafront. One house, Ye Olde Coffin House, is shaped exactly like a coffin. Legend has it that it was built by a young man for his love—not for morbid reasons but because her father told him that he would rather see her in her coffin than married to such a worth-less character. The suitor designed and built the coffin house and the father, impressed by the quick thinking, relented and the lovers married and lived happily ever after in their coffin.

The harbour and the quay are always busy with the comings and goings of the weather-and sea-worn fishing trawlers. The men of the sea work hard and the workers who take the catch that has been brought ashore still labour in uncomfortable conditions. If you are interested in the history of these fisherfolk, then the British Fisheries Museum on the quay will answer all your questions and give you a vivid insight into the perilous lives of the men and the growth of their industry.

Brixham's latest tourist attraction has the unusual name of **'Perils of the Deep'** and it is an experience that lives up to the name. Right on the quay you walk up the gangplank to board the mysterious 'Ahab', a dark deserted trawler—very eerie. On the bridge there is total stillness, except for the creaking of the wheel as it spins, unmanned. Radar is no help—you can try checking the charts but you will not have a clue as to your destination. Without warning a storm breaks around you and it is a moment when you have to make sure you have your sea legs as you try to make your way along the tossing gangway with the hurricane raging through every porthole.

The next adventure is the Bathysphere, which takes you on a voyage of discovery under the sea. From the shallows you sink slowly to the great depths where the earth's crust is still being formed.

In an underwater cavern you suddenly catch a glimpse of the softly shimmering silhouette of a mermaid. You go on to explore a sunken pirate treasure ship which seems full of ghosts and finally to the Abyss, where in the dim, flickering light you see the towering figure of Poseidon, ruler of the deep.

An unforgettable experience, if slightly exhausting. It is open every day from 10am with the exception of Christmas Day.

Incidentally, there is a good Park and Ride scheme at a site on the A 3022 as you enter Brixham from the Torquay side. It is operational from July 23rd to August 31st on weekdays only, but it does help. Brixham is not the easiest place to find parking space.

I quite enjoy going by ferry from the Princess Pier in Torquay, which has a half-hourly service in the summer, and you can get the added bonus of combined tickets for the ferry and Perils of the Deep from the ferry office.

In the last two or three years there has been intense activity by developers to build a Marina. The first attempt was by an American consortium who had grandiose ideas but ran out of money, and in the last few months it has been taken over by one of this country's major Marina Development companies.The completion of this project will radically change the way of life in Brixham and I am not sure it is for the good.

Whilst tourism is not ignored here, it has always had to take second place to the fishing industry, and so the character of the town has changed little over the centuries. More homes have been built on the outskirts but no one can change its narrow streets and its charm.

For such a backwater it has witnessed some remarkable events in history. On the morning of August 7th 1815 two ships rode at anchor off-shore, the *Bellerophon* which had come from Rochefort was one of them, and had Napoleon on board. This mighty, fallen emperor had one desire—to land in England and to meet the Prince Regent. This was denied and he was transferred to the *Northumberland* together with his travelling library, his little camp bed and his chosen few who were to accompany him to exile on St Helena. As he went over the side of the *Bellerophon* men stood to attention, drums rolled and there was not a dry eye amongst the crew.

Francis Drake sailed into Brixham with the first capture of the Spanish Armada—a ship that, once stripped of its armour and gunpowder, was taken to sea again and fired. The wind carried the blazing, lethal, unmanned vessel towards other Spanish ships whose fate was sealed without a shot being fired.

It was in Brixham that William of Orange stepped ashore for the first time to become King and end the Stuart dynasty. There is a stone and a boring statue on the quay which marks this momentous occasion. I think he might have been better portrayed.

For me Brixham will always stay in my mind whenever I hear that wonderful hymn, *Abide with me*. It was written by Henry Francis Lyte, vicar, for a quarter of a century, of the 19th-century All Saints church.

Brixham Harbour

It is a hymn that has been sung throughout the Christian world by people in times of great emotion. My father told me that in World War I it was sung by the men in the trenches and when they had finished the Germans would take it up from their dug-outs.

Edith Cavell spoke the last words of the hymn as she stood before the firing squad.

> Hold thou Thy Cross before my closing eyes,
> Shine through the gloom and point me to the skies
> Heaven's morning breaks and Earth's vain shadows flee:
> Help of the helpless, O, abide with me.

It has brought peace to thousands. We had it sung at both my parents' funerals and perhaps it gave the same comfort to its writer who wrote it in the dusk after evening service. He did not know that it was his last service in the church. He died not long afterwards. If you listen you will hear the bells of All Saints ring out his hymn every night.

Berry Head Country Park is a place well worth visiting as indeed is **The Berry Head Hotel**, a free house which offers a family atmosphere, a lot of fun and a great deal of comfort in all their bedrooms. Some have the most glorious sea-views and private balconies; the sort of rooms which would be hard to equal anywhere and certainly not at the prices that the hotel charges.

The Napoleon Steak Room is super. Everything is named after the remarkable general who, for so many years, threatened England and the rest of Europe. He would have been extremely pleased to see that he is in no way forgotten in this restaurant.

There are Bonaparte Starters, the Main Campaign which covers a whole range of steaks, Napoleon's Downfall, a fillet steak coated with the chef's pâté, topped with sliced mushrooms and encapsulated in a light puff-pastry case, accompanied by Madeira sauce and a bouquet of vegetables. 'Not tonight Josephine' includes Josephine's Downfall, a wickedly fattening concoction of ice-cream, whipped cream, hot chocolate sauce and finished with chopped nuts.

The Berry Head is a happy establishment and one I am happy to recommend.

Coming out of Brixham on the Paignton road you get your first glimpse of the majesty of Torbay. It is as blue on a sunny day as anywhere in the Mediterranean and every bit as beautiful.

Goodrington Sands are just off the main road. These wonderful beaches have for years given pleasure to families. They are both safe and clean and every amenity is there. I miss the donkeys who used to give rides to children in my young days, but with so many other major counter-attractions on the beach I do not suppose today's children feel the loss.

Just on the outskirts of Paignton is the zoo. It is a small word for one of the finest examples of wildlife and botanical preservation in the whole of the United Kingdom, and recognised for its enormous contribution by conservationists throughout the world.

I was lucky enough to meet Mary Talbot Rosevear, who looks after the marketing of **Paignton Zoo**. This lady is full of enthusiasm for her job, which she matches with a remarkable depth of knowledge. She came into it via a circuitous route, having worked abroad for the Irish Tourist Board in Germany, France and Switzerland and then met and married a Devonian, and luckily, after searching for a suitable job for over a year, the one at the zoo came up.

Over many years I have made several visits to the zoo with my children when they were young and later with friends from other parts of the country. It was always an enjoyable experience but, with the animals in caged concreted areas, it lacked something. This has all changed.

Most importantly Mary told me that the name is to change. It will be called the Whitley Wildlife Conservation Trust because the word 'Zoo' is too restrictive and does not indicate the level at which they operate both nationally and internationally. Nor does it describe the field study work and *in situ* projects within the zoo. The change of name will allow it to encompass all the work of the Trust which includes

Rhinoceros at Paignton Zoo

British wildlife conservation, as in the case of Slapton Ley in the South Hams, which is a site of special scientific interest. At the same time it will expand its horizons to include behavioural studies, other scientific studies within the zoo and in the wild.

Mary Talbot Rosevear finds the future tremendously exciting. Using Jersey Wildlife Preservation Trust, which used to be known as Jersey Zoo, as a role model, she would hope that Paignton would be on a par with the model in five years time.

To the layman this could sound almost as if it was going to lose its appeal to the general public, but that is definitely not so. It is a great day out and will continue to be so—only better. It is certainly good value, good fun and an interesting place to come, but it is also a place where children and adults can use the resources. There is no need to pity animals being taken into captivity from their natural habitat and locked up in cages. Within the gates there are 75 acres of open space for visitors to roam about. There is a genuine Nature Trail—and I use the word genuine because it is pretty wild and has not been manicured to make it look tidy. Of course you are not going to have to hack your way through a jungle but you get the chance of seeing much flora and fauna in their natural state because it has not been disturbed.

Behind the scenes there is another 25 acres devoted to breeding and education as well as many other things that have to be done to sustain this wonderful place.

I asked Mary what advantages Paignton had over a safari park. Her answer made sense. In a nature reserve or a safari park you run the risk of not seeing any animals at all because they are either hiding in the grass or well camouflaged. Here the animals are readily seen in safety but at close proximity in as natural a surrounding as possible.

Apparently some people complain that it is too natural and the vegetation grows too high. Difficult perhaps to change people's view of a zoo in which once upon a time everything would have been scrubbed and hosed down and if by chance an elephant did a whoopsy in opening hours it would have been removed immediately!

Three hundred and fifty thousand people go to Paignton Zoo every year, mainly in the holiday season from April to October. People living in the county come from a radius of fifty miles but seldom in the peak season. They know they will enjoy it more when it is quieter. Many of them are regulars and are members of the Zoo Society which entitles them, for an annual subscription, to a number of benefits, not least free admission to the zoo every day of the year.

Approximately 20,000 Devon school children come to the zoo every year and use the education units for both formal and informal education worksheets which they can use as observational sheets in the grounds. There is also a series of programmes - some of which are styled to assist the teacher in the new National curriculum and some are purely for fun.

Different things are scheduled at different times of the year. At Christmas there is a reindeer event when the children come along and meet the reindeer but they also have their attention drawn to other features, with touch sessions as well as observation sheets. In the future it is hoped to set up a summer school for advanced students. It all follows the brief of the Herbert Whitley Trust.

Over the next few years I believe, from what I have been told, that the botanical gardens will become one of the focal points here. I know they are hoping to bring the beautiful, mature gardens in line with Kew and to participate in the international movement to increase the number of source plants and particularly the endangered plants. It is a mammoth task. A botanist has just been appointed whose job it is to identify the plants that are on the ground and to feed this information through on computer to Kew which in turn will co-ordinate the information for Great Britain and feed it through to Geneva to the National Union for the Conservation of Nature which is a branch of the United Nations. As Paignton now swops animals on the basis of genetic diversity, so the same thing will be done for plants.

The zoo is open every day of the year from 10am except for Christmas Day.

Flowers and rockeries along the promenade and a wonderful park, man made out of a marsh in this century, are the outstanding features of Paignton, which sits between Torquay to its left and the red cliffs of Berry Head to its right. It is a gentle sort of place, complete with a pier and a very good theatre on the sea front. The sort of place that people of my age enjoy in the spring, autumn and even the winter but who will probably avoid it like the plague in the height of the season.

Hotels, guest houses, caravan parks and holiday camps abound. As you drive in from Brixham you will pass at least five caravan and camping parks. There is not one which is not well run and does not pride itself on its amenities. I have poked my nose in on several over the years and the improvement in the last three years has been staggering.

The guest houses stand side by side, street after street. These professional landladies know their business and many have families who have been coming to them for decades. Even in winter these days many of them remain open to cater for people wanting short breaks in a comparatively warm climate.

We talked of the Singer family, when I was writing about Totnes, where they used Bowden House for training horses. It was in Paignton that Isaac Singer ordered his new house to be built in 1871. He described what he wanted as a big Wigwam. Sadly he did not live to see this magnificent house completed.

His son, Paris Eugene, carried on the work and his love of things French is seen in the fantastic ceiling he commissioned for the house, which he renamed **Oldway**—slightly more in keeping with its grandeur than The Wigwam! The ceiling is a copy of the one in the Galerie des Glaces at Versailles. Paris Eugene, intent on gilding the lily, also

Oldway Mansion

installed a grand staircase and gallery made of marble, over which there is another wonderful ceiling, this time in the Italian style. By the time he had finished there were more than a hundred rooms at Oldway.

I can remember it as a country club in the 1930s and then, like the Palace Hotel in Torquay, it was commandeered by the R.A.F in World War 11 as a training centre. Once the war had finished it was bought by Paignton Council for £45,000, and has remained in their hands ever since. Parts of the house and the superb gardens are open to the public.

The parish church, with its medieval tower, will tell you that Paignton was a place of importance way before the Georgians and Victorians discovered it and turned it into a holiday resort. Most of the church is 15th century, but the west door is Norman. A fine vaulted 14th-century porch leads you to an even older doorway and four more doors lead you into a church that has an unbelievable wealth of carving, old and new, some in wood and some in stone. I have never been able to understand how these master craftsmen were able to make stone look like the most fragile Honiton lace.

Torquay climbs the hillside at the far left side of Torbay. As you come over the brow of the road from Paignton, there it is ahead of you, gleaming white against the sapphire blue of the sea below.

It is so sheltered from the north winds by its hills and fanned by the sea breezes on the south, that it becomes a haven to visitors at all times of the year. In Victorian days people came to recuperate out of season, but in the 1990s we are looking at the new phenomenon —people who take several breaks in a year and want a place to visit that will provide comfort, warmth and entertainment. Torquay has it all.

The climate has made it possible to produce wonderful gardens, and there can be none more beautiful than the Abbey Garden with its lily pool that runs down to the sea. Strange trees grow, delighting in the warmth. There are Chile pines, Japanese bamboos, Barbary almonds and the Dragon tree of New Zealand.

Torre Abbey is the most historic possession of the town. The ruins of the abbey, founded by one of Richard the Lionheart's knights, contain a wonderful 700-year-old barn, known as the Spanish barn. No connection here with sunny Spain, but named because about 400 Armada prisoners were housed here from a Spanish ship. Its roof is about 450 years old and it is 40 yards long. Originally it was used to house the monks who built the abbey. The abbey is surrounded by trees as if in protection. The 14th century gatehouse is still there together with two crypts, ruins of the chapter house and the church, including the old gateway to the chapter house. 16th-century Torre Abbey House is the home of the art treasures of Torquay.

Where do you stay when you come to Torquay? A difficult question which depends a great deal on what you want to spend, so I went to visit a number of places and I hope you will enjoy reading about them and be able to choose.

One of the very few hotels in the country that keeps up an immaculate standard is **The Palace Hotel**, Torquay. This is a 'real' hotel, stately, dignified, welcoming and yet has an underlying sense of fun about it.

It was not built as an hotel—in fact quite the reverse, for it was originally a Bishop's Palace known as Bishopstowe built in 1841 for Henry Philpotts, Bishop of Exeter. Christianity would not have been difficult to achieve in this glorious setting! However this Bishop was far from popular. Firstly his diocese was vast and Exeter was almost a whole day's journey from Torquay. One cannot blame him for preferring to

14th-century gatehouse of Torre Abbey

live in the more fashionable and far more agreeable Torquay. What was so wrong was his complete lack of feeling for the unfortunate people of Exeter who were in the throes of a cholera epidemic when he was appointed.

By the time it was known that he had voted against the First Reform Bill, he was so hated that the coastguards were called in to garrison the Palace.

The Bishop went on to cause more controversy and anger when he decided his role was to save the Church of England from Popery and to this end he hounded out of his diocese any priest who showed a tendency towards High Church. He caused more stir virtually than any other churchman of modern times, including the Red Dean or the present Bishop of Durham. When I looked him up in the *Dictionary of National Biography*, I read, 'His pugnacity gave him his chief reputation. A born controversialist and a matchless debater, he was master of every polemic art ... neither in intellectual power nor in force of will, nor in physical courage has he often been surpassed by Churchmen of modern times.'

He did achieve some good things in his time. When he first went to Exeter he found a diocese that had not changed since the Middle Ages and stretched from the borders of Somerset and Dorset to the Isles of Scilly. He planned a separate diocese for Cornwall with a cathedral in Truro and he also founded a theological college in Exeter. Perhaps the nicest thing to remember him by is the beautiful Bishop's Walk which wanders along the coast from Anstey's Cove at the bottom of the Palace's garden to a point at the nadir of Ilsham valley where the Marine Drive begins.

In 1921 it became the property of the popular and successful racehorse owner, Mr G W Hands, who changed its name to the Palace and its image to a hotel which grew under his creative direction until it became known as one of the finest 'guest houses' in the country. Then came the 1939–45 war and everything changed.

Almost overnight the hotel changed into an R.A.F Hospital and Convalescent Home for wounded R.A.F pilots. I still remember visiting there and the determined fun that was a hallmark of almost everyone of that age group. Sneaking out of the hospital for a night on the town was a regular occurrence, aided and abetted by some of the staff.

If you are privileged enough to look at a special visitors book kept in the office of the doyen of all hotel managers, Paul Uphill, you will see it is signed by service people who were at the Palace at that time and have since come back to stay. There are many and it is not only nostalgia that brings them back. It is the sheer professionalism of the hotel.

The hotel is famed for its sporting facilities. There are two squash courts, indoor and outdoor swimming pools, saunas, six tennis courts (two of which are indoor) and a nine-hole golf course.

There are numerous lounges where you can tuck yourself away after a stroll in the wonderful gardens. Even at night there is no need to leave the hotel for entertainment. Almost every night something is going on with music to suit everyone. The porters seem to know all that is going on in Torbay as well and can organise theatre tickets or whatever. There is even a children's nanny.

The food, the wines, the service are all superb and, as Paul Uphill's Assistant Manager said to me, 'When you work here for a while you feel as though you have shares in the hotel and it makes you strive for perfection.' Nothing is ever perfect but the Palace Hotel is as near as you will get.

The Meadfoot area of Torquay has always been one of the exclusive areas of Torquay and it was here, embracing a section of the coastline that runs from Torquay's Inner Harbour as far as Anstey's Cove, that the Victorians built their mansions. Today many of them have been turned into flats and some have disappeared altogether, but one of the beautiful villas still gracing the slopes of the Lincombes is **Frognel Hall** in Higher Woodfield Road.

Lord Bridgeman carefully selected this site for his winter retreat in the year 1860. Wise man! The outlook is delightful and sufficiently sheltered to be protected from the worst of the winter storms. It is set in two acres of secluded grounds overlooking the sea, and is both nationally and locally 'listed'.

The house has quite a strange history. The Bridgeman family stayed here until the '30s when the Hall was sold to a local family who remained the owners until 1978, at which time Lynne and Michael Hookings bought it with the intention of turning it into a gracious hotel.

It is at this moment that the strangeness creeps in. Lynne Hookings told me that when she and Michael first went to take a look at the house it had been shut up for a considerable number of years. Apparently the family came occasionally to open the windows and let a little

Frognel Hall

air in, but that was all. The house was just allowed to die but, for some inexplicable reason, not a single piece of furniture had been removed. Beds were still made up and the dining room table laid. Everything was covered with thick cobwebs and it was almost Dickensian. Lynne said she would not have been surprised to see Miss Haversham rise from a chair at the table. One wonders why this was allowed to happen.

It took courage, the sympathetic help of a good bank manager and a lot of gritty determination to get the house back in order to be able to open the doors for business. Two years were spent rewiring, re-plumbing, putting in new drains, new gas, new electricity and water systems, and of course, fire precautions.

Intimacy is what the Hookings have tried to achieve. The bedrooms all have names, no guest arrives at a reception desk and then has to wait to book in. You are greeted by one of the Hookings, or their very charming and pretty assistant, and taken into one of the elegant and peaceful drawing rooms before being shown your room.

I chatted for some time with Lynne and found her a lady of intelligence and determination who will not allow herself to be defeated by anything. She has time to take an active role amongst the Torbay Hoteliers and I do not think anyone would be stupid enough not to listen to her well observed opinions. She believes that Torquay needs to be protected from the insidious threat of light industry being brought to the area.

More should be done to attract visitors to Torbay all the year round and so keep hotels and guest houses in occupation enabling staff to be kept on and not laid off in the winter months. When you look around at the beauty of Torbay you can do nothing but agree with her.

Frognel Hall gets much of its business from tour operators who bring the more mature people. They love the atmosphere of the house and revel in the views from the gardens. For the first day or two of their stay most of them explore Torquay and all it has to offer, but towards the end of their visit they tend to come back and sit in the garden or gather in the bar.

The drawing rooms took my fancy with their fine marble fireplaces and original ceilings with delicate scroll work. In one recess Lynne has a super collection of Wedgwood mugs which I would love to own. One cupboard has glass doors hand-painted in the Victorian fashion.

Don't think for one moment that this is a hotel devoted to the elderly. It is not. The young in age and at heart will enjoy it. The lower ground floor is devoted to leisure for example. There is a television lounge, a games room, a sauna and solarium with exercise equipment to keep you in trim.

There are no parking worries and no traffic noises to disturb your night's rest.

At present Frognel Hall is open from March to November and over the Christmas and New Year.

What happens when, without warning, a long and happy marriage is severed by sudden death? For many people it is a time when you do not want to face the world, small jobs become mammoth tasks and decision making almost impossible. Time does heal but that luxury is not always available. Such a tragedy happened to the charming and unassuming lady, Mrs Downes, who is the proprietoress of **The Lindum Hotel** in Abbey Road. For thirty years she and her husband ran this hotel together, and. as she describes it, he had always been the O.C taking responsibility for all the major decisions and the maintenance. Three years ago he died suddenly and she was left on her own and still with a business that needed operating.

As I talked to her I could see the pain flit across her face; she is lonely in spite of all her friends who rally round, most of whom have tried to persuade her to sell the Lindum. I asked why she had not taken their advice. The answer was simple: she would miss it intensely. The hotel has so many happy memories for her and the thought of each new season, whilst causing some anxiety, is in itself a purpose for living.

This is essentially a quiet, comfortable two-star hotel. The bedrooms are all well appointed and en-suite. The menu is a mixture of English with a little French thrown in for good measure. The little bar is a focal point at night before dinner and frequently late on in the evening when people return to have a nightcap and chew over the day's events. It is these times that Mrs Downes looks forward to. More often than not there are people staying who have been before and are almost old friends. There is an air of quiet contentment about this very pleasant hotel.

People intrigue me and when I met Pamela Oatley at **Homers Hotel** in Warren Road, I wanted to know what had brought her into the hotel business. The answer I got surprised me. It was simply that she had stayed in the hotel several times and fallen in love with it. She was based in Bahrain where she ran a school and from this distance she pursued her aim to buy the hotel.

Homers Hotel

Her husband, Derek, had to be persuaded, first because neither of them had any experience of the business. I got the feeling that he was slightly reluctant and, whilst he appears from time to time, he still maintains his nomadic existence in his own career. She asked the owners if they were prepared to sell. The question was dismissed quite lightly with the reply that, 'Everyone wanted to buy Homers.'

However, she did not give up and eventually she was told to ring back after Christmas and when she did, to her surprise, the answer was 'Yes'. Her dream was beginning to come true. Some months later, after much stress, the papers were signed and she moved in, aided by a delightful young couple, Neville and Heather Sparks. Neville runs the restaurant and looks after the wines. He does it with a great flair and a love of the grape. The wine list is superb.

I asked him what he would choose from the list. He won a lot of brownie points when he did not give me a long lecture about what should be drunk with whatever dish, but gave a straightforward answer: Chateau L'Enclos Pomerol (Chateau Bottled) 1980. I have since tracked down a supply and he is so right—it is a delight to the palate. If I were staying at Homers I would have no hesitation in accepting his recommendations.

Heather bravely gave up a career in nursing to join Pamela and Neville at Homers. She still makes beds! Her role is a multiple one. Reception, bar, chambermaid, housekeeper—you name it and she does it with grace and charm.

Coming back to Pamela Oatley, this lady has a gift for organisation and imaginative planning. Every person who stays at Homers is made to feel that they are guests at a house party. All year round there are special events and occasions which are well thought out.

Christmas is an occasion on which Homers goes to town. This is truly a house party. The hotel only takes twenty-six people, so it is quite easy to get to know your fellow guests, some of whom have been coming here for many years. There is no stuffy breakfast on Christmas morning but a buffet with Buck's Fizz, croissants and coffee, which is fun and leaves room for the sumptuous Christmas lunch at 1.30pm.

Non-residents are welcome to dine at Homers in the restaurant Les Ambassadeurs, which has the most spectacular sea-views on the English Riviera.

The other side of the hotel business, slowly emerging, is corporate entertaining, which started because a director of one company stayed with his family and decided it was just the place for a company meeting. After several meetings, in which every detail was noted, it was agreed that they would take over the whole of the hotel.

In so doing Pamela was able to provide them with meals at whatever time they chose, and see that meeting rooms were organised with the appropriate equipment. The organisation was so meticulous that place names for the diners were arranged previously, making sure that members of the company sat at different tables every night. The company achieved their aims and it started a new line of business for Pamela. The minimum number she will accept to give a company sole use of the hotel is sixteen.

Pamela Oatley do you want to sell Homers? I too have fallen in love with it!

With the motto, 'If you care to choose, we choose to care!', **The Hotel Nepaul** states its policy quite clearly. It is a hotel which stays open all the year round, offering equal pleasure for a summer holiday or quiet out-of-season break. I have not stayed there, but the reports I have had from people who have give me sufficient confidence to say that I am sure you would be comfortable, well fed, enjoy good wine in very pleasant surroundings.

It is only 250 yards by private footpath from the hotel to the golden stretches of Abbey Sands, and wherever you look there are lovely views. Many of the bedrooms look out over the sparkling waters of Torbay and have their own private balcony.

Do not expect it to provide entertainment; it is a hotel that has no functions, does not take coaches and so keeps quite a unique atmosphere. You, the guest, are of prime importance and all the facilities of the hotel are at your disposal.

You can swim in the heated indoor swimming pool, play snooker or billiards or be completely idle sitting on the sun terraces and in the gardens, which all face south-west and catch the maximum sunshine.

The Nepaul has 'Mind Easer' mini breaks which must be a tonic for anyone feeling a bit jaded. A two-day break in an en-suite room with a sea-view costs as little as £63 per person between November and March and that includes dinner and a full English breakfast each day.

When I started enquiring about **The Victoria Hotel** in Belgrave Road, I discovered that I had happened on something very different. It is one of three hotels, all situated on a single six-acre site close to the sea-front, owned by a family, headed by Mr Laurence Murrell, whose management, planning and careful attention to detail have produced something unique in each venue. The other two in the group are the Derwent and the Toorak.

The Victoria is the South West's finest dancing holiday venue. The ballroom has a dance floor of over 2000 square feet—one of the biggest in the West Country. It really is an extraordinary place, a bit like a continuous 'Come Dancing' with a holiday thrown in for good measure. It is obviously a hotel for people who love dancing but there is no need to feel that you have to be an expert. Dance instruction is arranged in the morning and afternoons leaving you feeling confident to join the twinkling toes on the ballroom floor in the evenings.

In addition to the dancing events which the hotel organise themselves, there are also well established dancing house parties run by organisers who invite you to join friendly parties of dancers who regularly visit the Victoria. For these occasions availability is limited to guests booking direct with the organisers. The hotel will forward any correspondence or you can ring the Holiday Helpline 0803 291333 and the information you require will be forthcoming.

Once a year there is the English Riviera Dance Festival, during which there is Social Sequence Dancing, Modern/Latin American, Cabaret, and demonstrations by World Champions. Philip Wylie is the man behind it all and you can contact him for details of a package holiday to cover this enterprising event on 0895 632143.

The Toorak combines elegance with fun and offers some marvellous Themed Weekends, which tend to bring guests of similar interests together. Whatever the theme, genuine cuisine is served and includes wine or a complimentary aperitif. For the gala dinner on these weekends some guests join in the spirit of the occasion by dressing in the appropriate style. The Themed Weekend Break entitles you to use the entire range of entertainment and leisure facilities within the Torquay Leisure Hotels complex.

Last but by no means least in this group of hotels is **The Derwent**, which is great for a holiday at any time but does specialise in mid-week breaks which not only allow you to enjoy the English Riviera with its warm climate, but will take you into a world of interesting activities with something for everyone from quizzes, competitions and tea dances to whist, indoor short-length bowling and bingo. After the activities of the day there is dancing and cabaret at night and a fancy dress competition with a 'free holiday' as one of the prizes.

If you do not want to join in all the activity you will find there is plenty of room in which you can escape and just rest quietly.

I find it incredible that one can get so much and pay so little without some of the quality disappearing, but it is a fact that these three hotels all offer marvellous value for money.

What a pretty house **Orestone Manor** is! On the Teignmouth road it exudes tranquillity and you can almost feel the strains and stresses leave your body and mind as you drive up to the door. There is no disappointment either when you walk inside and find yourself enveloped in quiet comfort. Mike and Gill Staples own and run Orestone Manor and they set an example to their staff which affects the whole

Orestone Manor House

ambience of the hotel. There is nothing fussy or obsequious about the service, it is just well mannered and very welcoming.

I have never been over keen on the 'Star' system for hotels but the new awards made by the A.A. now cover quite a wide spectrum and are based not only on the standard of the furnishings, en-suite facilities, etc, but also on hospitality and the Inspector's personal view. It did not surprise me to learn that Orestone Manor has been awarded a 67% rating which is one of the highest awards for 3 Star hotels in Devon.

The hotel is open to non-residents and it is not only a pleasant place to dine but the *table d'hôte* menu is imaginative. I was in my element: I love fish and having looked at the menu decided to stick to the fruits of the sea all the way through. Amongst the four starters was a Danish fish salad, followed by Arbroath smokies in a cream and cheese sauce and then the most delicious lattice of salmon and sole served with shrimp sauce. The fresh vegetables were just that little bit undercooked which is perfect in my eyes and to my taste buds.

It would make a super place for a break and what a lovely hideaway for a honeymoon! If you are a golfer you will appreciate the excellent courses within easy reach, and for shoppers Torquay is full of temptations.

It is people that make places which is why, having chatted to Peggy Dobbin of **The Thatched Tavern** at Maidencombe, I came away thrilled with what she and her husband Richard had achieved and richer because I had listened to the extraordinary road she had travelled that finally, in her sixties, had brought her to Maidencombe.

Not so many years ago she had a house in Teignmouth which was

The Thatched Tavern

dedicated to the rehabilitation of mentally handicapped people who, having been institutionalised in many cases since their childhood, were suddenly thrust out into the unsympathetic, and certainly not cognisant, world. It was a brave enterprise. I can remember when the people of Teignmouth were up in arms at having these unfortunates in the town. They felt it put off holidaymakers. Thank God that there are people like Peggy who are not daunted by public opinion and are prepared to tackle a social problem.

Her success rate varied; sometimes she was fighting a hopeless battle and had to acknowledge that there were people who were beyond the help of laymen. In many cases though, by patience, love and just human fellowship, she was able to see people leave her and strike out into the world on their own, full of confidence, having put the nightmares of the past behind them.

When she decided to give up, her daughter took on the mantle and is still carrying on the same devoted work. Every week Peggy entertains some of them to lunch or a little something at the Thatched Tavern. They love it and it warms Peggy's heart when she sees what simple pleasure these people derive from such an outing. She told me that she feels as if they are all part of her family—and she is not lacking in children of her own either. They are a close knit and devoted family— the salt of the earth.

Having left Teignmouth with the intention of retiring, within three weeks she was bored out of her mind so she bought some holiday flats in Torquay—but that did not give her enough contact with people. Letting holidaymakers into their apartments at the beginning of the week and saying goodbye at the end meant nothing, and it was at that time she discovered that the Thatched Tavern was on the market. A small inn close to the beach at Maidencombe in a lovely sheltered spot with a beautiful view. It was a small business that did a good trade in the summer and then virtually shut up for the rest of the year. Just right for her husband and herself, Peggy thought.

They bought it just three years ago and from that moment on they have done nothing but build on in the most attractive manner. The bars are virtually brand new and yet they look absolutely right in company with the original part which is 300 years old. The whole building has acquired a warmth of atmosphere that can only stem from Peggy and her son John, who, with a dedicated staff, cope with anything up to 300 covers.

If you think I am ignoring Peggy's husband, this is untrue. This is a man who likes to keep a low profile but the extensions and mainten- ance are his forte in addition to being the strength behind Peggy.

The gardens in the spring and summer are full of colour and it is possible to sit outside and enjoy a meal quite late in the year. Last Christmas Day several people actually had their Christmas lunch in the garden.

I have not eaten there, but I did take a look at the menu and believe you me it matches the excellence of this establishment. There is a well- chosen wine list and both the food and the wines are incredibly good value.

When Peggy told me the story of the opening night of the latest exten- sion I hooted with laughter. They were due to open in the evening but they were nowhere near ready. Most sane people would have decided to put back the occasion for at least a month—but not Peggy. She cajoled and motivated, bribed and manipulated until she had her team working flat out. The guy artexing the walls found himself followed by her, brandishing a hairdryer, with which to get it to a sufficiently dry state so that the painter could slap on the emulsion.

By late afternoon they were almost ready for the influx of visitors but to Peggy's dismay the wholesalers had not turned up with supplies.

Fortunately she caught them before they closed and they told her that they did not think it sensible to deliver because their boss had been down that morning and returned to say that there was no possibility of the pub being opened that day. How wrong he was, he should have known Peggy better.

The latest enterprise is a beautifully appointed small hotel built alongside the tavern. Called Suite Dreams, it lives up to its name. The rooms are beautiful and so carefully planned. The ground floor rooms open out onto a terrace overlooking the sea and the rooms above have an even better view.

If you stay here you breakfast in a pretty room and then dine, if you wish, in the restaurant at the Tavern next door. It is a superb place for corporate entertaining or small company meetings and seminars. There are sixteen rooms in all and once breakfast is over that room becomes a well equipped meeting room. I know of one company who are using it shortly for business purposes but also inviting the wives as well. The wives will be delighted.

At the moment the prices are ridiculously low for what is on offer. I cannot imagine this being able to continue but Peggy says that it is because it is a new venture and they want people to get to know about Suite Dreams. My advice is to seize the opportunity whilst you may.

From the day that it opened its doors in 1866, **The Imperial** has been England's foremost resort hotel. It has the unfair advantage of an unrivalled site to start with. Standing in 5 acres of lush gardens, in a sheltered position, it commands a view across the English 'Bay of Naples'. Even I am not old enough to remember its very early days but I do remember being taken to tea there on several occasions just prior to World War II. It was quite awe inspiring to a child; the surroundings were impressive and I felt very small sitting up straight in a high backed chair with my feet dangling quite a way off the ground. Children were expected to be seen but not heard so there was plenty of time to gaze about.

Even now I can conjure up the resplendent waiter who served us, with his several minions in attendance to answer our every need. I remember the paper-thin brown bread and butter wrapped round pieces of asparagus—works of art in themselves—and the wonderful array of cakes of all kinds, including fresh cream meringues.

It was not many years later that I was there again during the war. Things were different, staff was scarce and food was in short supply, but the Imperial still had its aura of grandeur. It could have been a different story because only a sudden change of mind by the powers that be saved the hotel from being requisitioned. It had got to the stage when all the staff had been dismissed, including the General Manager, and the furniture stored away in a house taken over by the hotel for this purpose.

The change of plans meant near panic for the directors who, with no manager, no staff, no furniture and not even a bottle of wine in

The Imperial Hotel

the cellar, somehow had to recreate an establishment within this beautiful shell. Lady Luck smiled on them. The Chairman asked a member of the D'Oyly Carte family, who had an estate not too far away, if they knew of a suitable manager through their connection with the Savoy Hotel, London. They did and that is how the Imperial acquired a man who was to become one of the most famous hoteliers in this century, Michael Chapman. He was very young but from the moment he met the Board, they sensed that in him they had found someone who would rise to the challenge. The Imperial was quickly in business again.

The worse the bombing became in London the more people flocked to Torquay and the Imperial. Young R.A.F. officers were regular visitors whilst they did their initial training. I was told, when I was researching this piece, that the charge was half a guinea a day each. That is just over 50p today!

The ingenious Michael Chapman helped to ensure good food supplies by having a large part of the lawn in front of the West Wing dug up for vegetables, and local farmers supplied him with chickens in return for leftovers which they were able to use as chicken-feed. Gone were the asparagus rolls and the fresh cream meringues but never once were the standards of the hotel allowed to drop.

The Imperial did not escape the notice of the Germans and the summer of 1941 brought near disaster, but fortunately the bombs fell short and the damage inflicted was superficial. Guests who had tried to escape the bombing elsewhere were soon on the move but their place was taken by those who were not quite so chicken-hearted and knew that the Imperial would enable them to forget the war for a little while.

I remember dancing there on New Year's Eve 1942 to the strains of music from the band of Jack Padbury. The ladies were in ball gowns—

mine was made from some rather exotic curtains that were no longer in use at home! Men, unless they wore dress uniform, were expected to wear dinner jackets. It was the good side of the war. By this time too the 'Meals in Establishments Order' was in force and no hotel or restaurant could charge more than five shillings—or 25p to you. There was a control on service charges and on drinks, when they were available.

During all of this adversity, Michael Chapman kept the hotel going and by the end of the war he was Managing Director of the company and the Imperial was ready for a new beginning in peace time.

It was not until the early seventies that I had the opportunity of returning to the Imperial. Much had changed, it now belonged to Trusthouse Forte who, with infinite wisdom, made sure that Michael Chapman stayed at the helm, modernising and transforming this wonderful hotel into the best equipped resort hotel in Europe. It is history that he was put in charge of all Trusthouse Fortes overseas hotels and later its London luxury hotels, but his first and remaining love has always been the Imperial.

So much for the past, but what will you find there in the 1990s? Apart from the 17 suites, the 105 twin rooms and 41 singles, all superbly furnished, you will enjoy unparalleled service from the moment you arrive. Every meal is a gastronomic experience and there are varied sports and leisure facilities.

Gastronomic Weekends at the Imperial are famous the world over. They are extraordinary occasions. Every weekend is meticulously planned and apart from the serious eating it is also a great deal of fun.

The Imperial has recognised that much business today comes from companies who need first-class meeting rooms or conference halls and

Village of Cockington

probably require to house their people as well. The Imperial is completely geared for this and has a specially trained staff detailed to look
after these occasions. When I saw the Conference Tariff, I was agreeably
surprised at the reasonable rate.

My childhood gave me a taste for the Imperial and now I am approaching my second childhood, I have not lost it! It is a wonderful hotel.

The theatre has always played a prominent part in the life of Torquay.
Not so long ago there were two theatres, the Pavilion and the Princess.
The Pavilion is no more but it has been turned into an imaginative
shopping mall and is more than worth a visit. The Princess is home
to many productions throughout the year. There is almost always a
long running summer season with a well known star—this last year
it was Jim Davidson.

No one comes to Torquay without seeing Cockington. If you want
to see it at its best go early in the morning, soon after sunrise when
it is still. Later it will be swamped with visitors and all you will remember
will be the crowds and perhaps the thatched cottages. Seen early it
is as if you were back in the 16th-17th century when Cockington Court
was first built. It sits in a park with the church of St George and St
Mary close by. The church is even earlier with a tower that dates back
to the 13th century. I love the carved bench ends under the tower and
the two 15th-century stalls with misereres in the chancel.

A cut through the lanes from here brought me back to the Newton
Abbot by-pass, a busy road but one that has cut down the endless
traffic jams of not so many years ago.

Cockington Court

Just off this road and surrounded by narrow lanes and bridleways, meant for packhorses and pedestrians rather than the mechanised 1990s, take a look at Ipplepen, a village as old as time. Conan Doyle spent many a happy visit here with his friend Bertie Robinson, who lived at Parkhill House. Exploring Dartmoor was one of his great pleasures and he used to be driven in a horse and carriage by the Robinson groom, one Harry Baskerville. Now you know where the Hound of the Baskervilles originated.

It is only a mile or two up the road from here to reach the beautiful village of Abbotskerswell with its lovely old church of St Mary the Virgin, which still bears the scars of Henry VIII's men, who ransacked it at the time of the Dissolution. The lychgate is still there and is almost the oldest in the country.

There are many pretty thatched cottages and then suddenly you drive into a new housing estate in the middle of which is **Court Farm Inn**. Once a Devon long house it is now a very nice pub and restaurant. The building is full of interest from its flagged floors to the low beamed ceilings. When I was there a lot of changes were being made to improve the kitchens. One of the partners is a keen chef with a great deal of experience—he once worked with Keith Floyd. I do not know whether that was a good or bad thing but I do know that the food is enough to tempt anyone. Lunchtime is informal but the evenings are designed to make it a bit more of an occasion, dining at candlelit tables.

Kingskerswell is best seen from the train as you go from Torbay to Newton Abbot. From here you get a tantalising glimpse of the medieval part of the village with its thatched houses and the church of St Mary, first built before Domesday. From the car you will only see the new part which is home to over 4000 people and is really a dormitory for Newton Abbot.

Between here and the centre of Newton Abbot is an unexpected pleasure, **The Passage House Hotel**. It is very seldom today that one comes across a privately owned, purpose built hotel. Massive complexes belonging to the big groups seem to pop up all over the place but comfortable as they may be they cannot compete with owner managed businesses. The newest one I have had the pleasure of visiting is the Passage House Hotel which is off the road out of Newton Abbot going towards Teignmouth. There is nothing especially striking about the exterior of the building. Its position overlooking the estuary is undoubtedly its nicest feature. The area abounds with birds so there is always something to watch and although the hotel is near the main road it is incredibly peaceful.

The Haywoods who own the hotel also have the Passage House Inn, an old establishment just a few yards down the road from the hotel, and I feel it is probably their ability to make everyone extremely welcome there that has rubbed off on the new hotel. It is always difficult to stamp personality on a new building but in spite of the youth of the

Passage House you get an impression of well being from the moment you walk in. The receptionists actually smile and make you feel important—a rarity.

The hotel has been decorated in soft shades of blue with a tinge of autumnal colours, reflecting the water and the growth of trees and riverbank. It is incredibly restful and carefully planned. Each of the eight luxury Penthouse rooms has the name of a bird instead of a number. The birds are those that can actually be seen on the estuary. Choose from Swan, Kingfisher, Heron, Wren, Warbler, Curlew, Swallow or Nightingale. They are all charmingly furnished and have private terraces and stunning views. The Sandpiper Suite includes a private sitting room, a terrace and a hydro spa bath.

Even the ordinary Executive rooms, of which there are thirty, have satellite television and a mini-bar and in every room there is an original watercolour of the superb views from the rooms.

All this is very much like every good hotel but the Passage House is somehow different. It is basically geared towards the business fraternity who use the excellent seminar and conference facilities regularly. Much more use could be made of the hotel, however, by companies slightly outside the normal catchment area, who have perhaps not yet discovered its existence. It is a stimulating setting and would certainly benefit any company who needs to instil new energy into their people, whether it is a sales force or a boardroom.

Away from the business side the hotel runs special Break prices, which are available from Friday to Sunday inclusive, with breakfast and dinner included. There are special interest and activity holidays offered and anyone staying in the hotel has automatic membership of the Leisure Club with its swimming pool, gym, sauna, steamroom, hydro massage spa and jet stream. In fact everything you need for a break that combines fitness training with blissful relaxation. I think the prices are ridiculously low for such comfort, good food and facilities. As I write the price per person for a weekend break is £35 in an Executive room and £45 in a Penthouse room.

I will probably be accused of being unfair if I call Newton Abbot a railway town, but to me that is what it is. It is really because of its geographical position at the head of the estuary which has made it an important railway junction. It is here that the main line trains stop and you change for Torquay and Paignton. It is usually, too, where the restaurant or buffet car is removed, before the train goes on via Plymouth to Penzance!

It is not a town that attracts me but it is of considerable antiquity and a busy market place. Taking a look at the mother church, St Mary's, is well worthwhile. It stands alone at the top of Wolborough hill and has been there certainly since the 13th century, of which age the tower remains. It combines grandeur with grace and simplicity. The lovely arcades have wonderful capitals which include birds, animals and even snails resting on leaves.

Just to the east is Kingsteignton which lies across the River Teign from Newton Abbot. If you want an interesting experience then go and find **The Old Rydon Inn**, which once stood in the midst of fields and now sits bang in the middle of a Wimpey housing estate. It is a fabulous place. One table in the restaurant is over a well and you can look down through glass into the depths below. Another is inside a chimney breast. A private dining room is available, superbly decorated to look like a library. On a summer's evening dining on the patio beneath the grape vines is an enchanting experience. The food is out of this world and I have to admit that the prices tend to be a bit that way too. It is the sort of place to go for an occasion.

From here to Teignmouth is about six miles along a road that skirts the river and every now and then gives you a glimpse of the opposite bank. Sometimes I take the other road from Torquay which provides breathtaking views of the sea and later on to take a quick look at Stoke-in-Teignhead which lies in one of Devon's combes by the mouth of the Teign. You come to it from a height and as you drop down the winding lanes you will see the pretty cottages and the old church which must have been here in Norman times. When you look at the mosaics in the sanctuary perhaps, like me, you will wonder how so many years ago such work was done by Italian craftsmen. Where did they stay, how did they cope with the language barrier and how long did the journey take?

Coming in to Teignmouth by this route allows you to take a look at Shaldon with its church walls which meet the river at the foot of the toll bridge. It has become more commercialised over the years but there is still a quaintness about it which appeals.

Across the bridge and there is Teignmouth with countryside behind it and the vast expanse of the Channel ahead. I think that there is

Teignmouth

nowhere in the county that has a promenade to equal it. I can remember a Christmas morning almost twenty five years ago when, with my husband and three children, we walked in brilliant sunshine along the shore and could have believed ourselves to be in the South of France.

Teignmouth is a favourite holiday spot with its two miles of sandy beaches with the odd rocks, called the Parson and the Clerk, creating a mini-headland halfway to Dawlish. No one could call the town historic but it has a pleasant shopping area.

The Cliffden Hotel on the Dawlish road is wonderfully situated, beautifully furnished and totally unique. It belongs to the Royal Institution for the Blind and has been re-designed and furnished especially for them. You cannot stay there unless your sight is impaired or you are part of the guest's family. Brilliant idea isn't it?

If you have blessed the advent of the calculator, then you will be delighted to know that the inventor, Charles Babbage, was born here.

Teignmouth can claim one building unlike any other in the county. It is the peculiar church of St James which was built as an octagon round a 15th-century red tower. I do not find it beautiful but it is a matter of taste. The other oddity is a lighthouse at the south end of the promenade. It is only 25 ft tall and has stood there since 1845 but no one seems to know why.

What an enormous pity it is that **Teign Valley Glass Studios** and the House of Marbles at Broadmeadows, Teignmouth, has not room to expand. Sitting as it does, almost on the banks of the river, it would be perfect if at the end of a visit to this fascinating place one could have tea, perhaps overlooking the gently lapping water. It would also give them room to display their beautiful wares more extensively.

The examples of their work, in the brilliant range of colours, is stunning and you can actually see the glass being blown. No one seems to mind how many questions you ask either. Every piece is designed by Teign Valley and is completely hand-made by a small team of skilled glassblowers who follow the traditional methods handed down over the centuries.

I espied some paperweights which are made here and sold to the Paperweight Centre in Yelverton, which I have also visited. I would love to become a collector of these beautiful items and certainly the ones sold here are at an affordable price.

Marbles, in my mind, were only playthings for children, until I made my first visit to **Teign Valley House of Marbles**. Now I know what immense variations there are in colour, size, quality and price. The use of them to weight a vase to help flower arrangements is quite new, or at least it is to me. They look stunning in a glass vase and are functionally very satisfactory. The great joy is that you can use them time and again, unlike the green oasis stuff which crumbles after about the second time of usage.

By visiting the House of Marbles you get the opportunity not only to see the entire range, but also experimental pieces, samples and seconds which may be purchased at considerably reduced prices.

The Teign Valley Glass Studio is just on the left as you turn into the Broadmeadows Industrial Estate, which is a turning to the left on the Newton Abbot side of Teignmouth, just before you reach the turning for Shaldon. It is open on weekdays from 9–5pm and on Saturdays from Easter to December between 10–4pm.

I have never found anyone who does not enjoy the simple beauty of Dawlish. This little town, beloved by Jane Austen and Charles Dickens, never seems to alter. The river Daw runs right through its midst down to the sea over a series of little waterfalls surrounded by colourful gardens.

Brunel wished to bring his railway through the town but found the only way was to take it along by the sea, in and out of a series of five tunnels. It is a pity but does not detract too much, and think what joy it gives to travellers on the main line as the train wends its way along the coast. The views are unforgettable and sometimes at the height of a storm it is impossible to travel. I have been aboard a train when the seas have pounded the line and covered every carriage with a torrent of silver spray. Exciting and terrifying at the same time.

One of my favourite places as I drive along this part of the coast, past Dawlish Warren with its beach huts and wildlife, and Starcross where Isambard Brunel failed to drive locomotives by atmospheric pressure, is **Powderham Castle**, one of the quiet glories of Devon, built between 1390 and 1420. It has been the home of the Courtenay family ever since. Sir Philip Courtenay was the first occupant, the sixth son of the second Earl of Devon, from whom the present occupant, the Earl of Devon, is directly descended. Actually what I am saying is not strictly accurate because about three years ago the present earl, who is 73, decided to move out and make way for his heir. He has not moved far—merely to a house on the estate, but it has meant changes within the castle and some modernisation in the wing of the castle in which the younger family live. I am told that guests staying there now do not have to go on safari to find a loo for instance!

If you take a look at the castle you will see that every generation has made some form of alteration in order to keep up with the changes of their time. None of this has detracted from its beauty.

The story of the Courtenays is so extraordinary that it has inspired writers for centuries to tell the tale. Gibbon traces the rise of the house from a root established near Paris, Crusading Governors in Mesopotamia and giving a king to Jerusalem, as well as rulers to Constantinople. One branch came to England and for 600 years they have played their part in the history of this country.

Thomas was killed fighting for the Red Rose in the Wars of the Roses. Richard, beloved of Henry V, died in his presence at the battle of Harfleur. Henry fell foul of Henry VIII and was executed in the Tower. His son, Edward, fell in love with Mary Tudor and might well have

East front of Powderham Castle

married her had it not been in England's interest for her to wed Philip of Spain. Some say he might have become the Consort of Elizabeth I. The family has produced many bishops, one of whom became Arch-bishop of Canterbury in the 14th century. Other Courtenays too have played their part in the affairs of state.

Powderham church stands serene as it has done for five centuries. Inside is the original font and screens, some well-worn benches and reminders of the Courtenay family everywhere. Their names are recalled in many of the windows and their arms on the pillars. A 14th-century lady with angels at her head and a dog at her feet lies under an arch. It is not quite certain who she is but I am told that it is probably Elizabeth Bohn, whose daughter, Margaret, married a Courtenay and brought Powderham into their possession. Some Courtenays have nothing to remind us of them, except for a bronze plate, which was set up in memory of all the Courtenays buried here since 1566.

One brass inscription points out the esteem in which a young man, of humble origin, was held. John Dinham was born at Powderham in 1788 and rose to become one of the most respected men in Exeter. He never forgot his less fortunate friends and was responsible for build-ing some of the city's lovely alms-houses.

As a member of the general public you will only get to see this gem of a castle between May and October and only in the afternoons on Sunday, Monday, Tuesday, Wednesday and Thursday. For goodness sake, do make the effort, because it is quite unlike anything else you will see in the West Country.

Competing with the fame of the Courtenay family, when you have an ancestor who fought at Crecy, is a little difficult but one member of the family is at this moment quite likely to find himself in the *Guinness*

Book of Records. He is Timothy, the Tortoise who has lived at Powderham for at least 160 years, possibly longer and is considered to be older than that. He is a friendly chap and does not mind visitors one bit.

Having taken a look at many of our stately homes and wonderful National Trust properties I have become acutely aware of the enormity of the task and cost of keeping the fabric of our heritage. Seldom can a family, like the Courtenay's for example, sustain the cost without creating some form of income from the buildings themselves.

Powderham is no exception and my conversation with Captain Anthony Smith, who is the Administrator, was extremely enlightening. He has only been at Powderham since 1988, having come via the Merchant Navy and the Sir John Soane Museum in London. During his two years, with the encouragement of the family, he has started to open the Castle for purposes other than people like you and me who go there just for the joy of seeing such an historic building. He told me that one or two specialist companies who design wallpapers and fabrics asked if they could take a look at the existing papers and fabrics. This they did and in return the Castle is being given some curtains which will replace those frail with age, and wallpaper which will not be the original but which will be in keeping.

Powderham is available for conferences, for fashion shows, archery, clay pigeon shooting, deer stalking, concerts and even private dinner parties. Imagine dining in the wonderful Victorian Gothic banqueting hall with its minstrel's gallery and heraldic fireplace with its roaring log fire, or listening to a concert in the Music Room. This is undoubtedly the most elegant state room in the Castle, with its high domed ceiling, marble pillars and fireplace, designed by James Wyatt in 1790 for the 3rd Viscount, who enjoyed a lavish lifestyle. The candles in the large chandelier are lit and the room becomes magical.

Powderham is also a venue for wedding receptions and it would be hard to find a more beautiful or romantic setting.

I understand that working with Devon County Council Tourism department there is the possibility that Powderham will be included in one of the very excellent tours that the council operate for people staying in Exeter. This is good news because not enough people know of this superb castle.

Gerry Mosdel of Dartmoor Antiques in Ashburton, who is the organiser of something in the region of 140 Antique Fairs in Devon and Cornwall, used Powderham for one of his venues which was extremely successful and he hopes to make it an annual occurrence. I could think of a hundred and one different businesses who could use either the Castle or the grounds to great effect. What an inspirational place in which to work!

CHAPTER 4

Dartmoor

PLACES OF INTEREST

132 Buckfast Abbey, Buckfastleigh. Tel. No. (0364) 42882
117 Castle Drogo, Drewsteignton. Tel. No. (06473) 3306
112 The Miniature Pony Centre, Moretonhampstead. Tel. No. (0647) 432400
147 Morwellham Quay, Morwellham. Tel. No. (0822) 832766
107 Parke Rare Breeds Farm, Bovey Tracey. Tel. No. (0626) 833909
134 Pennywell South Devon Farm Centre, Buckfastleigh. Tel. No. (0364) 42023
125 Poundhouse Craft Centre, Buckland in the Moor. Tel. No. (0364) 53234
141 The Yelverton Paperweight Centre, Yelverton. Tel. No. (0822) 854250

What is unchanging about Dartmoor is the love affair that people have with it. It is almost like a good marriage: it is sometimes turbulent, sometimes inexplicable, mysterious, exciting, infuriating, but always beloved. Within its encompassing arms you wake in the morning never knowing what the day will bring.

People who live on the moor are a breed of their own, generous enough to want to share their love affair with outsiders and astonished if your reaction is not the same as theirs. No intrusion of man, since prehistoric times, has managed to conquer the wildness of this granite mass, some 130,000 acres in all.

There are fundamental lessons to learn about Dartmoor before you start exploring. It is a National Park, but that does not mean you have unlimited access. For example, it is an offence to drive a car more than 15 yards off the road.

You are asked not to feed the ponies because it encourages them to stray onto the roads, putting themselves and road users into danger. There is a severe fine for those who do not heed this request. One other important point is to take note if red flags are flying on the north side of the moor. This means that the army is at work. Disobey the warning and you could get shot.

It is not a place in which to take chances. People die of exposure on Dartmoor. The weather can change in minutes from glorious sunshine to impenetrable mists. On a summer's day it looks as if butter would not melt in its mouth—excuse the metaphor. Do not trust it. It is easy to get lost and very frightening. In heavy rain it becomes positively sinister.

I was on my way from Moretonhampstead across the moor to Buckland-in-the-Moor on an afternoon, beautiful in the autumn sunlight with the ever-changing colours of crag, shrub, gorse and heather delighting my eyes, when suddenly a black cloud descended and the heavens opened. I could not see through my windscreen and the sense of being isolated, in an unfriendly world, enveloped me. I missed Buckland-in-the-Moor altogether, having taken the wrong turning, but I was lucky enough to find myself minutes away from some people I wanted to see anyway. A stranger may not always have such good fortune.

The Bel Alp House at Haytor was once owned by a formidable millionairess, Dame Violet Wills. The lady had an eye for beauty, which she put to very good use when she significantly altered this Edwardian country mansion. It is a house of large airy rooms, beautiful arches and a wonderful atmosphere.

Since 1983 it has been the home of Roger and Sarah Curnock and their family, who welcome guests into this lovely house which they have furnished, elegantly and comfortably, with family antiques, paint-

Bel Alp House

ings and an abundance of house plants. There is a quiet restfulness in all the rooms and most of them have stunning views, across the rolling fields and woodlands, to the sea.

No guest ever arrives at Bel Alp without being greeted personally by at least one member of the family, who somehow always manage to remember your name. Sarah Curnock's mouth-watering cooking is something else that would always draw me back to the Bel Alp. Each evening she cooks a different, carefully planned, five course dinner, with one or two alternative choices. It is no good asking her the day before what she will produce. She may have some thoughts on it but it will all depend on what is available when she shops.

Sarah looks upon her task as though she is cooking for a private dinner party for somewhere around 16 people every day. She keeps a comprehensive reference of every meal and who the guests were, so that the next time they come she can ensure they do not get the same menu.

Bel Alp nestles into the hillside, 900 feet up, on the south-eastern edge of Dartmoor. On a sunny day there are many perfect places in the garden to snooze away an hour, or sit and drink in the sheer beauty around you. When I was there thunderous rain was teeming down but it did not detract from the breathtaking views, merely giving them another dimension.

Not the easiest place to find, I suggest that the best way is to turn off the A38 dual carriageway onto the A382 to Bovey Tracey. From there take the B3387, signed Haytor and Widecombe. Half a mile, fork left, and go straight over one crossroads. After one-and-a-half miles, cross a cattle grid onto the moor. Another five hundred yards fork left into the hotel drive.

From the stunning, awesome tors of Dartmoor through the leafy road that takes one almost into Bovey Tracey is quite a change, and when you turn off the road into **Parke Rare Breeds Farm** with its soft, undulating fields, it is a different world. The car park is set at the end of quite a long drive. You need to be prepared for quite a walk, so strong and comfortable shoes are a necessity.

It is run by the Rare Breed Survival Trust, which was formed in 1973 to prevent any further extinction of mainly British farm livestock. Many of the breeds that you will see are very rare indeed and I realised that if it were not for the work of this Trust, and others like it, so much of our heritage might disappear. Some of the animals can be traced back to prehistoric times.

It is educational, rewarding and marvellous for children, who will revel in being allowed to handle some of the animals at the specially designed Pets Corner.

Bovey Tracey, the traditional 'Gateway to the Moor', has been important since the days of the Normans, when the manor was held by Edric, a Saxon thane. In the last few years it has lost much of its peacefulness with the arrival of new businesses, who have taken the opportunity of entrenching themselves close to the A38. It still has delightful narrow streets and sits sedately on the hillside overlooking the River Bovey. Newcomers may not know some of the wonderful legends that exist about the town and if they did I am not sure they would believe them. Would you believe that Sir William Tracy built the 12th-century church of St Thomas à Becket as a penance for being one of his murderers? Not satisfied with one church, he built three.

Sir William's church went up in flames 150 years later, but what has been left for us to enjoy, is a 15th-century building with a 14th-century tower, which contains some of the finest treasures that Devon has to offer. There is a wealth of carving done almost 600 years ago. The screen has to be one of the finest in the county. Exquisitely carved and decorated with gilded leaves and green grapes, it has 31 Apostles painted on its lower panels. The medieval stone pulpit echoes the carving with more grapes and leaves.

The fine brass lectern brings us to another story. In the 17th century, James Forbes was the chaplain to Charles Stuart and also to the forces in the Netherlands and Germany. Having had enough of the hardships and discomfort of this sort of life, he settled down to become vicar of Bovey church, only to find himself ousted by the Puritans. He was able to save the Elizabethan chalice and the registers. Not only that, he preserved the fine brass lectern, which is an eagle with silver claws and three lions at its feet, by throwing it into a nearby pond, praying that a drought would not occur!

With the Restoration and the return of the king, James Forbes set to work to undo all the damage the Puritans had done to his church. The chalice was back in place, together with a pewter alms dish and flagon, which he presented to the church in thanksgiving. Finally the lectern was rescued, all traces of pond life removed from it. How proud he would be to know that his action saved one of about only 50 left in England.

Bovey Bridge was built during the Civil War and herein lies another tale. Royalists occupied Front House when it was attacked by Cromwell. They were playing cards and had not a hope of beating the number of men set against them. With great presence of mind they scattered

Water Wheel on River Bovey

all the stake money out of the window and whilst the poverty stricken Parliament men scrambled to retrieve it, the crafty Royalists escaped unharmed.

There is no doubt that battles were fought at Bovey and Chudleigh Knighton Heath and it is said that the ghosts of soldiers in Royalist and Cromwellian clothes still haunt the area. Unfinished business do you suppose?

An insight into the craftsmanship of the area, both present and past, is superbly displayed at Riverside Mill where **The Devon Guild of**

Craftsmen provide a changing series of exhibitions. The Museum of Craftsmanship takes you back over the years and brings it all into perspective .

On my way to Moretonhampstead I stopped at one of my favourite places, **Becky Falls**. It is high up in the solitude of Dartmoor and you approach it through glorious woods. On one side of the road there is a car park, where, if you have any sense, you will don stout shoes or wellies, before making the descent alongside Becka Brook, where the water cascades over and between massive boulders, until with a

Becky Falls

roar it reaches its peak and falls, in sparkling torrents, on its way to the sea. This enchanted world is at its best after the mid-winter rains. I saw it on a sunlit November morning when the autumn colours of the leaves and bushes added lustre to the silver grey of the tumbling water.

Moments up the road is the isolated village of Manaton, with its green nestling beside the church. It is mentioned in the Domesday book and seems to have been there forever. Overlooked by the lofty Manaton Tor, which if seen in the autumn, aglow with the berries of holly and mountain ash, will remind you that there are not many more shopping days to Christmas!

Away to the south the great rocks known as Bowerman's Nose look like a petrified sentinel guarding the rugged hills or a man with a sense of humour, wearing a cardinal's hat, playing God.

It is worth taking time to look at Neadon Upper Hall which is an unique example of a Dartmoor building in which the family and servants lived above the animal stalls. There are a number of interesting long-houses too—long and low, built of granite with windows that are almost hidden beneath deep thatch.

Quite by chance I pulled into the car park of **The Kestor Inn**. It is not a pretty pub from the outside but this belies the inner warmth that greets you. Fitted out with a lot of rough stone and comfortable tables and chairs, it is the epitome of a nice village pub. It is rich in wood and has a separate dining area.

I was filling in time between a visit to Becky Falls and my next appointment in **Chagford**. It was only just past 11.30 and lunch did not start for another half an hour but the staff took pity on me and very quickly I was served with a fresh granary roll accompanied by a side salad, pickle and several slices of beautifully cooked cold roast beef that was tender and still pink in the middle.

Having glanced at the blackboard which had a number of interesting and fairly priced dishes on it, I then nosied into the main menu and discovered that they did a full, traditional Sunday lunch for £5.95. If the meat served then is anything like as good as the cold joint from which my meat was cut, Sunday lunch must be a very enjoyable occasion at the Kestor.

Whilst Manaton remains essentially Dartmoor, Lustleigh to the east has changed completely in the last two decades. There was a time when this rural community lived simply in the beautiful valley of the Wrey. They gained their livelihood from small holdings and cultivating productive vegetable gardens, seldom venturing away. A journey to Exeter was a once in a lifetime experience. Nowadays the 13th-century church still stands. Look out for the mischievous carving of the small heads on top of the screen which was erected in Tudor times. The craftsman obviously had likes and dislikes; all the heads facing the chancel have a secret grin on their faces and those towards the nave, a scowl.

There is no longer a railway, village school or local bobby. The doctor holds a surgery twice a week and the children are taken by mini bus to school in Bovey. Once where there were cider orchards, a few stunted trees remain; it is more economical for the cider makers to import apples.

Village cricket still flourishes. At weekends you can sit and watch on a field, fringed with alders, and make believe that the noise and trauma of the 20th century does not exist.

Within my lifetime Moretonhampstead too has changed. Forty years ago it was a shopping centre for farmers and people living in outlying hamlets. It had everything that a community needed. Today the butcher is still there and the chemist, but the general store is no more and it is only recently that a baker has returned. It gets its livelihood mainly from tourists.

The Hampstead part has been added in the last century or so and most local people ignore it, calling the little town Moreton, derived from the Saxon Mor Tun. The 15th-century church of St Andrew, standing on high ground, has tombstones in the porch in memory of two

The Village of Lustleigh

French officers who lived in Moreton during the Napoleonic Wars, when they were on parole from their prison at Princetown.

What an extraordinary race we are! Given half a chance the French would have invaded and made Britain hell had they succeeded and yet we let prisoners wander at large. I wondered who paid for them and where their spending money came from. Do you think we were daft enough to provide that as well? Were they *persona grata* at social occasions or were society matrons warned to lock up their daughters?

Four major fires occurred between 1845 and 1892 and many of the old buildings were destroyed. Apart from the alms-houses, which were built in 1637 and narrowly missing demolition in the 1930s because they were not considered hygienic, the most stunning building, and the oldest, is Mearsden Manor, a reminder of medieval times.

I found it quite hard to believe my eyes when I entered the portals of **Mearsden Manor Gallery** in West Street; I pinched myself to make sure I was awake. It is absolutely full of the most beautiful objects that Liz Price and her partner, Mike Littlewood, have imported from Turkey, Thailand and China.

Large as life statues, carved in wood or cast in bronze, of animals and humans marry up with enormous copper containers catching the light. Turkish carpets are arrayed in all the glory of their rich colours. The jewellery room is full of necklaces, bangles, earrings, lapis and jade, whilst the walls are hung with original paintings and carved wood mirror frames. There are cabinets full of exquisite jade and one of the best collections of Chinese jade carvings and painted ceramics to be found in the country.

It is only three years since Liz and Mike took the brave step of acquiring this amazing place. Until that time, neither of them had any knowledge of this type of business. Liz worked in Local Government and Mike for British Gas. Neither occupations exactly compatable with the world of importing. Liz quite openly admits she did not even know how to operate a ledger, let alone anything else. Now she travels constantly and, between the two of them, they purchase enough goods to import six containers every year.

I asked her how she knew where to go and from whom to buy. In the early days the previous owner of Mearsden Manor took them and introduced them to his contacts, but now they just take it in their stride. Liz tells me that in Thailand especially, much of their business is with women, which quite surprised me. I have always thought of Thai ladies as gentle, retiring souls with exquisite manners, not tough business people. I am wrong; the Thai ladies are charming and courteous but they are skilful negotiators apparently.

Much of Liz and Mike's purchases are sold on to other establishments because the wholesale trade is a major part of Mearsden's business. I am glad that this does not deprive the Gallery of its lovely things. The criteria for what Liz and Mike buy is that it must be hand-made, of high quality and a sensible price.

At the end of your visit it is well worth being tempted into the oak-panelled tea rooms where you can get a light lunch or enjoy a piece of home-made cake with a piping hot cup of freshly brewed coffee or tea.

From Moreton the B3212 will take you to **The Miniature Pony Centre** which I would not like you to miss. It is the brainchild of Jane and Tony Dennis, two very exciting people. It all started when Tony retired from racing as a jockey and they decided to move from Dorking to the West Country. He opened a stud farm in the South Hams. In amongst the hunters and Arabs, Tony kept miniature ponies which were his wife's hobby.

After a while they found there was more interest in the miniatures than in the stud farm, so with great courage and a certain amount of good fortune, they purchased land from the National Parks, just before the law was changed, which would not have allowed the sale. For a year they worked round the clock, landscaping and doing everything to produce a centre in which the public could enjoy these delightful animals and gain a deeper understanding of the working and management of a stud. It took them two years before they were ready to open their gates in 1987.

The climate of Dartmoor is particularly suitable for the breeding of Shetland ponies, with the fresh, clear air and rolling countryside that provides shade and shelter in the form of hedges, trees and stone walls.

There are now around 100 ponies in the stud and they are amongst the very smallest in the world. Such tiny ponies are extremely rare and a large number bred at the stud have been exported. To qualify as a miniature, the pony must be no higher than 34 inches. Most of the ponies here are no taller than 32 inches and some are as tiny as 28 inches.

Minature Pony Centre

One question I wanted to know: was it man who, by contrivance, had made the Shetland ponies so small? The Dennises were quite adamant that the ponies were not dwarfed by starvation and sparse living conditions but rather it was the small pony who was able to survive this, whereas the larger horses and ponies could not. The proof of the pudding was in front of me; miniature ponies bred in the mild climate of the West Country, given ample food, do not increase in size at all.

The ponies love human company and they have a wonderful nature, which makes them ideal for the smallest member of the family. Because they are sturdy and strong they are easily ridden and also make excellent driving ponies.

The majority of foals are born in April and May. Once they have been weaned at five months, they are stabled in pairs for company and at the same time they are taught their manners and are halter broken.

There is even a nursery in a large covered barn which everyone can enter, and where you can make friends with baby animals. Rare miniature donkeys can be seen here and they just love someone to make a fuss of them.

It depends on how energetic you feel, when it comes to walking round the grounds. The lower walks will take you round the lakes and down to see the beautiful ornamental birds, whilst the higher walk leads to the goat paddock. If you want to walk further you can continue onwards and upwards to the larger paddock where you enter the fields and mingle with the ponies.

I had a lesson in grazing. It never entered my head that if you let nothing but ponies graze in pasture then the land would become 'horse sick'. To prevent this there is an intermixing with cattle, sheep and goats which keeps the paddocks healthy.

At the end of this delightful visit, I wandered into the restaurant from which there are superb views over the lakes. On a warm day, sitting out on the pergola or on the terrace is super and just the place in which to enjoy a meal, or indulge in a Devonshire cream tea.

One word of warning. Please do not feed the animals. The ponies are very well behaved, but the introduction of food creates jealousies amongst them, and they might bite or kick each other, with you in the middle.

To miss Chagford would be a crime. It is a sleepy place which has grown, over the centuries, round its village square. There are innumerable businesses which acquire their trade, not only from the people who live here, but from the many villages surrounding it. My purpose for visiting was to talk to Peter Smith, whose ancestors founded **James Bowden & Sons** in 1862, which today can only be called an emporium!

A most unlikely store in such a place and even more unlikely when I tell you the whole story. You can get every imaginable thing in this shop that calls itself an ironmongers. The building is one of the oldest in Chagford. When Peter Smith's great-grandfather started the business in 1862, it was known as the Vulcan Ironworks and was a smithy as

Chagford

well as agricultural equipment merchants.

Over the years, through marriage, other family names became associated with the business. In 1910 the Agate family had the local Bellhanging works and were to be seen carting massive bells on carts through the countryside to their destination. The last of these huge bells was hung in Alphington church in 1927. It is hard today to imagine how such heavy things could be carried, let alone hung, without the modern equipment we take for granted.

Every branch of this amazing family seems to have been innovative, none more so than the Smiths. Peter Smith's grandfather invented 'Silverlight', which few will have heard of, but it was the forerunner of Calor Gas.

The work of the smithy, went on until 1958. The local hand operated fire engine was also kept on the premises. It was a slightly Harry Tate operation to say the least. If the alarm was raised the horses had to be caught before they were harnessed to the engine. This gave the voluntary firemen time for a quick drink in the nearest hostelry so, by the time they arrived at the scene of the fire, the chances were that there was nothing but charred remains.

All this information came pouring up out of Peter Smith's memory whilst we sat in a tiny shop museum that he has created at the top of the store.

All around me were examples of past shopware, from tills to scales, bottles to buttons. Years of issues of local newspapers were stacked in one corner. The museum is not always open but if Peter Smith is around he will open the doors and take you in. If not you have to content yourself looking through the glass windows and door that shield all this memorabilia.

In an unashamed wish to pamper myself with a visit to probably the finest privately-owned hotel in Devon, I drove out of Chagford and took the side road to Gidleigh.

It is a tortuous one-and-a-half miles from Chagford to **Gidleigh Park**. It is a road that goes nowhere apart from one or two houses and finally ends up at the hotel.

There in front of me was a pretty, 1920s black-and-white house, sitting gracefully above a tiered garden that ran down to the River Teign. Once inside I had no doubt that everything I had heard about Gidleigh Park was true. It is a quietly sumptuous house, furnished with comfortable restraint and exuding an air of welcome and well being. There are no black-coated, superior, front-of-house managers here, just a friendly young staff who behave in the sort of manner one would expect from children of the household who are welcoming their parent's guests. While this delightful informality aligns itself with the relaxed but efficient service, Gidleigh Park will not lose its starring role.

Kay and Paul Henderson, an American couple, started Gidleigh Park in 1977. They were not hoteliers but knew precisely what they required from hotels in which they stayed in their extensive travels. The hotel's reputation was not achieved overnight by pouring millions into it, but by years of dedicated hard work and proving that if you provide the highest standards and maintain them, the world will beat a path to your door.

All of this would be of no use if the gastronomic standards were acceptable but not out of the ordinary. I am not sure whether the Hendersons were lucky enough to find Shaun Hill or he them, but the resulting 'marriage' of these three hotel keepers 'extraordinaire' is what will keep Gidleigh Park at the very top of the bestsellers list.

Shaun Hill, who is not only the chef but also the Managing Director, has a light-hearted approach to life which masks the intensity he feels about food and its presentation. He is blessed with that rare gift, a light touch in everything he sends to the table. His sauces have just the right balance, his pastry is unforgettable and his creative ability makes every meal a delight. In his immaculate kitchens his team of young chefs were busy preparing dinner. There is an inner happiness in that kitchen which comes from the maestro who is prepared to encourage his team to rise continually to greater heights—if that is possible.

Gidleigh Park is essentially a place in which to spoil yourselves, perhaps play a little croquet, tennis on the all weather court, or more energetically walk on Dartmoor. It is expensive but no one can possibly say that the money is not well spent.

The little hamlet of Doccombe with its pretty thatched cottages, nice tea room and Mill House which takes guests and has a thriving trout farm, is charming but my interest is its connection with William de Tracey, he who murdered Thomas à Becket in 1170. You will remember him from Bovey Tracey. Before his death in Italy in 1174, still desperately trying to make amends and ensure a place in heaven, he drew up a charter granting the manor of Doccombe to the prior and covenant of Canterbury cathedral, 'for the love of God and the salvation of his soul and the souls of his ancestors, and for the love of the blessed Thomas Archbishop and martyr. The income to be used for the clothing and support of a monk to celebrate masses for the souls of the living or dead'. No one can say that the man did not try to expiate his sins.

A little further east is Dunsford, whose wooded hills slope down to the River Teign. It is such an attractive place. The 15th-century church of St Mary's, which was restored in the mid- 19th century stands, high above the houses. You approach it by steep steps among thatched cottages and little cob houses. The view is stunning, reaching out over the heights and hollows of the Devon countryside.

In the church you can see an impressive Jacobean monument in the 'Fulford pew', dedicated to Sir Thomas and Lady Fulford, dated 1610. There is a recess below a window, which I am told might be the grave of Sir Baldwin Fulford, who, 500 years ago, rescued a princess from a Saracen's castle. It conjures up, in my imagination, a knight on a white charger riding bravely against all the odds to rescue a damsel in distress. His reward was to be made High Admiral of England, no doubt a great office but it does sound a bit stuffy after such an adventure.

This is a real village and in the centre there is a splendid pub, the Royal Oak, where I have enjoyed many a pleasant evening. Dunsford is a recognised beauty spot with a nature reserve in Dunsford and Meadhaydown Woods, run by the Devon Trust for Nature Conservation and owned by the National Trust. A visit in spring will remind you of Wordsworth and 'I wandered lonely as a cloud amongst a host of golden daffodils'. There are thousands of them everywhere.

If you want to wander southwards from here, you will come across

Farmhouse, Dunsford

Bridford, a Teign valley village since the Middle Ages. It is remote and beautiful, clinging to a south-facing ledge on the foothills of Dartmoor. Do not expect fine architecture but accept that it is a working community with its focal point the church of St Thomas à Becket, in which there is a superb screen and some interesting memorials.

From Heltor rock, a mile to the west of the village, you can see right across the wide open spaces and on a clear day it is not difficult to pin-point the red cliffs of East Devon.

I was amazed to learn that during the Napoleonic Wars people from Exeter, which is about nine miles away, evacuated themselves here as a precaution against an invasion by the French. I wonder if they knew about the French officers in Moretonhampstead. If they had, I doubt if they would have slept at night!

Another beauty spot is right on your doorstep from here. Canonteign Falls and Country Park, the property of Lord Exmouth, who has made it into a delightful place to spend a day.

Backtracking on the A382 from Chagford to Drewsteignton is a must for several reasons, not the least being a visit to the amazing **Castle Drogo.** It has the honour of being the last castle to be built in this country. Julius Drewe was responsible for it and he was the man who made a fortune by buying tea in China and selling it through his chain of shops, the Home and Colonial Stores.

He wanted the very best and it was to Sir Edward Lutyens that he went, demanding of that fine architect something totally unusual. Building was started in 1910 on a promontory which stands at least 1,000 feet above sea level and commands some of the finest views in the whole of Devon.

Lutyens plans were too ambitious. Julius Drewe had allowed £60,000 for the building and the gardens. It does not sound much today but, for something around the £200 mark, you could buy a four bedroomed terraced house at that time, which puts it into perspective.

What was built was a third of the size intended but it is still huge and Lutyens has managed to capture a sense of medieval times, even without the great hall and other rooms that his original plans demanded. The windows with their small panes are distinctly in the manner of Tudor times. There are many grand and stately chambers; splendid tapestries line the walls of the main staircase. The magnificent drawing room has views of Dartmoor from three sides and in the kitchen there is a table which will intrigue every housewife. It is round, made of solid beech and even the pastry boards have been curved to fit.

It has a feeling of home about it inspite of its size. Sadly, Julius Drewe lived only a year after it was finished but at least he had achieved his dream; a castle built in the medieval style complete with a chapel.

The gardens are lovely and you can even play croquet on the lawn if you wish. It is open from Good Friday until the end of October, daily 11–6. You can get coffees, light lunches and teas at the castle and there is reasonable access to the house and most of the garden for anyone in a wheelchair.

From Castle Drogo, which got its name from the Drogo who owned the manor in the days of Richard the Lionheart, it is only a stone's throw into the village of Drewsteignton, standing high above the wooded valley of the River Teign. It is a village of total charm with

Castle Drogo

its thatched cottages and a hilltop church from medieval days. It also has the oldest licensee in Britain, a 90-year-old lady who still runs the Drew Arms. It was not my intention to linger here I wanted to enter the enchanted land of Fingle Bridge and to persuade Jack Price of **The Angler's Rest** to tell me all about it.

You do not just arrive at Fingle Bridge, you have to go looking for it. It is hidden away at the end of a long, winding, leafy lane that seems to descend for ever, until, suddenly, there is a low pack-horse bridge which dates back to Elizabethan times, if not earlier, straddling a river dancing and cavorting as it plays with the boulders strewn in its path. Alongside the bridge is the Anglers Rest where you can get sustenance throughout the day and into the evening during the summer, but daytime only in the winter. The building is nothing very special, in fact I will openly admit to being slightly disappointed at its appearance—but that was just for a fleeting moment. Inside it has acquired quite an atmosphere, with its beams, stone-clad floor and rustic tables. The food is plentiful, well cooked and not wildly expensive. It's fun, and quite delightful, to sit outside eating a Devonshire cream tea and idly watch the beauty of the ever-changing trees that climb steeply up the escarpment hanging over the valley.

This summer, the beautiful and romantic Fingle Bridge has been repointed by a stonemason, John Bovey, whose intense interest in its history made it a labour of love for him. Once you cross the bridge you will find that the road comes to a grinding halt and many people wonder why. The paths leading away from the bridge were probably the way that merchants came with their laden pack-horses but, because of the difficulty of the terrain, nothing grander was ever developed. We can count ourselves lucky that this was so, otherwise Fingle Bridge might not have survived the wear and tear of men and vehicles over the years.

This was a great skirmishing ground for Cavaliers and Roundheads during the Civil War. I had no difficulty in conjuring up the picture of clashing swords meeting beneath the trees and on the bridge and then the sound of pounding hooves as men rode away at speed leaving the vanquished behind, probably wounded, maybe even dead. If you wander across the bridge and up into the woods you will find the little grave of a Cavalier.

Equally romantic is the story of the Price family, who have provided refreshment to fishermen and visitors at Fingle Bridge since 1837. Jack Price, the senior member of the family who are carrying on the tradition, is one of those lovely men who will chat to you for hours about the area and the family history.

It was his grandmother, Jessie Ashplant, who first started providing food for fishermen. She set up a little stall in the open air by the Bridge, totally unprotected from the weather. She would walk down from Drewsteignton every day and stay until dusk. Eventually she persuaded her husband to build her a lean-to shed which at least kept the elements at bay.

Jessie's daughter, Edith, married Harry Price and they continued the business. Harry Price was a fine painter. He never had a lesson in his life but if you look round the Angler's Rest you will see evidence of his work painted on all sorts of weird things—some on wood, some on cardboard and then varnished. All of them are about Fingle Bridge and he has captured the light and colour so beautifully that you feel you are looking at the real thing.

As the years have gone by, so bigger and better premises have been built. The next two generations of Prices are now running the business, and I do hope they will not be the last.

There are three Iron Age hill forts around Fingle Gorge. Prestonbury you can see very clearly from the bridge. Wooston is down river and if you see it on a spring morning with the sun behind you, it is breathtaking. The third is Cranbrook, higher up. At one time there were some small businesses across the bridge, charcoal, tannery and a mill, but they have all gone and all that is left is the sheer beauty of the river, the bridge and the trees and, of course, the Anglers Rest.

At Shilstone to the west is the best known of the cromlechs or dolmens in Devon, with the odd name of Spinsters' Rock. Legend has it that three spinsters put it in place, but fact says it is the remains of a Bronze Age megalithic tomb.

Spinsters' Rock plus pony

The B3212 cuts Dartmoor almost in half, allowing you to drive through the most spectacular moorland. As the road dips and winds, you will find yourself revelling in the constantly changing moods and colours. There are places where you can pull in, abandon your car and take off for a brisk walk. You may come across one of the thousand Dartmoor letter-boxes hidden away.

Letter-boxing is a pastime that has become increasingly popular and gives many people hours of pleasure searching for them. There are booklets available which explain it to you and give clues to where the locations are. Once you have unearthed one the rules say that, having used the official stamp, taking care not to deface the postage stamp on your letter or card and signing the visitor's book, you must leave them safely tucked away, taking with you only the mail that someone else has left for posting on. Just to keep you on the go it is quite likely that you will find a clue that will lead you to the next box. It is a bit like an unending treasure hunt really.

Along this road, too, you will see the medieval Vitifer Tin Mines and not much further on the **Warren Inn**, which stands at the highest point on Dartmoor. It is a great pub. There is always a roaring fire in the vast fireplace which until recently had been fuelled with peat and had not been allowed to go out for 100 years.

It is a lonely spot and I sometimes wonder how the landlord manages to remain constantly cheerful when there are days up here which are so cold, damp and dreary that no-one in their right minds would want to be in residence. I have been in there a time or two when the weather has been appalling, and his welcome has always been friendly and reassuring. You can get a good meal or a bar snack and when the weather is right there is no finer spot anywhere.

One wayfarer stranded here was given shelter and put in a room in which there was a wooden chest. Being inquisitive, he could not resist opening this Pandora's box and he got his just desserts for doing so. Inside was the dead body of a man. All through the night he tossed and turned, quite convinced that he had come across a den of thieves and murderers. When morning came he went downstairs for his breakfast and was told that the body was that of the landlord's father whom they had not been able to bury because the ground was too hard to dig a grave!

As you go along the road keep a look out for Bennet's Cross, a granite edifice probably of the 14th century. If you are wondering who Mr Bennet was, the answer is that he probably was not! The most likely reason for the name is the corruption of Benedict and it is likely that it was the work of one of the monks from a local monastery. It is certainly a waymark and it is one of three that you can find on this road.

Postbridge will halt you in your tracks with its famous packhorse bridge crossing the East Dart river, where water jostles for position as it hits the colossal loose stones.

This bridge, with its trackway, is probably as old as anything you will see in this county. It stands 1,400 feet above sea level, so you can imagine how wonderful the views are, especially if you climb Laughter Tor, three miles away. I suspect it got that name because it reduces even the fittest person to a wimp on reaching the top. All around are prehistoric remains and more fragments of the Stone Age than anywhere else on Dartmoor.

If you are in search of a riding holiday—and what better way to see Dartmoor?—then a sojourn at **The East Dart Hotel** is for you. You can either take your own horse or allow the owners, Brian and Liz Drayner, to organize your mount. The hotel is the home of four packs of foxhounds and two hunts, so the busy bars and restaurant are magnets for those loving this sport. The stories told get more and more graphic as the convivial evening draws to a close.

Postbridge

On the road between Postbridge and Two Bridges there is a gate, a few yards beyond Parson's Cottage, which lets you into the enclosure in which Crocken Tor stands. It is quite an easy climb to the summit and an important place. For hundreds of years up to the 18th century, the Stannary Parliament met here. There were 96 members who ran the Stannaries under the command of their Lord Warden. Their job was to make the rules for the tin mining industry in Devon. It seems an odd place to meet but it was chosen because it was the most central point on Dartmoor.

Andy and Margaret Duncan who own **The Cherrybrook Hotel**, just near here, are warm hearted people who, in the two years that they have been in residence, have endeared themselves to many people who want to stay on Dartmoor. Cherrybrook is an old farmhouse which, with a little careful incorporation of outbuildings, is comfortable, unpretentious and ideal for anyone who wants to walk or explore. The Duncans had no idea what to expect when they started because it was their first venture into hotel-keeping. Perhaps it is because of their naivety that they have become so successful. Every day they learn something new about the moor and willingly pass on their knowledge to their visitors.

Andy told me that he reckoned he had seen the wild, large black puma that has stalked the moor for years. He came almost face to face with it one dark night when all he could see were luminous eyes, set in a dark face, too far apart to belong to a domestic animal. In the morning, large paw marks confirmed his belief that this was no house cat.

He reminded me also of the spectre of the 'Hairy Hand' that haunts the road between Postbridge and Two Bridges. It has put in a an appearance in recent years. Even the vicar saw and felt it—it caused him to fall off his bike!

From here the mood has taken me to turn left and drive along the B3367 which will bring me back into Ashburton, but allows me to tell you about some delightful places not far off the road en route.

The centre of an amazing number of outdoor activities is **Wydemeet Farmhouse**, a beautiful and secluded granite house built early this century. It is situated in the quietude of the Swincombe Valley just close to Hexworthy. It is in Dartmoor's solitude that so many secrets are hidden and that is why a super couple, Jan and Kevin Chamberlain, run **Mountain Stream Activities** from Wydemeet.

If you enjoy the challenge and excitement of outdoor pursuits as well as loving the ruggedness of the moors, you will not find a better holiday than the one on offer here. Amongst the many choices are climbing and abseiling, for which the Tors, rivers and sea cliffs of the area provide a wide variety of climbs suitable for the novice or the experienced. Safety is obviously vitally important and all the specialist equipment is maintained to a very high standard. Everyone must wear a protective helmet and will always be secured by a safety rope. Kevin also ensures that there is an appropriate pupil/instructor ratio.

You must be sure to bring a windproof jacket if you want to go canoeing, which is very exciting. You are taken out either, on the river, down to the coast or to a local reservoir. You need not worry if you are totally inexperienced; the instructors have infinite patience.

One of the best attributes of this splendid holiday was being taught the correct way to navigate across the wild moorland, learning about all the correct equipment to carry, and the techniques involved in route planning and orienteering. You can go on an expedition that will last up to a week and include camping.

Orienteering, for those who wish to become extremely proficient and enjoy a challenge, is another planned activity. These courses are of varying difficulty and great fun. It is one good way of trying to seek out some of the famous Dartmoor 'Letter-boxes'.

These are just a few of the activities that Mountain Stream offers. Staying at Wydemeet completes the picture. Do not expect luxurious accommodation because what is on offer is a sturdy bunk bed in a large bedroom which you may share with anything from four to eight people. Adjoining the bedrooms there are separate shower, washing and toilet facilities. Downstairs there is a large, comfortable dining room and lounge which have roaring log fires and spectacular views of the moors.

It is just as well that there is so much physical activity because Jan Chamberlain's food is wholesome and filling. You will never leave the table hungry.

A recent addition has been a centrally-heated chalet which adjoins the farmhouse and is available as a self-catering unit for up to 16 people. This has been designed with easy access in mind for disabled people, who are made very welcome.

To get further details on this excellent venture contact Mountain Stream Activities, Wydemeet, Hexworthy, Devon, PL20 6SF, or telephone Kevin on 03643–215.

A strange custom existed up to the mid-19th century. On Dartmoor if a house could be built, with a roof in place, between sunrise and sunset, then the house and all the land around it became the builder's. The only such cottage I know that still exists is Jolly Lane Cot at Huccaby near Hexworthy.

Tom and Sally Satterly chose Midsummer's Day to set about their task and by sunset they had succeeded. This meant that they were free from bonded employment. In her later years Sally used to be seen sitting in her front doorway talking to passersby and frequently singing old folk songs. She knew so many that Sabine Baring Gould visited her on one occasion just to write down the songs for posterity.

On Sally's death the men carried her across the tors to Widecombe for burial and rested the coffin en route on the last remaining coffin stone on the moor. It can have been no easy task to be pall bearers for miles over rough terrain.

Dartmeet: Where the East and West rivers join

Past Dartmeet and on to Poundsgate, Widecombe in the Moor can be seen from miles away with its tall church tower built, 400 years ago, by tin miners, in thanksgiving for the thriving industry. It is dedicated to St Pancras and known as the cathedral on the moor. On one of the roof bosses they left the tinner's symbol of three rabbits, each with an ear joined at the top to form a triangle.

In 1638 the 135-foot tower almost caused the death of many people when it was hit by lightning during a service. For a long time it was believed to be the work of the Devil and his hounds as they rode across the sky.

For centuries the village remained almost unknown and it was not until 1850, when the vicar decided to hold an annual fair and Sabine Baring Gould, the vicar at Lewtrenchard popularised an old folk tune, that Widecombe became world famous.

There will be few who do not know the old song 'As I was going to Widecombe Fair wi' Bill Brewer, Jan Stewer, Peter Gurney, Peter Davey, Dan'l Whiddon, Harry Hawk, Old Uncle Tom Cobleigh and all'. If you are one of the few you may rest assured that you will be told the story of Uncle Tom Cobleigh and his grey mare. Whether he was fact or fiction is strenuously argued. What is fact is that a Thomas Cobleigh was born in the village of Spreyton in 1762 and died there in 1844. It could well be that he brought his motley crew with him to Widecombe for the fair.

Widecombe is a delightful place with one of the best Dartmoor skylines, with huge boulders and outcrops of bare rock all round.

To take a glass of ale in **The Rugglestone Inn** is an experience you will not often have. It looks far more like a cottage as originally built. The first licensee was in 1850. He was a farmer and stonemason, and then the Lamb family took over and have been running the inn ever since. What is odd about it? It has no bar; you order your drinks in a narrow taproom which opens on to a passage and then you take your drink to what I suppose would have been the front parlour. Nothing has been done to modernise it, apart from the installation of electricity in the 1960s—and therein lies its charm.

Buckland-in-the-Moor is a different kettle of fish. Standing high on Buckland Beacon with the Ten Commandments carved in the stone beneath your feet, you are 1,280 feet above the sea, looking out as far as the Devon coast at Teignmouth and Torquay and below Holne, where Charles Kingsley was born, and nearer still Holne Chase.

What a beautiful hamlet it is, with some of the loveliest thatched cottages I have ever seen. On a hill stands the small 15th-century church with carved bosses in the porch and old tiles under the tower. The 15th-century screen is a gem with painted panels and a red and gold frieze. On one side are paintings of the Annunciation, the Wise Men and saints, and on the other some odd grey figures.

When you look up at the clock you will see that it does not have numerals. In their place are the words, 'My Dear Mother', and its bells chime out, 'All things bright and beautiful'. There is no official explanation for this curiosity but legend has it that it was placed there by a man in memory of his mother. This remarkable lady, when told the news that her son had been lost at sea, refused to believe it. Every night she lit a candle and placed it in the window to guide him home. Her faith was rewarded; he did return. When she died this is how he repaid her faith.

The Perryman family have farmed here at Southbrook for 40 years, surrounded by incomparable beauty. One hundred years ago the farm

Church, Buckland in the Moor—'My Dear Mother' clockface

had the unusual distinction of having a combined out-building which dealt with everything from stabling to threshing and meant that the farmer and his men could work under cover. When this barn block fell into disrepair a decision had to be made to determine its future. There was a possibility that planning permission could have been obtained to turn it into cottages, but David and Angelina Perryman felt they wanted to give something back to the community, and decided to turn the buildings into a Craft Centre.

This happened three years ago and now the old buildings have a new lease of life. Downstairs is a shop selling all sorts of Devon crafts. Alongside it is a pleasant restaurant where once the horse was harnessed to the wheel that operated the thresher. The old stone walls have not been covered and you sit at rustic tables enjoying the good home cooked food. Stew and dumplings never tastes better than when it is served here on Sunday at lunchtime.

The Perrymans have two daughters who both work in this busy place. I have a sneaking suspicion that it is more for love than money, but their smiling faces and enthusiasm are a tonic.

As you wander round the building you will find various craftspeople at work. There is one workroom devoted to the making of dolls-houses and all that goes into them. Quite enchanting. Another where model soldiers leap to life from the skilful hands of their creator. Fine marquetry work is the work of another, and there is a lady saddler.

Take your time in looking round this centre, which is at the heart of a working stock farm, but most of all stop at the head of the stairs where there are some benches. Sit yourselves down and take a look at the view from the wide window. It is breathtaking and stretches for miles.

There is no charge for walking around but I will be amazed if you are not tempted to put your hand in your pocket to buy something or at least sit awhile and have tea.

It is not often that one finds a village of less than 300 inhabitants with so many talents. I unearthed them at Holne by reading the first newsletter of **The Holne Chase Hotel**,' The Bromage Bulletin', edited by the young master of the house, Hugh Bromage, who runs the hotel with his parents. Holne is just up the Princetown road from Ashburton, a drive that takes you along winding roads, through a canopy of trees

Holne Chase Hotel

and then across a narrow bridge over the Dart. It is so pretty and so peaceful.

Dartmoor Cider is made only a mile away from the hotel, which offers it to the guests. Whilst you are eating the excellent food, a major factor in this lovely hotel, you will see, among the condiments, Dartmoor Mustard, which is ground and blended in Holne.

The Bromage family are talented without doubt. Since 1972 they have been running the Holne Chase Hotel and gaining friends throughout the world. You turn off the country road into a drive that runs between tall trees which are a playground for grey squirrels who dance across the driveway right in front of you, with a complete lack of regard for their safety. You are asked politely not to exceed 5mph, so perhaps the squirrels understand this.

The house is a happy one. Totally informal, and both you, your children and your dogs will be welcomed by one member of the family or another. It has an air of graciousness about it which makes one feel at ease. The dining room looks out over the wonderful view to the tors beyond with trees and rocks providing an ever changing colour against the sky.

People come back again and again to Holne Chase for different reasons, but one must be the excellence of the food. The head chef, David Beazley, has recently returned having left three years ago to fulfil an ambition to set up and run his own restaurant. Having built up that business and earned a coveted place in the *Good Food Guide* he has returned to Holne Chase determined to repeat the achievement for the hotel.

The smiling lady who is the Restaurant Manager at Holne Chase is none other than his wife, so it is a powerful team. Not only is the food good but it is equalled by the service.

Theme Dining is to become part of the way of life at Holne Chase and I think it might be fun. The objective is to explore the cuisine of other countries. For example, the authentically prepared dishes in the Bavarian evening will feature those unpronounceable items, knackwurst, bockwurst, sauerkraut and weinerschnitzel, accompanied by the strong beers and wines of the region. I understand that it is the intention to find an Oompah band to grace the occasion but that guests will not be required to wear Lederhosen!

Many companies use Holne Chase quite regularly for their business meetings. Something I fully understand. The facilities are right and the peaceful, out of this world atmosphere has to be conducive to clear headed thinking.

I cannot imagine anyone would find it difficult to occupy their time whilst staying at Holne Chase but just in case you are keen fishermen, let me tell you that the Dart, with its tributaries, can provide some wonderful sport for salmon peel (sea trout) and brown trout. It is a spate river, so water conditions are important. The hotel has a mile of water, single bank, fly only. The season is March to September and for hotel residents there is no charge, but you must have your own equipment. Fishing is also available on Duchy of Cornwall water at a nominal charge. All fishermen must have a River Authority Licence however, which may be purchased at the hotel.

If you want to ride, Holne Chase has some of the best stables on Dartmoor within less than a half-hour's drive. If you are a beginner do not despair, tuition is available. Foxhunting can usually be arranged in season.

The Bromage's have a number of short holidays based on exploring Dartmoor which are available between November and March.

The area has a long Christian history which may be explored on foot across the moor as a 20th-century pilgrimage or, maybe, like me, you like your Christianity to be a little more gentle and would enjoy discovering the wonders of Buckfast Abbey where the monks follow the rule of St Benedict and the Office is sung daily.

Ashburton is a town of contrasts and beauty. In 1305 it was designated a Stannary town. Tin mining and the wool industry brought great wealth and with it the building of some fine houses. One in North Street still remains. It was a 17th-century gambling house, known as the Card house. You will see the reason why because of the clubs, diamonds, spades and hearts that form the pattern on its slate-hung facade. What is now the ironmongers on the corner of North Street was once the Mermaid Inn where the Roundhead, General Fairfax, had his headquarters after defeating the Royalists nearby. That many people were Royalists, and were prepared to risk their lives hiding them, is evidenced by the little carving of a man on horseback on one of the houses—a sign that Royalists were safe there.

Whether to be encouraged to visit **The Golden Lion** because it is the headquarters of the Monster Raving Loony Party, headed by Screaming Lord Such, or to stay away because of it, is your decision. If you decide against it, you will be missing an opportunity to visit a place that is totally out of the ordinary. It is, primarily, a thriving market town pub, busy with locals who come in for the fun, the good beer and food. The comfortable bedrooms make it somewhere not too expensive to stay and from which you can explore the moors, the coast and take a look at several National Trust properties in the immediate vicinity.

Alan Hope and his wife Norma are the landlords of this establishment. They are both members of the Raving Loony party and Norma seems to be the mainstay of the administration. Alan is a larger than life character who has done more than ruffle the feathers of the staid Ashburtonians since their arrival 12 years ago. He was once the leader of a rock and roll group and brings live music to the Golden Lion regularly. If you can get him to talk to you about his record collection you will discover that he has one of the largest in the South West.

I wondered where Screaming Lord Sutch acquired the money to fight elections and almost always lose his deposit. The telephone rang at least three times whilst I was talking to Alan and Norma and each time it was a newspaper or a magazine wanting to write an article about him, for which they were willing to pay; the question was answered. The publications concerned might be a little different from the normal political journal, but why not? I am sure *Club International* and *Razzle Magazine* will do him proud! The membership of the party is interesting, too. People from all over the world belong.

As a member of Ashburton Council, I suppose it would be possible for Alan to become the Portreeve, a Saxon heritage. The name comes from 'Port' or market town and reeve, an official. Today the Portreeve is the social head of the town. The role does carry duties. He has to join the Leet Jury of Ale Testers and Bread Weighers and one evening he is obliged to knock on the door of each public house to try a sample of their beer. It is as well that Ashburton is quite small because there are ten pubs and it would take quite a lot of stamina to visit them all. The Bread Weighers weigh the bread from the baker's shop and providing it is satisfactory, a certificate is given together with a piece of evergreen. The custom now is for the bread to be auctioned at the local recreation ground whilst everyone is enjoying a ram roast.

Nine times a year there is a market, one of which, in October, is for the sale of Dartmoor ponies.

Behind the Bank House, in West Street, there is a delightful house which is the home of **Dartmoor Antiques**. On entering, my first reaction was one of disappointment because I expected to see more than just one room in which treasures were displayed. It was my meeting with Gerry Mosdell, the owner, that opened my eyes to the world of riches stored up in this small room.

He is an antiquarian bookseller and collector with a passionate love of books of the 18th and 19th centuries. You have only to listen to him talk about caring for his collection; the oiling of leather covers, the gentle repair of a slightly damaged page, to realise that here is a man with a vocation. As I looked round the higgledy-piggledy room, a collection of dolls-houses caught my eye. These are his wife's great love and she has over 40 of them complete with all the little pieces of furniture, people and equipment. These two gentle, charming people share Dartmoor Antiques with other collectors who display china and other pieces. It is only open on a Tuesday and Friday . It is the sort of place where you can pick up something you will treasure without it causing you, or your Bank Manager, too much pain.

In the course of our conversation I found out that Gerry is the organiser of no less than 140 antique fairs every year which take place anywhere from Bristol to Penzance. At these fairs he gathers together exhibitors and collectors of every possible type of antique. He tells me that he has a regular following of enthusiasts who will travel wherever a fair is taking place. The circuit was first started twenty-two years ago and has grown in momentum every year. This dedicated man virtually does all the work in getting the fairs organised, from sending out the mailing lists to setting the scene in whatever the venue might be.

If you would like to exhibit or would like to know the dates on which fairs are held, just write to him at Dartmoor Antiques Centre, Off West Street, Ashburton, Devon TQ13 7DV or telephone him any evening on (0364) 52182.

The 15th-century church tower is beautiful with delightful double buttresses, a charming turret, and over the west door three niches. In the centre is a gentle Nativity scene and at the sides are St Catherine and Thomas à Becket. It is a church full of treasures and one to be savoured. In the churchyard I found a grave of a French officer who had been paroled in Ashburton. I had not realised that there were places other than Moretonhampstead where this happened. This grave has an offshoot of the willow growing by Napoleon's grave at St Helena. Planted, so I understand, by a French visitor years later.

It is quite a good moment whilst you are in this neck of the woods to go about six miles up the A38 to Stover where you will find the extraordinary Trago Mills, an out of town shopping centre with a difference. It is an offshoot of the original, which lies in the Glynn valley between Liskeard and Bodmin. You can buy just about everything there

Miniature train around Trago Mills/Stover International Caravan Park

and enjoy a remarkable day out at the same time.

It has **Stover International Caravan Park** as its neighbour. One of the finest sites in the country, it has just about everything and, in the words of its brochure, is a site 'Designed and built for caravanners by caravanners'.

How many times have you been disappointed by a glossy brochure which looks gorgeous, promises you the earth and then when you arrive it just does not live up to the promises made? I can promise you, hand on heart, that if you send for a brochure from Stover you will be seeing and reading precisely what is there.

It could not be better sited for exploring Devon. It is only 8 miles from Torquay, Paignton, Babbacombe, Teignmouth and many other superb beaches. Dartmoor is on the doorstep with its wild beauty that is hard to match anywhere in the U.K.

I always enjoy a day at the races, and with Exeter and Newton Abbot racecourses within easy reach, you can be sure of a good day's racing. Greyhound race meetings are held at Newton Abbot racecourse every Tuesday and Thursday and at the County Ground stadium, Exeter, on Wednesdays and Saturdays. Newton Abbot racecourse also plays host to Stock car racing.

In addition to the caravan park there are spacious, fully equipped chalets, and planning permission has been obtained for 4 and 6 berth static holiday caravans which, I am quite sure, will be up to the high standard set everywhere.

Steam enthusiasts will enjoy the miniature steam locomotive and passenger train which chugs around the boundary with Trago Mills every few minutes and, if you like using your camera, the sunsets make fabulous photographs for your album.

If I had to pinpoint what I liked best about this excellent site I would say that it is the aura of peace that surrounds it, largely due to the efficient manner in which the whole place is run.

You may bring your dog with you, providing it is not a fighter, but you will find that there are rules for dog owners which are enforced rigidly. Because it is so super you do need to book well in advance. The number to ring is 0626 821446

Buckfastleigh, just south of Ashburton, is a charming place of narrow streets set between the River Dart, the Mardle, Holy Brook and the Dean Burn, which flow in from Dartmoor. It has grace and a character of its own, although it is often overshadowed by **Buckfast Abbey** just up the road.

Seldom have I seen or heard anything quite so dramatic as Buckfast Abbey at night during Compline. The monks come silently down the aisle, the only sound the swish of their long robes as they pass by, the only light a bidding one high over the altar. As they reach their stalls, they push back the cowls from their heads and the service starts. Its simple message is chanted and reaches out to every corner of this

Buckfast Abbey

great building. One cannot doubt that God is present.

The most impressive thing about Buckfast is that the present abbey was rebuilt by just four monks, who at the outset had no experience of this sort of work at all. They just used commonsense and dogged determination, coupled with the sure knowledge that God was with them. One of these monks is still alive and living at the abbey.

The first monastery was founded in AD 1018, in the reign of Cnut. In 1147 the abbey was rebuilt and transferred to the Cistern order. After the Dissolution on 25 February, 1539, years of decline and dereliction followed, until the complete restoration of the monastery by this small group of Benedictine monks. Work began in January 1907, based upon the original Cistercian foundations and the final church stone was laid in July 1937.

The exterior walls of the church and domestic buildings were built of local blue limestone. The window arches, quoins, coping stones and turrets of the tower are in mellow Ham Hill stone, a little softer than the limestone.

Dedicated to the Virgin Mary, the Lady Chapel has some of the most amazing marble mosaics, using marble taken from ancient Greek and Roman buildings. The marble floor depicts the biblical Tree of Jesse, symbolising Christ's descent from David and his father Jesse, and was made in the abbey's own workshop. There are four ambulatory chapels, the chapel of the Blessed Sacrament gives a modern touch to the abbey, and is a place for quiet prayer for the monks and visitors. The astonishing colour of the glass in the windows almost distracts one from prayer. The incoming light reflects above the High Altar producing a stunning effect.

The chapel of St. Benedict is dedicated to the father of western monasticism. Born as a Roman aristocrat in AD 480, Benedict decided to live life as a hermit and later wrote his rule for monks, which is as valid today as it was over 1,500 years ago.

Monasteries need to be self-sufficient to survive as they are not funded by churches or the state. They are like a huge family rallying around to support each other and the communities' older generations. In the middle ages Buckfast gained much of its income from the wool trade. Today a farm is run by the monks and is better known for its honey and tonic wine than its wool.

It has been difficult for the monks here living within the Benedictine rules which made it quite possible for them to be sent to other monasteries. This caused problems, when loss of experienced and trained monks from their duties at Buckfast, held up essential work. Now when someone joins the community he becomes a Buckfast Benedictine and does not move.

Bees have always been kept at Buckfast Abbey and Brother Adam has been head beekeeper for the last 70 years. Over the years he has developed a new bee known as the Buckfast bee, and has gained recognition world wide, and an OBE. The queens are held in isolation in Dartmoor but have 320 hives around the abbey grounds, local farms and orchards. Together with the honey that has become famous, so too has the wine made in the monastery cellars. Buckfast tonic wine is sold all over the world.

Buckfast was not always as relaxed and until the 1940s was one of the strictest communities. They were only allowed to talk for an hour a day and sign language was developed. They even had to kneel when speaking to the Abbot. During the war Buckfast became a fire station and outside influences crept in.

There are many things to see and, if you are male, no better way to witness the life of a monk than to actually take on that role. This is possible, as every year about 250 retreatants come to Buckfast to stay usually three or four nights. All walks of life enter this calm and peaceful retreat, among them writers, accountants and students doing their A levels; all looking for rest or spiritual enlightenment. There is no charge but the guests are invited to contribute.

When you go to see the Abbey allow sufficient time to sit awhile and drink in the beauty of this astonishing building. Look up to the roof and see the magnificent paintings. Read the various pieces of history that are laid out for you. Take note of the little balconies from which sick monks can take part in a service even if they are bedridden.

You will always find one or more of the monks in the abbey who are more than happy to tell you about its history and their work.

Another unusual sight is the presence of a Methodist chapel within the grounds. Seldom used for services, its doors are always open for anyone who wishes to go in. I am told that the offetory here is frequently greater than that of the nearest operational Methodist place of worship! I am not quite sure how it got there.

Just on the edge of Buckfastleigh, and moments off the A38, a fairly new **Little Chef** has emerged as being one of the best in the county. The food is no different than any other in this chain but the staff are wonderful, slightly more mature than usual and attentive to your every need. I give them full marks and wish it were emulated elsewhere.

There is a splendid Butterfly Centre and Otter Sanctuary at Buckfastleigh and also the home station of the Dart Valley Railway, but I was in the mood for something completely different: **The Pennywell South Devon Farm Centre**. It is only one-and-a-half miles down the road at Lower Dean, so if you are coming from either Plymouth or Exeter watch

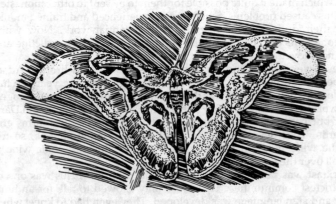

Butterfly Centre

out for the Lower Dean exit on the A38.

Pennywell is organically farmed and it took me back to the days when

I was working as personal assistant to the Hultons, who owned the prestigious *Picture Post* magazine. They purchased an estate in Gloucestershire which was derelict. There was no electricity and the land was sour.

It became my duty to get this place re-established and to see that it was farmed organically. We are talking about the 1950s when such an idea was rare. I have never been one to be slow in taking up a challenge and this was certainly of mega proportions. Where does one begin? I bought a book by Violet Bonham Carter called, *The Living Soil*, in which she described how it should feel. I can still see myself, complete with wellies, walking across the untilled fields picking up sods of earth and turning anxiously to chapter four, page seven or whatever, to see if what I had in my hand answered the description in the book!

The husband and wife team, the Murrays at Pennywell, have no such problems. They are dedicated to organic farming and have achieved enormously high standards, winning themselves some prestigious awards en route.

Make sure you take your camera when you visit here. It will provide you with a record of one of the happiest and most instructive days out that you could wish for. You have the added bonus of wonderful countryside overlooking the Dart valley to top it.

There is no doubt that animals and plants thrive on this chemically free environment. You can try your hand at milking a cow or goat, feed the poultry, pick up free range eggs or wander along the farm trail. The Murrays have thought it out so splendidly that you will find there is always some other activity in which you can take part when you have completed another. My grandchildren think it is the greatest place ever, particularly when they are allowed to ride on the play tractor.

I listened to people asking endless questions which were all answered with enthusiasm and total patience. Things like how much does it cost to rear a piglet. Or do chickens really produce 250 eggs a year.

Children and adults are encouraged to cuddle a calf, or pick up a piglet or any other animal for that matter. There are no restrictions, you can wander anywhere. All that is asked of you is to obey the Country Code and use commonsense.

At the end of your visit if you are a trifle weary you can sit down and have what is known as a Pennywell snackette or a super Devonshire tea.

Pennywell is open from Easter to October 3l, seven days a week from 10am-5.30pm.

There are two really super hotels in this neck of the woods; either of them would be a pleasure to stay in but in both cases I think it is the excellence of their food that would keep me returning.

Sue and Lawrence Cowley own **Glazebrook House** at South Brent. To find them take the Marley Head exit off the A38 coming from Exeter. You will see a signpost for South Brent which you follow and not far up the road there is a police station on your right. Just a little further is the road that leads to Glazebrook clearly marked. From Plymouth it is simple; you leave the A38 at Carew filling station where it is signposted Avonwick and South Brent. Follow the South Brent road and you will very shortly see the turning to the Glazebrook.

Glazebrook House

It is an elegant, spacious mid-Victorian country house on an elevated site amidst four acres of rhododendrons, azaleas, camellias, mahonias and other plants which light up the garden with colour that lasts through most seasons of the year. It is a totally relaxed house which reflects the attitude of the Cowleys. They want you to feel at home and enjoy staying with them.

In the past few years the Cowleys must have spent a fortune on refurbishment and how beautifully that money has been used. Every bedroom is now ensuite and decorated in charming Laura Ashley wallpapers and toning fabrics. There are four-poster beds and most rooms have that warm antique pine furniture. The pretty restaurant looks out on rolling countryside which sets the scene for the excellence of the dishes that will be set before you. Great pride is taken in the way in which the table d'hôte, à la carte lunch or dinner is presented. All the meals are freshly prepared and the wine list is a delight. The prices were a pleasant surprise as well.

Cowleys have specialised in functions. Nowhere could be more charming than Glazebrook House for a wedding reception. The rooms will take anything from 6 to 200 people. This space is used, too, for conferences and seminars and sometimes for concerts.

South Brent has acquired several new housing estates in recent years but in bringing the population up to about 3000, the newcomers have ensured that the village stays alive. The main street has not changed all that much in hundreds of years. The Anchor Inn has been there since 1546, when Henry VIII granted the village to Sir William Petre of Torbryan. Almost next door is the Old Toll House with its board of tolls payable by farmers bringing their sheep and cattle to market and to the four fairs which were held annually between 1850 and 1950. The market and the fairs have gone but it is still lively and a pleasant place in which to live.

St Petroc's church has been there since the 6th century. It was enlarged and rededicated in its present form about 1436. It has the dubious distinction of being the only church in England where a priest was murdered apart from Canterbury Cathedral. This murder cannot be laid at the door of Sir William Tracey either. It happened at the end of Vespers, sometime in 1436, when, for no known reason, the vicar John Hay was dragged from the altar by one Thomas Wake. The congregation sat there stupefied as the unfortunate cleric was hauled through a small doorway and, with the help of accomplices, beaten to death.

Heeding the directions from the A38 for Glazebrook you will be on your way to finding **Brookdale House** at North Huish. As you come

Brookdale House

off the A38 head for Avonwick rather than South Brent. In Avonwick turn right as you come to the Avon Inn and then first left signposted to North Huish. Climb the lane to the top of the hill and turn right where it is signposted Brookdale Hotel. At the bottom of the hill turn right and Brookdale House is first on the left.

Brookdale is a house acquired by Carol and Charles Trevor-Roper in 1986 after they had been searching for a hotel to purchase. Not finding anything that met their requirements, they asked estate agents to find them a country house which they could convert, and Brookdale is the result. The house was run down and it took guts and many gin and tonics to undertake the alterations that would make the house as the Trevor-Roper's wished. The first year was spent entirely in doing this but it was worthwhile. Ever since they opened the doors of this gracious house, people have been coming to Brookdale.

Many years ago I had the privilege of meeting the historian, Hugh Trevor Roper, who was a friend of my father-in-laws and so I know a little of this distinguished family's history. It came as no surprise to me that Charles Trevor-Roper has this intrinsic ability to hit on the things that are essential to imbue a house with a sense of history. Staying at Brookdale is a privilege and one to be cherished. Little in the way of advertising has ever been done; most people come because of word of mouth—what better way?

The restaurant and the kitchen are the heart of Brookdale House and make use of the wealth of local produce available in South Devon.

The policy of Devon Fare, whom I have talked about previously, stands out a mile in this super establishment. The Trevor-Ropers do stick by the local community. Peter Hayford from Lower Bearscombe Farm provides them with free range quail, guinea fowl, Aylesbury and cross-bred ducks, as well as quail eggs. Mark Lobb from Stoke Fleming supplies game in season and all the fish comes from the Brixham Fish Co-operative. Chris McCabe in Totnes provides the guaranteed additive free meat. From Buckland-in-the-Moor, Charles Staniland grows the herbs, specialist vegetables and delicious strawberries in his organic garden.

I was delighted to learn that the cheese comes from Ticklemore Cheese in Totnes. Langage Farm plays its part, too—they supply traditionally produced cream and free-range eggs.

Brookdale House has six bedrooms in the main building and two smaller bedrooms in Brookdale Cottage some 25 yards from the hotel. The rooms are all beautiful with some nice antique pieces in amongst the furnishings.

It is a point to remember that Brookdale does not permit dogs nor children under the age of ten.

Dinner is always a set price of £25, for which you get a truly memorable meal, with a number of excellent choices. Just to make you envious, and I hope, rush to the telephone to book your table, I am going to tell you about one or two of the dishes you may find on the menu.

Braised lamb's tongues served in a Filo tart with a warm red and green pepper vinaigrette, or steamed fillets of lemon sole with samphire and a star anise sauce to begin with.

Roast best end of Devon lamb with noodles and a rosemary butter sauce or well roasted leg and lightly roasted breast of free range duck with a honey and ginger stock sauce accompanied by perfectly cooked fresh vegetables, as the main dish.

Then a super cheese board—like Shaun Hill at Gidleigh Park, Terry Rich, the head chef, does not believe in serving cheese at the end of the meal. Some of these cheeses you may not be familiar with but try a little piece of each—it is an adventure for your taste buds.

Who could resist summer pudding with clotted cream and a summer fruit sauce or mango and strawberry meringue with a mango sauce to complete the meal?

Coffee is served in the lounge accompanied by petit fours, by which time, if you are like me, you will have become an ardent fan of Brookdale House.

Charles Trevor Roper has a keen appreciation of wine—that too runs in the family! His list is so carefully chosen and contains gems. He is an entertaining host and a very knowledgeable man who does much for the reputation of true Country House hotels.

The part of Dartmoor bounded by Princetown and Tavistock to the north and Yelverton to the south is very different from anywhere else on the moor. Princetown is the most isolated. Famed because of its sinister prison which even sends shudders down the spine of the most hardened criminal.

The forbidding walls were first raised in 1806 by French prisoners-of-war who were forced to erect their own goal. It must have been appalling. Even on a summer's day Princetown is never the warmest place and in the swirling mists of winter penetrating rain eats into one's very soul, so these poor devils must have hated the guts of every Englishman.

In 1812, the French prisoners were joined by hundreds of captured American sailors who built the church. Its beautiful east window lights up the greyness of the interior. It was donated by American women in memory of two hundred of their kin who died in captivity. There is also a memorial inscribed to Sir Thomas Tyrwhit 'whose name and memory are inseparable from all great works in Dartmoor'. It was this wretched man who suggested that Dartmoor prison should be built, a memorial of which Devon is not proud.

The little town is a mecca for hundreds of tourists who come, armed with cameras, to take pictures of the prison and perhaps to catch sight of a prison work party going about their task. It has brought a lot of business to the town which has to be considered a bonus I suppose.

The happiest place in Princetown is **The Plume of Feathers** due to the skill and warmth of James and Linda Langton who have been the owners since 1968. James is the son of the man who started the Rock Complex at Yelverton, now operated by James's brother. It was the first building to be erected in Princetown in 1785 during the reign of George III.

Here you will get good company, good ale and super food. The beamed ceilings are the originals and with slate tables, copper lamps and open log burners, it has a thoroughly comforting atmosphere.

Without in anyway detracting from the antiquity of the pub, the Langtons have a camp site for dormobiles and tents just across the car park. It is the only one on the moor. In a sort of hostel, known as the Alpine Bunkhouse, you can stay in what are effectively two dormitories with ten beds in each, a kitchen, dayroom, toilets, showers and drying room—something you will find essential on Dartmoor. If you prefer something a little more sophisticated there are three letting rooms within

Plume of Feathers

the Plume. Children are welcome and a special adventure playground has been designed for them.

From Princetown you can opt to go west towards Tavistock or south on the B3212. I am going to take this latter route first.

Yelverton's post code covers a wide area but the village is divided by the main Plymouth to Tavistock road. It is a popular residential district for people working in Plymouth. It will always have memories for me because during World War 11 it had Harrabeer aerodrome on its doorstep, which for some months was the base of 193 Squadron who flew Typhoons, and I was madly in love with their leader!

Today the aerodrome is no more; the overgrown runways are used for people to park their cars on a Sunday afternoon whilst the children climb up the rocks or over the old bunkers. The ice-cream vendors do a roaring trade. I used to take my children there when they were young and, as I sat on the grass in the sun, I had only to close my eyes to conjure up those fraught days of the 1940s. I could hear the aircraft taking off and landing. I could recall the absence of lost pilots at the end of a day's flying. It was not the done thing to even talk about them. It was not a lack of feeling or respect, just the sheer necessity of carrying on with life whilst waiting for the next order to scramble.

There is a small community which really is part of Yelverton but has the odd name of **Leg O'Mutton Corner**. The derivation of that name is simply that if you look at the shape of the cluster of buildings it does look like a joint of meat. Apart from that it is a thriving place and very much the focal point of the several small villages spread about nearby.

As always, the village shop, owned by Anne and Tony Merriott, is the general meeting place. I arrived there promptly at nine o'clock one morning to find a constant stream of people in and out collecting their papers or returning videos.

Many of the roofs are flat or at least squat. They were not built like that but became so because the aerodrome was alongside Leg O'Mutton Corner. As the planes came down the runway for take-off they could not get sufficient height quickly enough to rise above the houses—and so surgery was required to ensure safety. At night the church spire had a red warning light on it to safeguard the returning squadron. They were a tremendous bunch of men. We used to frequent the local hostelries in the evenings, especially the Royal Oak at Meavy. Usually the squadron mascot came along as well—a duck with a penchant for beer. By the end of the evening the duck was almost always paralytic!

There is an excellent Chinese restaurant and an equally good Thai house. One of the best we have been to. It is very much an acquired taste but once hooked on it the addiction needs attention frequently. However, what will always bring me back here is **The Yelverton Paperweight Centre**.

On my first visit I had no idea what to expect as I walked through the door into a room full of well-lit cabinets and showcases, housing paperweights of every conceivable shape and size. It was the radiance of the colours that first struck me. Then I began to take more notice of each individual piece and wanted to know more.

This is where the Yelverton Paperweight Centre becomes so special. Kay Bolster, who owns the business, together with Susan Portchmouth, worked for the late Bernard Broughton, whose collection forms the base of the Centre. He was an incredible man who first started showing his collection in Truro in 1968 and later moved to Yelverton. His love for these beautiful objects and for the history of paperweights rubbed off onto Kay, who had no knowledge at all when she started working for him. It was her instinctive love of beautiful things which had surrounded her in her formative years, that developed in the years they worked together. When he died, Kay bought this unique business and, with the invaluable help of Susan, she has built a tremendous following all over the world. These two charming and knowledgeable ladies will talk to anyone and make a point of doing so, showing the uninitiated, like myself, some of the facets of the world of paperweights.

There are some 800 paperweights on permanent exhibition and in addition Kay commissions weights from Caithness, Selkirk and Whitefriars.

I fell for the Millefiori weights, which consist of a great variety of ends of fancy-coloured tubes cut sectionally, at right angles with the filigree cane, to form small lozenges or tablets; and these, when placed side by side, and massed together by transparent glass, have the appearance of a series of flowers or rosettes. If you think I have suddenly become an expert on paperweights, I have to confess I am cheating. When I left I was so enthralled by what I had seen that I read avidly anything about paperweights that I could find. When you see all the different types, the flowers, the whirls, the pinchbecks, the butterflies—even reptiles—all encapsulated in beautiful glass, I am sure you will be as eager to learn more as I am.

Collecting paperweights need not be a costly business, although the most expensive one in the world cost £88,000 not so long ago! Here, one can start at the modest price of £2.50 rising to somewhere around £500.

The Yelverton Paperweight Centre is unique; as far as I can discover there is not another one in the country. Admission is completely free; there is also free parking and it is open from the week before Easter until the end of October, Monday to Saturday 10am to 5pm and in winter from November to Easter Wednesdays 1pm-5pm and Saturdays 10am–5pm or by appointment. Kay is delighted to welcome parties providing you telephone her first. The number is 0822 854250.

Sir Francis Drake has always been one of my heroes and so Buckland Abbey, a 13th-century Cistercian monastery which was once his home, is a favourite of mine. It nearly came to a sad end when the last of Drake's family, Captain Meyrick, wanted to sell the Abbey. He himself has estates at Yarcombe.

Buckland Abbey

Drake was acutely aware of the power that wealth brought, as indeed were most of the buccaneering Elizabethans. He acquired vast estates. Elizabeth I gave him the manor of Sherford, between Plympton and Elburton, now part of Plymouth and in the same year, 1582, he purchased part of the manor at Yarcombe from the Drakes of Ash.

By the time of his second marriage, he had added the manor of Sampford Spiney to the rest of his property. This lovely old manor house is now in the hands of one of Drake's descendants, Andrew Spedding and his wife. 'Spud' Spedding is well known to the sailing fraternity and a great friend of mine. I detect in him something of the spirit of Drake. His adventures would make a book in itself as I am sure his friends would agree. If ever you want to know something or somebody in the world, he is the sort of man who might not know himself, but he always knows a man who does!

These properties stayed within the Drake Abbey estate until the first break up of the West Devon part in 1942. Fortunately in 1946, when Buckland Abbey came on the market, Plymouth found a benefactor in Captain Arthur Rudd, a Yelverton landowner who came forward to buy the Abbey and then gave it to the National Trust. The gift was conditional. The Abbey had to be restored and, on completion, the City of Plymouth should take over the responsibility and open the Abbey to the public as a Drake Naval and West Country Folk Museum.

From Yelverton if you wander the lanes you will come to Burrator, the man-made reservoir that feeds Plymouth. It is absolutely beautiful and surrounded by spectacular moorland. There is a walk that will take you right around the edges and others that will lead you up to the tors from which, you might think, you were in Switzerland.

Sheepstor is along one of these little roads. It is merely a collection of small houses but one which belonged to the white Rajahs of Sarawak, sits overlooking a water garden which is entrancing.

The romantic story of the two men of the Brooke family who became the rulers of Sarawak is one that appeals to me. They both lie buried in the 15th-century churchyard at Sheepstor, a constant reminder of two men who devoted their lives to the people of Sarawak to whom they brought peace and prosperity.

James Brooke was born in India in 1804 whilst his father was serving there. He was sent back to England to be educated but returned to India at the age of 16 as a cadet in the infantry. After one battle he was left for dead but was saved by a friend. It took him so long to recover that the Army had no further use for him. After his father died he inherited £30,000, a fortune in those days. Uncertain of what he wanted to do, he bought a yacht and set sail for nowhere in particular. In 1839 he reached Sarawak to find a civil war in progress. His help was readily given to repel the revolt and in gratitude he was asked to remain and become the ruler of the province. The mixed bag of races did not make it easy. He had to contend with Christians, Chinese, Malays, Moslems and, worst of all, head hunters.

He struggled for years against piracy and head hunting, spending his own fortune to establish a land which was peaceful and prosperous. The British Government did not want to know but he did find one ally in Baroness Burdett-Coutts, a member of the banking family. She was in love with him and is believed to have proposed marriage, which he rejected but he did not reject the money she loaned him when he was penniless. He always repaid it. By 1852 he had just about achieved his goal when his nephew, who was ex-Royal Navy, came out to join him. He was persuaded to change his surname of Johnson to Brooke and carried on the name and the work.

It was still a volatile place and in 1857 the Chinese sacked the capital, Kuching. It caught Sir James unaware and he escaped by plunging into the river and swimming away in the dark. To the rescue came Charles and with a force of Malays and Dyaks beat off the Chinese.

Sir James died at Sheepstor in 1868 and Charles took over in Sarawak. There can have been no stranger or more prosperous community anywhere in the world. He managed to educate his unruly pirates and headhunters, provide schools, roads, a railway, waterworks, telegraph, telephone and radio. By now the British Government was only too ready to acquire Sarawak as a Protectorate.

Charles came back to Sheepstor for a holiday in 1917 and it was here he died and lies at rest not far from his uncle, under a rough moorland stone.

At Meavy the 500-year-old oak tree stands propped up on the village

Royal Oak at Meavy

green right in front of the village's own pub, the Royal Oak. It is an unique inn, actually owned by the parish. Once a 12th-century church house, it was rebuilt in the 18th century and renovated in recent years, but it has still managed to keep its ancient atmosphere.

There is a little round house on the Yelverton to Tavistock road at Horrabridge, which once was a Toll House and is now called **The Saddler's Shop**, but belies its name and stocks the antiques that Bob Howes and his wife Pat sell to discerning and often regular customers. People come from quite a distance to see what has been acquired and

I hasten to tell you that all their treasures are not housed in this tiny 19th-century building.

Bob Howes is a true antique dealer. He followed in his father's footsteps and from a very early age learnt to love and respect beautiful things. His main joys are 18th- and 19th-century paintings and clocks; subjects in which he is extremely knowledgeable. He is a quiet, unassuming man and it takes a little bit of effort to get him chatting. Once having achieved that you are talking to a man who can do nothing but enhance your own enjoyment of fine craftsmanship.

He made me aware of the changing face of the antique world. The general public are much more alive to the value of things, brought about by programmes like the Antiques Road Show. This makes Bob's purchasing life a lot more difficult. He has always treated vendors with fairness and courtesy but he says the problem now is that there are fewer vendors and frequently those who ring and ask him to come and see what they have, are merely looking for a free valuation rather than to sell.

Much of our heritage now goes abroad, which is another blow to English dealers. I wondered how long it would be before the number of antique shops dwindled almost to nothing unless one were dealing in the top echelon. Bob's reply to that was, 'Quite soon. The non-true dealer will go very quickly. In other words the man who just goes into the business to make money and not for the love of it. That sort of man or woman would not have the patience to seek out what is still to be found.'

If you are anywhere in the vicinity of Howes Antiques, give Bob a ring first on Yelverton 853929 or 852109 to make sure you can meet up with him and his wife.

Occasionally I stop at the Half Way House at Grenofen just along the road from Howes Antiques. It is one of those pubs that you can easily pass by before you realise it is there. I can recommend that you don't. A friendly establishment with a sizable car park, it is a great place for food and drink.

The road wends its pretty way down the hill to the little bridge and then on to Tavistock, one of the nicest small market towns in the county. It always has a sense of well being and shopping there is a pleasure. I do not know anywhere else that still has the old fashioned Grocer's shop with everything that is best of the past incorporated in it. You can get just about every kind of delicacy from Crebers and I go in there whenever I am in Tavistock for the sheer joy of it, rather than necessity which drags me to Sainsburys or Tescos.

Tavistock is probably one of the oldest parts of Devon to be inhabited. Settlements of tin found on the surface no doubt attracted pre-historic man. Its most important son was Sir Francis Drake who was born here and you will not be allowed to forget it. Who would want to lose sight of the country's greatest Englishman anyway? I wonder how many children even get to hear about Drake's exploits in their schooling today.

Shabby treatment for a man who was born into an age when the people of these islands were prisoners of the sea. Drake set them free and took ships into unchartered waters, bringing rich prizes home. He terrified and broke their enemies, making sure that by the time he died there was no man on earth who would dare flout a British ship at sea. Sailor, buccaneer, favourite of Elizabeth 1, he never knew upon his return to the shores of England whether he was going to be treated as a hero or have his head chopped off in the Tower for treason. His crew adored him and he never lost a ship.

The Abbey to all intents and purposes governed the little town and

Tavistock Town Hall and 12th-century Abbey Gatehouse

its markets so when Henry VIII gave the Abbey estates to his friend, John Russell, the first Earl of Bedford, it must have meant considerable change. By this time the trade in wool had brought the town new life and prosperity, and everything went swimmingly until the Civil War when the town was held for Parliament by the Earl of Bedford but changed hands no less than six times.

You can still see the stones of the old abbey in the heart of the town around the square laid out by the Duke of Bedford, who spent his mining royalties in doing so. It is a remarkable place with a fine old church, the town hall and the Bedford Hotel, now a distinguished part of the Trust House Forte empire. The river runs at one end and on its banks the ruined walls of the abbey.

In the vicarage next to the hotel are the most picturesque fragments of the abbey and the Great Gate with the abbot's prison in the ruined tower above it. Betsy Grimbal's Tower is also here. She was a nun who was loved by a monk. He, perhaps from a sense of guilt, perhaps from rejection, murdered her.

So much has happened here. One of the young abbots became so great, he was chosen to crown William the Conqueror. One of the first printing presses in the country was set up here and in the medieval church I have witnessed the sadness of death when a young American girl buried her mother beneath its wonderful pinnacled tower, wide nave and glorious gables. One of the three aisles was built for the Clothworkers Guild, with a lovely roof of carved beams and bosses. The font is 500 years old; who knows, Drake might have been baptised in it. The church is a place of peace and exploration and worthy of your time to look at its treasures.

By chance I found out that the unpretentious **Cornish Arms** in West Street is an excellent spot for a quick, sustaining lunch in comfortable surroundings. I didn't think from the outside that it was a pub; it looks more like a restaurant. I liked it and so did my purse!

Many small villages surround Tavistock, all of which are worth seeing. On the Okehampton road there are the two Tavys, Mary and Peter, the twins who grew out of settlements either side of the river Tavy. Each has a church linked together by a bridle path and a little bridge. Peter Tavy has a very old pub which is charming. It once was the home of Jennifer Clulow, the seductive lady who appears in the Cointreau advertisements and was an announcer for Television South West—a useless piece of information.

As you drive on through Mary Tavy you will see the engine house of Wheal Betsy, which was part of the extensive workings of an old silver and lead mine. Women worked on the surface of this mine breaking up the ore. They were known as Bal Maidens. Bal is an old word for mine which is more often in use in Cornwall than Devon.

At one time Mary Tavy housed Wheal Friendship, the largest copper mine in the world, later producing arsenic which was exported from **Morwellham Quay**. That is a very interesting place to visit. You will find it on the Callington road out of Tavistock. It has been completely restored to its original glory and is a favourite tourist attraction.

Gibbet Hill was once the gruesome place where wrongdoers were hung and left dangling at the end of the gibbet as a deterrent to anyone thinking of stealing sheep or becoming a highwayman. The condemned were kept waiting for their execution in a cage at the foot of the hill on the Brentor road.

This road leads you across some of the most beautiful stretches of the moor and before very long you will see Brentor church high up on the tor as near to our Maker as you can possibly get. A strangely beautiful place with a dedication to St Michael de Rupe. There are several legends about how it came to stand, 1100 feet above sea level, and only accessible after a difficult climb. My favourite is the one where the church was being built at the foot of the hill but every night the stones that were laid were removed and rebuilt at the top by the devil, because he reckoned that no one would love God enough to climb the rough tor for worship. It took 700 years for him to be proved almost right! Now there is a chapel in the village itself and the church on the tor is seldom used.

Another tale tells of a wealthy merchant who got caught in a terrible storm at sea and vowed that if his life was spared he would build a church on the first land he saw, which was Brentor.

The village is one of those that has been left alone by developers and the small community thrives—mainly farming, but for such a small number the people have a wealth of talent. There are quilt and cushion makers, someone who makes quite beautiful ceramic model houses, photographers and leather workers. Then on the outskirts there is a water garden supplying exotic aquatic plants—and **Devon Herbs** where I met Sally Wetherbee.

At the top entrance to Devon Herbs in Burns Lane, North Brentor,

Devon Herbs

I watched two men working at the intricate business of building a rough stone wall from hundreds of pieces of mellow stone in all shapes and sizes. It is all part of country craftsmanship and delightful to observe. This was just a part of the new gardens being developed by one of the most valiant and enterprising women I have met in a long time.

Having parked my car, I wandered down through this restful garden, which is surrounded by the tors of Dartmoor, amidst glorious scenery. A small pool full of goldfish on my right and a delightful oblong small garden patch to my left brought me to the steps that led down to the front door of Thorn Cottage where Sally's cheerful voice called, 'Come in, the door's open,' even before I had knocked.

This lady, still in her thirties, started the small nursery, specialising in cultivating a wide selection of culinary, fragrant and medicinal herbs, in 1983 with her husband Hugh. They both knew he had cancer, which for a while was in remission but reared its ugly head again two years ago. For the last year of his life, knowing that he was incurable, they still continued to plan the gardens for the future. The result is a wonderful, living memorial to a courageous man from which many people can draw comfort. There is nothing morbid about Sally Wetherbee or her garden. She radiates energy and enthusiasm for what she is doing and readily admits that she is on a learning curve every day. What she has done is to make the cultivation of herbs easy to understand for simpletons like me who get utterly bemused by experienced gardeners using Latin names. When I left Thorn Cottage, the home of Devon Herbs I felt I knew just a little more about what to pot, what to plant, what would grow tall and what could well be used as a border plant.

But this is not all that the enterprising Mrs Wetherbee tackles. She obtained planning permission to turn what was a derelict old smithy into a charming, functional holiday home, which has another purpose. In the winter Sally is going to use her other talents, cooking and home economics, to run one day and half day courses to teach the use of herbs in the art of cooking. The main room of the Smithy has a super fitted kitchen along one wall and it leaves sufficient room to seat up to twenty people coming to these courses.

Not the easiest place to find, I may say. If you have been to see St Michael's church atop Brentor, then just go on along that road and take the second turning right after Brentor Inn.

Opening times to the public are from April to mid September, Friday, Saturday, Sunday and Bank Holiday, 11am-5pm. At other times it is strictly by appointment. If you are unable to visit it is worthwhile sending for her catalogue and taking advantage of the efficient mail order service.

Crisscrossing the lanes from here going towards Lamerton I drove to **Countryman Cider** at Felldownhead, absorbing the beauty of the trees and hedges, highlighted by a wonderful autumn morning.

It takes a while for countryfolk to accept newcomers, but the polite good mornings that first greeted Anne and Bob Bunker when they bought Countryman Cider just over a year ago, have now changed to friendly smiles. What a fascinating couple they are. Bob has that clean cut, sparkling eyed look about him that denotes a sailor. I was not surprised to discover his love of the sea but I was full of admiration when I found out that he was one of the first men to tackle the single handed transatlantic crossing way back in 1964.

Perhaps it is the same dedication and courage that inspired him to take on the pretty daunting task of rescuing Countryman Cider when it was almost non existent. For many years in the hands of the Lancaster family, Countryman Cider had flourished but when Horace Lancaster decided to retire he sold it to people who were not as keen nor exper-

Countryman Cider

ienced and the business suffered.

With determination, Anne and Bob have cleared out the rotting barrels, rejuvenated the press and fought long and hard to obtain the right size and shape containers which hold exactly the measurements laid down by the E.E.C. They built themselves a super house in what was an old barn and planted out a new orchard, which for sometime looked like a War Graves cemetery, each tree marked with a cross and protected by a white covering. Now the little trees are growing stronger daily and every day the Bunkers take one step towards their goal.

Lay people, like myself, take it for granted that the packaging for any goods we buy is acquired simply, but this is not the case with Countryman Cider. It is a constant struggle to find suppliers prepared, or able, to make the right size containers. Even when success has been achieved in finding a source, there seems to be no guarantee that delivery will be on the promised date. This is a malaise that damages a growing business and one that, sadly, seems to be prevalent throughout the country.

If any reader is a potter and can supply Countryman Cider with pots of the requisite size, then get on the telephone (082287) 226. You will be welcomed with open arms by the Bunkers—you might even get some free samples!

I asked where the apples come from, and the answer was largely from the generosity of people who responded to an advertisement for cider apples and turned up at Countryman Cider, some with a van load and some with plastic bags full. Cash was not what the donors were after; they were far keener to receive some cider as their reward. In my ignorance I thought that all apples were suitable for cider-making but this is not the case; the true cider apple is very pithy.

It is not only locally that the cider is sold. Bob has opened up accounts all over Devon and Cornwall, in the Home Counties, London and the

Midlands—and he is constantly increasing his contacts. With the meticulous attention to the stages of cider-making, he has achieved outstanding results and my research—a secret excuse for tasting—has confirmed that the end product is some of the finest to be found anywhere in the country.

Anne looks after the shop where you can buy the cider on draught, dry, medium or sweet, or mixed to your own taste. It comes in 5 gallon, 5 litre and 2.5 litre containers or in bottle sizes of 1 litre and 75cl. I must confess to a preference for the attractive earthenware jars or bottles rather than plastic containers. Mead can also be bought here as well as some interesting country wines and cider vinegar.

If you have never cooked with cider, talk to Anne about it. She has tried out many recipes successfully and has put the method down on paper. You can buy these recipes in the shop as well. If you love fish you will find she has some particularly succulent suggestions for you to try.

To get there take the A384 from Tavistock and about five miles along the road you will come to the village of Milton Abbot; pass through this sleepy place and approximately one-and-a-half miles further on there is a right turning signposted for Bradford Kelly. Just follow the road not much more than half a mile and you will see the nice, rough brown-stoned building on your right.

There will be many of you who will not forgive me for leaving out some of your favourite places on Dartmoor. In mitigation I ask that you will accept that one chapter could never do justice to such a fantastic part of the county. I just hope I have written enough to attract those people who have never set foot on the moors.

CHAPTER 5

East Devon

No-one had prepared me for the sheer beauty of **Combe House Hotel**. It is only two miles from Honiton off the main A30 London to Exeter road, and so I imagined a country house set in nice gardens and probably quite similar to other country hotels I had visited. How wrong I was. I chose to wander the lesser roads from Sidford, taking a left-hand turning, just a few yards on from Putts Corner.

The narrow lane twisted between high hedgerows, at times affording a glimpse of the Blackdown Hills in the background. The sun's blaze

Combe House Hotel

lit up the glorious gold and orange of the autumnal leaves and everything around me was still. Occasionally passing signs for Combe House, on and on I went, to the little village of Gittisham with its wide street, pale stone houses, lovely old cob-and-thatch cottages, and its church enshrining 500 years of the community's history.

Turning into the winding drive through magnificent parkland it brought me to the front of this stately Elizabethan mansion, originally founded in the 1400s. Some of the attractions of Combe are the perfect serenity, beautiful walks and fine views; all of this I could appreciate as I sat in my car, in awe of the grandeur about me, almost hesitant to open the heavy main door in case I would be disappointed.

How foolish. The entrance hall with its carved panelling says 'welcome', and from that moment it was what I felt. The smell of log fires burning came from the main hall, across the way was the Pink sitting room where I awaited my host, John Boswell. To be in one of England's oldest country mansions gave me joy, and a recognition of an atmosphere inherited from past generations.

Combe can boast some illustrious owners since the days of the Norman Conquest and their taste in fine architecture, furniture and decor is still evident. The Boswells have merely added to this distinction by bringing cherished furniture, books and pictures from Auchinleck House, their ancestral home in Ayrshire.

John Boswell, a direct descendant of James Boswell, the biographer, and his wife Therese first came to Combe in 1970, since when they have worked unceasingly to create a hotel that they themselves would like to stay in. To claim success is an understatement; together with their sons and their innovative ideas they have achieved total grace and comfort combined with excellent service, facilities and the glory of past.

I suppose that one of the greatest compliments they could be paid was by another hotelier and her husband, Pat and Frank Grudgings, who have the Tytherleigh Cot Hotel at Chardstock. Their's is a totally different establishment with its own charms. More of that later but hearken to their comment, 'Ah, Combe House, that is where we go when we want to be pampered and spoilt.'

It is pampering in the nicest possible way. Nothing ostentatious, every room has its own character, bedrooms are spacious and gracious, individually named and decorated to suit its own style with the most ingenious ways found to create en-suite bathrooms. No mean feat in a house this age. All have superb outlooks through mullioned windows, little jars of home-made biscuits, and a letter explaining who is who in the establishment. On many of the walls Therese Boswell's exquisite paintings are hung; this unfairly talented lady not only paints extraordinarily well but she is also a sculptor.

John Boswell is a less extrovert Robert Morley (I hasten to add in character only) who has that deprecating manner and a keen sense of humour. As he showed me the two beautiful dining rooms he was almost apologetic of their slightly theatrical appearance, but dining should be distinctive in a house such as this. The rooms are wonderful and, when candlelit, are quite special.

I discovered that John has a great fondness for racing. His forays into this sport of kings has attracted many racing people to Combe House, and a great talking point in the bar is all the pictures covering the walls of the room.

Try it for yourselves. The number is Honiton (0404) 42756.

The delightful village of Gittisham is ideally placed for easy access to the fine golf courses at Honiton, Sidmouth and Budleigh Salterton. For beaches, Sidmouth and Branscombe are within spitting distance. Horse riding is easily arranged, and the hotel has fishing rights of approximately a mile and a half on the River Otter's south bank.

My purpose in visiting Honiton was to find out why it is slowly dying. Chatting to people clearly revealed that the town could not survive on tourism, and apart from Express Foods there was no major industry. It is not a happy place and really needs help. I thought that once it had been by-passed it would blossom, instead of being a driver's nightmare. Sadly, not so, only a great deal of unemployment and poor wages for those who were in work.

Elizabethan times accounted for its initial prosperity; lace makers were much sought after and business flourished. It was also reputedly the first town in Devon in which serges were made. The wide High Street is typical of a late Georgian coaching town with some fine 18th-century buildings. I browsed through Allhallows Chapel, for 300 years used as a schoolroom and now an interesting local museum, with a wonderful display of Honiton lace and craft demonstrations. Here I found evidence of the happy town it once was.

It is still worth visiting or staying in Honiton, however—exploration of the main street and little alleyways are rich with finds. Possibly not

Honiton High Street

enough to justify a long stay in the town but I do recommend it as a base for exploring East Devon.

There is only one reasonable place in which to stay and that is **The New Dolphin Hotel** in the High Street. It is a comfortable, unpretentious pub run by Peter and Pam Beazeley who came here three years ago. It was a totally new trade for them and Peter told me that it has been more than a shock to the system! I do not think either of them realised how tough it would be. Running a pub is arduous enough without the current financial climate, which has deprived them of many company representatives, their main residential trade.

If you decide to stay there you will find them a friendly couple and most interesting to talk to. The two bars are very different. In the public bar, used mainly by locals who call in almost daily for a pint and a chat, there is a very good bar menu. I thoroughly enjoyed the pleasant lounge bar; reading the various documents of bygone days which decorate the walls, I discovered that only 60 years ago you could stay here for five shillings a night.

The food at the New Dolphin is excellent, the wine list more than acceptable and the service friendly.

I asked Peter Beazeley why he thought that Honiton folk did not go to Exeter to work, if jobs are not readily available on their home ground. A return rail ticket costs only £2.50 taking just 20 minutes. To my surprise he explained that people are loth to go away from the town; indeed a number of the 5,000 strong community have never been to Exeter.

I was especially interested because Mike Wharton, of the Economic Development Growth sector of Devon County Council, told me that Exeter cannot find enough people to fill the clerical vacancies in the city, created by its expanding number of businesses. You would think that there must be some relatively simple answer in achieving a marriage of convenience to help the economy of both places. Conversely, there is a shortage of suitable work in Plymouth with insufficient jobs for the white-collar brigade, making Devon County Council eager to bring more industry to the city.

If I were using Honiton as a base for sightseeing, I think I would first take a look at the little hamlet of Yarcombe. Still owned by descendants of Sir Francis Drake, now named Meyrick, there are tenant farmers round here who until this day pay rent to the family. Yarcombe is situated between Honiton and Chard on the A358, almost at the gateway to Devon. Dorset and Somerset are on the doorstep, yet it is only a tiny hamlet with a few houses, scattered farms and an ancient church, St John the Baptist.

Probably little changed since Saxon times, then named Erticombe, it was owned by Earl Harold, of Battle of Hastings fame. It was renamed Herticombe in Elizabeth I's reign, when the Queen granted part of the Manor to Robert Dudley, Earl of Leicester. Subsequently sold to Sir Richard Drake, the third son of John Drake of Ashe, it was in turn conveyed to Sir Francis Drake, to whom Elizabeth granted the remainder of the estate. Quite a history for a tiny place.

In amongst the hamlet there is a 14th-century monastery which has been converted into a pleasant hostelry, and the old village school which has been transformed by Robert and Jill Little into **The Belfry**, a small luxurious hotel with only six bedrooms.

The Belfry is not suitable for children under 12 years, basically because of the design of the building. I shamefully admit my delight at this: much as I love my grandchildren, there are times when I could well do without their exuberant noise!

Driving from Yarcombe through the Blackdown Hills, in and out of the small lanes, is pleasurable. From here I went to call on Frank and Pat Grudgings at **The Tytherleigh Cot Hotel** in Chardstock. This is a unique business that has realised two people's dream. Pat was once a secretary and Frank worked with teams overseeing the country's conversion to natural gas. Their ambition was to run a hotel and when Frank, 12 years ago, was able to take voluntary redundancy they invested it all in an establishment in King Arthur's country, at Tintagel.

It is a village in which I once lived and I know that it has always been difficult for hoteliers to survive there; unsurprisingly, they soon realised they were making a loss. Fortune was not totally against them, however, and they sold it making a 50% profit having acquired invaluable experience in the art of hotel keeping.

Many less courageous folk would have retreated to secure employment, but not these two. They opted to buy the Tytherleigh Arms at Chardstock, just three miles outside Axminster. This time there was an established clientele which expanded considerably as they started introducing good food and various other pub comforts. With the

The Tytherleigh Cot Hotel

satisfaction of increasing turnover between 1980 and 1983 from £60,000 to £189,000, their dream took a new turn. They decided they had had enough of living over the shop and bought a listed 14th-century thatched cottage half a mile up the road, leaving Frank's sister and brother-in-law to live at the Tytherleigh Arms.

This is where the fun starts, because almost from the day they moved in they have been creating the Tytherleigh Cot Hotel. The pub did not have room for visitors to stay, an evident need, so money was raised and an extra four bedrooms were built. Slowly new buildings have been created out of derelict barns around the cottage. When I was there this time, I was shown the bedrooms, which are all in different little buildings surrounding the cottage. Each has been created from stone matching the original and, inside, the rooms are delightfully individual. The walls are rough-cast stone in shades ranging from rich cream to the hues of polished wood. The warmth of colour in the new range of Laura Ashley fabrics, used for drapes and bedcovers, provide a dramatic and imaginative complement.

A contrast to the above is found in the charmingly light and pretty Conservatory restaurant. It's ambience entices you to linger after a super dinner, sipping the excellent brandy, and perhaps catching the sound of the water outside cascading from the fountain and waterfall into the lily pond. An extra delight for anyone with a predilection for cheese is the hotel's cheeseboard. The Cheeseman literally calls once a week and it is almost as much a ritual making the selection as it is choosing the first-class wines on the wine list.

One of the additions, since I wrote about Tytherleigh Cot two years ago, is the first floor conference suite overlooking the swimming pool and the surrounding countryside. With all modern facilities from projectors to video monitors and cameras, it can accommodate 25 in theatre seating, and has a separate syndicate room for up to 10 delegates.

Pat and Frank in making their dream real have never relied on the auspices of a benevolent fairy; their own determined efforts, long hours and the support of their great team of staff granted their wish.

Three miles down the road from Chardstock, Axminster comes into view, currently a horror in which to drive until the by-pass is built. The curious shape of the town centre, dominated by the parish church of St Mary's, does nothing to alleviate the traffic. However, when you consider its town planning evolved through the last 2,000 years, perhaps it is no wonder!

Upon entering St Mary's, I was flabbergasted to see a church so wonderfully carpeted, with it's pews set back far beyond the norm so that one can take in its magnificence. The shock should be expected perhaps as Axminster is the home of carpeting. One of the earliest Axminsters made, in 1775, can be seen in the Guildhall in which is also housed the original Market Charter dated 1210.

Thomas Witty pioneered the carpet industry in Axminster, having discovered the technique from the Turks. His first carpets were produced in a little building alongside the church, and so important was the completion of each carpet that the church bells were rung in celebration.

Musbury on the A 358 between Axminster and Seaton is much in the news at the moment of writing; here South-West Water Authority want to build East Devon's desperately needed reservoir. It is being ferociously contested by the local community. Who can blame them? The march of progress invariably hurts someone.

The fascinating connections of Drake with Musbury are worth mentioning. His kinsmen lived here for generations, some rising to even greater heights than he, and their memorials in the church make most interesting reading. John Drake, depicted together with his wife kneeling at a prayer desk, was the father of Sir Bernard, who was knighted upon becoming an Admiral by Elizabeth I. A lasting memory of him and his wife is present as well -- also one of his sons, John, and spouse. Another Sir John Drake is remembered by a stone in the aisle. It was his daughter, Elizabeth, who married a Sir Winston Churchill, known for having lost all his estates and wealth trying to prop up the toppling Stuart throne. Their children are the stars of this story. Arabella was a royal favourite and John became the first Duke of Marlborough.

Ever onwards, completing the round trip from Honiton to Yarcombe, Chardstock and then Axminster, you find yourself passing the turning for Dalwood on the way back to Honiton. Not a particularly remarkable place except for Burrow Farm garden, a large bog garden in a Roman Clay Pit creating such fertile soil to produce a profuse display of azaleas, rhododendrons and roses. A wondrous sight at the right time of the year. Also, the National Trust own **Loughwood Meeting House** at Dalwood. Nearby Kilmington was a stronghold of Baptists about 1653 and this simple, unadorned building was for their regular use until 1833. Surviving intact, it can now be seen throughout the year by one and all.

The sea beckoned me next and so to one of my favourite parts of the Devon coast. Seemingly not quite of the 20th century, Seaton, Sidmouth and Beer, have altered little since coming to prominence in Victorian times. Sheltered in Lyme Bay, all sharing shingle and pebble beaches and the dignity of yesteryears, these are not places to visit if you want a sophisticated life.

Sidmouth springs into frenetic activity for the annual Folk Festival which has become the Mecca for entrants world wide. The first time I saw it I could not believe that there were so many variations of Morris Dancing and Folk Singing, let alone the clacking Clog Dancers.

Once over, Sidmouth returns to its demure, elegant self. You can stroll along the Regency Esplanade where, as a child, Queen Victoria was pushed in a little carriage by her father, the Duke of Kent. He would stop people and tell them to look carefully at the little girl for one day she would be their Queen. The Kents lived quietly trying to escape from creditors; the Duke drove regularly to Salisbury to collect his mail rather than let them trace him to Sidmouth. It was from one of these trips that the Duke ultimately caught pneumonia and died, leaving Victoria heir to the nation.

Their house is now **The Royal Glen Hotel**, owned and run by Orson and Jean Crane, whose sensitive understanding of the house's historical value has kept it much as it must have been in the young princess's time. There is even a bullet hole in the window of Victoria's bedroom which happened when a small boy shooting at sparrows missed his target and the bullet smashed one of the nursery windows. It missed our future monarch by inches.

The Royal Glen is a charming place in which to stay, and I am delighted that the Cranes are such sympathetic people, allowing nosey non-residents like myself to take a look at Victoria's early home.

I used to be a regular visitor to Sidmouth and one of my great pleasures was to browse around a little museum in Field's Department Store in the Market Place, which houses vintage toys and trains. Memories of my childhood surged back as I looked at the Dinky Toys, both English and French, Hornby trains, Meccano sets, and Cadbury's Cococubs which were given free with a tin of cocoa!

One of the most gentle and loving of places in Sidmouth is **The Donkey Sanctuary**. For the last 20 years Mrs Elizabeth Svendson MBE has devoted her life to the care and welfare of donkeys. This remarkable woman, furthermore, in 1975, increased her work to include handicapped children. Utilising the donkey's gentle nature, they were taken to special local schools where the children could ride and pet these loving animals.

Once Elizabeth realised that children, who had lost the capacity to

The Royal Glen Hotel

find any pleasure in life, responded with huge grins and laughter to these attractive beasts, she knew that a proper Centre was needed. In 1978 the Slade Indoor Riding Centre was opened. Since then hundreds of children have visited and benefited from the Slade Centre, but for Elizabeth Svendsen aiding local children is not enough. She dedicates herself even further to help as many as possible throughout the country; her charity, the Elizabeth Svendsen Trust for Children and Donkeys, is her way of achieving that aim.

The Trust's goal is for all major towns to have a small unit, consisting of a team of specially trained donkeys along with a qualified riding instructor and a suitable vehicle to transport them around. During the summer months the teams will visit special schools in their areas. Elizabeth Svendsen hopes eventually enough interest and funds can be generated to enable indoor riding centres to be built all over the country.

Between Sidmouth and Seaton is Branscombe, sprawling over two miles through a valley that is a delight. I love the thatched cottages and the narrow streets which have not widened since medieval times.

Beer, the place not the drink, is a particular personal favourite; little more than a fishing village which attracts an influx of visitors in the summer, but unlike many similar seaside haunts, it does not die in the winter. The inhabitants have all sorts of activities, from amateur dramatics to coffee mornings. They are such friendly folk, too—quite willing to talk, especially the fishermen. Some of the older ones will tell of the days of smuggling which was rampant here. The notorious activities of one Jack Rattenbury are especially popular. He, it would seem, had in some way been in league with Lord Rolle, lord of the manor. It is difficult to pinpoint the relationship but Rolle history discloses that the infamous Jack was given a pension by his lordship.

Lord Rolle lived at **Bovey House** just off the Beer to Sidmouth road. Turning into the drive of the house (one I would not care to walk at night) you can well believe in the spirits which reputedly haunt the trees to either side. One wonders, though, if these spectres were not the smugglers' inventions conjured to deter unwanted visitors, whilst they stored their ill-gotten gains in the house. Certainly no one within living memory has seen a ghost.

Bovey House

Today Bovey House is an entrancing hotel. Built in the 16th century, it once belonged to Catherine Parr, to whom it was given by Henry VIII as part of her dowry. The opportunity to stay in an historic house is rare, so seize this chance if you can. It is owned and run by Geoffrey and Pamela Cole with their daughter Jacqueline and her husband Lee Gosden. They have been at Bovey for five years and have brought it back from a rather run-down business into a thriving, happy house which delights everyone who stays or dines here.

The family have enhanced the beauty of the house very cleverly, even at times courageously. A huge 15th-century fireplace was discovered in the oldest part of the house, and round it they have created the tremendously popular Inglenooks Bar with its own 'eating house'. Jacqueline reflected that upon their arrival at Bovey the fireplace was bricked up and the flagged floor was covered with linoleum. Such unappreciative and moronic behaviour leaves me incredulous.

The main dining room is wonderful, with Tudor linen-fold panelling, heavily beamed ceiling and Delft tiles round the fireplace. Here, candlelit dinners are an experience. The exceptional quality of the food and wine list seem almost incidental bonuses.

Upstairs the bedrooms are all different shapes and sizes and with, in most cases, through great ingenuity, bathrooms or en-suite showers.

It must have been a plumber's nightmare getting through the enormously thick walls. My favourite room, at the heart of the house, is the King Charles bedroom which has a fantastic coffered ceiling depicting the Merry Monarch hiding in the infamous oak tree at Boscobel. The whole room is panelled and reeks of history. If you sleep here, you may well imagine you are not alone because of the odd groans that happen in the quiet hours—be assured it is only old timbers settling down for the night. Ceilings seem to be a feature of Bovey. The drawing room, originally the house's medieval hall, captures the elegance of the 18th century with its stunning Adam ceiling. There are Delft tiles round the fireplace here too.

Bovey House is open all the year round with the exception of Christmas.

Actually in Beer, high up on the New Road, is **Mullions**, a friendly seven-bedroomed hotel run by Val Andrews with a little help from her husband, Les. The people who come to stay in this comfortable house, with wonderful views over the sea, return year after year. Some, Val tells me, are married couples who used to come with their parents as children. It is that sort of place. Everyone feels at home and incredibly well cared for. All the meals are freshly prepared, using homegrown vegetables and fruit, by Val, an excellent cook who relishes experimenting with new recipes.

When we were chatting, Val explained that the years have brought a change in the pattern of holidays; guests no longer sojourn for the annual two weeks but prefer shorter breaks. She further added that people were far more adventurous in their eating habits than previously, which pleases her enormously.

Mullions is only open from Easter to the end of November. During the winter months Val and Les try to take a holiday, and the rest of the time is spent in keeping the house in apple pie order. Situated high up, the only drawback is it is a bit of a climb from the beach and the village; guests though are always warned before a booking is accepted. I think you will like this lady, I certainly did.

Another place with magnificent views over Seaton Bay and the Axe Valley is **Seaton Heights Hotel and Leisure-Activity Centre**. In five acres of beautifully kept grounds, there are 26 Motel units, each well appointed and flexible, enabling them to be used as double, twin or family rooms. The catering is imaginative and sensitive to the needs of young families as well as the more sophisticated palate.

Apart from being able to enjoy the general attractions of Seaton you can also take advantage of the Leisure Centre's plethora of activities: squash, badminton, five-a-side football, volleyball, indoor cricket nets, and there is a sauna and solarium plus a spacious outdoor heated swimming pool.

It is in use all the year round and has found a lot of favour with the business community, who use the excellent conference facilities. The function rooms are also made available for wedding receptions—

occasions in which the hotel specialises. Such care is taken in the planning that it has to be a great weight off the mind of any bride and her parents.

Seaton has that rare item today, a tramway. It is even more a rarity to find a tramway working on an old railway line. Once run along the promenade at Eastbourne, and doomed when the promenade's extension was planned, the tram was rescued by the enthusiast who cares for it today—a considerable benefit for Devon. The hour's journey travelling the three miles aboard the double-decked tram, through the Axe and Coly valleys along the route of the old railway, will take you to Colyton, one of the prettiest small towns in Devon.

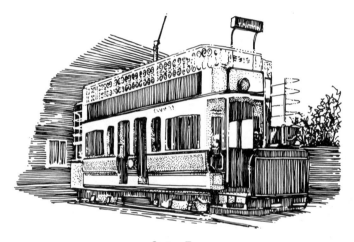

Seaton Tram

Colyton was settled as early as Saxon times and has a number of very attractive buildings. It stands at the mouth of a beautiful combe running into the Blackdown Hills. There is something very satisfying in walking along the many combes in this parish with their network of lanes linking farm to farm. Most of them have been there since medieval times and I wondered what the hedgerows housed then. They are beautiful now and alive with wildlife.

The village's 13th-century parish church of St Andrew has been altered over the years, of course, with the aisles being rebuilt in 1765 and 1816 giving the arcades a curious style. If you look closely at the stone parclose screen, erected by the incumbent, Thomas Brerewood, who held the living from 1524–44, you will see the initials T.B. and a briar bush. Obviously a pun on his name and evidence of a sense of humour which appeals to me.

When you have finished wandering take yourselves to **Rosemary Cot-**

tage for refreshments, whose scones and cream are excellent. It was once a butter store, a blacksmiths and a granary, but as a delightful tea-room it has found its true vocation.

Another place in which to get a superb cream tea is the **Southern Cross** at Newton Poppleford. For years I used to pass this attractive cottage and never stop because of the traffic. Now it is comparatively easy to get into the car park and more than worth the effort to be rewarded by such delicious and wickedly wanton food.

From here it was an easy run to Ottery St Mary or to Otterton. I tossed a coin and it came down in favour of Ottery. If you believe in fairie-folk, particulary pixies, this is the place for you. The large and beautiful collegiate church of St Mary, which almost looks like a twin of Exeter Cathedral, is home to a marauding band of them! Their life's work is to try and abduct the church's bellringers in order to prevent them ringing out their joyous peals. To banish this threat, someone has to say 'Bless my Soul' after which the pixies disappear until their

Ottery St Mary Church

next opportunity. The secret password has worked so far and never once have the bells failed to be rung, except during the 1939–45 war of course, when all bells were silenced, only to sound if invasion was imminent.

There was once a whistling cock on the weather-vane of the church. It really did whistle in the wind when a storm was brewing. After 600 years it needed repairing, so in 1977 modern technicians tackled the task but sadly were unable to replace the whistle. The new one screeched and had to be stopped, so perhaps the pixies won that round.

Ottery, like so many places, has an annual carnival which takes place on November 5th. Nothing strange in that but here young men rush through the main street carrying barrels of flaming tar, a sight worth beholding.

The town has stood for a 1,000 years. It is a pretty place, named after the river, in whose valley it lies. You will find the **Stafford Hotel** is a friendly place in which to stay; nothing pretentious or out of the ordinary, but the food is good and reasonably priced. It is especially recommended if you have young children; the owners having a young family themselves take childish problems in their stride.

Although two horrific fires in 1767 and 1866 unfortunately destroyed most of the thatched cottages in Yonder Street and beyond, Ottery still has many fine Georgian buildings. One fine example, in Silver Street, is a superb restaurant, **Oswalds**. The proprietor, whose name regretfully I forget, is also the chef and is famous for his mouthwatering sauces.

On the B3176 Ottery St Mary to Talaton road is **Escot Aquatic Centre and Gardens**. Unusual from most tourist attractions, its converted 18th-century buildings house an astonishing collection of tropical and coldwater fish, from Koi to Piranhas. There are birds, reptiles including an alligator and a python, rabbits plus many other animals in an open plan setting. They are all for sale, that is apart from the alligator and python. It is not this that makes the place so special, though. Here there is a two-acre walled garden, thought to have been built from the rubble of the original Escot House which burnt down in 1790—some of the bricks are visibly charred. South facing, the walled garden was built as a vegetable garden, supplying the needs of Escot House. Sadly, in the appalling gales of January 1990, much of the east and west walls were destroyed.

As in the case of many of these fine gardens, the horrendous cost of propagation and labour caused the decline of production, and by the 1950s and '60s its only harvest was soft fruit, for sale to local markets. Even this became unprofitable by the 1970s and the garden was leased to a local nursery for growing trees. In 1983 the garden was returned to the present owners, the Kennaways, and Escot Aquaculture used the land to create ten, 30-metre covered fish ponds.

The story then becomes very interesting because Parklands Farm became available, and was converted into what is now the retail centre, allowing other, more suitable wetland on the estate to be used for ponds. The Kennaways, therefore, in 1988 took the decision to recreate the old walled garden. The filled in ponds gave birth to the Victorian rose garden, which I think is perfection, and with the original paths to tread and a charming pergola, it is a delight. In giving this garden new life they also unearthed the original well which now serves all the water requirements throughout the farm.

Following the garden's north wall you will reach what is known as the Wilderness and the wild boar enclosures, built in an area of overgrown Christmas trees. Naturally at home in the forests of Europe, wild boars are very shy creatures and have a tendency to hide themselves away, lying in shallow scrapes which they have made. Continuing along this path you come to a bridge, on the eastern side of which is Rose Cottage, a private residence, and past which between April and July is a breathtaking blaze of rhododendrons and azaleas in full blown and spectacular beauty.

The northern reaches of the Escot Estate provide other outstanding views, the glories of the Devon countryside, and it is from here our gentle meander led back to Escot House, the seat of the Kennaway family—right in the front garden, actually. The house is private but the path leads around and past the mews building to arrive once more at the aquatic centre. It is approximately a 45 minute stroll of which every moment is a sheer pleasure. Push-chairs are manageable along the path but it is harder going for wheel-chairs, and the cafe will always provide delicious cream tea rewards afterwards.

Escot is open every day from 10am-6pm, with the exception of Christmas Day until the 1st January inclusive.

Somewhere I am totally happy to linger is in the **Domesday Mill** at Otterton. What a fantastic place and how nearly it was ruined by former owners without a sense of history. Fortunately, a teacher of Medieval Archaeology, Desna Greenhow, lived directly opposite this gem. Having watched its gradual decline she managed, once the mill was vacant, to acquire the lease from the Clinton Devon Estates, and two years in which to see if she could do something with it. Twelve years later she is running Otterton Mill not only as a tourist attraction but, as originally intended, a mill working as it has been, grinding grain, since before the Norman Conquest.

When I drove into the car park I was not at all sure what to expect. I was immediately greeted by a bevy of visitor friendly chickens who cackled away and part escorted me through a small alleyway into the midst of a hive of industry. Several of the barns and old buildings have been turned into craft workshops for local crafts people. You can watch John Stafford working with wood, and next to him a potter who produces some delightful work which captures exciting autumnal colours on a greyish green base. He told me that he changes the colours from time to time, but is never quite sure what they might be.

One remark he made I found fascinating. He stated, quite firmly, that he and Barnstaple clay were not compatible. Eschewing the Devon clay he buys his from Stoke-on-Trent. It never occurred to me that working with clay could vary. Alas, to me clay is clay.

At the top of some very steep wooden steps is the studio of Tamarisk, who produces individually crafted stove enamelled signs which she hand paints. There are four basic shapes, oval, arch, rectangle and circle, into which a design of your choice can be skilfully created. The motif list is extensive covering birds, flowers, animals, transport, buildings, trees, leaves and finally fruit. One of these would make an excellent Christmas present. She has a super mail order service which allows you to select your shape, motif and colours. The prices start from as little as £30 and go up to approximately £120. She is doing extremely well at Otterton and has a full order book, so if this interests you get in touch quickly. It takes a minimum of eight weeks to receive your sign. Her telephone number is 0395 67595.

Another of the mill's studios is devoted to stained glass, an art form that I love, and a further one to painting. Then there is the bakery which, using the mill's various flours, makes and sells cakes, bread, scones and pastry. It supplies the Duckery restaurant, situated in the old barn, which opens every day during the summer but is closed on weekdays during the winter. The food served is all home grown and you can have lunch or tea or just pop in for morning coffee. The smell of freshly baked scones and cakes will make the latter highly unlikely—it is far too tempting for even the strongest will.

The Duckery Gallery above the restaurant always displays paintings and sculpture by several artists working in the West Country, all of them for sale. It is an interesting mix of styles and concepts and thoroughly enjoyable.

Across the little bridge, over the water in which the wheel turns, is the co-operative shop where all manner of local crafts are sold. The museum, above the shop, is worth the visit to Otterton alone. Illustrations show the working of the mill with explanations at each point in the tour. On the stone floor a relief map shows sites where other mills were in lower Otter Valley, and there are also displays of stone-dressing tools and the different stages in making a cog.

I was enthralled watching the two water-wheels and the mill machinery, part of which is wooden and part cast iron. The wheels vary in age from the 18th to the 19th centuries, and the great spur and crown wheels have applewood cogs. Milling, on average, occurs only three days a week, but the machinery and restored wheel turns every day. Guided tours for groups must be booked in advance, although the miller often takes groups round informally on summer afternoons.

Desna Greenhow, with the support of her husband, has given so much to Otterton Mill. There can be no real financial benefit from the venture because it is so costly to maintain, but for her it is a labour of love and one I hope she will go on doing for many years to come.

Otterton itself, which in the 16th century was a port until a shingle bar silted up the estuary, is a large village already with proposals to build even more houses; I sincerely hope it will not get too big and lose its character. More houses inevitably mean more cars and the road through the village is quite busy enough already. It is a lively community who organise all sorts of events throughout the year—one of which reminded me of the childhood game of Pooh sticks, but in this instance it is an annual duck race where model ducks are dropped over Otterton bridge to float downstream.

On my way to Otterton I had stopped for a short while in East Budleigh. What a pretty place it is with some delightful cob-and-thatch buildings. Sir Walter Raleigh was born just a mile west of the village at Hayes Barton, which is a fine example of a Tudor house.

Hayes Barton

I have always been attracted by bench ends in churches and the parish church of All Saints has more than sixty, most of them 16th century, if not older. They had been splendidly carved, probably by local craftsmen, and I had an hour or so of immense pleasure looking at them.

The church is mainly 15th century although it was sympathetically restored in 1884. Decorating its walls are several memorials to the Rev Ambrose Stapleton and his family. He was a beloved vicar who cared deeply for his parishioners, but like his counterpart at Thurlestone, he is better known for his involvement in the smuggling industry, rampant in the early 1800s. Many a barrel of brandy was stored in his vicarage which was perhaps marginally less reprehensible than the vicar of Thurlestone who used the church roof!

No distance at all from East Budleigh is Budleigh Salterton, one of Devon's most charming and unspoilt places. There is a gentle brook running right through the street that houses the friendly shops. The brook starts its run at Squabmoor, a drab name for such a beautiful spot adjoining Woodbury Common.

Like most of the beaches along this part of the coast with its red cliffs, the pebbles do not entice you to walk barefooted—but it is of no importance, the scenery makes up for any minor inconvenience. After a busy day I sat in total contentment watching the world about me and thanking God for it.

The oldest seaside town in Devon, Exmouth, is almost next door to Budleigh Salterton. The Romans used it as a port, in the 19th century it was a fashionable watering place and today it is a popular family holiday resort. Not the most attractive place architecturally, apart from the rather distinguished houses on the Beacon, where Lady Nelson once lived at No 6 and Lady Byron at No 19. Even these are strange houses. From the front they are beautiful but at the back nothing short of a mess. It was the practice at that time for the developers to build outstanding facades, and let the owner decide on the rest.

What a sad lady Nelson's widow must have been. Upon her death she was buried in the sublime cemetery attached to the church at Littleham just two miles away. In this incredibly overcrowded burial ground, her tomb, a copy of Nelson's in St Paul's Cathedral, albeit less ornate, rests under a great yew tree.

The town has grown enormously in the last decade with new housing estates galore. The Royal Marine base at nearby Lympstone has created quite a different atmosphere in the town, too. Many of the service wives now live in the Exmouth area.

One of the very special places in Exmouth is **A La Ronde** in Summer Lane. It has been acquired by the National Trust this year so we will still be able to visit this unique, beautiful oddity, with its sixteen sides

A La Ronde

and octagonal centre. Each of the twenty rooms has the most stunning views of the sea over twelve acres of parkland. Built in 1798 by two spinster ladies, Jane and Mary Parminter, dedicated their lives to the upkeep of the house. All around the gallery at the top, the walls are covered in sea shells, every one of which they collected and put in place themselves. A La Ronde is quite astonishing.

To the east there is the chapel Point-in-View with a school and almshouses close by. Erected in 1811, Point-in-View was a Dissenting Chapel whose purpose was to promote Christianity amongst Jews. Jane Parminter was buried here. The almshouses, four in number, were built to house spinsters over the age of fifty, one of whom was required to teach six pauper girls in the school. Preference was given to applicants who were Jews converted to Christianity. Jane Parminter decreed that on the anniversary of her death the little girls were to receive each a 'stuff gown, a straw bonnet, a linen cap and a Vandyke tippet'.

One other wish in her will was that the oak trees on the A La Ronde estate 'shall remain standing and the hand of man shall not be raised against them, till Israel returns and is restored to the land of Promise'.

As all seaside resorts, Exmouth has many places in which one can stay from small and excellent bed-and-breakfast establishments to high-class hotels. One I especially like, and which is ideal for families, is **Devoncourt** in Douglas Avenue.

The hotel stands in four acres of lovely, mature sub-tropical gardens which slope gently towards the sea overlooking two miles of golden sandy beaches. You could almost imagine yourself on the Continent as you sit under the palm trees looking out over the uninterrupted sea view.

The hotel is well appointed. In addition to the normal bedrooms, which all have en suite facilities, there are some delightful suites, all with a private lounge and some with panoramic sea views.

Devoncourt has excellent recreational facilities. You can take a dip in the indoor or outdoor heated swimming pools, relax in the sauna, indulge in a steam bath or find stimulation with the whirlpool spa. There are two solariums on the premises and a snooker room which contains a world championship standard table. You can test your skill on the fourteen hole putting green, croquet lawn, and an all-weather tennis court.

What you have just read is no more than one would see in almost any hotel brochure, but what needs stressing is the friendly service and fantastic value for money offered by Devoncourt. For example a 'Bargain Break' of two nights or more would cost you £77 per person for two days in which is included bed, breakfast and a superb three-course carvery meal with coffee.

Driving out of Exmouth, past the Royal Marine base, one comes into the Saxon village of Lympstone. It shelters in a little valley from which the fishermen could reach the water and the yeomen could till the fields. Its church, of the Nativity of the Blessed Virgin Mary, was dedicated in 1409. It has not always been a peaceful place of sanctuary though. The tower was used by both sides in the Civil War being high enough to sight their guns to fire at ships coming up river attempting to relieve Exeter. The church was rather viciously restored in 1860, but it is still a lovely place of worship.

If you want a place to stay which has style and is not too expensive, Ebford Manor Hotel, at Ebford, is super. Quietly elegant, good food and wine and nice grounds. It is equidistant from Exeter and Exmouth.

Almost into Exeter is Topsham. Be careful how you pronounce the name. The 'S' goes with Top rather than with ham! In Napoleonic times it was a flourishing port but declined steadily afterwards and it is now home to boatyards and boat builders and a host of small marine craft who sail on the estuary. I love its grace and elegance. It has one main street with a number of 14th–17th-century buildings.

Topsham

Every now and again you come across a little alleyway, fascinating to explore, which leads down to the river. It has some super restaurants, far more pubs than it needs and overall a general sense of well being; a perfect resting place after our journey.

CHAPTER 6

Exeter

There are many counties envious of Devon's good fortune in having Exeter as its capital. It has everything. The River Exe wends its gracious way through the heart of the city, stopping every now and again to prepare itself for the opening of the swing bridge which lets small coasters up stream for unloading, much in the way it has for centuries. The jewel in the crown is the magnificent cathedral which dominates the city centre and dictates much of the life-style immediately around it.

Exeter is Roman, Saxon and Norman; it has walls and a tower built by Athelstan, the first King of England, but most of all it is Medieval. There are still miles of quaint streets and passageways, rambling walls, a plethora of churches and of course the cathedral bequeathed to us by many generations of the finest builders, apart from its Norman walls and tower. Of course the 20th century has crept in and much has had

The Historic City of Exeter

to be changed, but on the whole it has been done with the greatest of care and dedication to the preservation of all that is good. One of the reasons that it can sustain its beautiful buildings is because of the ever increasing business that comes to the city.

Industry and commerce have flourished in Exeter for centuries but probably never so forcefully as today. Companies throughout the U.K.

seek to relocate here. There is little opposition from their staff either, once they have seen the amenities that Exeter has to offer and the glorious areas within easy reach of the city in which they can live.

Shopping is a pleasure, with the big stores living comfortably alongside medieval buildings. As in most county towns there are innumerable small shops which entice—most of them hidden away in the enchanting alleyways. It is people who make businesses interesting and in Caroline Boa I struck gold.

One might wonder what a Trout Farm at Umberleigh in North Devon has to do with a little shop called **Devon Foods** in the narrow Gandy Street, which you reach by turning right down an alley way by Topman. The answer is that Robin and Caroline Boa own and run **Head Mill Trout Farm** at Umberleigh. It was from here that Caroline started producing her own range of pies, quiches and pates which are now well known.

This enterprising lady joined with seven other home-based ladies to form Devon Harvest, all individual businesses but uniting from time to time to produce what the customer required. Each had her own speciality and the enterprise grew in strength until Devon County Council encouraged them to become larger and rename themselves Devon Fare. This did not appeal to Caroline who likes her independence and also thought her integrity might be threatened if she were asked to sell something she did not care for.

Caroline found the little shop in Gandy Street, installed a kitchen and opened her doors selling nothing but Devon Foods. The name remains but it became apparent, very rapidly, that restricting the stock to strictly Devon based produce was not sensible. When I walked in I discovered the shop full of all sorts of exciting, unusual delicatessen items that are so hard to find. The quiches are wonderful and the variety of pates superb.

The University brings her quite a lot of business but when term ends it seems to pick up elsewhere. Caroline has a regular clientele who use her for dinner parties and buffets. They just ring and tell her the number of people who have been invited, and she does the rest. I would suspect that Caroline knows most of her customers and is on Christian name terms with them. She is that sort of lady.

On the counter I saw a tray of marzipan animals and little people, all individually sculpted. These are made by someone else and sell extremely well. Caroline told me that not long ago she received an order for a number of them and each had to be applicable in some way to the guest dining in the house of the customer. Imagine a beautifully laid dinner table, shining silver, gleaming crystal—and there on the dinner mat in front of the guest a serpent or a pig perhaps. The mind boggles. I wonder if the recipients recognised themselves?

Caroline also does marvellous hampers by mail order for Christmas or special occasions, which will include some trout pate from the trout farm.

Gandy Street is a gem with its various shops, restaurants and little off-shoot alleyways, but it would be infinitely poorer without Devon Foods.

All the time you are wandering in and out of the alleyways you will probably be getting ever nearer the **Cathedral**. Such is the dimension of its beauty that I find it hard to do it justice on paper. Gazing at the outside will give you hours of pleasure and probably an aching neck. I love walking along the little Cathedral Close and Southernhay with its beautiful buildings, almost entirely occupied by professional people rather than residents. Perhaps I will walk in the garden of the 14th-century bishop's palace, with its fine trees taking shade from the great walls of the cathedral. Certainly I will look at the Deanery where Catherine of Aragon stayed a night on her way to meet her fate—Henry VIII. I wonder how she felt.

Exeter Cathedral—west front screen

There are Norman arches that lead into cobbled courtyards with graceful wisterias. Over the cloisters is a room in which the Librarian works, surrounded by 8,000 books—and amongst them the wonderful Exeter book which Leofric gave to the cathedral. It is beautifully written in ink and contains about a third of our Saxon literature. . . .And so it goes on, but I always know that at the end of this little meander I will come to the final glory, the sweeping majesty of this incredible cathedral.

The two great Norman towers, one of which has 100 arches, have stood for eight centuries; the piers and arches and the roof for six. The west front is covered with three rows of statues. There are angels, prophets, soldiers and kings, fighting for their places amidst the priests and apostles. St Peter sits above them, almost as if he is looking down on an unruly mob.

Once inside I am always mesmerised by the beauty around me. It is almost like being in a heaven in which modern man is allowed to go about an ordered, peaceful existence which in no way lacks purpose. There is no strife, no threat of war, no anger, just a great sense of the presence of God in the most wonderful surroundings. If there is any cry for help at all it comes from the need to keep this treasure safe. The years are telling on it and constant war is waged against decay. This takes an immense amount of money which is mainly raised by the public. It is not only money that is needed, craftsmen are continually at work and some of them are getting much older. Finding replacements becomes quite a battle in itself.

Colonel Woodcock is the Administrator and, whilst I envy him his job which enables him to work in such wonderful surroundings, I am quite sure that he must feel he carries an onerous responsibility. He does so with grace, charm and a steely determination, leading his troops in the unceasing battle.

Exeter is blessed with many fine churches, some of which are never used but most have stories attached to them. One entrance into the Close is by the tiny church of St Martin with its porch looking across to the cathedral. It is quite easy to disregard this little gem because of the stunning beauty of the Elizabethan structure alongside, which

Moll's Coffee House

was known once as Moll's Coffee House. The tiers of windows lean out and are crowned by a little gallery. Its front reminds one of an old ship—not surprising because it was here that Drake used to meet his captains. Nothing much has changed since his time. The oak panelling is almost black with age, and there is an intriguing gallery painted with 46 different coats of arms. The most fascinating sight though is the whole front of the low room, which is glass. I am told there are no less than 230 panes and no two the same size.

St Petrock's church has a bell that is more than 500 years old, yet its parish is no bigger than the ground the church stands upon. Then there is the Norman priory of St Nicholas which is almost 900 years old, and so I could continue with St Mary Arches, the curious church of St Mary-at-Steppes and the quaint 16th-century church of St Thomas—a church with a difference. It is the only one in the county in which a vicar was hanged from his own tower in the rebellion of 1549. There is another little piece of history attached to this church. General Gordon of Khartoum fame arrived at the door of this church with the intention of seeing his grandfather's grave. Before he could cross the threshold he was handed a telegram summoning him to the War Office in London. Once there he was ordered to Khartoum from where he never returned.

If you enjoy churches you will have a field day in Exeter. I never have enough time to see all I want and I have lived in the county for almost 66 years.

Apart from the cathedral, none can compare to the **Guildhall**, whose walls have stood for 650 years. It makes sure you will not miss it for it thrusts itself out into the busy main street, in amongst all the 20th-century buildings. I can almost hear it saying 'I bet I will be here still when you are long gone.' Quite right too. Can you imagine C & A or Marks and Spencers still being there in 600 odd years?

Inside it is quite lovely. The hall has a superb roof with gilded beams, from which hang dazzling candelabra. The city arms were carved and painted for Elizabeth I to give to Exeter in Armada year. Displayed elsewhere are royal and other gifts that have been collected over the years, including a sword used by Nelson and some of the rarest seals in the land. One dates back to 1175 and is believed to be the oldest in the country.

Next door there is something quite different but equally ancient. **The Turk's Head**, which has been a hostelry since 1330, is now a Beefeater Steak House. Its owners retained its pub downstairs and created eating areas at other levels so that you can choose your venue. If you want just to eat and be away from the hustle and bustle of the bar, then a rear entrance takes you to the attractive first floor where food is foremost in everyone's minds.

The Beefeater chain has a standard which it maintains throughout the country and the Turk's Head is no exception. Good food, well presented at acceptable prices, makes it a very popular place.

Fred and Caroline Cairns are a young couple who have managed the Turk's Head for just over 12 months, during which time they have wrought a remarkable change. The pub had a reputation for hooliganism and troublemakers which spoilt the enjoyment of many people who were just looking for somewhere pleasant to eat. This was not, and still sadly is not, an unusual happening in the centre of Exeter at night. It is something that has driven a lot of people away from the city centre for their evening's entertainment and cost the restaurateurs and the publicans a lot of trade.

When the Cairns were sent to the Turk's Head as relief managers they were thrown in at the deep end. It was just before Christmas, staff morale was low and the clientele needed taking in hand. These two achieved this and to their delight were confirmed as permanent managers. From that time Fred has used all his training in the business and much of what he was taught in the police to change the reputation of the Turk's Head. The Turk's Head is now an enjoyable, safe place to be.

He has a good relationship with the young Royal Marines, who are training a few miles away at Lympstone and use the bar of the pub as their local at weekends. He tells me that a group of fifteen of them will arrive. One will be the 'duty' man. He will not drink for the evening and his task is to keep a watchful eye on his mates to see that they do not get too boisterous. It works splendidly. They all have a good run ashore and go back to their barracks without causing themselves or anyone else any trouble. Perhaps we should insist that more of our youth spend 15 weeks training time with the Royal Marines!

This sort of behaviour has a roll-on effect which helps to keep the rest of the young customers in hand. The louts have learnt that they are not welcome and will not be served with a drink, so they have disappeared. With this firmness of touch Fred and Caroline have brought old and new customers back into the restaurant and are delighted at the increase in trade.

The bar is a fun place to be, noisy yes, but that is what the young enjoy. There are regular theme nights which prove very popular and of course the excellence of the bar snacks makes it a magnet for people at lunchtime.

The age of the building causes headaches when it comes to maintenance, but the atmosphere created by so much history makes it worth the hassle. The floors are uneven, there are beams everywhere and on the walls there are shelves full of books which have been acquired over the years. Some, I am quite sure, are of great value and I do wonder if the books, for which an antiquarian bookseller would give his eye teeth, should really be there. I would have loved to have climbed up and had a closer look at them.

No building of this age could be without a ghost, and the Turk's Head is no exception. No one seems to know who it is but the spirit in question delights in causing loo doors to stick in the staff quarters and manages to lock the occupant in quite frequently. I wondered if it was the spirit of the Turk who was the last man to be decapitated in Exeter, hence the name of the pub!

Whilst we are talking about eating out in Exeter there are two very special places, totally different but each delightful in its own right.

Opposite a public car park in Mary Arches Street there is an archway; go through it and you come into a world of enchantment. **St Olave's Court Hotel** is a building acquired from the Church Commissioners some few years ago and has been developed into an oasis of peace under the guiding hands of its owner, Mr Clarke.

Even had he not produced a charming, friendly and informally elegant place in which to stay, I would still have been tempted to remain, just to savour the pleasure of the peacefulness away from the traumatic bustle of the centre of Exeter.

I was there in the middle of the intense heat of August, but in the restaurant, which draws its daylight from a glass dome in the ceiling, the soft cream and golden furnishings coupled with the greenery, which is profuse, produced a sense of fresh coolness. It is a particularly intimate restaurant which has its own name—'The Galsworthy'. The night before my arrival guests had enjoyed their delicious dinner, sitting at candlelit tables on the lawn across the courtyard, almost unaware that they were in the middle of the county town.

It is without doubt the owner and his daughter Michelle who have created this delightful place and their charming hospitality has rubbed off on their staff. The chef has been with the Clarkes since they started. He loves the West Country and although his brilliance would enable him to get a place wherever he wished, Exeter has become his home, and guests at St Olave's are the beneficiaries. All meals are prepared freshly to order and so a little patience is required, but the result is more than worth waiting for.

Wine has always been a pleasure to me and I was delighted to find that Mr Clarke has a pioneering spirit in this field. He is not afraid to bring to his excellent wine list the ever increasing selection of wines from all around the world. His current list is aimed at a cosmopolitan approach without in any way jeopardising its structure.

Lunchtime sees this quiet place come to life. Business lunches are very much the order of the day. It is a place that removes stress the moment you come in through the archway and the sheer ambience of the restaurant would make the cut and thrust of business that much more enjoyable.

It would be fair to say that the majority of guests here come from the business community. People in the process of being relocated by their companies find St Olave's a temporary home.

For the second place I was told to take the first turning to the right in Bonhay Road into Tudor Street. I was looking for **The Tudor House** and I found it unbelievable that a building of such antiquity could be part of a street which seemed to me to consist of factories and warehouses—but there, tucked away on the left hand side opposite a late 20th-century monstrosity, was this gem of Elizabethan England.

Today it is a wonderful restaurant owned by one of England's outstanding women chefs. She offers a marvellous à la carte and table d'hôte menu, amongst which there is always a very special vegetarian

The Tudor House

dish. This unassuming lady has no less than six entries in the leading guides to her credit and as her partner, Mr Clive, is a wine buff, there is also an outstanding cellar.

It must be wonderful to work and live in this fabulous house which has not changed since the day it was built, which one assumes is 1450, as stated on the flagstone at the portal. Apart from the main banqueting hall there are small, intimate rooms. Every room has the original beams and relatively low ceilings.

In 1628 Isaac Burche, who was appropriately a malster of the city, lived here with his family. Nothing has changed since then except for the furniture which has been so carefully chosen in colour, shape and content that it blends beautifully with the richness of the gleaming wood. Like all houses of this age there are endless steps and stairs which add to the charm but can make it a little awkward for the elderly, the disabled or wheelchair users. Mr Clive tells me that this minor problem is easily overcome, because there is a wide door at ground level and with prior notice guests can be directed to this entrance where assistance is readily at hand.

In the 1970s the Tudor House was lovingly and painstakingly restored by a Mr Lovell, with no assistance from the city fathers or any other group. He spent so much time and money on this labour of love that it bankrupted him. He certainly suffered but the work he undertook has allowed this wonderful place to continue as it does today.

It was Mr Lovell who developed the Leat Room, named after the 1000-year-old mill leat which still runs outside its windows. The magnificent hand-carved ceiling is not Elizabethan but done by the man himself. It is an incredible piece of work and gives a superb atmosphere to the room, together with the Gobelin tapestries which adorn the walls.

The Leat Room is used for luncheon and dinner functions, and private celebrations. You can take drinks in the Tudor or Rose bar first and then choose from the seven menus available. The room is available for conferences with facilities that belong strictly to the 1990s, including conference packs, video, T.V. and flip charts.

Hotels abound in the city, many of them small, comfortable and friendly but it is of the bigger ones that I want to write mainly because of their history.

Cathedral Yard in Exeter is one of the delights of Devon and to stay in **The Royal Clarence Hotel**, in one of its bedrooms overlooking the floodlit cathedral, is a privilege.

Two hundred years ago the Royal Clarence was the first inn in Britain to receive the title 'hotel'. Lord Nelson stayed here and so have many Royals including Czar Nicholas 1. I wonder what they would have thought of the careful restoration that has taken place over the last couple of years.

The Royal Clarence Hotel

If you are an architectural buff you will be intrigued and delighted by the differing styles which have been introduced ever since the original building in the 14th century. You will see that every one of the 56 bedrooms and suites is richly furnished in Tudor, Georgian or Victorian style, which in their own way tell the story of the colourful history of the Royal Clarence.

Dining in the Raleigh restaurant is to be gastronomically spoilt, waited on by quietly efficient staff, who unobtrusively see to your every need.

Caring for staff is one of the policies of Queens Moat Houses, to which the Royal Clarence belongs. When I was talking to a member of staff in another one of their hotels, I discovered that she and her husband, who were having one of those troublesome spots in their marriage, stayed for a weekend in one of the best suites here for just £10 a night. It gave them a chance to sort themselves out and to me it underlined the fact that to get the best out of people who work for you this sort of consideration pays dividends.

It says on their brochure, 'Peaceful elegance and undisturbed comfort makes the Royal Clarence more than worthy of its distinguished reputation'. It could not have been better phrased.

In spite of the damage that Hitler managed to inflict on Exeter in World War II, it still retains some truly beautiful buildings with a strong Georgian flavour. An indestructible part of the tradition of Exeter is the dignified **Rougemont Hotel**, just a few yards from the High Street.

David Reynolds has been the Manager here for over ten years; backed by the Mount Charlotte Group, he has steadily enhanced the hotel's image, bringing it in line with the very best of modern day hotels and yet never once allowing the dramatic quality of its splendid rooms to be decimated. His impeccable standards are reflected throughout the hotel and he demands nothing from his staff that he is not personally prepared to give.

Originating from the Midlands, he is yet another man who has not the slightest desire to leave the West Country for greater glory. I doubt actually that there is a better hotel in the Mount Charlotte Group than this one.

The history of the Rougemont always intrigues visitors. Originally the site was occupied by a debtors prison and was said by one occupant that it was the worst he knew in all England. To this day some of the basement areas of the hotel remain as they were in the days of the prison. There is a tunnel which runs from the basement to the present site of the museum situated across the road. No one knows quite what its purpose was, but it could have been an escape route for prisoners or even a safe place for wealthy guests. One person who might know, if only she could talk, is The Grey Lady, who is sometimes seen walking the staircase in the early hours of the morning. She was a guest when the hotel first opened, but for some reason she gassed herself in her room and has never found peace since. The flagpole stands at the front of the hotel on the grisly spot where prisoners were hanged, and in the cellar of the Drakes Bar, until quite recently, old shackling irons were still attached to the walls.

It was in 1876 that the building of the hotel commenced and for the sum of £21,000 plus another £11,000 for furnishings and fittings the Rougemont was able to open its doors on the 29th May 1877. It was a splendid occasion and the local paper stated that, 'If the venture was not attended with success this would be due to an ungrateful public, and not any fault of the directors.' It has flourished ever since, although there have been times when its prestige slipped a little. Today, however, I am happy to report that this hotel is very much alive and kicking and offering an excellent service to anyone who stays within its hallowed portals.

The city business people make great use of the function rooms, both for dinners and for more mundane seminars. Americans think it is great and there is an ever increasing number of foreigners who come once and then again.

At Christmas the hotel is virtually full, and a good many of the guests are people who have been coming every Christmas for the last five years or so. They obviously enjoy it and from the hotel's point of view it must be very helpful having a nucleus of people who all know each other helping create the sense of a house party.

In one of the little pamphlets which the hotel gives its guests, there is a suggested walk which really takes you into the heart of the city. It is quite a way so you will need comfortable shoes, but it is more than worthwhile. From the front of the hotel you turn right into Queen Street, leaving the museum on your left and coming to the High Street. This allows you to see some of the most exquisite timber-framed Merchants Houses of the 16th and 17th century; on your right there is quite a mishmash of shop fronts which vary from the 16th to 20th century. Turn right and you come to the Guildhall with the Turk's Head next door. Further down on the same side is Parliament Street, the narrowest street in the world—so be careful you don't miss it.

At the bottom where the four ancient main streets meet, you turn right into St Nicholas Priory built about 1070, the surviving west range of which is now a museum. Bartholomew Street next and then into Fore Street again and down West Street to the bottom of the cobbled Stepcote Hill, once the main thoroughfare leading to the West Gate and the river crossing. At the bottom of the hill is the 'house that moved'. A wonderful house that got in the way of progress but was far too historically valuable to demolish, so literally it was rolled to its present position in the 1960s. Next on to the Quay. This area, with its massive warehouses and beautiful Customs Houses built in 1675, reminds you sharply of the one time importance of the maritime trade to the city. If you have the time you can take the little ferry across the river and visit the **Maritime Museum**, which is fascinating.

Leave the Quay by the steps alongside the 'Prospect' and continue up Southernhay. From here you pass into Cathedral Close dominated by the superb Gothic Cathedral with its 12th-century towers.

In Princesshay there are underground passages and the line of the old Town Wall is marked by crazy paving. A left turn takes you into Castle Street and there is the Norman castle, or what remains of it. Left again brings you to the Rougemont Gardens, laid in the 18th century. On the right is the only remaining piece of the Norman castle defences, the Gatehouse. Rougemont House to the left contains pictures of archaeology and history of the City and County. If you go through the small gate cut into the Town Wall and into Northernhay Gardens, a turn left will bring you back to the Rougemont Hotel more than ready

Cobbled Stepcote Hill, terminating in St Mary's Steps, is believed to have been the medieval 'main road' out of town

The Customs House, Exeter Quay

for a meal, a large drink or even a cup of tea. Whatever you require the hotel will have it for you and you will once more be enveloped in a cocoon of comfort.

Whilst no-one could call the new Trust House Forte hotel historic, I am delighted to report that it is extremely comfortable and well run. It has the great attribute of being situated just at the foot of Southernhay, making it extremely convenient for the city centre. I have found it a very useful place to park my car whilst I go about my business and then return to the hotel for a very good snack lunch.

A totally different type of hotel, built specifically in the mid 19th century for the comfort of travellers on the Great Western Railway at Exeter, was an hotel of the same name. The arrival of the motor car started the decline of the railway and after nationalisation the Great Western Railway ceased to exist, but for thousands of people throughout the world **The Great Western Hotel**, St David's Approach, Exeter, has become a Mecca. Much of this is due to a brave Austrian hotelier, Mr Krombas, who had the courage to take on the hotel which for years had been a white elephant and had taken more than one owner into bankruptcy.

I had visited the hotel several times over many years and felt saddened by its decayed state, but under the present management it has got its steam up and flourishes. Somehow Manfred Krombas and his wife Pauline, assisted by their very able young manageress Diane Hancock, have created a tremendous atmosphere. When you walk in it feels more like a friendly local pub than a formal hotel. The 'Loco' and 'Brunel' bars retain many of the characteristics of an old railway inn. There are old prints and sketches of steam railways decorating the walls. There is even the original nameplate from the 'Corfe Castle' serving as a great reminder of the age of steam.

Every year, railway enthusiasts of various societies gather here for their get togethers. They come from all parts of Great Britain and some from overseas. Situated so close to the station it is a wonderful place for dedicated train spotters.

Apart from the excellent food served in the Brunel restaurant, at a very reasonable price—a three course meal offering a wide selection of dishes cost me only £8.95—the 44 bedrooms, most of which have private bathrooms, are comfortable and have every modern convenience. It is within easy walking distance of the centre of the city.

For companies wishing to hold a medium-size conference it would be ideal. The conference room is on the first floor of the hotel and holds up to 35 delegates for meetings. All the facilities you would expect are available. Paddington is just two-and-a-half hours away on one of the regular express trains.

If ever there was a case of a theatre not knowing to which community it belonged and therefore seemingly having allegiance to neither, this is the **Northcott Theatre** in Exeter.

I remember how thrilled we all were when it was first built—the first new theatre in the South West for many a year. It was at a time when we were all deprived of good live theatre. Touring companies did not like coming west of Bristol, Plymouth still had the old Palace Theatre and a little civic theatre on Plymouth Hoe, but it was all shabby and second rate. The Northcott was to be the shining star.

Over the years the star has grown less bright. Plymouth has stolen much of its brilliance by building the Theatre Royal right in the heart of the city where, not only does it attract big names and new shows, it also creates its own. Roger Redfern, its director, brought us *Shadowlands* with Nigel Hawthorne and Jane Lapotaire in 1990 which, as we all know, went on to the West End, won several awards and is now doing brilliantly on Broadway. The question in my mind is why Plymouth and not Exeter?

I have talked to one or two people about this and it seems to me that because the theatre was built on land given to the city by the University, it has found itself isolated from the people of Exeter. The student population make little use of it and the lack of parking does not encourage any but the most ardent of theatregoers from the city to make the trek to the campus.

What is the solution? It does not keep a sufficiently high profile in the city or the surroundings. If you were to run a market research exercise you would find that the vast majority of the people of Exeter know of the theatre's existence but they have not a clue where it is nor what it offers.

The theatre has everything that it could wish for except a good site. It dithers a bit in artistic direction, but I understand by the time this book is published there will be a new, dynamic Artistic Director who has strong beliefs. It would be wonderful if he could polish up the theatre's image, give it several shots of adrenalin and make the people of Exeter wake up to the fact that they have a splendid theatre in their midst which should be used for seeing productions and as a meeting place for friends.

One splendid building in Exeter is **County Hall** from which the business of the county is conducted. Not the place that many visitors would go to, but I arrived there one morning wanting to dig a bit into how the future of the county was seen. I met Peter Hunt, the Countryside Officer, a helpful, friendly man whose abiding passion is the prevention of outsiders coming into the county! I quite understand his viewpoint in many ways, because the more people we attract the more difficult it becomes to look after roads, housing, hospitals and the environment. At the end of the day I suppose it will be the political masters who make the decisions, irrespective of the value of that decision to the county.

Peter Hunt is a writer as well as an officer of the County and I can see that he may well have a divided loyalty when he puts pen to paper. I watch, with interest, for his articles in the *Western Morning News*. I am glad the county has him fighting in its corner against the intrusion of too much that we do not want.

If you want a first-class Holiday Park that is near enough to Exeter to allow you to explore, you will not do better than **Springfield Holiday Park**, Tedburn Road, Tedburn St Mary. It has a well-deserved reputation as one of the highest rated parks in the South West and is situated in beautiful, peaceful countryside with marvellous views. The Park

County Hall

covers an area of nine acres, half of which is laid out in terraces and the rest with level grass.

Terry and Carol Aisthorpe are the resident proprietors and they make sure that the high standards that have been set are maintained. There are fully equipped luxury caravans for hire, all of which are sited so that you can enjoy the views. There is room to park your car adjacent to the caravan.

The facilities are super. A heated swimming pool is set in a large patio which acts as a sun trap. The toilet/shower blocks have individual washing cubicles for complete privacy. They have also hand driers, shaver points and hair driers. It was the sparkling cleanliness that I especially approved.

For touring caravans there are electric hook-ups and throughout there are refuse, fire and drinking water points. The Licensed Park Shop has just about everything you need including a wealth of tourist information.

Children will love the adventure play area and the games room, complete with video games, pool and table tennis, will entertain all the family. Dogs are welcome but they must be kept on a lead.

Quite close by is **Fingle Glen Leisure Complex** which has a nine-hole golf course, a driving range and a first-class restaurant. There are several good pubs and eating houses within walking distance.

It is not difficult to find. From the north take the A30 signposted Okehampton from junction 31 at the end of the M5. Go along the dual carriageway for eight miles and then take the right turn lane signposted Tedburn St Mary. Turn left at the roundabout signposted 'Springfield Park' and the site is on the right hand side of the road through the village.

Crealy Adventure Park on the main A3052 from Exeter to Sidmouth is one of those places that makes a great day out for the family, or if you are noble minded grandparents, it will ensure your enjoying the day as well as your lively grandchildren. A definite plus as far as I am concerned.

Pet Guinea Pigs at Crealy Animal Farm

It is described as a great farm adventure and it is just that. The children can make friends with the animals, pet the rabbits and guinea pigs and even have a go at feeding the calves and lambs from 11am and 3pm.

You will find that there is a fantastic Treetops Adventure Playground which will keep children occupied for ages and at the end of it all you can go into the Crealy Park restaurant and enjoy excellent food which is served throughout the day. I made a complete pig of myself on an exceptionally good cream tea.

Finlake Touring Caravan Park and Leisure Park is quite unique. It is just off the A38 on the road from Exeter to Plymouth, near to Chudleigh. It is clearly signposted from the main road. I thought it was just another park which offered good service and good value to those who either brought their own vans or rented the ones available. It is much more than that. For example it not only has a 130-acre site which combines peace and tranquillity with its own lakes and woodland, it also has a lively and well-equipped Holiday Complex. Every kind of activity and entertainment is available for all ages.

It is one of those places that offer something all the year round. Winter Weekend breaks are good fun. At Christmas and New Year there is a special programme laid on. There are 'Over 50's' weeks which are dedicated to people no longer quite so young but who enjoy a get together and good entertainment. For all these events you may bring your own touring caravan or stay in one of Finlake's luxurious, heated Scandinavian Lodges.

Chudleigh is a charming and interesting place enhanced by the superb **Ugbrooke House**, home of the Clifford family. It is set in a valley and surrounded by a beautiful landscaped park with two lakes, which were contrived by the inimitable Capability Brown. Inside there are simple Adam interiors but with that well-proportioned, light and airy style that is his hallmark. You will probably be surprised by the ornate chapel which is Italian Renaissance at its best and quite a contrast to its prim Adam front.

The house was built by Thomas Clifford, the favourite of Charles II. A statesman, he is always remembered as one of the five who formed the first of all Cabinets, the Cabal Ministry. He was a brave and valiant soldier, fighting with all his fervour in the war with the Dutch in 1665. It was rumoured that he was a Roman Catholic and under the laws of the land it became impossible for him to remain in office. The strange anomaly is that he built his Protestant chapel in which he is buried but he refused to avow that he was a Protestant or deny that he was a Catholic. What we do know is that his self-enforced retirement from public affairs broke his heart and he hung himself in August 1673 at the age of 43.

Chudleigh's coaching inn once housed William of Orange after he landed at Torbay, and from one of its windows he spoke to the towns-folk. They were gratified, but his English was so bad that it is doubtful if they understood one word of what he had to say.

The motley coloured 14th-century church is worth exploring for its unusual bench ends if nothing else, and not far off is the rewarding sight of a delightful glen from which the water cascades to the rocks beneath. Then there are the unusual Chudleigh Rocks and Pixie's Hole in which prehistoric animal bones and other relics have been found. The walls are covered with initials carved by youth of the past, including Samuel Taylor Coleridge and his brother. Nothing much changes does it?

From Chudleigh I like the little lanes that take me across country back to Exeter via Hennock first of all. Here, high up on a hill, 600 feet above sea level, overlooking the Teign valley and very close to the beauty spots of the Kennick and Tottiford reservoirs, the population of 230 souls live a peaceful existence seldom troubled by the outside world. The bus calls once a week to take them shopping but otherwise they are comfortably self sufficient with a good village shop, which is also the post office, and a nice old pub, the Palk Arms.

The 12th-century parish church of St Mary, built of granite, still has its original medieval font and one of the most beautiful old oak rood screens in Devon. Hidden behind a stone wall is the medieval thatched rectory and adjoining it is a fine tithe barn which is the village hall.

A dead end road leads past the church and a row of cottages and then you come to **'Longlands'**, a listed building mentioned in the Domesday book. It was this house that I had come to see and more particularly to meet the owners Derek and Cynthia Steele, their daughter Deborah and her husband Alastair.

Longlands is no longer just a farmstead but a flourishing Field Study Centre, created by the Steele's. Catering for 40 or more children coming from schools all over the country and abroad to take up residence for a five day course, it aims to stimulate their minds, enhance their image of the countryside and send them home both academically and physically healthier.

It was in the early 1980s that the idea first began to take shape. Cynthia was a primary school teacher devoting quite a lot of her time to Field Study trips which she found frustrating. More often than not she and her colleagues would find themselves and their charges staying in an hotel, out of season, where they were on sufferance. The owners merely wanted to find some way of making money in the off peak season. After breakfast every day they were no longer welcome and more or less forced out until the evening. Generally there were very few facilities available for the children to collate what they had learnt in the outdoor explorations, and it was just not satisfactory.

Cynthia believed that a purpose-built centre in which the children could stay, and in which there were classrooms, workshops and leisure areas, would be the ideal solution—but where, how and with what? It was just a dream, but if you keep dreams in your sights long enough they tend to come true. This one did. Derek was offered early retirement from Heinz where he had nineteen years experience of product development. He grabbed it, they sold their house in Gerrards Cross and set about the search for a suitable place.

The site needed to be in Devon because daughter Deborah, also a teacher, wanted to be part of the scheme. She is married to Alastair Sandels, a forester who works on Dartmoor, and they had no wish to move out of the county. Several times they thought they had found the right place but for various reasons each time it came to nothing, and then one day, hey presto, there was Longlands, a 15th-century manor house, with attached Saxon longhouse, on the edge of Dartmoor National Park. It even had outbuildings and stables.

I wondered how this quiet village had reacted to the idea of 40 children descending on their blissfully peaceful surroundings. Derek told me that they had received nothing but co-operation from the people of Hennock. I suspect that his diplomatic approach to them, smoothing the path before the venture started, helped considerably. They have also been able to offer part-time employment to women in the village which otherwise would not have been available.

The outbuildings and stables have been cleverly converted to include dormitories, a refectory, classrooms, laboratory, a library and common room, and it is all set in 45 acres of grass and woodland facing right over the Teign valley. It could not be a better place to realise Cynthia's dream.

This is a very disciplined place. Children come here to learn, not to play, but in so doing they have immense fun and quickly become steeped in the rural atmosphere.

Longlands is a real family business. Cynthia teaches primary school pupils and makes all the domestic arrangements, as well as running crafts classes for local women. Deborah takes the GCSE and A-level students, and her forester husband helps, in his spare time, with environmental studies and woodland ecology.

It falls to Derek to head the business side. Fortunately he is also good with his hands and capable of coping with plumbing and electrics as well as all the general maintenance. He is also the farmer, looking after the holding and handling the flock of Pol Dorset sheep, some of which are fattened up to provide food for Longlands. His aim is to have a lambing every month so that there is always something for the children to see.

Working and living together as a family is not always easy, something I know about from my own experience, but they have all learnt to give each other space and it does help that they each have their own particular skill. Their home, into which I was welcomed, has that right sort of feel about it that instinctively tells you it is a happy place.

Next stop Doddiscombsleigh, which stands high on the hills lining the valley, through which the Teign flows to the sea. A visit to the church is a must, because it has some of the most glorious medieval glass windows in Devon. When you leave the church you have no distance to go to reach the **Nobody Inn**, a place of charm, warmth, good hospitality, super food and a landlord who wins every prize going for the quality of his wines and innkeeping. His wine list is incredible and not only can you drink it on the premises, you can also buy from his considerable stocks to add to your meagre wine rack at home. Unusually, he runs a mail order wine business, which is highly successful, and because of his great knowledge, which he happily shares, you can buy the best bottles at the best prices.

It is an odd name for a pub and there are several versions of how it acquired such an unwelcoming title. This has been a pub far longer than its name. It was once terraced cottages, the end one being a cider house. Over the years it has had additions by converting stables or outhouses, but it still looks more like a large cottage standing in its pretty garden rather than a pub.

There is always someone in here and you can stay if you wish in the comfortable bedrooms. You will not be greeted shoddily as people were once. Legend has it that an unknown landlord refused to answer when travellers knocked on the door so they believed there was nobody in and the name has stuck.

The more likely reason for the name, which came into being in 1937,

Nobody Inn

before which it was the New Inn, is one confirmed by a retired policeman in 1970. This story says that after the death of the landlord in 1937 an empty coffin was buried. The pall bearers thought the coffin was light but as the dead man had been ill in hospital for some time that was reasonable. The coroner's office was suspicious after the rumours got around and issued an exhumation order to permit the grave to be opened. The retired policemen was a young constable at the time in the coroner's office and remembered the order being granted. He was not able to say however that 'No body was in'.

Only a mile and a half from the boundary of Exeter city, a remarkable couple run **New Barn Farm** in Manstree Road, Shillingford St George. It is not an ordinary farm, because in addition to the rearing of beef cattle and growing wheat, they have diversified into growing a large variety of flowers for dried flower arrangements; they grow grapes to make their own Manstree white wine and there are acres of soft fruit which you are invited to pick. Gerry and Day Symons are very busy people but so organised that one feels the whole operation runs without a hitch.

The fruit farm rejoices in the name, '3F's, which is an abbreviation of, 'Fresh and Freezer Fruits'. Gerry Symons is always looking for something new for his fruit farm. He grows tayberries, a cross between a raspberry and a blackberry, which make super jam and are also very easy to pick. There are Worcester berries, a cross between a blackcurrant and a gooseberry, and a sort of loganberry-shaped blackberry, which is known as a sunberry. In addition, there are all the standard fruits— gooseberries, currants, strawberries, raspberries, etc. An American variety of strawberry, the Totem, is particularly good for freezing. It doesn't defrost into a mushy mess.

With the unpredictability of the weather and the seasonal nature of fruit, it is always advisable to ring before you come to pick. You can ask the day's prices at the same time. Free fruitbaskets are provided and you will be offered water and a towel to wash your hands afterwards.

'Ever Joy Dried Flowers' are sold in a shop on the farm, where you can buy sufficient to make an arrangement for yourself, or you can leave it to the experts and order something for a special occasion. Offices and hotels find this sort of service very useful. It can be done by mail order and, being a lazy shopper, I can well imagine ordering presents of these beautiful flowers for my friends at Christmas or birthdays.

For lovers of wine, the vineyard produces grapes which make a delicious medium-dry white table wine, sold under the Manstree label, of course.

The A377 out of Exeter takes you to Crediton and some super small villages and hamlets that run off it. The superb church which stands back from the road gives one a chance to observe its noble proportions. The foundations were laid by the Normans and it is over 200 feet long with a central tower and four turrets. The nave, and the thrillingly beautiful windows in the aisles, are 15th century. The 13th-century lady chapel, with its fine double piscina, was used as a school for 300 years.

It is almost cathedral-like in its majesty. The nave has six bays and a great reredos at the west end. Everywhere there is intricate carving, especially the chancel stalls, delicately designed with thistles, grapes, roses and acorns, but what I love most is the rich glowing colour of the windows which seems to permeate everywhere.

The Thatched Cottage

It is quite unusual to find a small guest house, with only three bedrooms, carrying the English Tourist Board's Three Crowns. The Tourist Board rating, if anything, underrates **The Thatched Cottage**, just two miles from Crediton on the Barnstaple Road. You have to keep your eyes open for a left turn signposted Coleford and as you turn, you turn sharp left again almost immediately into the drive.

The first thing that strikes you is not the pretty thatched cottage but the incredible panoramic view over rolling farmland and hills to Haytor and Dartmoor some 25 miles away. It seems to go on forever and, because of the varying types of countryside, the colours are ever changing. I discovered later the sheer pleasure of sitting outside on the small patio in total peace, watching the sky hang low over the far away tors, clouds lifting and falling, sometimes scurrying before the wind that blows in from the north coast.

Daphne and Michael Nightingale are the lucky owners of this delightful house. It is run as a business but visitors are treated as though they are welcome friends. The bedrooms, charmingly furnished, face the wonderful view that I first saw.

The Thatched Cottage dates from the reign of Elizabeth I and was built of cob, which to the uninitiated means a mixture of mud, dung, straw and stone. Once two cottages, it was used by farm workers on the estate with two rooms up and two down in each.

Believe it or not, there were as many as twenty people living in this small space. Conditions were very primitive; water was obtained from the well in the yard; you can still see the pump although the well has been filled in. All the cooking was done over open fires; the bread oven stands in the hall. Also there is what I believe may well be a post carved by Grinling Gibbons, supporting the stairs. It is quite beautiful and, if not his work, then it was certainly done by one of his pupils. It would not have been part of the house originally, but probably brought in from a defunct church.

Following the first world war, the Thatched Cottage is believed to have been a 'haven' for the countless 'men of the road' who roamed the area. The owners were allowed free rates if they were prepared to give anyone calling some bread, water and shelter. There was a large shed attached to the cottage which was left permanently open.

There is a firm no smoking rule which I applaud but apart from that there are no restrictions whatsoever. Breakfast is a feast, cooked superbly by Michael. You can have almost anything you want—the locally made yoghurt is totally foreign to anything one buys in the shops, the eggs will be fresh, free range, the bacon cooked to perfection and if you love sausages then you will be in your element. The Nightingales go all the way to Hatherleigh, some twenty miles away, to buy them from a Mrs Edwards who is renowned for making probably the best sausages in Devon.

It was the Nightingales who told me about about **The Fox and Hounds Eggesford House Hotel**, a few miles further up the road on the A377 going towards Barnstaple. The hotel is completely surrounded by the forest where the very first forestry trees were planted over 50 years ago. It is a wonderful place for those who love walking, fishing or just want to enjoy the peace, warmth and comfort of an extremely luxurious hotel (once a coaching inn).

You feel as though you are a guest in a country house rather than a visitor at an hotel. This is very much due to the owners, Mr and Mrs David Ingyon, who bought the hotel late in 1987 and have devoted considerable time, money, energy and loving care in bringing it to the standard that it enjoys today.

The en-suite bedrooms are superbly appointed, some of which have four-poster beds and after settling in you come downstairs to a pre-dinner drink in a bar which is brimful of character. The dinner that follows is worthy of the hotel, impeccably presented and served by charming staff.

The hotel owns some seven miles of private salmon, sea trout and brown trout fishing on the rivers Taw and Little Dart which has been a Mecca for fishermen since Victorian times.

The Garden Cottages, adjacent to the hotel, used to be part of the stables but have been imaginatively converted and can be used as lettable rooms on hotel terms or as self-catering units. All the rooms are fully centrally heated and have every comfort one could look for. A cooker and fridge are in the kitchen/diner. What an excellent place it would be for a family, especially if father was a keen fisherman. He could fish to his heart's content whilst mum took the children off to explore the many wonders of North Devon which even in winter are exciting and stimulating. Mothers will probably hate me for this but it could possibly be a compromise; perhaps for half term?

The bar of the Fox and Hounds, with its character log fire, is a haunt for many people who live within the area. It is a welcoming place and if you just want to stop there on your travels for a drink and a bite to eat you will find an extensive menu of good bar snacks.

Between the A377 and Tiverton to the east, there is a wealth of small villages and hamlets which, over the years, have given me hours of pleasure. The nearest to Eggesford is Coldridge, with its 15th-century church of St Mary in which, under an arch, lies Sir John Evans, park-keeper to Henry VIII. My imagination probably does run riot, and I have no doubt that I fantasise, but I think I might be forgiven for trying to compare a park-keeper of today with this Tudor gentleman, whose territorial duties must have been vast. Just about all the land in this area would have belonged to his master. The church is lovely with a chancel floor covered in glazed tiles as old as the Tudors themselves. In one window of 15th-century glass, the boy king, Edward the Fifth, is depicted in a brilliant blue robe holding a mace. Over his head, rather like a vast jewelled halo, is a crown in addition to the one he wears. There are some wonderful bench ends too, which cannot be less than 500 years old.

On the other side of the road, at Lapford, you will find a winding village street which seems to climb for ever from the river Yeo. There is a nice mixture of old and new houses and the 16th-century village pub is a jolly place to be, with its open fireplaces and beams.

We also come back to our old friend William de Tracey here. Apparently as part of his penance for the murder of Thomas à Becket, William enlarged the Saxon chapel in 1180 and the church was dedicated to St Thomas of Canterbury. According to village legend, however, Thomas was not appeased, and at midnight at the time of the annual village revels he has been seen, dressed in robes and mitre, riding slowly round the church and then down through the village. Mark you, the pub is close by!

Passing through the centre of Morchard Bishop, is the Two Moors Way, which is a splendid walk. A stone near the school marks the mid-way point.

Its wonderful church has stood for about 650 years, high on a hill, commanding glorious views of Exmoor to the north and Dartmoor to the south. One of its greatest beauties was its medieval screen which, some time in the 19th century, was broken up and allowed to rot. It looked as if it was gone forever but, with a bequest from the seventh Earl of Portsmouth and several other people, sufficient money was garnered and a wonderful craftsman, Herbert Read, was able to restore it. It now looks as beautiful as ever. If you seek out a clergy desk you will see it is beautifully carved—this too was done by the redoubtable Mr Read, who presented it to the church at the time of the rededication of the screen.

The village has many attractive buildings and has become a favourite place for commuters to settle. It is a conservation area so new houses have to fit into the pattern of the village. No modern house could ever compete with the thirteen attractive thatched cottages, standing like pretty maids in a row, in Fore Street. Built in the late 18th century they are, reputedly, the longest row of thatched cottages in the country.

From here I am no distance from Cadbury, a small village amongst the hills, with wonderful views over the Exe valley. The tall church tower which has stood for over 500 years dominates all around it at first sight, until you realise that it, in turn, is overshadowed by the mighty Cadbury Castle. Standing 700 feet up, it is a fort of the ancient Britons. Nothing much left now other than two ramparts enclosing a great space. It was here that General Fairfax pitched his camp in the Civil War.

Fursdon House stands just a mile away. The Fursdon family have lived in this beautiful house, or its forerunner, since the signing of Magna Carta. I love browsing in churchyards which always have so much history to relate. The yard, which surrounds the 15th-century church, is the last resting place of many members of this family. They must have worshipped here regularly. Perhaps they were responsible for the installation of the complete panel of ancient glass which has an extraordinary representation of the Crucifixion. Jesus is dressed in

Fursdon House

purple, white and gold and coming from five wounds are long lines of red. Underneath this haunting depiction are the words, in old English, 'Is it nothing to you, all ye that pass by?'

So much beauty and history is crammed into the scenic village of Bickleigh. It has everything; a castle, a river flowing under a superb bridge, thatched cottages, an award-winning mill and two very good hostelries.

Bickleigh Castle, once the seat of the Courtneys and Carews, is now the home of the Boxall family. It stands on the banks of the river Exe and there has been some kind of fortified dwelling on this spot for 900 years. The group of buildings remaining cover almost every period of English architecture. The moat has become a delightful water garden and the major part of the 14th-century castle still standing is the gatehouse. In one of the rooms is the Armoury which is full of weapons, cannons, guns, suits of armour and a helmet and breast-plate of a Cromwellian soldier.

It was this castle that General Fairfax stormed when he was encamped at Cadbury. He managed to destroy the fortified wings on either side of the inner courtyard. These wings were replaced by a typical Devon farmhouse, complete with cob walls and a thatched roof; unexpected but utterly charming. The only other part of the castle to survive Fairfax's onslaught was the thatched chapel. It is thought to be the oldest building in Devon. It may well be, for it was built in 1090. On the door there is a sanctuary ring. I was not sure before I came here what its purpose was. The explanation is that anyone, criminal or political, needing sanctuary, could take refuge inside for forty days, the equivalent time that Christ spent in the wilderness.

For some years this beautiful building was allowed to fall into disrepair and suffer the indignity of being used as a cattle shed. In 1929 it was

Bickleigh Castle

restored and its beauty has been shared ever since. One of its treasures particularly appealed to me: a sermon timer, not unlike an egg timer, was turned over by the priest before he delivered his sermon which was likely to last a full hour. Imagine standing up all that time and being bored out of your mind—there were no seats so you could not even enjoy a quick catnap. There would have been some stone seats round the walls for the elderly, the halt, the lame and the very young, but it would not have been very comfortable.

The sermon timer reminded me of my young days. I was taken to chapel every Sunday when I stayed with my maternal grandparents, who were devout Methodists. My grandfather had built his own chapel and ruled his band of elders and the ministers with a totally un-Christian rod of iron. Before the service started the family and the servants were seated in the pews. My grandfather presented everyone with their collection money. The amount depended on your age and standing in the household. This was followed by a piece of liquorice cut from a long stem with his gold penknife. We sucked this during the sermon to stop us fidgeting. When it came to the sermon Grandfather would take his large gold hunter watch from his waistcoat pocket, place it somewhat noisily on the pew shelf, settle back and close his eyes. I was never sure whether he slept or not but I was sure that on the dot of twenty minutes his eyes would open, fix like a laser on the minister and remain there until the man rapidly brought his discourse to an end. If it was not quickly enough for Grandfather he would start coughing, and it was a brave man who denied him!

Traditionally the Minister joined the family for Sunday lunch and if the unfortunate had overrun his allotted span Grandfather would talk, at length, about people who liked the sound of their own voices!

The Cromwellians, incidentally, overcame the problem of no seating in church. They invented the folding seat and there are several examples of these remarkably comfortable seats in the Bickleigh Chapel.

The entrance to the gardens of Bickleigh Castle is either by the picturesque bridge over the moat or through the fine pair of 18th-century Italian wrought-iron gates. In the spring the gardens and orchards are covered in golden yellow daffodils and other flowers. There are rare shrubs, azaleas, roses, a centuries old wisteria, two Ginkgos, uncommon trees and some topiary. Beyond the lawn, at the rear of the medieval building, rises a huge mound, once part of the fortifications but now covered with almost every variety of rhododendron. It is quite a climb to the top but what a reward you get when you make the effort. You are looking down on the whole of the castle, the village and the church beyond.

I am going to leave the hostelries to last. You may well need them to resuscitate you at the end of a busy day. Bickleigh Mill Devonshire Centre just off Bickleigh Bridge offers something for everyone and it is not surprising that it has won so many awards. There has been a mill here for hundreds of years and it certainly appears in the Domesday Book. It is the most comprehensive gift, garment and cloth centre in mid-Devon. The water wheel is no longer used to drive the machinery which ground the corn but it is still there, turning, and forms the centrepiece of the mill, around which there are a number of craft workshops.

The 19th-century farm is run without recourse to machines. They rely on oxen and shire horses for power. There are rare cattle, sheep, pigs, donkeys and all kinds of poultry. You can help with collecting the eggs or even try your hand at milking and cream separating which takes place daily. It brings home how hard farming must have been in those days. I think it is a hard life even today. Unrelenting really, even on Christmas Day milking must be done and the animals fed.

Henry Williamson of *Tarka the Otter* fame would be delighted to see that there is an Otter Centre here which is dedicated to the preservation of the short clawed otters, much like Tarka.

If you do not want to visit the pleasant restaurant you are invited to make use of the Picnic Centre which has benches and tables placed so that, whilst you are eating, you can watch the feathered life at Birdland. This is a naturally landscaped water garden enclosure which is home to all kinds of exotic birds: penguins, flamingoes, crested cranes, ornamental duck cockatoos and parrots.

The Motor Centre is something quite different. It offers a complete pictorial history of motorised transport and has examples of some of the most coveted veteran, vintage and post vintage vehicles. They are all in running order and used frequently. I spotted a De Lorean in a garage near the Trout Inn. I wonder if that will ever join this illustrious collection?

The Fisherman's Cot, an inn and hotel, sits on the edge of the bustling river, just off the arched 16th-century bridge, which was rebuilt in 1809 after severe floods.

It is a long, low building with plenty of parking space. A nice place to visit at any time of the year. During the summer months the doors open onto the river bank and you can take your drinks and food outside. In the winter the warmth and comfort of the long rectangular inn makes

Fisherman's Cottage

it a comfortable place to be. I could spend hours sitting at one of the tables in the window just watching the water flow along on its way to the sea. It tumbles out beneath the bridge in an enormous rush and then steadies itself as it passes the Fisherman's.

Graham and Susan Dove have been here since August 1990 and have plans in hand at the moment to improve the service. They have a difficult task. As I write the food is brought to table by friendly waitresses which works well in winter, but in the mad rush, in the height of summer, it sometimes becomes impossible to track down people once they have given their orders. This causes displeasure on both sides. Graham told me he is keen to set up a buffet service which will offer the same food but be handled much in the way of a carvery. He feels that everyone will be happier. I can understand his problem but I have to admit to preferring waitress service. This will not affect the restaurant which will remain silver service.

If you would like to stay here you will find it is friendly and the rooms are simply, but well, furnished. The aim is to acquire a two star rating but in my view this has been reached already.

Just along the road going towards Tiverton is the 17th-century **Trout Inn** owned by a remarkable young man, Simon Van Den Begin. What an attractive place it is. You open the heavy door into a low beamed bar from which other rooms stem off. It is spacious but intimate with no obtrusive music. Even on a wet winter's day it was busy at lunchtime.

People come out here from Exeter and from Tiverton for lunch and dinner, as well as people who live more locally. Most of the people I saw had come to eat although there were a few standing at the bar obviously enjoying a drink in these friendly surroundings.

Simon has progressed in the licensed business from smaller pubs always with the desire to serve good food and wine. His last pub was the Thatched Cottage at Bovey Tracey. What he has brought to the Trout Inn is the essential ingredients for an innkeeper: a warmth of personality, a sense of humour and a desire to build up and retain a contented clientele.

The Trout has been the village inn since time immemorial and so he did not have to make an atmosphere; it was already there. What he has done is to improve the quality of the food, at the same time keeping the prices low so that it is possible for people to come out for lunch, even if they are living on a limited income.

In keeping with the name, Trout appears many times on the menu. It comes locally from the Bellbrook Trout Fishery at Oakford. Try the stuffed trout pate—baked and stuffed with chicken liver pate—it is delicious. If you are not a lover of fish there are many grills and dishes such as duck, honey glazed with a wild berry sauce. There are a host of simple dishes as well and a super salad bar. Stuffed peppers appear on the menu for vegetarians as well as dishes like cauliflower and broccoli au gratin.

The Trout Inn has three letting bedrooms which are extremely comfortable and reasonably priced.

Tiverton is a place that grows on you. I used to hate it before it was by-passed. Traffic was horrendous and you never got time to stand and stare. The prettiest way to approach this very old town is by the Exe valley road. It goes back to Saxon days when it had fords across the Exe and Loman, and it is where these two meet that the town looks down from its high ground between the rivers.

Tiverton Castle built by the Normans is still important to the town. There are only remains now; the main gateway still stands, there is a square and a round tower and battered walls. In the round tower one can see the handiwork of Fairfax once more. His troops pounded away at the castle and there is a sizable hole made by cannon ball. It is an impressive sight and was once the home of the powerful Courtenays.

It was the wool merchants who provided Tiverton with many of its finest buildings. Right by the medieval gateway of the castle is the 15th-century St Peter's church. Its spacious windows glisten in the afternoon's sunlight highlighting its pinnacles and battlemented parapets. The centuries have not destroyed the wonder of the carvings on the outside walls. Look for a bear that creeps along a hollowed wall, a monkey holding fast to its baby and the proud lions which crouch on the buttresses. On the north side there are two vast gargoyle heads and more carved animals interspersed with odd human faces.

John Greenway, one of the wealthy merchants, ensured that his memory would live on. He spent a fortune in 1517 adding the porch, a chapel and an aisle on the south side. The carvings are breathtaking. He will never be forgotten whilst over the porch of the chapel it says:

> Have grace, ye men, and ever pray
> For the soul of John and Joan Greenway

He started life as a poor weaver and died one of the greatest benefactors the town has ever had. There are tributes to him and his wife in many places in the church and also to two other wealthy and philanthropic merchants, John Waldron and George Slee.

It is a fine church and will give you pleasure if you are prepared to take your time and be prepared to get a crick in the neck from looking upwards continuously to absorb so much that is beautiful.

The most famous of Tiverton's sons is Peter Blundell, who made his fortune after starting out as an errand boy. He used to fetch and carry for the kersey makers—a cheap roll of homespun cloth. He saved enough pennies to buy a roll and then sold it. From the profit he traded again and very soon became a merchant marketing other men's kerseys. He was hardworking, thrifty and energetic. He prospered and acquired great wealth and an estate. He never married but he was intent on

Old Blundells (former school), Tiverton

doing something about the education of boys. He conceived Blundell's School, which sadly he did not live to see finished, but it has stood in the town ever since and educated many of the finest young brains in the land. For more than three centuries it has been one of the most famous schools in the country.

The rivers are not the only waterways in Tiverton. The reach of the **Grand Western Canal** has been lovingly and carefully restored and is now open to the public who can enjoy the gentle trip, by horse drawn boat, along this beautiful canal as far as East Manley, where you can disembark and take a short walk to the aqueduct, which crosses the disused Tiverton railway line.

Going back to talented people, I am reminded of my visit to **The Tiverton Craft Centre** in Bridge Street. It was closed for lunch when I arrived there and just looking through the window at what could be seen might have not interested me enough to wait. I am glad I did. Once inside, and talking to the two very charming and intelligent ladies who were on duty that afternoon, I was made privy to all the happenings in this centre. It is not just a shop selling local craft wares, which are delightful in themselves; it is the other activities that ensue.

I learnt, for instance, that there are no less than twelve hundred potters in and around Tiverton who come to the Craft Centre to buy the materials they need. Other groups come to ceramic classes and learn about decorative art on pots. One room is the studio of a picture framer. It is a hive of activity and a place in which one can buy anything from a postcard to a delightful watercolour.

In amongst all the 18th- and 19th-century buildings in the principal streets you will see the Town Hall, which is a delightful piece of Victorian imagination. It has a distinct touch of the baroque and I think perhaps the architect had a passion for things French. It is especially charming in the summer when it is further adorned by a profusion of hanging baskets.

Where do you stay when you are in this area? Two very nice places come to mind and each very different. The first is remote, unusual and you might perhaps think you had gone back to the days of P.G. Wodehouse. From Tiverton you go towards Uplowman and then take a turn up a little lane which wanders for three-and-a-half miles until it reaches the village of Huntsham; keep going and you will come to **Huntsham Court**. Once you have discovered it you will want to keep the knowledge all to yourself in case too many people get to hear about it. I almost feel guilty about putting this piece on paper .

It is owned by Mogens Bolwig, a Dane who was once a travel agent, and his Greek wife, Andrea. A copywriter would find it extremely hard to describe Huntsham in any sort of commercial manner. The Bolwig's do not view their home as a business. All they are concerned about is making a sufficient income to cover their overheads, keep this superb Victorian house in apple pie order and, more importantly, have fun and intelligent conversation with their guests.

This is not a place to come if you are a telly addict and cannot bear to miss an episode of Coronation Street—there are no televisions. The Bolwig's are dedicated to making their guests forget they are staying in a hotel at all. There are no locks on the bedroom doors and definitely no direct dial telephones in the rooms. At night you are invited to help yourself to a drink in the self service bar whilst you get acquainted with your fellow guests. It is highly likely that Mogens will invite you to join him in the cellar to choose the wine for dinner. The food is superb and by the time you sit down at the single, long dining table you are amongst friends and about to enjoy that finest form of all entertaining, a dinner party.

There are only 14 bedrooms at Huntsham and each is named after a composer. The Beethoven room has the most extraordinarily large bathroom in the middle of which sit two mismatched Victorian baths. While you lie back and enjoy the luxury of bathing in such a depth of water, you may well find yourself listening to an aged console radio telling you that the Home Service is on the air. On the way into the bathroom you will pass a miniature library of books amongst which may well be a *Reader's Digest* for 1954. It is an experience.

No one minds if you come down to breakfast at mid-day. The charming Australian girls who wait at table are not in the least put out by such behaviour. Afterwards you can choose to be active if you wish and ride a horse, play tennis on the all-weather courts or shoot a few clay pigeons. A sauna, mini-gym, table tennis, billiards and bicycles are also available. There is no urgency about anything. It is restful, remote and a complete tonic.

It would not be too hard to recognise that the Bolwig's are music lovers; they have a wonderful collection of over three thousand records and cassettes, mostly classical with a leaning towards opera. You are welcome to play them at any time and perhaps dance to the music of the twenties and thirties after dinner.

Many years of hard work have gone into creating Huntsham, which is a masterpiece. I just hope that it will continue successfully for many years and that the dinner table will resound with laughter and conversation. Huntsham is the greatest of fun but please do not even attempt to go there if you prefer the commonplace.

Only a mile on the Tiverton to Bampton road is **The Hartnoll Country House Hotel**. It is just seven miles from the M5 at Junction 27. The Georgian building is set amidst the rolling fields and woods of the beautiful Exe Valley, right on the edge of the tiny village of Bolham. It was once the Dower House to Knightshayes, which belongs now to the National Trust and is open to the public in the summer months. A super place to visit, incidentally, and a good reason for choosing to stay at the Hartnoll.

With some 45 years behind it as a Country House Hotel it has settled down to a delightful place in which to bide awhile. Not as unorthodox as Huntsham and certainly a little cheaper, it has eleven rooms in the hotel proper. In a cottage annexe, just yards away from the hotel foyer, there are another five rooms, all beautifully furnished. These rooms are particularly good for anyone who does not wish to climb stairs or for pet-owners. They have direct access to the car-park in the motel fashion, without being anything like those soulless places.

The restaurant, which is open to non-residents, offers a mixture of traditional English and French dishes with just that something extra produced by the chef and his team. Dining at one of the tables looking out over the fishpond and the mill stream is a great appetiser. The staff are well trained and extremely courteous. Quietly observant of customers' needs, is how I would describe them, I think.

The Hartnoll is open all the year. Throughout the winter months you can get some extremely inexpensive weekend and special activity breaks. The hotel is particularly proud of their association with the internationally renowned Shalden Shooting School, where novice or expert can shoot a variety of sporting clays, under the expert eye of the School's owner and senior coach, Rod Brammer.

I liked the oak panelled Function Room with its huge open log fireplace which is available for banquets and business meetings. It can seat up to 200 in comfort for a formal or informal meal, and up to 300 for a theatre style meeting. With such pretty gardens combining with the function room, it would be a super place for wedding celebrations, particularly in the spring and summer.

It is certainly worth talking to the management if you are looking for a business venue. I was very impressed with the range of residential and non-residential delegate rates, suiting every occasion and every budget.

Two more places in this part of Devon were on my itinerary. Bampton first. You should go there if only to discover the ducks and the tablet on the west wall of the 15th-century church. It says:

> In memory of the Clerk's son
> Bless my little iiiii's
> Here he lies
> In a sad pickle
> Kill'd by an icicle
> In the year 1776

One wonders who put it there and whether it was done without realising its humorous side. Churchyards are always rewarding. The houses are mainly of the local quarry stone and much of it is 18th century. In medieval times the village was ruled by the all powerful Bourchier family, who were the Earls of Bath.

Come to Bampton on the last Thursday in October and you will be able to take part in the annual fair which has been the event of the year ever since Bampton got its charter in 1258. It used to take place over three days but that has been whittled down to one over the years. It was originally set up for the sale of sheep and as a get together for people from far and wide; ponies were included later. These days it is just an excuse for a jollification which everyone enjoys.

The Swan Inn close to the parish church is one of the nicest places in which to stay. I believe it was built originally to house the craftsmen who were building the church, in the early 1400s, so that will help you to envisage the splendid historic atmosphere greeting you as you walk through the portals. Ever since those days it has been a hostelry of some kind with different owners. It is mentioned in the deeds of the property that the Lord of the Manor, probably one of the Bourchiers, sold the premises to his coachman for one pound.

A small village, to the south east of Bampton and slightly north east of Tiverton, excited my curiosity. Holcombe Regis was mentioned in the Domesday Book, when it had a 1000 acres and was worth the vast sum of £10! The Bluett family were lords of the manor from Tudor times and they have their chapel in the small Perpendicular church. The Bluetts built Holcombe Court, a fine Tudor mansion which lies in its walled grounds, sheltered by a wooded hill overlooking the village.

Holcombe Regis

Nothing curious about any of this but when you learn that much of the carving in the Court was done by Spanish prisoners from the Armada, that Dutch refugees carved the large Court pew in the church, and that tough American servicemen billeted there during the Second World War were frightened out of their wits by the persistence of an unknown ghost, then, if you are as nosey as I am, you do want to take a look.

There is an unique textile mill just two miles off the M5 at junction 27. **Coldharbour Mill** at Uffculme has existed on this site since Domesday. It is quite an experience to visit this historic working factory, which has been producing yarn since 1797. I took my time as I watched the various processes of worsted and woollen manufacture, from combed fleece to knitting wool and woven cloth. The finished products you can purchase in the mill shop which also sells some locally made garments.

With beautiful weather on the day of my visit, I was able to spend a therapeutic hour wandering gently round the mill grounds and gardens, taking in the lovely views of the unspoilt Culm valley. The Waterside Restaurant, where I was served with a super cream tea and a piping hot cup of coffee, was the pleasant finale of my outing.

The car parking space is vast and Coldharbour Mill is open all the year round; from Easter to October daily and in Winter from Monday to Friday.

I wanted to see **Whitmoor House** at Ashill, quite close to Coldharbour Mill. Richard and Ann Trussell live here and have done so since 1983 when they bought the 17th-century house and the estate to pursue their twin interests, the cultivation of grapes to produce wine for their winery, and the propagation of orchids.

Their background gives no hint of their present business. Richard was a doctor teaching at a university in East Africa and Ann taught maths. The only similarities are that modern methods of orchid propagation, involving tissue culture, is akin to some medical techniques.

The orchid house is an exotic experience. Large white Cattleya orchids bloom and the flower will stay beautiful for as long as two months. The mixture of colours, purple, white yellow and sometimes a touch of pink, blend together sometimes in large cultivated sprays, sometimes in the much smaller flower of the wild orchid. I had never been a great orchid enthusiast until I looked, and then listened to Ann Trussell. It reminded me a bit of a visit to Florence and to the Uffizi Gallery where there was a display of Botticelli paintings. I had always thought of this great artist as being a rather wishy-washy master of colour, but the moment I walked into the Botticelli room I was stunned by the blues and greens and pinks of his pictures. It was a similar experience at Whitmoor.

The acres of Madeline Angevine grapes produce a delicious medium-dry white wine and they also have black grapes in order to have red wines on their list. Cider made from home-grown apples, as good as any I have ever tasted, is another Whitmoor speciality.

In order to see all this for yourself it is necessary to ring before 9.30am or early in the evening to make an appointment. You will be invited to taste the wine and cider and I am quite sure you will come back with bottles to add to your wine racks. If you are thinking of going there in a party beware that you are not more than twelve in number. The lanes are so narrow that nothing bigger than a minibus can reach Whitmoor. The telephone number is Craddock (0884) 840145.

Have you ever watched sheep being milked? It was a new experience for me when I visited **Waterloo Farm** at Clayhidon, Cullompton. Tony and Yvonne Trotter care for a flock of Friesland sheep. The friendship and affection between the Trotters and their sheep is quite remarkable. The moment their familiar footsteps are heard, the sheep come running to greet them, each wearing a little bell, and it all sounds like Julie Andrews and *The Sound of Music*!

Even the situation of the farm is reminiscent. It stands high on the Blackdown Hills, on the borders of East Devon and Somerset, with magnificent views across the valley.

The milking parlour and the machines are like toys compared to the larger version used for cows to which I am more used. The ewes walk up a ramp to a platform to get attached to the pumps and then a minute or so later they walk down the other side. They seem totally contented with their lot and whilst awaiting their turn munch away at food, which looks a bit like muesli but which Yvonne says is a mixture of rolled oats, soya beans, flaked maize and sugar beet.

The milk is made into very creamy yoghourt which is high in protein and fat but easily digested. Apparently, it is ideal for people who are allergic to cow's milk. I am not sure I would want to drink it in preference to my normal pint, but it had a very pleasant mild taste. The yoghourt, however, is delicious and decidedly moreish. It needs no additives and is super for cooked or uncooked dishes. I tried some on my breakfast cereal and I have also used it mixed with chopped mint when I have lamb.

The Trotters have some letting rooms, so if you wish to stay here and see more, you will find them delightful.

In order to arrange a convenient time to see the sheep being milked or perhaps catch a glimpse of the newly born lambs in their bright yellow plastic macs—yes it's true, they look a bit like Norwich City on a Saturday afternoon—just ring the Trotters on Hemyock (0823) 680273.

In Silverton I learnt about an old Devonian saying 'Us can't all live in Vore Street'. Almost every village in Devon has a Fore Street, which was where all the people of importance lived originally. Silverton is no exception; it was built with just one main street and the rest has grown gracefully around it. It had the good fortune to be bypassed as early as 1819 so it has never been subjected to the roar of 20th-century traffic. In spite of two horrific fires in 1837 and 1878 there are still some very pretty cob-and-thatch buildings from the 16th century.

The village is a favourite place for commuters who find themselves equidistant from Exeter and Tiverton and able to live in these delightful surroundings.

I wonder if any of the newcomers ever look at the magnificent yew tree in the churchyard and think that men tramping home from Agincourt may well have rested against its massive trunk. It has stood there since the 1100s, way before the present church of St Mary the Virgin was built in 1450. There is no doubt that there was a church there at the time, even the record of past rectors goes back to 1273.

On the west side of the B3181 Exeter—Cullompton road you will find **Killerton House**, a National Trust property and one from which they carry out the administration for all their properties in Devon. How I envy those who work here. The house is glorious. It was rebuilt in 1778 to the design of John Johnson and is the home of the Acland family. Its wonderful, gracious rooms house superb paintings and furniture and, in addition, the Paulise de Bush collection of costumes, shown

Killerton House

in a series of room tableaux of different periods from the 18th century to the present day. The materials of the earlier costumes put to shame the man-made fibres we use today and the workmanship that went into the design and creation of each outfit is quite incredible.

The 15 acres of hillside gardens are a delight in themselves and I could spend a day happily in the grounds alone. One thoughtful touch is the provision of a motorised buggy which is available, with a driver, to take those of us not so young or perhaps disabled for a tour of the higher levels.

The park is open all the year during daylight hours and the house opens on Good Friday and closes at the end of October. It is as well to remember that the house is only open to visitors from Wednesday to Monday 11–6pm. If you wish to bring a party or want any further information just ring Exeter (0392) 881345.

Another large village, a few miles from Silverton, is Thorverton where, in the main streets, you will find a channel stream. This is something peculiar to South Devon villages. In Thorverton though it continues with smaller channels running in the streets. The reason is preventative medicine! At least that is what a Victorian rector's daughter thought when she suggested them after a serious outbreak of cholera.

You will remember when I was writing about Exeter, earlier in this chapter, that I mentioned Devon Food and Caroline Boa. I said also that she and her husband ran a trout farm. This is where I want to take you next. It is going totally in the opposite direction from Thorverton but if you get back onto the A377 and go towards Barnstaple you will come to Head Mill Trout Farm if you take a turning off to the right at King's Nympton on the B3266.

The Boas started the farm beside the River Mole in 1979 and it has been labour intensive ever since. I was told that 50 tons of trout are produced each year in the 16 large tanks. At any one time there can be in excess of a quarter million trout in the tanks.

You can buy the fish, freshly caught and cleaned. If you have a long journey home then they will be laid on ice and packed so that they will be in prime condition on arrival. Having eaten them you will want more and this can be arranged, because Head Mill has an efficient mail-order service for the smoked trout, covering the whole of the U.K.

Head Mill Trout Farm is open from 9am-6pm daily or if you wish to telephone the number is Chulmleigh (0769) 80862.

Umberleigh, which is the official address of Head Mill, is a nice rural village. The valley is beautiful and bisected by the River Taw. The film of Henry Williamson's book, *Tarka the Otter*, was filmed here and it has been a favourite spot for nature lovers and fishermen for generations. Henry Williamson also wrote *Salar the Salmon*, and it is still possible to see salmon fighting their way upstream, frequently watched by the eagle-eyed kingfishers and herons. It is not unknown, either, for an otter to be sighted.

In the village pub, **The Rising Sun**, you will hear endless fishing stories, a good many of them supported by the pictures on the wall. The late Eric Morecambe loved fishing in this area and there he is, showing his catch in a splendid photograph, minus his pal with the fat hairy legs!

One curiosity is the little wooden church built on leased railway land. Under the terms of the lease the church has to be painted brown and cream, the old Great Western Railway colours!

If you go into the local in Chulmleigh and get talking to the old men of this tranquil small town, they may well tell you about a remarkable woman who lived in East Street. Charity Joint was a carrier, one of the most important means of links between towns and villages. She must have been one tough lady for she collected coal, beer and other goods from Eggesford station. She had the strength of a man and she could drink most of them under the table. One of her roles was a sort of Securicor task; she was employed to take the town's police sergeant and constable to South Molton to collect their wages. Can you imagine that happening today?

CHAPTER 7

From Bideford to Lewtrenchard

230 Castle Inn, Lydford. Tel. No. (082282) 242
213 Commodore Hotel, Instow. Tel. No. (0271) 860347
218 Fosfelle Country House Hotel, Hartland. Tel. No. (0237) 441273
228 Heathfield House, Okehampton. Tel. No. (0837) 54211
212 Kenwith Castle Hotel, Abbotsham. Tel. No. (0237) 473712
219 Lake Villa Hotel, Bradworthy. Tel. No. (0409) 241342
231 Lewtrenchard Manor, Lewtrenchard. Tel. No. (056683) 256 or 222
217 Manor House Hotel, Woolfardisworthy. Tel. No. (237431) 380
223 Orford Lodge Hotel, Torrington. Tel. No. (0805) 22114
219 The Pig's Ear, Bradworthy. Tel. No. (0409) 241342
214 Riversford Hotel, Bideford. Tel. No. (0237) 474239 and 470381
226 White Hart Hotel, Okehampton. Tel. No. (0837) 52730
221 Woodford Bridge Hotel, Milton Damerel. Tel. No. (040 926) 481

PLACES OF INTEREST

222 Dartington Glass, Torrington. Tel. No. (0805) 22321
218 Hartland Abbey, Bideford. Hartland 559
226 Lambretta Preservation Society, Nr. Okehampton. Tel. No. (0409) 221488
230 Lydford Gorge, Lydford. Tel. No. (082 282) 441/320
226 Museum of Dartmoor Life, Okehampton. Tel. No. (0837) 52295
227 Museum of Water Power, Nr. Okehampton. Tel. No. (0837) 850046
217 Milky Way Dairy, Woolfardisworthy. (0237) 43255
215 Northam Burrows Country Park Centre, Bideford. (272) 79708
227 Okehampton Castle, Okehampton. Tel. No. (0837) 52844
224 Rosemoor Garden. Great Torrington. Tel. No. (0805) 24067
213 Tapeley Park Gardens, Instow. Tel. No. (0272) 869528

The new fast link road from the M5 at junction 27 has made it so much easier to get from London or the Midlands to North Devon. For years the tedious journey stopped all but the most intrepid traveller from attempting a short break in the Bideford, Barnstaple, Ilfracombe area.

It was deprivation of the worst kind. There is nowhere lovelier and now I can tell you about some really super places to stay which are within striking distance at weekends.

Kenwith Castle Hotel at Abbotsham, Bideford is definitely different. You approach it by going over the new bridge at Bideford, straight on at a small roundabout and approximately one mile later turn right on to the B3236, signposted Westward Ho!, then left, signposted Abbotsham.

Kenwith Castle Hotel and Country Club

It was originally a stone built farm. By the 1600s it had become a manor house which was later given castellations and a neo-Gothic front facade; one of the best in the country. It really is delightful and is a listed building for its architectural design.

Imagine what a lovely sight meets your eyes as you drive in. The buildings sit low, and sedately, looking out over a lawn that leads down to a trout lake so well stocked that you can fish it all year long. The gardens, beautifully laid out, have lots of interesting nooks and crannies which are sun traps. It is so peaceful and greets you with welcoming arms, taking all thoughts of the stresses and strains of life from your shoulders.

Inside there is everything for your comfort; the splendid entrance hall and the residents' non-smoking lounge are decorated with genuine tapestries. In the superbly panelled cocktail bar there is a marvellous Adam fireplace and I am pretty sure that some of the woodcarving is the work of Grinling Gibbons. The bedrooms, 14 in all, have en-suite facilities. A heated outdoor swimming pool in ornate gardens, hard tennis courts, and a games room with table tennis, will make sure you remain fit and keep down the weight that you will inevitably gain if you indulge in the excellent food and wine.

A few miles out of Bideford, on the Barnstaple road at Instow, is **The Commodore Hotel**, owned and personally managed by Mr and Mrs Woolaway. He is someone who has lived in the house all his life and his ancestors have been in the area for 300 years, so there is little he does not know about the history. He will tell you that the building was not established as an hotel until 1969, since when it has had a steadily increasing reputation. You really could not ask for a nicer site, just above the sea front. It is pristine white and has an almost Continental air about it.

Instow is a haven for sailing, waterskiing and windsurfing, so it is not surprising that during the summer months many people come to enjoy these sports. Others come because they are content to spend the sunny days under the umbrella tables or sunbathe on the lounge chairs, fascinated by the constantly changing waterfront scene. You can enjoy a casual meal out here, indulging in a traditional Devonshire cream tea, or something more substantial, if you wish.

The sea-facing rooms with their balconies are my favourite, although every bedroom is individually furnished, and all have en-suite bathrooms. The hotel is immaculate and says much for the care and attention that the Woolaways give to it. They have been joined by their son, Gary, who has been brought up in the family tradition. He and the rest of the staff are cheerful, efficient and do everything within their power to make your stay memorable.

The busy kitchens produce an extensive à la carte and table d'hôte menu with dishes created by a seasoned brigade of six chefs, who use the wonderful variety and quality of local produce. Clovelly crab, lobsters from Lynton, Torridge salmon and mussels from Fremington appear regularly, together with Tapely pheasant and Exmoor venison in season. Eating this delicious food, sitting in the elegant dining room watching the spectacle of the sun setting over a watery horizon, is a recipe for complete enjoyment.

The Commodore opens all the year round offering special 2, 3 and 4 day autumn and winter breaks as well as Christmas, New Year and Easter programmes.

I took advantage of a two-day break here in January, when the weather was not particularly kind, but within the hotel I was cosseted, extremely well fed and housed. £74 is what it cost me, which included two nights accommodation, a full English breakfast and dinner. My days were spent wandering round the pannier markets of Bideford and Barnstaple, where I managed to pick up some presents for friends, and one afternoon I took myself across the river on a ferry to Appledore. It is here that the two great estuaries of the Taw and Torridge meet. Charming and picturesque are two suitable words for the old world beauty of the little street that runs up from the quay. Anyone with the slightest talent for painting will itch to get their materials out, and for those of us unable to do so . . . well we can just stand and stare.

Tapeley Park Gardens were not open in January but, if you are in Instow between Easter and October, it is open daily except Mondays, and has a super Italian style garden with many rare plants. **Marwood Garden** near Barnstaple is equally attractive. It is a private garden and has been created around two small lakes. You can visit here throughout the year.

The Riversford Hotel in Limers Lane, Bideford is another charming establishment. It has the air of a country house and stands in three acres of gardens, looking right over the Torridge. By no means isolated,

Riversford Hotel

it still manages to create an air of total seclusion and tranquillity. Ten minutes walking will bring you into the heart of Bideford. This is a family owned and run hotel. Maurice and Merrilyn Jarrad and their two sons work hard insuring that all their guests enjoy their stay.

The bedrooms have been modernised and furnished with style, there is full central heating, which is super in the winter months. I have not stayed in the hotel, but I have a friend who has whilst recuperating from an operation, and she told me what immense pleasure she took from sitting in the window of her bedroom overlooking the river. She described it as therapeutic and her doctor as miraculous! The care and attention she received was something she will never forget and she tells all her friends about it.

Sailing, water skiing, and canoeing can be arranged locally. The safe sandy beaches attract surfers and wind surfers, and if you want to bring your boat there are free moorings; the hotel has its own slipway.

Within the grounds you can play badminton, putt a ball or two, or just relax. In the off-season breaks you can still acquire a tan in the solarium or work off some of the excess weight that you have acquired from eating so many good meals, by using the Ergometer exercise bicycle.

Northam Burrows Country Park would be a good place to spend a day whilst you are here. There are 650 acres of sand-dunes, saltmarsh and pasture. On the sea-shore is the fascinating natural barrier of the

Ringed Plover and Seashells (Northam Burrows Country Park)

Pebble Ridge, fringed by a two-mile stretch of superb sandy beach, with magnificent views across Bideford Bay from Hartland Point to Baggy Point. On a clear day the island of Lundy can be seen looming out of the waters of the Bristol Channel.

Incidentally, you can take day trips by boat to Lundy from Bideford and Ilfracombe.

For a family outing the County Park is ideal, although its proximity to the sea-shore and estuary and its variety of natural features makes it of particular interest to the specialist. The sea is safe for bathing, with car parking space adjacent to the beach—something I always found a godsend when my children were young. We always seemed to have so much stuff with us! At Westward Ho! the sandy beach gives way to rocks, full of pools and damp crevices packed with sea-shore life. The rolling Atlantic breakers are good for surfing and surf-canoeing, while the more sheltered waters of the estuary are perfect for sailing. Large expanses of open space in the park provide ample room for the championship course of the Royal North Devon Golf Club, attractive picnic places and a specially designated horse riding area.

Bird-watching and walking are other attractions of Northam Burrows. The estuary salt-marsh is visited by large numbers of waders and ducks, particularly in winter and during the spring and autumn migration.

This salt-marsh, known as the Skern, is one of the most accessible and convenient bird-watching sites in North Devon.

For walkers there is free access to most parts of the park and the South West Peninsula coast path follows the shore-line from Appledore to Cornborough and beyond. From the coast path it is possible to experience the loneliness of the estuary at low tide, even at the height of the summer, and to admire the breathtaking views from Kipling Tors. The estuary itself is often busy with small fishing boats, trawlers and coasters plying to the sea-ports of Appledore and Bideford.

No one should come to North Devon without visiting Clovelly. It is unchanging and an artist's paradise. Forget your car; you will have to leave it in a park at the top of the village. I would recommend low-heeled shoes for the descent along the cobbled street which tumbles down for half a mile to the sea. On either side are old cottages with

The village of Clovelly

flowers and creepers climbing up their walls. Unless you are of Olympic fitness standard you will be forced to stop every now and again to catch your breath. You will be grateful for it because the scenery is unforgettable. High above you trees reach for the heavens whilst below the sea sparkles in the sunshine.

The little village of Buck's Mill is frequently quiet and the beach deserted. Not much happens here but for a restful day it is ideal. It is essentially a scenic fishing port and has a spectacular waterfall. I went there when I was staying at nearby Woolfardisworthy, pronounced 'Woolsery'. This busy village revolves around the centre with its thriving village shop, an 18th-century thatched pub, the Farmer's Arms, a post office, village hall and a fine Wesleyan chapel. The parish church of All Hallows has some beautifully carved 15th-century bench ends; the one of the Crucifixion is unmutilated, and very rare. You will have gathered by now that I am a mental collector of these marvellous carvings. It is one of the first things I look for in a church. It is rumoured that Old King Cole was buried here and a tomb of a knight, still retaining its original greens and gold, is named so by the villagers.

Woolsery is lucky enough to have the **Manor House Hotel**, parts of which date back to 1122. It stands in pretty gardens right in the heart of the village. What a happy house it is, the hospitality is generous

The Manor House Hotel

and the amenities are enough to make any old soul merry. The bedrooms have en-suite bathrooms and all the other modern requirements. The cosy panelled bar is absolutely right for a pre-dinner drink whilst you mull over the day's happenings. Whisky drinkers will approve fully of the 20 fine malt whiskies on offer!

The glorious country air is enough to make even the most pernickety eater hungry, and having once seen either the magnificent table d'hôte or à la carte menus, the problem will be deciding which of the delicious dishes must wait for another day. Whoever plans the menus has the taste buds of vegetarians at heart too. A separate menu is devoted to providing a richly varied choice.

A visit to the **Milky Way Dairy** makes an interesting day out, but I prefer nearby Hartland Point, where there are some of the most breathtaking seascapes in the country. You can walk to the lighthouse or visit the museum, which charts all the wrecks on the local coastline over the last 200 years.

Hartland is a place that goes to no other town, which is part of its charm. From it you can easily reach Clovelly, Bideford, Bude and Holsworthy, as well as Exmoor and the Lorna Doone country. If you go through it you will go past Hartland Abbey to the wonderful St Nectan's church at Stoke. It is one of the finest churches for miles around and a place in which you will want to spend hours. Take a look at the coloured glass windows; you will see, amongst the many famous figures, King Arthur and the Holy Grail, and if you look at your map you will notice that Tintagel, the legendary home of King Arthur, is within striking distance.

The coast is harsh and storms sweeping in from the Atlantic stir the seas into a maelstrom which crashes against the rocks. They have been the graveyard of many a stricken ship lured onto their treacherous points.

Seldom have I seen better value for money than **Fosfelle Country House Hotel**, close to the pretty village of Hartland. You can stay in this delightful 17th-century manor house, set in six acres of land with its rose gardens, rhododendron woods and undulating lawns, for the ridiculous price of £27 in an en-suite double room. That is not just for bed and breakfast but for an excellent evening meal as well.

The proprietors, Mr and Mrs Underhill, have a true feeling for the needs of their guests. Families are very welcome, indeed there are special family rooms. The atmosphere of Fosfelle has been created by these two very hardworking people and of course it rubs off on their staff, who are a friendly bunch dedicated to making sure visitors are comfortable and enjoying themselves.

At such an inexpensive price one could reasonably suppose that the food might be restricted in choice and in quantity. That is definitely not so. Breakfast offers a full English meal or something lighter for those who are conscious of their weight and cholestrol level. The table d'hote and an extensive à la carte menu at dinner time, using local meats and vegetables and locally caught seafoods, makes it difficult to choose. The wine list is not vast, but it has quite obviously been selected after a great deal of thought, both for its content and price.

If you need a special diet or are a vegetarian you merely have to inform the Underhills and it will be arranged.

There is a cosy bar, a games room for children, a television lounge and a delightful patio on which to enjoy a drink on a balmy evening before dinner.

It is not just a hotel for summer days. The centrally heated rooms throughout and the log fires make it welcoming at any time of the year.

Hartland Abbey stirs the romantic soul of everyone who goes there. It is the sort of place that would inspire Barbara Cartland to write one of her famous books. It dates from the 12th century, is situated near a wild, isolated coastline, has monastic origins and has been lived in by the same family, although frequently inherited through the female line, since the Dissolution, when Henry VIII gave it to William Abbott, the Sergeant of his royal wine cellars. It was much larger then and over the years many changes have been made. Half way through the 18th century the Great Hall and Chapel were demolished and the level of part of the remaining building was reduced. On this foundation it was rebuilt in a style known as Strawberry Hill Gothic, and externally it remains much the same today.

In the mid-19th century Sir George Stucley owned the abbey and he loved things Gothic, particularly the type of architecture practised by the eminent Sir George Gilbert Scott, who was responsible for the Albert Memorial. He asked Sir George to design a new front hall and entrance in this manner. You can see the result today in the Inner Hall which has the old panelling brought from the Great Hall and painted to enhance the Gothic atmosphere.

Sir George also directed Gilbert Scott to produce something in the mode of the Alhambra Palace in Spain, which he had visited. The result was the unusual Alhambra Corridor, with its blue vaulted ceiling stencilled in white.

There are many lovely rooms but my favourite is the Top Corridor in the Queen Anne Wing. The paintings are superb and I am envious of the set of rare oak Hepplewhite chairs, but it is the view from the window that makes it extra special. Through the trees you can see the tower of St Nectan's Church and on the skyline a curious arch, which seems to have no purpose, but you will learn that it was a two-storey look-out used to warn the abbey against approaching pirates and wreckers whose activities were rife on this coast.

The grounds are outstanding and the valley is still as beautiful as it must have been to the Abbots, Luttrells, Orchards and Stucleys who have been lucky enough to live amongst this majesty for centuries. The present owner is Sir Hugh Stucley.

Hartland Abbey is open May-September on Wednesdays, Bank Holiday Sundays and Mondays, from 2–5.30pm. Dogs on leads are allowed in the grounds.

One of the few medieval houses licensed to be fortified is Weare Giffard Hall, between Bideford and Torrington. Like Hartland Abbey it is steeped in history. Henry VIII thought it romantic and brought Anne Boleyn to stay here. Journeying took so long then that it must have taken them over a week from London just to reach the house. You can see their entwined initials incorporated in the stained-glass windows of the Great Hall. Of the defences, only the gate-house now remains; the rest was razed by Cromwell, who for some reason also left the hall untouched.

On the Bude road just outside Holsworthy I met a remarkable couple, Tim and Jennie Horn and their two Vietnamese pot-bellied pigs, Clarence and Cleo. Tim and Jennie bought **Lake Villa**, a small hotel, just about 18 months ago and since then have wrought a complete transformation. The hotel has become secondary to the fascinating pub they have built out of the stables and outbuildings alongside. It rejoices in the name of **'The Pig's Ear'**. When I walked through the door I thought I was in a pub that had been there for years. Somehow these two, together with a little help from their friends, have created a bar that looks as though it has been there for ever, complete with atmosphere.

Weare Gifford Hall

It must have taken enormous courage to sink all their money into this undertaking. When I first saw it, because of its isolated position, I wondered how on earth they could make it pay and from whence did they attract custom. During the summer months it is not so difficult because it is a road much used by holidaymakers and the happy informality is ideal for families. Children are very welcome, the garden is there for their use and, as I write, a real adventure playground is being built for them. Cream teas are served out here on summer days, and all the year round Jennie's super food is available. She is Burmese and specialises in curries which have become a byword. The menu covers a wide range of other well cooked dishes as well and in the restaurant charcoal grills are the order of the day.

The growing number of people who come in winter from quite a wide area around them speaks volumes for the success of this venture. They come for the fun, live music and entertainment at weekends—and the food of course. If you look at a map you will see that Bradworthy is off the beaten track but it is within easy distance of Holsworthy, Bude, Bideford, Torrington, Okehampton and Launceston.

The hotel is still called **Lake Villa** and here you can stay in comfortable rooms for a very reasonable sum. Ideal for families, particularly at night when the children are tucked up in bed, leaving the parents free to go into the pub and join in the fun.

This is not the only pub the Horns own. They have the Blue Peter in Polperro, Cornwall, which they took over four years ago and have turned that also into an outstanding success. Not surprising because they are two of the most likeable and enthusiastic people I have met. They have a tremendous sense of humour and take everything in their stride.

Another place in the middle of nowhere between Holsworthy and Great Torrington is Woodford Bridge, a quite unique place and very unexpected. I thought I was going simply to look at a nice country hotel in pleasant surroundings and no one was more surprised than I at what I found.

For something like 500 years there has been an inn on the present site of **The Woodford Bridge Hotel**, providing sustenance for travellers journeying from the market town of Holsworthy to the port of Bideford.

Ducks on the pond at Woodford Bridge Hotel

The River Torridge crossed the main road, almost exactly half way between the two towns and, in the days before transport, this meant a day's journey on foot with a herd of cattle or a flock of sheep, in either direction.

There is the remains of a large Roman fort close to the hotel, so the Romans too must have found this a strategic position, keeping a watchful eye on the marauding Saxons wanting to pinch the Cornish tin and lead. On a steep, south-facing slope in the hotel grounds are the remains of an ancient Roman vineyard, which provided the legionaries with wine, starting a precedent which has never ceased.

So we have an interesting place to begin with, but that is just the background. The 15th-century thatched coaching inn is full of original oak beams and old world charm and blessed with one of the West Country's finest game fishing rivers running through the garden. I would not have minded spending a few days in such a warm, happy atmosphere and eating super food. The hotel has a fine restaurant which offers a choice of à la carte and table d'hôte menus, whilst in the bar bistro there is a wide selection of bar lunches, light snacks and special menus.

That is just the beginning of what is aptly described as 'The Woodford Bridge Experience'. The Woodford Bridge Country Club is a private luxury resort, complete with everything you need for a holiday at any time of the year. It is exclusive, as accommodation is limited to 51 lodges. A once only payment secures all the privileges associated with this unique resort for a minimum of 80 years.

By joining you become eligible to use the facilities of the magnificent Clubhouse and Hotel, together with all the sporting and leisure amenities provided by the site. The lodges in which members stay are beautifully furnished, ideal for families and tucked away deep in the countryside. They are light, airy and spacious and have been carefully set in the side of a natural coombe, landscaped with lakes and waterfalls cascading into the River Torridge.

The flexibility of the system for the use of members is a boon. Your membership gives you the right to the amount of time you want to use the club properties, at a fraction of the cost of buying a whole property. You are not restricted to the same dates every year, and you can book any time within your chosen season to suit your holiday plans. The cost of the membership depends on the season of the year and the number of days occupancy you require.

Membership of Woodford Bridge allows you to enjoy a superb holiday and the use of its sports facilities all the year round. It also brings with it membership of Resort Condominiums International, the world's oldest and largest holiday exchange organisation. This allows you to exchange your holiday ownership time at any of 1,500 holiday resorts in 60 countries around the world.

Devon never fails to surprise me. I believe I know it well, and then, out of the blue, I come across the Woodford Bridge Experience!

It is also an experience to spend time in Great Torrington and particularly at the factory of **Dartington Glass**, an industry which brought life and employment back to the people of this town which stands high up above the River Torridge.

The Dartington Crystal story begins in the beautiful surroundings of Dartington Hall, 50 miles away across Dartmoor towards Totnes. It was here, in 1925, that Dorothy Elmhirst, an American heiress with an unusual degree of social awareness, and her husband Leonard, a Yorkshireman who possessed a winning combination of vision and practicality, bought the medieval ruin and began turning it into the centre for a social and economic experiment.

The English countryside had suffered from rapid depopulation as a result of the industrial revolution, and much of British agriculture was no longer economic. With Leonard's vision and Dorothy's wealth, they set up an enterprise, the Dartington Hall Trust, which was dedicated to rural regeneration, and which became involved with a wide range of activities, including farming, weaving, forestry, establishing a saw-mill, and education.

By the 1960s the Trust, having achieved its objectives in the south, turned its attention to North Devon. Since the decline of the wool trade the working population of the area had declined at the rate of 6% a decade, and was badly in need of a broader base of industry and commerce to provide the kind of employment opportunities which local people had to seek elsewhere. It was hoped that a glass factory, making English lead crystal by hand in the traditional way, would not only provide work for local people, but also opportunities for them to develop specialised skills and improve their quality of life.

The company started manufacturing in June 1967 with a work force of 35, and it was three years later that the scheme came to fruition. It was a gamble that paid off; Dartington Crystal has become Britain's leading manufacturer of plain crystal, exporting to 50 countries, and synonymous worldwide with quality and innovative design of handmade crystal.

With a workforce of nearly 300 and retail sales in excess of £20,000,000 per annum, the company has not only achieved its original objective of contributing to the local economy, but Dartington Crystal has also become one of the West Country's leading tourist attractions, receiving over 200,000 visitors each year.

It is a fabulous place to visit and you can watch the whole process from the visitors' gallery. Within the brick arches and around the central circular furnace of a replica 18th-century glass cone, Dartington has established a Studio glassmaking workshop, where traditional handworking skills can be observed at close range.

The Studio glass movement gained its momentum from technological advances in small furnace design in the United States. From the 1960s this movement, involving individual artists and craftsmen using glass as a medium of expression, has flourished, spreading throughout Europe and Scandinavia to the Far East.

At the Studio workshop, master craftsmen explore and refine skills handed down across generations, to make reproduction pieces using authentic methods, and undertake production work for an international field of the leading Studio glass designers of today. A number of these designers, in addition to creating their own individual pieces, work closely with Dartington on its current product range. A new dimension is also evolving in limited editions and unique pieces that exhibit the successful integration of Studio and factory skills.

The Museum is excellent, it not only houses a record of the unique establishment, growth and development of Dartington Crystal, it has also assembled a historical collection of glass and its usage in Europe from the 17th century to the present day, through acquisitions and the generous support of private individuals and public collections.

Visitors are welcome on the guided factory tours, from 9.30–3.30pm, Monday to Friday throughout the year. The glass centre, shop and restaurant are open 9–5pm, Monday to Saturday, and on Sundays during the summer.

I went to visit **The Orford Lodge Hotel**, Torrington, only to find that it had been sold and was in the process of being converted into a self-catering complex with six luxury self-contained apartments. There are two charming riverside cottages to let as well. Tarka Cottage is already in use. It stands on a bank of the river Torridge in landscaped gardens with streams, waterfalls, mill pool and a working waterwheel where Tarka the otter hid from the hound Deadlock, in Henry Williamson's famous book. Close by, standing in quiet splendour, is Orford Mill, once the country house hotel.

If every apartment and cottage is as luxuriously equipped as Tarka Cottage the occupants can count on an enjoyable stay. The minimum booking is for three nights; everything is provided, including bed linen and towels. No pets are allowed.

To get to Orford Mill you go south of Torrington. Take the A386 and turn left into the B3320. The entrance is about 200 yards up on the right, before you reach **Rosemoor Garden**, belonging to the Royal Horticultural Society.

Rosemoor is described as a Garden for all Seasons. It is a place of tranquil beauty. The original garden was created by Lady Anne Palmer, who presented it to the Society together with an extra 32 acres of land. Within the first eight acres there is a wide range of plants in a variety of beautiful settings. The garden is of interest at any time of the year. In spring and summer it is the colour which commands attention. The rhododendrons do their best to upstage every other shrub and plant but they have stiff competition from the glorious roses, the many flowering trees and shrubs, bulbs and herbaceous plants. In autumn it all changes and you find yourself amidst the golden glow of autumnal colours.

With the additional 32 acres of land, the Royal Horticultural Society have been able to start work on many new features, including two Rose Gardens with over 2000 roses, and extensive herbaceous borders.

The new Visitors Centre sits in a lovely garden setting and within it is a restaurant, a shop and a plant sales area where you will find the staff more than willing to help you with your purchases. I found them particularly helpful in explaining how to cope with some of the rare and unusual plants propagated from specimens which can be seen growing in the garden.

Rosemoor is open daily from Easter until the end of September from 10–6pm, and 10–5pm during October. There are full facilities available for the disabled.

Either side of the road from Torrington to Okehampton there are pretty villages, the most well known is Sheepwash which, since the 18th century sat, minding its own business, then it was designated a conservation area and almost overnight it became a tourist attraction. The four picturesque streets converge on a central square which has everything. An old chestnut tree watches over two cherry trees and the village pump. The church looks down benignly and the inn, a mecca for fishermen, is crowded in by thatched and colour-washed cob cottages. The 260 inhabitants all work hard, mainly in farming which is in their blood. You will see more tractors in the village square than cars!

There is a story about the village bridge. In the 17th century there were only stepping stones across the river and one day, when the river was in spate, the only son of a villager, John Tusbury, was drowned whilst crossing. John was devastated and immediately found money to build a bridge. Not satisfied with just building it, he made sure that he donated enough money from his land to maintain it as well. The Bridgeland Trust was formed and, on his instructions, any surplus money was to be used for the benefit of the people of Sheepwash. To this day the income provides money for cases of hardship, helps in the upkeep of the church and chapel, makes sure the pensioners and children have outings and usually something for the elderly at Christmas.

Iddesleigh is interesting too. It has a 15th-century church and in it, behind the organ, is a cross-legged effigy of a Crusader. Jack Russell, the famous hunting parson, who gave his name to the Jack Russell terrier, was curate here from 1830–36.

The 'Farms for City Children' project operates at Nethercott House. It is an educational charity set up in 1973 to give city children direct experience of living and working on a farm. Over a thousand children a year reap the benefit of this fine experiment.

At Hatherleigh you can be sure of hearing fishing stories. It is a charm-

A thatched linhay at Deckport, Hatherleigh

ing little place, where fishermen come for a quiet holiday, determined to capture the biggest salmon or trout in the river.

There are some towns that fail to get the attention they deserve, and I often feel Okehampton comes into this category. It is a market town, selling the agricultural produce of the surrounding area, but for the visitor it is a superb centre for touring and exploring Dartmoor. The Georgian **White Hart Hotel** stands solidly opposite the handsome town hall of 1685, which was once a town house and converted to its present use in 1820.

I attended a Farmers Union dinner in the White Hart once with my husband, who was the guest of honour. Unfortunately because of road-works we arrived late and had little chance, before we sat down at table, to meet people. I found myself sitting next to a rosy-cheeked, mature man who smiled readily, said little in response to my chatter about farming, apart from the occasional yes or no. I found it hard going but he seemed contented enough. After dinner and the usual speeches I met several other people and eventually asked who my din-ner companion was. 'Ah, Joe, good man, stone deaf mind you but one of the shrewdest antique dealers in the county.' All the seeds of my conversation had fallen on stony ground! If he heard anything at all of my conversation, he must have thought I was mad.

Next door to the White Hart, surrounding a pretty cobbled courtyard, is **The Museum of Dartmoor Life** which is part of the North Dartmoor Museums Association. Alan Endacott is the Curator and the driving force behind the enterprise. Alan has been in love with Dartmoor from an early age, and a collector of anything remotely connected with the Moor. It is this collection, together with donations from all sorts of people, which has helped to furnish the museum. This particular part of it is set in a old mill and tells the story of the people who have lived and worked on Dartmoor from prehistoric times. Nothing stuffy in the presentation. It is lively and everything is simply explained. In one part there is a reconstruction of domestic and working life, another has displays of minerals and prehistoric relics. Farm implements and vintage vehicles stand by the blacksmith's and wheelwright's shops and there is a fine working waterwheel.

Alan and his committee are well aware of the need to keep changing the exhibitions, so if you have been once already, come back again because you will find much has changed. Schools have begun to use the centre regularly and one of the museum's main tasks is to ensure that the displays tie in with the national curriculum.

In addition to the museum there are craft shops in the courtyard. The Crafty Cat is full of old and new quality local crafts, lace, soft toys, quilt ware, dried flowers and arrangements, pottery and bric-a-brac. The Opal Studio has opal and gem cutting demonstrations, plus a wide range of exclusive and inexpensive jewellery, rocks, minerals and leather goods. Guaranteed jewellery repairs are a part of the service as well.

Within the courtyard is the Dartmoor Visitors Centre which opens its doors to offer advice and information on where to go and what to do in the area. The people who run it, like Alan Endacott and his colleagues, are all enthusiasts and you will find them very helpful.

There is a walk that one can take between Okehampton and Sticklepath, part of the Tarka Trail, which will take you to the **Museum of Water Power** at Sticklepath, which comes under the jurisdiction of the the Dartmoor Centre. Finch Foundry was a 19th-century waterpowered factory producing sickles, scythes and shovels. Now it is an unique museum with working waterwheels driving ancient machinery.

The foundry was started by the Finch family in 1814 when William Finch, the village ironfounder, got the villagers to help him dam the river about half a mile above the road bridge, and from there they constructed a leat which travels down through Sticklepath before it joins the river again. This provided William with the power he needed and soon the business expanded, taking over the corn and woollen mills and making cutting tools for the china clay workers, the farmers and the miners of Devon and Cornwall. At one time there were seven members of the Finch family employed here as well as 20 local men. The arrival of mass produced tools from the Midlands killed the business and by 1960 it was bankrupt. It looked as though this remarkable place would be lost to posterity, but along came Richard Barron, a descendant of the Finch family, and he made it his business to rescue the foundry and turn it into a Museum of Rural Industry. He was not to live long enough to achieve it, but the project was taken on by Bob Barron and his sister Marjorie, and Sticklepath, once called 'the village of water wheels', still has what can only be described as a museum of the greatest possible historical and educational value. Bob Barron still keeps a watching eye over it but it is Alan Endacott and his associates who are responsible. We should be eternally grateful.

Finch's Foundry is open March to mid-November, 10am-5pm, Monday to Saturday plus Sundays from June to September.

Okehampton Castle is a glorious ruin. Established by the Normans as the seat of the first sheriff of Devon, the castle was largely rebuilt in the 14th century as a lavish home for the Courtenays, Earls of Devon. No one has lived here since Henry VIII had the castle dismantled, but you can still see the whole plan of the ancient fortification, the 15th-century entrance tower, banqueting hall, the kitchens, 13th-century chapel and the Norman keep. It is in a wonderful woodland setting and you can walk through the old Deer Park. I think it is a magical place in which to picnic alongside the river, especially if you have taken advantage of the Soundalive personal stereo tours which fire the imagination and keep you wrapt in the cocoon of history long after the tour is over.

The castle is open from Good Friday—30th September from 10am-6pm daily and from October until the end of March from 10am-4pm, Tuesday to Sunday.

There is one lady I would like you to meet. Her name is Jane Seigal,

Okehampton Castle

who owns **Heathfield House**, situated 800 feet above sea level on the outskirts of Okehampton. She runs this country house primarily for people who enjoy the moors. Since she was 18 it had always been her ambition to live on or close to Dartmoor. Heathfield House literally backs onto the edge of the northern part of the moor, well placed for wonderful walks if you are so inclined, or a drive for miles in the most haunting scenery you will ever see. Jane has converted quite an ordinary house into a comfortable home; every bedroom has an exceptionally high standard and all are en-suite with either bath or deluxe power showers. She is a superb cook and housekeeper which one would think would take all her time, but not a bit of it. Jane is so well organised that part of staying at Heathfield is walking with her on the moors, to all her favourite places. She will take you to little-known spots and point out to you, on the way, the bird life, which is her great love, as well as all the flora and fauna. You will see High Willhays and Yes Tor, both 2000ft high and waiting to be climbed. You will hear tell of ancient legends, such as the Ghost of Lady Howard, burned as a witch after murdering her four husbands in the 17th century, and whose ghost is still said to ride from Okehampton to Tavistock on wild Dartmoor nights .

One fairly long walk is as far as Throwleigh (pronounced 'Ow' as in cow). What a pretty place, unbothered by time. It has a beautiful village cross, a church with a thatched lychgate and an ancient thatched church house surrounded by other attractive cottages.

Jane is not a bossy walker! You can take the walks at your own pace and enjoy them. If she is not with you, she will map a route out for you, or perhaps direct you somewhere other than the moors. There is so much beauty around Okehampton.

Higher Shilstone, Throwleigh—Saxon Longhouse

This is a non-smoking house, which I think is a blessing, but one needs to be forewarned. Probably part of the great pleasure in staying at Heathfield is that there are only four rooms so it is never crowded and at night everyone tends to sit around after dinner, sipping a glass of wine and chatting over the day's activities. There is a sense of bonhomie and well-being that strikes you the moment you enter the front door.

It is as well to tell you how to find Heathfield House. Travelling west through Okehampton, take the left-hand road at traffic lights. Go past the police station on the left and the post office on the right. Take the next major road to the right (Station Road). Go up this road for about 500 yards, keep to the left-hand fork at the fountain. Proceed for another 400 yards and you will see an old railway bridge. Go under the bridge, up a fairly steep road with woods either side. After approximately 150 yards, the road opens up and there is a little unmade road going slightly left and a small road sharply to the right, but if you continue steeply up the hill, through some rustic wooden gates, you will see the house in front of you with a car park to the right.

Near Okehampton, at 'Kesterfield' Northlew, another lady is carrying on after the death of her husband. Rachel Karslake runs **The Lambretta Preservation Society**. This private collection was started by her husband and it is unique. In it you will find vintage scooters from the first of 1947 through to the last in 1971, including three-wheeled types such as the Rickshaw, fire engine and the BL Innocent Mini, with all the posters and publicity items. Racing machines, the old and new, are all here. It is the only collection of its type in the world. There is even more to see with the addition of the die-cast toy section which features pre-war Dinky toys, a collection of 'Models of Yesteryear' including rare prototype and pre-production models together with the main feature of Toy and Model Tractors, with over a thousand items, from old to the present day.

Camping and caravan sites are available to visitors to the Collection. For 1991 opening times to the Lambretta Collection ring (0409) 221488.

L stands for lovely and there are few lovelier parts of Devon than Lydford and Lewtrenchard, my last ports of call in this chapter, a mere eight miles from Okehampton.

Lydford Gorge is an unsurpassed beauty spot, now in the care of the National Trust. Water pours off the moor onto its boulders with a ferocity that would overshadow a witches cauldron. It once was home to a band of villainous red-bearded robbers with the unlikely name of Gubbins, led by Roger Rowle, the self-styled Robin Hood of the West, whose story Kinglsey told in *Westward Ho!* They caused misery to the local village of Lydford and trepidation to travellers. Good does come out of evil. Debauchery, intemperance and inter-breeding brought their reign of terror to an end; they disappeared. Now you can stand on the little footbridge looking 300ft down the gorge and see nothing but nature at its most beautiful and mysterious.

Alfred the Great had a hand in the founding of Lydford. It was one of his four moorland burghs and was sited on a hill overlooking the river Lyd. Less than a mile downstream it was possible to ford the river—and so the name Lydford. The Danes burnt it down in AD997, probably because of the mint which was operating and producing coins known as Lydford Pennies, some of which are still in existence and can be seen in the 16th-century **Castle Inn**, a favourite haunt of mine.

This inn is right next to the castle and is one of those snug, country inns that welcome you instantly. You can stay in one of its ten well-appointed bedrooms, some of which look over Dartmoor and the others over the garden. Downstairs the Forester's Bar, in which meals are served, is warm and attractive with low lamp-lit beams, a vast collection of old plates, and a great Norman fireplace ablaze with logs in winter. If I am being strictly honest then you must be told that the fireplace was not built in Norman times but from the stone nicked from the castle! It is here you will see the Lydford Pennies.

The Tinner's Bar is used by the locals, and a lot of regulars who come from quite a distance, to enjoy the hospitality of the Castle. Quite deservedly, the Castle has a good reputation for food. There is a buffet luncheon table available from Easter until the end of October and always at weekends throughout the year. Bar meals are served at lunchtimes as well as in the evenings. Every night the à la carte restaurant is open for business and has a wide menu which includes much local produce. It is as well to book a table.

I always expect the pub to be haunted but as far as I know there has never been a sighting. However, when you consider the appalling things that happened in the castle it is surprising that no spirit took refuge. All that remains of the castle now is the keep, but for a long time it was used as a prison for Stannary Law offenders. These tinners had the so-called privilege of being tried by their fellow tradesmen under the unique Lydford Law. Quite horrendous was the outcome. More often than not the offender was hung, drawn and quartered in the morning and the trial held in the afternoon. What if the man was innocent? You can sense the evil surrounding the remains of the castle even today. You will never see a bird; they have an inborn alarm system that steers them away from evil.

The church is older than the castle, and stems from the 7th century but it is mainly 15th century. Inside it safeguards the old village stocks and has the most wonderful bench ends anywhere, some 69 in all. Carved with every conceivable flower, bird, fish and animal, they are a joy. There is even one presented to the church by King Edward VIII which has a figure of Edward the Confessor holding a model of Westminster Abbey. The fine oak screen, with a fan-vaulted canopy, is in memory of Daniel Radford, who restored the church and made the gorge accessible.

Look around the churchyard and you will spot the fascinating epitaph to George Routleigh, watchmaker:

> 'He had the art of disposing of his time so well that his
> hours glided away in one continual round of pleasure and
> delight till an unlucky minute put a period to his existence.'

A mile or so away is Lewtrenchard, a quiet and lovely place in the valley of the Lew. Hidden in the woods is the 15th-century church, so tiny that it seems full of benches and a fine old screen. Sabine Baring Gould was rector here for 43 years and he was in his 90th year when he was laid to rest in the churchyard in 1924. He gave so much to the world apart from the restoration of this lovely church and his wonderful hymns.

I will probably offend every professional hotel manager in the country when I say that a managed hotel never has just that something extra that it acquires when the owners are resident and active in the day-to-day running. There will always be exceptions to the rule, of course—Paul Uphill at the Palace in Torquay for example.

Lewtrenchard Manor at Lewdown is a prime example. It is first and foremost the home of James and Sue Murray, who would make you feel at ease and quietly pampered wherever they resided, but Devon is lucky inasmuch as they acquired Lewtrenchard three years ago and set about bringing this entrancing house back to being a superb residence. There are only eight guest bedrooms, which keeps the numbers to a manageable house-party size, and the only additional people are those who come here for dinner in the delightful dining rooms.

The restaurant has a tremendous reputation far beyond the locality. The chef, David Shepherd, has been there some time and runs his skilled team with the dedication that only a true lover of the gastronomic arts could attain. It is an experience to dine here enhanced by the loveliness of the surroundings and the quality of the wines.

As I walked in my nose twitched, inhaling the unmistakable smell of logs burning. A marvellous place, built about 1620 on the site of

Lewtrenchard

an earlier dwelling recorded in the Domesday book, this house has the mantle of love enveloping it. It has a strange history and it is amazing that it has retained so much beauty after some appallingly bad treatment over the years. Empty for some years, it was then let to a number of tenants, used to billet Army officers during the war and then run as a hotel and a function venue by several different people who neither had an understanding of the business nor a love for the house. Thank God that James and Sue decided to leave South Africa where they were farming and had the desire to run this sort of hotel.

It was the childhood home of General George Monk, first Duke of Albemarle, who, himself, had some tough times before he found fame and fortune. In 1626 his father was forced to sell the Manor to a relative, Henry Gould, in order to raise money to get his son out of prison where he had been sent by Cromwell. The Goulds most famous member was Sabine Baring Gould, the composer of hymns who gladdened my childhood with the rousing 'Onward Christian Soldiers'.

It was Sabine who embellished Lewtrenchard and made it quite out of the ordinary. He was an intrepid traveller and a compulsive collector which resulted in his bringing home interesting architectural features, so much part of the house today. Who else would have acquired the most ornate wood carving in Bavaria with the intention of installing it in the ballroom? The floral carving is a bit over the top as it trails from the floor to the ceiling, alongside and over the fireplace, until it joins the equally decorative plaster figures above one's head. It reminded me of an Austrian concert hall.

Over the mantelpiece in the Hall there is a fine, probably medieval, carved panel, held up by two beautifully carved Victorian pieces of mahogany. It does not offend in the least; Sabine had a genius for putting the right things together. The gallery which runs the length of the central part of the house is superb. There are comfortable sofas everywhere and more panelling with yet another wonderful ceiling. It is here at Christmas that the carol singers come and sing round the piano.

Every bedroom is spacious and you can look out through leaded windows onto the 11 acres of gardens or beyond to the 1,000 acre Lewtrenchard estate which entices you to take walks. Sue Murray has a wonderful eye for colour and she has refurbished every bedroom quite beautifully. Both she and her husband, James, understand and love Lewtrenchard which means that the house responds.

There are still original pieces of furniture and many family portraits of the Baring Goulds on the walls. Sabine's sister Margaret haunts the house, in the friendliest way. She must enjoy all the careful restoration that James and Sue have done.

You could fill every day of your stay in and around the estate, with trout fishing in the river or in the well stocked lake, shooting, or horseriding. The morning I was there a young American couple were having immense fun clay pigeon shooting. If you want to go further afield, then there is the 365 square miles of wild Dartmoor to explore. St Mellion championship Golf Course is only 20 minutes or so away. Plymouth and Exeter, both steeped in history, are within easy reach but I would suspect that you would get as much pleasure from all the little villages, inns and churches as the more sophisticated cities.

At the end of the day you will come home to this glorious house and its friendly owners, dine supremely well and then sleep in the greatest comfort in a room named after one of Sabine's hymn tunes. 'Now the Day is Over' perhaps?

I discovered that the Murrays belong to an association of hoteliers called Pride of Britain. Every hotel in it is an owner-run country house hotel, with the exception of the few in London, which are special places too. Having met John and Therese Boswell and their sons at Combe House, Gittisham, about whom I have already written, and also Tim and Pauline Ratcliffe, who own the superb Lutyens House, Little Thakeham at Storrington in Sussex, I am very happy to say that any hotel in 'The Pride of Britain' must be a superb place to stay if they match these.

CHAPTER 8

North Devon

PLACES OF INTEREST

Barnstaple claims to be the oldest borough in England. It is certainly ancient and crowded with memories of the past, but of recent years the present has crept upon it and the town has become the business centre of North Devon. Much of the old has had to give way to new roads to contend with the growing industry.

It is over 600 years since Barnstaple's first bridge was built across the Taw and its inner arches are still there. There is no longer a quay, from which men sailed to fight the Armada and Hugenot refugees arrived seeking sanctuary. In its place is the quaint colonnade, called Queen Anne's Walk. Merchants used to gather here and transact their business around the Tome Stone, a flat round pedestal. It is still there to remind us that a contract was sealed once a merchant had put his money on the stone.

An inscription to James Wilson should not be missed. The course of history might have been changed, had he accepted the freedom offered to him by his Spanish captors if he would pilot the Armada up Channel.

Barnstaple has its share of interesting places to visit. The almshouses are particularly attractive, the Old Grammar School Museum is well designed and the North Devon Leisure Centre has something for all.

Seven miles north-east of the town is **Arlington Court**, home of the Chichester family until the death of Miss Rosalie Chichester at the age of 84 in 1949, when it was taken over by the National Trust. With her death came an end to the Chichester's association with North Devon

Horse and carriage outside the front of Arlington Court

that had started about 1385. Rosalie was a woman of passionate interests, particularly in birds and animals. An ardent traveller, she collected things from everywhere, shells, minerals, china, pewter, model ships and so on. This she left behind and the list is so lengthy that it is impossible for more than a fraction to be shown at any given time to the public.

The present house was built in 1820, of stark design. It is the inside that is elegant. There are some lovely rooms, although Miss Chichester's father nearly ruined it with the alterations he made. In his time the size of the house doubled, not to its glory. He lived his life always wanting bigger and better things, all of which outstripped his resources, leaving Rosalie an inheritance that was nothing more than debts, and took her almost 50 years to pay off. She loved Arlington and, in spite of the burdens of her inheritance, she kept the house quite beautifully.

There is plenty to see and in the grounds are the descendants of the beloved animals that she cared for so deeply in her lifetime. Miss Chichester made her land a sanctuary for birds and animals and to their number is added now Shetland ponies and Jacob sheep which roam the parkland. Larger horses are there to pull the brake which carries visitors to the stables, where there is a superb collection of carriages set up by the National Trust.

Arlington Court is open from Easter to October, Sunday to Friday 11–6pm. From November to March it is only the garden and the park that is open during daylight hours.

I am always impatient to move further north or deeper into the countryside because of its sheer beauty. The countryside first, I think, because I want to leave my favourite to last.

The A361 is a springboard to many good places. Looking for somewhere to stay presents no problem. I would recommend **Downrew House** at Bishops Tawton to anyone, providing they do not have young children.

I could not wait to find out what it was that brought five men—three Germans, an American and an Englishman—to a quiet 16th-century country hotel in North Devon. To get there I drove into Bishops Tawton from Barnstaple and at the BP garage I turned left up Codden Hill. The road climbed higher and higher, with the occasional opportunity to gaze down at the wonderful autumn-tinged countryside. After about a mile I came to Downrew, parked my car and entered the old white door to be greeted by a charming man, who was busy painting the wooden struts on the staircase. He had no need to be apologetic at this unorthodox welcome. Bruce Hendricks is the American in this quintet and his easy charm made me feel instantly at home.

His English partner, Clive Butler, then took charge of me and we went off to sit in a very comfortable drawing room, furnished as a country house should be, with furniture that is meant to be used and not sat upon gingerly. It was from him that I got the information I was seeking.

The three Germans are purely sleeping partners at present, and it is Clive and Bruce who have grappled with the task of running a successful hotel. 'How did it come about?' I asked. It was then I discovered that all five had worked in the oil industry, mainly in Third World countries, but sometimes as far east as China. It was whilst they were all working in Ghana that the decision was made to find a suitable hotel to buy in the U.K. Slightly different from the world of oil, but apparently they had all had considerable experience of entertaining in their homes and felt that this was what they wanted to do.

Downrew is not the place to stay if you want to be starchy and formal. It is warmhearted and delightful. The bedrooms are comfortable and en-suite of course. The dining room has a wonderful bow window which allows the light to stream in, and those inside to gaze out across the garden. Bruce has a flair for cooking and originally did it all himself, but now they have a very able young chef, who works with him, to produce some truly memorable meals. One very popular dish on the menu is the roast saddle of rabbit, something I had not tasted since my childhood days. If you are lovers of wine you will find the list pleasing. The range in price is from £6–£60, but if you enjoy a glass of claret I think the house offering is excellent value.

The swimming pool is one of the unexpected pleasures at Downrew. It is a sun trap, which makes it a marvellous place to sunbathe, relax and just cut yourself off from the world.

Dogs are very welcome visitors here but they are not allowed indoors. Like the dogs belonging to the house they have their own quarters and have a wonderful time cavorting in the garden or going out with their owners walking, or exploring North Devon.

I was present when some guests left the hotel and they could not thank Bruce and Clive enough for the wonderful time they had spent there. They hoped to return next spring. I can just imagine how lovely it would be at that time of the year. The gardens would just be beginning to bloom and the grass at its greenest, backed by the height and elegance of the trees. It is certainly a hotel that does beckon one back and where else would you go to find an American oilman who speaks fluent Chinese or an Englishman fluent in German and Arabic?

Bishops Tawton is the home of one of the most unlikely Grade II listed buildings—a three-seater outside loo, the property of Ernie Smith, who will tell you that it has not been in use for thirty years or more. A sight to be admired but not used!

The delightful village of Chittlehampton has its own saint Urith, and once a year she is honoured with a procession from the lychgate of the old church at the top of her square, to the site of her martyrdom. As if in protest at her death, a spring of water gushed from the ground and flowers have flourished there ever since. Each year the well is blessed, and the procession returns to the church to sing her special hymn and for the children to lay freshly picked posies on her tomb. For 12 centuries this ritual has been carried out.

Cobbaton is close to Chittlehampton and here there is something very unusual.

It must be two years since I was last at the **Cobbaton Combat Collec-**

Under a canopy of limes, seen from St Hieritha Church's doorway,
Chittlehampton

tion. I enjoyed that first visit and the enjoyment was only enhanced
this time. It is owned by a fascinating man, Preston Isaac, who has
spent all his life collecting just about everything, but mainly from the
1939–45 period. If you are as old as I am, it is full of nostalgia. There
is sheet music which takes me down memory lane to the tunes that
we used to dance to during World War II. Preston has compiled a
number of wartime recipes and all the sorts of bits and pieces from
the war years that I remember so well. Apart from these items there
are over 50 vehicles and guns, tanks, armoured cars, trucks, carriers,
artillery, weapons and radio equipment.

This year there are some new vehicles, those surplus from the Warsaw
Pact. It is a super place to visit in a totally unexpected place.

Preston Isaac told me that he never intended to have such a collection
but somehow it got started as a hobby and then got completely out
of hand. I am glad it did because it reminds people of my generation
of all the trauma and misery of war but brings back too the fun we
all managed to have even though life was tough. For younger folk it
will give them an insight into the past which should not be forgotten.

From April to the end of October it is open daily, from 10–6pm. If
you want to go in the winter you will need to ring and make an appointment. The telephone number is (07694) 414.

What a nice little market town South Molton is. Nothing particularly
outstanding about it, but it has such an air of well-being and in its
midst is a hotel of outstanding beauty.

It is curious how names have an association. To me Whitechapel was
linked to London and not a pretty place, but here was I arriving at
Whitechapel Manor, South Molton and experiencing one of the most

pleasurable moments in the thousands of miles I have travelled compiling this book. Much of the credit for this is due to the owners, John and Patricia Shapland, who are very special people. It was their tenacity that restored this gracious Elizabethan manor house to its former glory, adding discreet touches of luxury to give one the modern day comforts without in any way detracting from the original features and unique atmosphere.

Its setting is unspoiled English countryside, with wonderful views over woodland and meadows, close to the Exmoor National Park and yet within easy reach of so many places.

The first recorded owners were the Peverells in 1162. The present house was built by Robert de Bassett around 1575. He was an illegitimate son of Edward IV and got himself into trouble when he made an unsuccessful bid for the throne on the death of Elizabeth I. Two years later he forfeited his title and the only way he could buy a pardon, granted to him by James I, was to sell his lands and manors. The D'Amory family were the next owners of Whitechapel Manor, and their love of things beautiful brought about the installation of a magnificent Jacobean carved oak screen and William and Mary panelling and paintings.

The house has something different to excite you in every passage and room. The dining room occupies one wing and has the sort of quiet elegance that can only heighten one's anticipation for the food to come. You will be served in the most professional manner by John Shapland, a member of the family, or some charmingly resourceful and polite young women. In that respect it reminded me a bit of the Bel Alp at Haytor. The maestro in the kitchen is Thierry Lepretre-Granet, whose innovative menus use only the very best of produce. He is given an entirely free hand by the Shaplands and the results more than justify their faith in this fine chef.

Imagine dining on Scallops cooked under pastry in a light stock with carrot and leek julienne and a flavouring of chervil, parsley and tarragon, followed by grilled fillet of beef with Meaux mustard sauce and a pastry basket of vegetables. The cheese board next and then passion fruit mousse with its sauce. A wonderful meal accompanied by a really good French wine. I still conjure up the delight the meal gave me.

There are ten, beautifully appointed bedrooms here, each named after the ten previous owners, all with private bathrooms, colour television and direct dial telephones.

I wondered what staff problems might occur here, for it is truly off the beaten track, although it is only 30 minutes from the M5 motorway (junction 27). You take the A361 and then a turning to the right just as you reach South Molton.

In North Road, South Molton is an all weather attraction, **Quince Honey Farm**. It is quite unique and world famous. The exhibition of living honey bees is acknowledged by experts to be the best in the world. It matters not whether you are a casual visitor or a serious student, the innovative design of many living exhibits enables you to learn the fascinating facts in an interesting and entertaining environment.

The observation hives, which open before your eyes, are behind glass and can be watched in complete safety. Posters, photographs and video shows complement the live action.

Free parking is available and there is a super three-acre area where you can picnic. I would suggest that you make sure you have your camera at the ready.

Quince Honey Farm is open daily 9am-6pm, from Easter to September and from 9am-5pm, October to Easter.

Do you like Devon cider? If you do, Hancock's Cider is made at **Clapworthy Mill** by the family who have been producing this liquid nectar for five generations and won prizes galore for its excellence. It is a pretty place with a mill stream complete with ducks. You can picnic, if you will, and go home laden down with bottles of cider to remind you of your visit.

Jon and Fiona Water, a couple who spent some time in Canada taking people trekking, have returned to Exmoor to run **Twitchen Waggon Tours**. I spent a wonderful day with them. Aboard this sedate method of transport, pulled by shire horses, you can relax and enjoy the splendour of the scenery. You choose from one of three trails which will stop at suitable old inns and historic places. Fiona packs a super hamper, full of traditional fare if you ask her to do so, or you can eat at one of the inns.

The church of St Mary at Molland, close to Twitchen, is outstanding. Built somewhere in the 16th century, it escaped the monstrous hand of the Victorian restorer and what remains is a charming interior, plastered and whitewashed with box pews and a canopied three-decker pulpit. There is a series of monuments to the 17th- and 18th-century Courtenays and something I had not seen before, a double heart-stone used as a receptacle for the hearts of one of the Courtenays and his wife.

You cannot fault the beaches of Braunton, Croyde Bay and Woolacombe. Marvellous places for people who enjoy water sports. If you want somewhere rather special and not too expensive in which to stay I sincerely recommend the AA/RAC two star **Kittiwell House Hotel and Restaurant** in Croyde. It was formerly a Devon Long House, dating back to the reign of Elizabeth I. The original features with its plaited, thatched roof and white painted cob-stone walls are still there. Inside there is a wealth of panelled walls with low ceilings and inglenooks. Modern comforts have been installed, but so cleverly that none of the olde worlde charm and congenial atmosphere are lost.

The restaurant is open to residents and non-residents every night with a choice of two menus, table d'hôte or à la carte. Jim and Yvonne Lang are the resident proprietors, whose skill is reflected in the successful manner in which the hotel is run. They look for all-year-round business and offer special Activity Breaks. With a championship golf course just 5 minutes away at Saunton, the game provides an ideal excuse

Kittiwell House Hotel and Restaurant

for a break. Clay shooting is another popular sport and there are special shooting weekends. Tuition is available if it is required.

Beach and moorland riding is available all the year round. From Croyde you can actually gallop along three miles of golden sand, or, just as exhilarating ride over Exmoor and, in particular, through the Doone Valley with all its beauty and mystique.

Coastal and rural walks abound in this area of Devon, taking in some of the most spectacular scenery you could wish to find. Maps, guides—including humans—are available at Kittiwell, and if you send a list of your requirements ahead of your stay the hotel will furnish you with the necessary maps and point you in the right direction.

Wildlife weekends are wonderful. Trevor Beer, an expert who also owns a conservation reserve, will guide you. Such a special feast of interesting subjects are covered in these weekends—incorporating films, lectures and trails. It is an area full of legend and beauty.

Ilfracombe tends to die in the winter, which is an enormous pity. It is a quaint town and surrounded by a magnificent coastline.

Life is full of surprises and none quite so surprising as **Dedes** in Ilfracombe. This looks like a small hotel-cum-pub which faces the promenade and the beach. I suppose that is what it is on the surface, but go through the door and start talking to the Cawthornes who own this remarkable establishment, and you will understand my feelings.

The name Dedes, an odd one, comes from the pet name for Jackie Cawthorne's aunt. It is a family business and when Jackie married Ian Cawthorne he was brought into the business as well, but with a difference. His love of shooting—sporting clays in particular—has led to Dedes becoming the leading centre for the sport in the West Country. Through-

Ilfracombe Harbour with Lantern hill behind

out the winter Dedes plays host to shooting parties who stay in the hotel, go out to the shooting ground, owned by the Cawthornes, during the day and return afterwards to eat the excellent food served in the Wheel Room Restaurant and drink at the bar.

All sorts of people come for these breaks which are supremely well organised by Jackie and Ian. Jackie loves shooting, too, but seldom gets the chance to get out these days because of the extra work in the hotel brought about by the success of the clay pigeon and game shooting programmes.

Ian Cawthorne is a senior C.P.S.A. qualified coach who has been approved to teach the 'Move, Mount, Shoot' method perfected by John Bidwell, former F.I.T.A.S.C. World Champion, and the famous 'Stanbury Method' taught by Alan Rose and his superb team at the West London shooting grounds. Ian has Ray Hulston to help him as the full-time coach. He has had many years experience of teaching sporting clays and is on hand at all times for any advice and help required. He is also well known, I understand, for his patience and occasional wry comment!

The ground is set in a beautiful natural valley with a multi-stand sporting layout, including a very high pheasant stand. There is also a Pro-trap layout providing excellent F.I.T.A.S.C. practice with automatic traps.

All stands have chipping paths and have been expertly laid out to be variable to one's own degree of competence.

There is a separate starter layout as an aid to the coaching of novice shots. The Cawthornes are constantly improving the ground, adding new facilities, making sure that it lives up to its reputation as the finest shooting in the South West.

This is a subject about which I knew nothing, but lack of knowledge seems not to be a disaster. In a short holiday you can be coached until you become a reasonable novice shot.

There are specific holidays normally comprising 3 or 5 nights, half-board accommodation and daily shooting sessions at a fully inclusive price.

Novices do not hold back the experienced, which is great because it means that perhaps a wife or a girl friend can get the chance to learn without being a worry to their other half. Of course in this enlightened era it could well be the woman who is the crack shot and the male the novice. Whatever, Dedes is the place to be. The Cawthornes motto is 'Good food, good shooting and good company'. People come back to them time and time again, year after year. I am not surprised.

Supposing that shooting bores you rigid, do not worry, you will still enjoy Dedes with its charm and atmosphere. Ilfracombe has much to offer in the summer months. Dedes is proof positive that you can get just as much fun in the winter months if you look for it.

Museums can be daunting but no one could possibly say that about **Ilfracombe Museum**. It is quite the friendliest of places, run by a team of dedicated people, who do it far more for love than money. Mrs Slocombe is the Curator and has been for some years. This lively lady will not mind me telling you that at 63 she is almost the youngest member of the team! Her assistant, Mr Stephens, is many years her senior—but what a mine of information he is. His memory is fantastic. Born and bred in Ilfracombe there is little that he does not know about it.

The museum was founded in 1932 by a noted explorer, Mervyn Palmer who brought to it all that he had collected in his many years in South America. Added to this was a considerable number of items donated by many people returning from the colonies to retire. Whilst these collections are still there, they did not make the museum the fascinating place it is today. It was far too serious and did not inspire young people at all. Since Mrs Slocombe took over, a great deal of time and attention has been given to building educational links with schools and acquiring the right sort of exhibits to kindle youngsters' imaginations. Nothing is ever purchased for the museum; it is all donated—so much seeking and persuading has been done to collect all sorts of memorabilia.

One cabinet is devoted entirely to cameras throughout the ages, another to razors, yet more to bits and pieces from the Second World War and to the days when the railway used to come to Ilfracombe. Costume is the most recent addition. There are dolls, coins, drawer upon drawer of butterflies, guns, jewellery; all of it carefully labelled and the donor's name shown.

There are frequent visits from various groups who delight in the friendly way in which they are greeted and the fact that no-one is too busy to talk to them and explain. In one of the back rooms there are shelves full of every issue of the now defunct Ilfracombe newspaper;

this throws light on much that has happened in the town.

It is Mrs Slocombe who has been the driving force behind the new programme at Ilfracombe Museum. She and her colleagues are certainly seeing the reward for their hard labour in the increasing number of people who come to see the museum, which stays open all year round. It costs very little to spend time in this fascinating place and when you leave you will probably feel as I did. I had not only been stimulated but had made new friends as well.

If you have any items that the museum could use they would be delighted to hear from you.

It was one of the museum members who told me to look out for the house on Lantern Hill which once was a medieval chapel. In the 14th century there were no lighthouses to guide the mariner but sometimes the church lent a hand, and at its own expense displayed a light for the benefit of passing ships. This house used to be the Chapel of St Nicholas with a projecting window on the seaward side in which a lantern was placed. This came to an end at the Reformation, when it became a private house. The occupants were caring folk and continued the practice by displaying a light on the roof gable. Today there is still a light surmounted by a weather-vane in the shape of a fish. I understand that it was put there about 1819, about the time that Ilfracombe rose from its quiet obscurity as a fishing village and started developing into a major resort. It is nice to think that people still care.

The little square at the back of the harbour was almost deserted on a damp October lunchtime, when I called in at the Royal Brittania, for a quick drink and a sandwich to sustain me before I went on my way further into the depths of North Devon.

This is more an inn than hotel, with famous traditions and a long interesting history. It was the haunt of Lord Nelson and Edward VII loved it and made it his headquarters for a west country tour, presenting the inn with the lamp that hangs over the entrance to this day. Smugglers too found the Royal Britannia a good port of call. I can fully understand why.

In contrast to the miserable weather outside, the bar of the **Royal Britannia** was warm and welcoming. It is a cheery place with a good local following that prevents it from dying a death as so many places in Ilfracombe do out of season.

Almost every table was full of people, either taking a lunchtime drink or enjoying some of the pub's excellent food. The blackboard menu offers a whole range of daily specials at extremely low prices. There was a choice of Hot Pot or Cottage Pie, or simply a good honest Ploughman's with crispy bread. What took my fancy were the well-filled fresh crab sandwiches which I saw some people ordering. I love crab and this looked the real McCoy. My choice was a good one. The sandwiches were served well garnished, the bread was fresh and not of the plastic variety.

Upstairs there is comfortable accommodation where, at the end of a day possibly deep sea fishing (which can be arranged for you), sleep will come easily, tucked up in the well-sprung beds.

If you come to Ilfracombe in the summer you will find it bustling. Holiday entertainments and activities are there for the taking. I think I like it best though when it has put on its winter overcoat and it is quiet. The scenery then takes on a different look. Rolling breakers crash into the boulders beneath the Promenade and the wind breathes fresh, sharp sea air into your lungs. It is a time for brisk walks and a return to the warmth of a good hostelry like the Royal Brittania.

A totally different hotel is the **Ilfracombe Carlton**. It is a quiet, rather stately sort of place which comes to life with the very lively tour parties who fill the hotel most of the year. Normally middle-aged people, they come to have fun and this is exactly what the Carlton provides. The food is simple home-cooked fare and plenty of it. Every day something is arranged to entertain the guests and at night there is dancing and frequently a cabaret. The rooms are comfortable and the bar is a meeting place for guests and for locals. Many of the business fraternity use the hotel for lunches and the function rooms are frequently full.

The Carlton would like to be able to welcome more business people for conferences or for training courses. It is a little difficult to persuade potential clients to come quite so far into North Devon. It is a great pity because the facilities are here and the price is right.

Creating the right environment for a holiday which is neither to be spent in a top quality hotel nor, at the other end of the scale, a simple home providing bed and breakfast, but giving comfortable, pleasant accommodation at sensible prices together with masses of free amenities—this is quite an undertaking. John Fowler has done just that, however, by offering six ways in which to enjoy a superb self-catering holiday.

This friendly, unassuming man has been welcoming visitors for years but his policy has never changed, and the proof of success comes from over 65,000 people who enjoy a John Fowler Holiday each year. Many of them keep on coming back for more.

The venues are **Ilfracombe Holiday Village**, Ilfracombe Holiday Village Motel, Devon Coast Holiday Park, Westward Ho! Beach Holiday Village and, in Cornwall, Downderry Beach Holiday Village. The sixth option is Country Cottages—privately owned farmhouses, country cottages and seaside properties located in both Devon and Cornwall. Most of these are tucked away, secluded places surrounded by wildlife—ideal for anyone who just wants peace and quiet and time to recharge their batteries.

The thing that struck me about John Fowler Enterprises is that the standard does not drop. Every bungalow, cottage or apartment is fully furnished complete with colour TV and covers just about everything you can possibly need down to kitchen utensils. All you have to bring with you is bed linen and towels. Cleanliness is a priority and you will find your accommodation spotless.

All this may sound fairly normal in any decent holiday venue but here is the twist that makes John Fowler different: some people will love the fun and bonhomie of a holiday village and enter into everything that is going on. Others may want to experience the fun sometimes but be able to remove themselves from it. What has been achieved is a perfect balance. In Ilfracombe the village is set above the town and sea and has wonderful views. The focal point is the 56ft heated swimming pool which is kept really warm from late May until mid September. There is crazy golf, children's play areas, a sauna and a solarium. The licensed club is free to residents and there is regular entertainment, discos and live bands.

Children love the entertainment centre with the latest video games and pool tables. The shop, launderette and very fairly priced 'Country Kitchen' restaurant complete the amenities.

Now if you want to be different and stay in the Motel perhaps, or take advantage of Devon Coast Holiday Park which is quiet and secluded, you still get the free use of all the amenities of the Holiday Village. I think it is a brilliant solution. I can just imagine mum and dad and the children staying in the village and the grandparents opting for the Holiday Park, yet all being able to meet up and join in the fun without any extra charge if they wish to. I know it is probably what I would do if I were away with my daughter and son-in-law and my three grandchildren.

The Westward Ho! Beach Holiday Village carries on the high standards of Ilfracombe. The advantage here is that the bungalows are virtually on the beach. Wonderful beach it is too, some three miles long with excellent surfing. It is recognised as one of the safest and cleanest beaches in Devon. Westward Ho! is within five minutes walk and is quite an amusing place to be, with good restaurants, bars, dancing and a putting green.

John Fowler deserves full marks for his attainments and he is not a man to be complacent so I am sure the standards will always remain high.

Chambercombe Manor is a house that you really ought to visit. It is only a mile from Ilfracombe off the A399 Combe Martin road. You may think it looks rather unpretentious, just a pretty farmhouse where not much will have happened over the years. How wrong you are. There was some sort of dwelling here in Saxon times. In the Domesday Book it is shown as being held by 'Robert', after whom came Sir Henry Champernon, from whence came the house's name. The manor house dates from then but was extensively altered in Tudor times.

It is likely that someone of great importance was coming to stay and, to provide appropriate accommodation, the Minstrel's Gallery was removed to make way for a pretty dressing room. This did not provide all the space, so the Great Hall was divided into two storeys to make a new bedroom. It is a wonderful room bordered by a plaster frieze of grapevines, with a Tudor rose in the centre. The richly carved bed is of the same period and it has an intriguing hidey-hole for valuables,

Chambercombe Manor

cunningly concealed in a diamond-shaped boss on the tester.

Next to the fireplace is an odd cupboard once used as a confessional, with the priest concealed in the Priest's Hole behind the wainscot panelling. Above the mantel is the arms of the Grey family, who were descendants of the Champernons, and it is believed the room was made ready for the pathetic Lady Jane Grey who ruled England for nine days before she was beheaded.

The Champernons were reputedly wreckers—a favourite pastime for Cornishmen and Devonians who lured unsuspecting ships on to the rocks and then looted them, frequently killing crew and passengers. This leads to a gruesome story about the manor. In a narrow passage leading from the Tudor bedroom, through a hole in a partition you can see a very small, dusty room discovered in Victorian times by the then owner. When he investigated it further he found a hidden bedroom in which, on the remains of a fine bed, lay the skeleton of a woman. She was aboard one of the wrecked ships and, because of her wealth and jewels, was brought to Chambercombe and after the occupants of the house had stolen her jewellery she was left to die.

It is thought that there is a tunnel connecting the house with nearby Hele beach which was used by smugglers and wreckers no doubt.

I have only told you a little about this romantic and sinister house. You will find out more when you visit.

It is open from Good Friday to September, Monday to Friday 10.30–

12.30; 2–4.30pm. Closed on Saturdays but open Sundays from 2–4.30pm. You can picnic in the grounds but no dogs are allowed.

Before you get into Combe Martin you will come across the extraordinary **Watermouth Castle**. You should allow at least three hours for your visit. You pay one price and that covers absolutely everything for the time you are there, except for food. Its position makes it fabulous anyway but apart from that it has to be one of the U.K.'s most exciting and unique all weather attractions. Inside there are nostalgic displays, brilliant sights and sounds, breathtakingly beautiful coloured waterfalls, haunted dungeons and magical fairytales that come to life before your very eyes. The landscaped gardens have even more to offer.

Children love 'Once upon a Time', a haven of fantasy and fun that give them pleasure for hours. They enjoy playing in an ocean of plastic balls, imaginative soft play areas, and going on train rides, as well as seeing fascinating animated fairy tales.

Combe Martin seems quite tame after all that excitement but it too has a lot to offer.

From running a successful residential home in Minehead to operating the busy **Glenavon Manor Holiday Park** at Combe Martin must have been quite a brave thing to do, but Frank Farmer and his wife, Dorothy,

Glenavon Manor Holiday Park

seem to have made the transition remarkably well. The position of the Holiday Park is fantastic looking right out over the sea in what is one of the most spectacular parts of North Devon.

Glenavon was built in the last century as a country mansion, standing in over 11 acres of landscaped grounds and natural woodland. Although it is in the heart of the village it really lives a quite separate lifestyle.

In a relaxed, friendly atmosphere you can stay in comfortably furnished apartments in the main house or choose one of the pretty apartments in what was once the old coach house. In addition to this there are purpose-built holiday chalets, well sited quality caravans with mains services, W.C. and shower, or, if you are needing to count the pennies, budget caravans with mains services, W.C. and hot water will offer you perfectly adequate accommodation. The main purpose of any holiday is to get out and about and see as much as possible anyway.

If you prefer swimming in a pool rather than the sea, then there is a good size heated pool plus a smaller, shallower pool for little ones to splash around in. There is a super children's play area as well with a splendid buccaneer pirate ship, swings, roundabouts and slides—and a sandpit for toddlers.

Like all good parks there is a Club House, shop and launderette and colour television in all accommodation.

It was no surprise to me to find out that, throughout July and August, Glenavon is always packed out, but it seemed to me that a holiday spent here at Easter or, possibly, early October would be ideal. The caravans and apartments all have heating so it would not matter in the least if the weather were a bit chilly. What it would allow you to do is explore this wonderful area in comparative peace. The safe and sheltered beaches with sand and rock pools at low tide become a paradise for people who like to walk.

Combe Martin has one of the longest village streets in the country and a strange 18th-century inn, **The Pack of Cards**. It was built by a man who is said to have been a great gambler and from his winnings he built the inn to resemble a child's house of cards, with each storey smaller than the one below and chimneys arising from every possible corner.

A little further along is **Higher Leigh Manor**, an excellent hotel which combines much of the elegance of a country home, without being too puffed up to accept those who are looking for a traditional seaside holiday complete with bucket and spade. Most of the bedrooms have superb panoramic views of the countryside and the sea. The food is excellent, combining the best of English and Continental cooking. Open all the year round, the high standard and personal service make it a particularly good place in which to stay.

Behind the hotel and under the same management is, **Combe Martin Wildlife and Leisure Park**, which opens from Easter until October from 10am-5pm. Apart from the animals and the birds it is a delight just to stroll around the 15 acres of beautiful natural woodland which includes Ornamental Gardens, Tropical Plants and Rare Trees.

There are nine species of monkeys and apes living in the park. They live in a tropical type environment which has lots of water and natural surroundings. The otter sanctuary is one of the finest I have seen and feeding the two grey seals is great fun. I love it there.

Coming from Combe Martin towards Lynton there is a left turn signed

Coulsworthy House Hotel. I would not have missed the turning for all the tea in China. It is a pretty house, parts of which go back to the 16th century. It sits sedately looking out over the fabulous spread of countryside rolling down to Combe Martin and the sea.

Coulsworthy Country House Hotel

However, it was not the hotel so much that I enjoyed as the people who run it. I was greeted in a friendly fashion by Luther Blisset, who promptly cocked his leg and relieved himself all over the rear wheel of my car. Having achieved that, he accompanied me into the house where he handed me over to his master, James Anthony. Apparently that is his normal pattern of behaviour on the arrival of strangers!

James and his wife Pat, together with their daughter Alison and husband Mark Osmond, plus James's sister and his aunt, combined all their resources not so very long ago and bought Coulsworthy House. They had no experience in running a hotel but Alison was a trained Home Economist with a rare talent for cooking.

Having found Coulsworthy they set about making it a delightful country hotel. There is nothing pompous or pretentious about it, the bedrooms are charmingly decorated and furnished with their own bathrooms. Downstairs the pretty dining room is just the sort of restful place in which to enjoy Alison's fabulous meals. I may say it would not do for anyone trying to diet to stay here; the temptations would be too great. Her standards are uncompromising and wherever possible she uses locally produced ingredients. The results are always delicious.

The family have all settled into their various departmental roles within the hotel. Mark is a natural behind the bar and this becomes the hub of the hotel before dinner and frequently continues afterwards. The family are adept conversationalists and have that wonderful ability of getting total strangers talking to each other.

If you ask for a mineral water here, you get a pleasant surprise when a glass of crystal clear water is poured for you from a bottle labelled Coulsworthy Spring Water. You will also find bottles in your bedroom. Yes, it does come from their own spring and is delicious.

The six-acre grounds are partly wooded and include a heated outdoor pool, a grass tennis court and a playable, but slightly odd shaped, croquet lawn.

The Anthony entourage may not have known much about hotel keeping when they started but there is no doubt that now the hotel is run by a group of dedicated professionals who are also great fun to be with.

This is almost Exmoor; you can feel the change in atmosphere and what better place from which to explore it than the linked villages of Lynton and Lynmouth. Two totally different places in which to stay are The Neubia Hotel in Lynton and The Rising Sun in Lynmouth.

The Neubia was built as a farmhouse in 1840 and with a great deal of skill, Brian and Dorothy Murphy, have managed to merge the past with the present and produce a very comfortable, friendly hotel. Not large (it only has 12 bedrooms) the international reputation it has gained since their arrival in 1978 is well deserved. For a good many people one of its great advantages is the car park, because most hotels in Lynton have no space at all for cars. I prefer to believe that it is the excellence of the personal service, together with Brian and Dorothy's feelings about food, that have given the hotel its recognition.

Talking to them you begin to understand that they take food extremely seriously. They trust no one but themselves to do the cooking which is imaginative and varied. To them cooking is an art and every meal is specially prepared from the best ingredients and with the utmost care. If you plan to explore Exmoor, a picnic lunch will be provided. At dinner they specialise in Cordon Bleu cuisine, using, as far as possible, fresh produce—sole and skate from Lynmouth Bay, Lyn salmon in season, local cheese and dairy products.

Dorothy is a vegetarian so she has a particular interest in these dishes, as indeed they both have, and will cater for vegan, diabetic, coeliac and other diets. For these they would appreciate advance notice.

At the end of each day their guests return for dinner and invariably take a drink in the snug bar that adjoins the dining room. Dinner is an unhurried meal and is perfect for anyone returning after a strenuous day out.

In winter the house is warm and is well suited for anyone wanting to take a winter break. Exmoor is wonderful at any time of the year and sometimes the solitude out of season is so beneficial. The Neubia would certainly be an excellent base.

In the 14th century, **The Rising Sun** at Lynmouth was dispensing hospitality to travellers as it does today, but I would take an even bet that then, and in later centuries, many of them were smugglers or seafaring men, mulling over their hauls, making brazen or surreptitious plans for the next smuggling run. You can feel this sense of history as you

The Rising Sun, Lynmouth

walk into this very pretty thatched inn, which today, not only upholds its innkeeping tradition but, without losing one ounce of its charm, has become a first-class hotel.

Ten years ago when Hugo Jeune returned to Lynmouth and acquired the Rising Sun, he must have wondered if he would ever achieve the standard that he required. The place was a mess and in need of absolutely everything doing to it. How do you retain all that is beautiful and right about its antiquity and at the same time made good the wear and tear of 600 years. He described it to me as a cobweb which had to be worked around so that not one strand was broken. Miraculously and thankfully he has been successful.

It sits overlooking a small picturesque harbour at the mouth of the River Lyn where it joins the sea. Inside, the uneven floors, the crooked ceilings, thick walls and fine oak panelling in the dining room and bar endorse its age. When you climb the fairly steep stairs to your room you will occasionally have to duck your head to avoid the old beams. Entering your bedroom you will find it restful and charming. It is quite simply furnished in pine using every last bit of space. Somehow, Hugo Jeune has managed to give every room its own private bathroom. No mean feat in a building this age. If you are lucky enough to have a room in the front you will be able to gaze out through the little leaded windows at the vast expanse of sea with all its changing moods.

The Jeunes are lucky in having a very good staff and in Lynda, their housekeeper, a lady who has been at the Rising Sun for 13 years and knows and loves every nook and cranny of the place. She was kind enough to show me round the bedrooms and it was quite apparent that caring for the Rising Sun was not just a job to her.

She took me out of the hotel and up a steepish slope alongside, until we came to **Shelley's Cottage**, which belongs to the Rising Sun but is totally separate if you wish it to be. It even has its own kitchen. It is where the famous poet P.B. Shelley spent his honeymoon with his 16-year-old bride in 1812. It would have been romantic then and still is today with its double bedroom with a four-poster bed, sitting room and private garden with quite spectacular views. It really is something special.

Shelley wrote of it, 'The climate is so mild that myrtles of immense size twine up our cottage, and roses bloom in the open air in winter.'

The poet was not the only famous writer to stay here. R.D. Blackmore, who gave us *Lorna Doone*, wrote much of this book whilst staying at the Rising Sun. I can well understand how he found it a place of inspiration. Sitting with a word processor in front of me does not inspire me but I am quite sure that if I had a room in the Rising Sun that looked out over the sea and I knew that I was going to be rewarded by a fabulous dinner at the end of the day, inspiration would not be far away.

Open all the year round, the Rising Sun offers some very good value Harbourside Breaks from February until June and October until December inclusive, with the exception of Bank Holidays. Because the hotel is not suitable, children under five are not taken.

Hugo Jeune's family have long been associated with Lynmouth. He is in fact Lord of the Manor. A title passed down to him through his family but meaning little in today's world because the Manor has long gone; it was sold to the Council in 1908. However the Lord of the Manor does have certain rights laid down in the deeds. For example he can own the seashore as far as a knight can throw a lance!

It was just about ten years before the Manor was sold that Hugo Jeune's grandmother opened Sir George Newnes's fabulous railway that climbs vertically up the cliff from Lynmouth to Lynton. The land on which the railway was built still belongs to Hugo. He also has half of mile of fishing rights where keen fishermen can catch some of the best salmon anywhere. It is free for anyone staying in the hotel apart from the local authority fee.

When I first read *Lorna Doone* I was not sure whether it was fact or fiction. Visiting Doone Country makes sure that I choose to believe it to be fact. It is so romantic and beautiful—totally different from its neighbour Dartmoor. Covered in gorse and heather, there are wooded ravines and exquisite little stone villages to reinforce the validity of the story.

Lynton stands 500 ft above the sea looking down on its sister village of Lynmouth. A solid ring of hills protects it from the worst of Exmoor's rain and the tree-covered Summerhouse Hill makes sure it is shielded from the gales sweeping in from the sea. You will find the buildings are mainly Victorian because it was during this time that they discovered what a marvellous place it was for a holiday.

There are places you must see. The poet Robert Southey described the breathtaking Valley of the Rocks as 'rock reeling upon rock, stone piled upon stone, a huge terrific reeling mass'. Watersmeet, as its name suggests, is the place where the tumbling waters of the East Lyn converge with the Hoaroak Water, which cascades down a rocky bed in a series of waterfalls. You should leave the car behind and explore this wondrous place on foot.

One of the lovely villages is Brendon, on the banks of the East Lyn, which is spanned by a fine packhorse bridge. The old church lies some two miles outside the village along a wooded valley. It is an odd, mystic place, surrounded by trees and slightly dark because of it but it has some fine coloured windows which pick up whatever sunlight is allowed to seep through.

Lynmouth, where I end my journey through Devon, is a place of towering cliffs and swirling river valleys which paid the price for so much beauty in 1952, when disastrous floods swept right through the village, destroying everything in its wake and many lives were lost. Part of the quay went and so did a curious edifice, known as the Rhenish

The village of Lynmouth

Tower, originally used for storage of salt water for bathing purposes. Before rebuilding started the East and West Lyn rivers were widened, and strong walls built to prevent a recurrence of the tragedy. The Rhenish Tower was reformed and the picturesque cottages rebuilt. Today they are a medley of colour amid gardens, bright with roses, fuschias and other shrubs.

This is the third book I have written about Devon. I know it and love it but I still feel as if I had just scratched the surface. I understand fully why Devonians call it 'God's own country'.

A–Z Index to Cities, Towns, Villages and Hamlets